Paige looked at each of the people in turn, all of them filthy from their chins down to their necks. A kid in his early teens locked eyes with her and snapped his neck to one side. What had started as some kind of fit quickly turned into something much worse as the kid violently twisted his head as far as it would go. Paige pulled the door open and bolted outside just in time to hear the loud crunch as the kid's spine gave way.

The sight of the teen standing there with his head dangling from atop its severed spine was enough to freeze Paige in her tracks. His eyes still blinked and his mouth still moved as he spoke into her brain and ears at the same time.

"I can go anywhere I want now," he said.

"Henry?" Paige whispered, "Is that really you?"

Marcus Pelegrimas's Skinners

"A hell of a lot of fun. . . . Fans of Jim Butcher and Laurell K. Hamilton will definitely want a bite of this!"

—Jonathan Maberry, Bram Stoker Award-winning author of *Patient Zero*

"Action packed. . . . Plenty of cinematic gore and wisecracks will keep readers coming back for future installments."

—*Publishers Weekly*

"Peels you right down to the nerve. A must-read."

—E. E. Knight, author of the Vampire Earth series

By Marcus Pelegrimas

Skinners
BLOOD BLADE
HOWLING LEGION
TEETH OF BEASTS

Forthcoming

VAMPIRE UPRISING

SKINNERS
BOOK 3

Teeth of Beasts

MARCUS PELEGRIMAS

An Imprint of HarperCollins*Publishers*

This is a work of fiction. Names, characters, places, and incidents are products of the author's imagination or are used fictitiously and are not to be construed as real. Any resemblance to actual events, locales, organizations, or persons, living or dead, is entirely coincidental.

EOS
An Imprint of HarperCollins*Publishers*
10 East 53rd Street
New York, New York 10022-5299

Copyright © 2010 by Marcus Pelegrimas
Excerpt from *Vampire Uprising* copyright © 2010 by Marcus Pelegrimas
Cover art by Larry Rostant
ISBN 978-0-06-146307-5
www.eosbooks.com

First Eos paperback printing: May 2010

HarperCollins® and Eos® are registered trademarks of HarperCollins Publishers.

Printed in the U.S.A.

10 9 8 7 6 5 4 3 2 1

To Dad. It's never too late.

SHINNERS

Teeth of Beasts

Prologue

Hunger clawed at Henry Bartlett's gut like a wild animal scratching at his innards. He didn't have the aptitude for a job and his hands were growing too shaky to be any good with a hunting rifle. Having spent most of his years keeping away from loud noises and the men who made them, Henry hung his head low and allowed his stringy light brown hair to cover his sunken face. He pulled his arms tight against his torso in a way that made him look more like a paltry collection of twigs covered in wet parchment than a man in shabby clothes. Somehow, his bony legs supported his weight and the crooked ridge of his spine kept him upright.

After scraping together what money he could, the thin, twitchy man found his way to the Easter Lake Saloon and calmed his nerves with whiskey that tasted like the bottom of a rusty bathtub. He silenced the growl in his belly with a bowl of greasy soup. The saloon was always noisy and filled with more shadows than the flickering lanterns could repel. Some of them were only inky stains upon the wall, but others lived, walked, and watched from the darkness. A few of the shadows were cast by men who stank of blood that had dried onto the clubs hanging from their belts. Henry could see the scars upon the stalkers' hands as they lifted dented mugs to their lips. Bleating everything from boast-ful songs to blasphemous insults from drunken mouths, the locals didn't pay any mind to the new arrivals. When one of the shadowy men approached Henry's table before all the soup had been drained from his bowl, the locals were given a different kind of show.

Henry sank his teeth into the man's wrist while the rest of the bloody men surrounded his chair. Only one was brave enough to step forward without drawing his weapon. His kind face was covered by long gray whiskers. Henry tried to have a word with him, but was dragged away by the others as the entire saloon laughed and hollered at the spectacle. Once outside, he felt his bones twist beneath his skin and some-thing sharp push through his gums. The men spread out and forced him into a stable. Scents of horseflesh, manure, and hay mixed with the creaking of wood and the wet patter of blood dripping from the men's hands onto the floorboards. As the men encircled Henry, they jabbed at him with clubs that had sprouted into long knives and pitchforks. Before long the one with the beard strode into the stable carrying a net that had been treated with some kind of foul-smelling tonic.

Henry grabbed a pitchfork that was poked into his side and bit into the face of the man wielding it. Everything after that was a rush of blood, movement, and pain. There was a brief moment when he was entangled within the net, but he scraped at the ground to crawl beneath the strange ropes. Once he made it into the fresh air, Henry ran until the settle-ment was well behind him. The shadowy men were gone when he returned. Even the remains of the one with the pitchfork had been scraped off the stable floor and hidden away.

The incident was ruled a drunken brawl that several of the saloon patrons declared had been started by Henry. He was jailed and served his time huddled in the back of a filthy cage, trying to avoid his foul-smelling cell mates. Upon his release, he tried not to think about the cravings that made him scratch at his own skin and grind his teeth until they cracked and splintered into jagged spikes. He took walks every night, breathing fresh air while choking on the desire to pull the clothes from his back just to feel the warm spray of blood cover his skin.

He'd never learned a trade, but had picked up a knack for climbing in through other folks' windows and helping himself to a few poorly guarded trinkets, which provided him with enough money to take back to the saloon. Within moments after walking through the tavern's familiar doors, he spotted a pair of women sitting at a table near the back of the room.

"Evenin', misses," Henry said as he lifted his chin and put on a shaky smile to try and mask the new hunger clawing at his belly.

Their dresses might have been frayed and tattered, but both of them were filled out quite nicely. Ample breasts swayed as the sweet-smelling females shifted in their chairs. Painted smiles grew beneath world-weary eyes as they looked Henry up and down. One of the women had hair flowing freely over her shoulders that was as bright and golden as Henry's had once been when he was a child. The other's was much longer, black as coal, and loosely bound by faded ribbons.

"What have we here?" the golden-haired one asked. "I'm Shalyn and this is Tricia. Want to buy us a drink?"

The dark-haired whore leaned forward to reach between Henry's legs. "Or would you rather buy something else? You carrying something for me in there?"

Henry swallowed and dug out what little money he'd stolen during one of his most recent walks. "This is what I got."

After taking Henry's stock in the blink of an eye, Tricia shrugged and said, "That'd be enough for one of us. You can get us both for a bit more."

"Really?"

She nodded.

Shalyn placed her hand upon her body and rubbed suggestively. "I give my word it'll be worth it."

As her promise rolled through Henry's ears, he swore he could feel their hands rubbing against his bare skin and lingering beneath his clothes in the spots where his blood was running the warmest. Before he could question the ghostly touches, his money was gone and Tricia was leading him away. She dragged him out through the back door and took him into an alcove between the saloon and a row of out-houses. After pulling down his britches just enough to get her hand inside and between his legs, she put on a lurid smile and vigorously worked him. Henry leaned back and waited for the craving in his belly to subside.

Before too long, it did.

"There now," she said as she stood up and wiped her hands upon her skirt. "You liked that?"

"Yes."

"It only gets better if my friend comes along."

"Really?" Henry asked.

She nodded with the certainty of a fisherman whose hook was sunk in deep. "Better than you could imagine."

Henry closed his eyes for a moment and tried to imagine, but could only feel the craving gnaw at him with freshly sharpened fangs. After letting out a hard breath, he asked, "How much for the both of you?"

When whispering the sum into his ear, she made sure to brush her lips against his skin. She lingered for a few mo-ments, allowing her hair to brush against the side of Henry's face, and then turned away. "You know where to find us."

"But . . . that's a lot of money."

"It'll be worth it," Tricia promised with a backward wave.

The twitch of the woman's hips caught Henry's eye. The sway of her arm reminded him of a broken doll. The plump curves of her breasts called to him like tender meat already falling off the bone. When he pressed his fingers to his nose, he could still smell the sweat from her shoulders.

Henry's breath caught in his throat, so he shook his head as if to snap it loose from his neck. The tingling she'd put into him was still working through his legs, and he had no doubt that both women could give him things to dream about for years to come. But he didn't have enough money. He didn't even have enough to buy the whiskey that usually got him through the hard times. As the cravings rumbled inside of him, he went for another walk.

The wind felt good against his face. The ground was solid and comforting. It didn't take long for him to catch a scent that led him to a shack built within a stone's throw of the lake on the edge of town. Henry couldn't find an open window, so he scraped at the door until it came away from its hinges. The house was quiet enough to be empty, but there were others inside who stank of anxious perspiration. He could hear them whimpering to each other as they tried to hide in a root cellar beneath the kitchen floor. There was no money or valuables to be found, so he sniffed around the kitchen for something to eat. A few strips of venison still dangled from his mouth when he turned toward the scrape of old boots upon the floor.

"Get out of here!" a tall man in long underwear shouted as he stomped in from another room. The man put on a stern face, but was tussled after having been roused from his bed by the intruder. Angry eyes sighted along the top of the shotgun in his hands.

Giving in to his craving, Henry drove his shoulder into the man's midsection and rammed him into a nearby table. The shotgun went off, but the only thing Henry felt was a thump against his chest as his feet scraped against the floor and his muzzle was buried into the gaping maw of the man's savaged throat. The cravings were subsiding, but he kept pulling flesh from bone even after the man had stopped trying to defend himself. When he looked up, Henry could hear petrified sobs coming from beneath the kitchen floor. Scents of dried spices and preserves drifted up from that space, mingling with an aroma that was just as tempting as the sweat that had trickled so beautifully along the back of Tricia's neck.

Henry pulled at the floor with his bare hands to reveal a woman and small child huddled against each other, surrounded by shelves of dusty jars. Spittle dripped from his lips to land upon the child's brow as he peered down at them. Their screams were loud enough to sail across the lake as Henry jumped into the root cellar and turned it into a grave.

* * *

He was sleeping on a woodpile behind the third house he'd visited that night when the shadowy men found him. They surrounded Henry and knocked him senseless before the one with the beard showed up. Their net smelled different than the last time, and when they tossed it over him, every bit of strength was sapped from his body. He fought back using teeth that were crusted in blood, but the men's weapons burned like lantern oil that had been dumped into his wound and touched by a match.

"How many did you kill, boy?" the man with the beard asked.

Covering his face with both hands, Henry squealed, "I didn't mean to! I was hungry, is all. I was hungry. Just hungry. Just hungry."

The man studied him with cold eyes and a face that didn't show the first hint of fear. "Do you know what you are?" he asked.

"Bartlett's my name. Henry Bartlett."

"That's who. I want to know what."

Before he could try to put together an answer, Henry's nervous stomach kicked up its contents, filling his mouth with the taste of meat that was stringier than beef and sweeter than venison.

One of the other men pressed a sharp wooden blade to his throat and snarled, "He's a damn monster and he killed Avery. What else do we need to know? I say we finish him off and hang his hide from my barn."

The bearded man pulled the other one aside and spoke to him in a harsh whisper that Henry could hear perfectly well, no matter how much the other man tried to cover it up. "We already did our worst and that thing still got away. Have you men even hunted a Full Blood? It ain't like those devil hounds we tracked through the plains or the leeches we burned out of Fort Griffin."

"You're supposed to be the one with the answers, Jonah. Do you have one now or did we come all this way just to toss a net around this son of a bitch?"

When Henry caught the bearded one looking back at him, he quickly averted his eyes and scraped at the spot where the ground met the net. This time, however, his hands didn't have the strength to make a proper trench.

"We don't have the tools needed to kill a Full Blood," Jonah said.

"Then who does?"

"Nobody in these parts. Maybe nobody in this country."

"Damn it all to hell," the third man bellowed as he pounded Henry on the side of the head with an angry kick.

"Stop it!" Jonah snapped. "Leave him be. Just because we don't have the tools now don't mean we can't make some. And since this one here doesn't seem fully grown yet, he may be the best test subject we could ever ask for."

"To hell with your doctorin'," the second man growled. "If we can't kill it, we can weigh it down and drop it in the lake. This net of yours seems good enough to do the job."

"No," Jonah said sternly. "We're taking him back to the reformatory. Help me load him into the wagon."

Henry spent the next several days in an even smaller cage, jostling in the back of a wagon while chewing at the rusted iron shackles clamped around his wrists and ankles. When he was finally unloaded, he thought he would be meeting his Maker. Instead, he was introduced to a place called Lancroft Reformatory. The walls of the big house up front smelled like clean mountain rock, and the mortar holding the second building together reeked of sulfur and strange metals. When he saw Lancroft's tall walls and ornate doors for the first time, Henry thought a picture from a storybook had somehow come to life. The closer he got to the castle, the more he thought he'd been granted a reprieve by the Almighty himself.

He was dragged through Lancroft's doors by two of the men carrying sharp, magical sticks while Jonah strode ahead and quickly disappeared within another room. Inside, the temple walls were sandy and smooth. There were words chiseled into them that Henry couldn't read, and when he reached out to touch one with a cautiously extended fingertip, a skinny old fossil of a man in a black preacher's robe slapped his wrist.

"Hands to yourself, please," the preacher scolded. "Do not disgrace the Good Word with your sinner's touch."

That talk didn't bother Henry much, since he'd heard plenty of it when he went to Sunday mass with his pa. The big fellows shoved him with hands that weren't quite as scarred as Jonah's, or they sometimes pulled him by the chains attached to his arms and legs. If he looked to one side for too long, he got a quick swat on the back of his head.

"Eyes forward, please," the old man behind him chirped.

His room was one of many off the short hallway in the southern wing. The doors were a lot thicker than the ones in that house with the root cellar beneath the kitchen. The floor was a whole lot sturdier too. Of all the doors along that hallway, only one of them was open.

"This where I gonna live?" Henry asked.

The old man tapped one of the big fellow's shoulders, which brought the whole group to a stop. "See out there?"

Henry saw the preacher's callused hand from the corner of his eye. When he looked in the direction the old man was pointing, he winced in expectation of another swat. The blow didn't come, so Henry took a longer look. "I see the window," he said.

The preacher lowered his hand and stepped forward. He reminded Henry of his grandpa. His grandfather was nice, but brittle.

"See outside the window? See what a beautiful sky the Lord has given to us this fine day? See the green grass?"

"Yes," Henry sighed.

"This is the last time you will be seeing it as you are now. When you are deemed worthy to leave this place, my work will be done and you will see that grass again. You will look upon those hills with clean eyes and you will thank God for this chance to have your spirit purged before you are cast into the fiery pit for all eternity. Wouldn't you rather serve your penance here than in eternal hellfire?"

"Yes."

"Of course you would." With that, the preacher nodded to one of the big fellows, who then took hold of the top of Henry's head and twisted it sharply away from the window.

Henry's first reaction came as naturally to him as pulling in his next breath. But before he could sink his fingers into the man's throat, the chains around his wrists were pulled taut and one of the other fellows prodded him with a thorny club that drew more of Henry's ire than blood. That was merely a prelude to the boot that thumped between his legs. He tried to stand up but couldn't make it halfway before crumpling over. Piss dribbled out of him like boiling water, and blood flowed freely from the welts left behind by the clubs.

"You see what your violence brings?" the old man asked as he shook his head and walked to the open door. "You will see the error of your ways soon enough, for you shall have nothing else to distract you."

As Henry was dragged the rest of the way down that hall, frantic eyes stared at him through small rectangular holes cut into the other doors. Henry's cell was open and waiting for him. It was square just like the rest and set at the old man's eye level.

Except for a copper pot in one corner, the room was empty. Even though Henry could see no windows, it was fairly well lit thanks to a small, oval-shape that had been cut into the ceiling, which allowed a fair amount of sunlight to trickle in. The hole was surrounded with more words that Henry couldn't read, and so were the walls.

Looking up at the ceiling as if he was on the verge of tears, the preacher clasped his hands and smiled as if he was peeking beneath a woman's lifted skirts. "That is the eye of our Lord," he said.

Henry looked at the old man and then back to the ceiling. "It's just a hole."

"So says a sinner. The eye of our Lord is always open, always looking down upon you. It is your salvation just as it is your only light. If there is good in you, He will see it."

Settling into a corner so his back was against the wall facing the door, Henry winced. "I suppose."

"Cherish the words around you," the preacher said as he ran his fingertip along some of the symbols near the door. "They will keep you from sinning again."

Henry felt a pulse roll out of the wall and press him into his corner. A dank, musty odor drifted through the room and felt as if it was curling in on him like a fist. When the preacher finished his tracing, he nodded to the big fellows and backed out of the room. The chains were taken from Henry's wrists and the guards left without a fuss.

Once the door was shut, Henry Bartlett had nothing in his world but a moldy piss pot to fill and the eye of the Lord to watch over him.

Three years later Henry had settled into his routines even better than he'd settled into the corner of his room.

Twice a week his pot was emptied.

When he was brought out of his room, his head was covered by a sack cinched shut by a leather strap around his neck so he couldn't see the other residents. A few screams could be heard at night, but it was hard to tell which came from other mouths and which were simply churning within the shadows.

The words on his wall hurt when Henry touched them, so he figured they were filled with the same hellfire as the preacher's sermons. Those lectures, filled with more words about the evil in Henry's soul and the hard work needed to purge it, rolled off of him like the rainwater that trickled in through the hole in his ceiling.

Outside his room, Henry tried to peek through a loose stitch in the bag covering his head. If he wasn't sneaky about it, rough hands snapped his head to one side and shoved his chin down against his chest. One time, he tried to bite the man who did it to him. There had been a crippling blow delivered to the small of his back, followed by a kindly voice that informed him, "You will see nothing but the words of salvation and the eye of our Lord."

If he behaved himself while he was in a room that smelled like food, Henry was allowed to roll up the bottom of the bag just enough to get some oatmeal into his mouth. He saw nothing but a few shadows while he ate. Heard nothing apart from the muttering and chewing of the folks around him. Felt nothing but the lead weight of the peculiar writing on the walls and the greasy filth that stuck to the bottom of his feet.

More than anything, Henry wanted to go for one of his walks. Whenever he strayed too far from his assigned path, the big fellows would come with their sharpened sticks to force him back to his room. He got flustered during his first month at the reformatory and pulled off one of those men's arms. The wooden clubs had rained down upon his head until he heard a loud snap inside his neck. He could barely lift his chin for a while after that.

The old preacher came to check on him, and so did Jonah. It was one of the few times Henry laid eyes on the fellow with the beard who'd kept the others from hanging him as a murderer. But Jonah didn't have any kind words for him. He did, however, seem mighty amused by the crackle of broken bones scraping against each other as Henry's head swung loosely at the end of his neck.

After he'd acted up again, Henry was dumped into his room and wasn't allowed out of it again. His food was brought to him and shoved through the hole in his door. The meals tasted rotten and smelled like they had been pulled up from the bottom of a mossy lake. He ate what was fed to him and got one of the big fellows' fingers as well. Jonah came along later to put a different bag on his head and tightened the belt until he went to sleep. When he woke up, he heard a voice that was clearer than the rest.

"You can hear me," it said.

Henry snapped his head up and smiled beneath the burlap sack. Putrid slime dribbled from his mouth and his breath felt like a wave of flame upon his ravaged throat when he muttered, "Yes. I hear you."

"Be quiet in there," one of the big fellows outside demanded.

Henry couldn't see the guard, but he'd long ago become accustomed to the fact that they were always watching. When he strained to turn toward that other voice, Henry reflexively kept his chin pressed against his chest. "Can you hear me, God?" he asked.

"Of course I can hear you," the soothing voice replied. "You are the only one worth listening to."

Trying not to let the Lord know how confused he was, Henry replied, "God is good."

"And you are too . . . Henry."

That last word brushed through Henry's ear like velvety fingers stretching through his mind; warm and itchy.

He caught a hint of light through the rough material of the sack. After the door was pulled open, a thick hand clamped down upon his head, sending a painful crunch through his neck.

"Eyes and head down," the guard said.

"But I hear God talking to me."

Henry was knocked face-first to the floor so another familiar voice could reach the large ears flattened against his skull.

"Blasphemy!" the preacher said. "You know better than that! Be silent and reflect upon the harm you've inflicted."

The belt was taken off and the bag peeled away. Henry sat in his corner with his head tucked against his chest and turned to one side. It hurt too badly to lift it, so he let it hang. The churning in his belly grew stronger, but the only other food he got after that night was damp, salty bread.

Insects skittered across his floor. They pinched his toes and chewed at the small of his back, but that didn't bother him anymore. He had a friend other than Jonah, so he let the ants skitter among the roots of his coarse fur and waited for his next conversation with God.

Ten years later Henry still couldn't read all those words on his wall. But the one thing he knew for certain was that the preacher had been right. The Lord looked down on him all the time. No matter how much Henry wanted to look up into that eye, his crooked neck wouldn't allow it.

That's when Henry Bartlett knew he was never going to be forgiven.

He would never clear the stench of his own filth from his nose.

The mites would never stop crawling through his hair.

He would never be able to eat something besides oatmeal, bread, or the occasional bit of stolen meat.

He would never be let out of that room.

It took a lot of strain, but he finally managed to look up to the unblinking eye of the Lord to feel some of the strength the preacher had always gone on about.

One day, God told him to dig.

Henry crawled to the door with his head cast down and his legs only moving below the knees so as not to agitate the lice infesting his groin. Settling next to the door, he scraped at the same spot he'd started on a few years ago, using nails that had hardened to jagged, calcified implements. His eyes narrowed to intense slits as he pulled at the wood and scraped against stone. His head wobbled and the voices rushed through his mind. Every splinter he pulled away brought him one step closer to freedom. Every bit of pain slicing through his hands spurred him on and chased away the need to sleep.

"You're doing well, Henry," God whispered. "I'm so proud of you."

"Uh . . . me too. I mean me for you . . ."

"I know what you mean to say, Henry. I can read it upon your heart."

"Thank—"

"Bless you," God purred. "And keep digging."

The Lord's eye was casting a dark red light into the room by the time someone approached the door. Reflexively backing into his corner, Henry saw a new set of eyes look in through the little window of his door.

"Back up or you'll be hurt," the unfamiliar man said in a thick accent. His face took on an angry hue and he asked, "You been damaging Lancroft property again? You were told what would 'appen if you bloodied up another door."

Henry knew what he wanted to say, but the words wouldn't come.

"He will obey you," God told him. "Place the words into his mind."

It wasn't easy, but Henry did his best to keep his thoughts together when he said, "Open the door."

"Shut yer hole!" the guard said.

"Think the words," God urged.

So Henry thought, "Open the . . . open . . . door . . . open . . . open door . . ." Despite Henry's trouble, the guard twitched in a way that revealed he was hearing the voices too. To keep the words straight in his head, Henry packed them into an orderly strand. "Open . . . thedoor. Openthedooropenthe-dooropenthedoor!"

As soon as the door moved, he charged forward. He reached out with clawed, desperate hands and grabbed for the first piece of meat he could grasp. Since his shoes had been taken away months ago to teach him the value of keeping his piss pot upright, his toes were free to dig into the cracks of his floor and steady himself when he pulled the guard down. The other man felt no bigger or stronger than the child who had hidden in that root cellar.

"Someone get this animal offa me!" the guard shouted as he slammed his club upon Henry's back.

Heavy footsteps stomped down the hall, but they didn't arrive quickly enough to keep the guard's blood from being spilled. More men came, and they brought their sharpened sticks with them, but they all seemed to get smaller as Henry's muscles swelled and the Lord screamed inside his head to finish what he'd started.

Henry's fingernails tore through one guard's uniform before shredding the flesh of another. Bones splintered easily in his grasp until he finally got to the tender meat he craved. After being stabbed and cut by those sharp sticks, he was forced away from the guards and back into his corner.

The lumps within Henry's chest rustled impatiently. They wriggled and clawed at his insides to keep him going as he gnawed on the dark, tender meat of the guard's heart. When that was gone, he chewed on one of the fingers that had become lodged in his fur after being torn from its hand. A nub of bone lay wedged in his throat. The ears, he saved for later.

As Henry became too tired to push against the weight of the symbols upon his wall, he swore he could feel himself shrinking down. Shriveled tendons in his neck had pulled away from his collarbone. With those rubbery chains broken, his head rolled freely upon his shoulders, flopping from side to side as his arms snaked around his twisted body. Perhaps he was wasting away like the preacher had told him he would. Before he fell asleep, a friendly bearded face peeked in at him through the hole in his door.

"How did you get that guard to open the door?" Jonah asked.

God insisted that he not tell, so Henry didn't say a word.

Jonah smiled knowingly, as if he shared a secret with his favorite patient. "You tricked him some way, didn't you?"

Henry turned away from the door. "I didn't trick nobody, mister."

"We'll be seeing plenty more of each other, my friend. You might as well start calling me Dr. Lancroft."

Chapter 1

Times were rough.

At least, that was the sentiment that stuck with Cole after his brief trip to Seattle. He'd been anxious to take care of some professional business after a nice long road trip in a rental car that came equipped with better air-conditioning than his old apartment. It was supposed to be a time for him to hang his arm out the window, feel the summer wind blow through the dark crop of hair stretching from a scalp that was normally buzzed to within an inch of its life, and listen to some music. Before getting too far away from Chicago, he'd stopped to purchase a new GPS so he could make the trip without having to rely on old-fashioned maps. There was a GPS function in his phone, but dropping some cash in an electronics store was another form of comfort to go along with the rest of the trip. After a few hours of fiddling with the options, he settled upon the voice of a British woman to tell him when to turn and which side of the road to shoot for.

Along the way, he'd slept in hotels that offered the barest essentials, ate his complimentary breakfasts, stocked up on gas station candy and spicy beef jerky, and had a generally perfect trip to the West Coast. Not long after his arrival at the offices of Digital Dreamers, Cole heard those dreaded three words.

"Times are tough," Jason Sorrenson had told him.

Cole's ears were still ringing from the constant flow of wind past his face when he'd been given that little tidbit. "I know times are rough," he'd said. "At least I didn't have to sell a kidney to afford the gas to get here."

"You drove all the way from Chicago?"

"Yeah, it was nice."

Instead of wearing his standard-issue Mariners cap, Jason had finally conceded to the fact that he and his hair were parting ways. Like many amicable separations, the man was left feeling beaten and somewhat ashamed. Most of the people in the building were clad in anything from T-shirts to light sweaters, but Jason was dressed to fit his role as their boss. His white shirt was starched, buttoned, and crisp. Slacks were freshly pressed and suspenders were straight out of a catalogue that must have fallen behind a sofa eight years ago.

"I wish you would have let me know you were driving all the way out here," Jason said.

Cole glanced at the small group of programmers leaving a large break room on their way to the newly refurbished room marked ART AND LEVEL DESIGN. All four of the sun-deprived professionals wore Digital Dreamers badges, smelled of cigarette smoke, and couldn't have been more than a year or two out of college. "I did tell you I was coming," he said. "Remember my e-mail?"

"You've sent a lot of e-mails, Cole. You've also made a lot of promises, but I've learned to take them all with a grain of salt."

"Well, that's why I came out in person. I wanted to run some new ideas past you, go over some ground rules, and define some terms for a new contract."

Jason's eyebrows flicked up as he mused, "Define some terms? That sounds official."

"It is."

"Are you moving back to Seattle?"

"No. I thought I'd—"

"Then I can't use you," Jason interrupted while digging a tissue from his pocket and wiping his nose.

Cole stood in the wide hallway until another group of new faces ambled past him. When he looked around this time, he spotted fresh paint on walls adorned with awards that were won since he'd left, pictures of teams he'd never met, and sketches from games he didn't recognize. "You can't . . . what?"

Rather than ask Cole to follow him, Jason simply led him into the break room. A set of double doors opened into a space that would have been Cole's favorite hangout if he was still in high school. Rows of arcade cabinets lined the walls on either side. The farthest wall played host to vending machines offering snacks ranging from the "diabetic nightmare" end of the spectrum all the way down to "brantastic." Fridges, microwave ovens, and a soda machine filled the rest of the perimeter. The rest of the space was cluttered with tables and chairs. Forget high school. He wouldn't have minded spending time there now.

Jason walked straight through the break room and out a glass door that led to a fenced-in courtyard populated by an ironic mix of smokers and people who wanted fresh air between work sessions. Blowing his nose and then tossing the tissue into a trash can, he mumbled, "Probably getting that damn virus that's hitting the rest of the country."

"You mean the Mud Flu? Yeah, that one sounds like the Black Plague of our generation. What's it give you? The sniffles? Some crap in your throat? Big deal."

"Yeah, I guess I don't know what's worse. Having the press try to terrify us with a flu or having the Internet make us think there are werewolves in Kansas City."

"So," Cole said without mentioning the fact that he'd met those werewolves personally, "you get a new batch of rookies from a career fair at a technical school and I'm out?"

Slipping his hands into his pockets, Jason replied, "We've had this discussion before. There's a place for you here, but only if you can make a genuine commitment to your job. *Hammer Strike 2* is going to be announced, and I'll want your input on that. If you can be a real member of the development team, you're more than welcome. Otherwise, your contributions will have to be reduced to creative input and design ideas."

"I've already been knocked down to work for hire," Cole pointed out. "Now I'm just a consultant?"

"Times are rough. We don't have the funds to pay a team as well as a bunch of freelancers."

"But I've been with Hammer Strike since the beginning!"

"You're not here anymore, though. That's the problem." Jason sighed in a way that Cole recognized from countless meetings with testers, marketers, or anyone who was either difficult or dense. "You know how we always wondered how companies could keep so much dead weight on the payroll?"

Cole nodded.

"It's like how I always wondered how a gas station could stay afloat when there was one on every corner," Jason continued. "Or how so many restaurants could stay in business. When times get tough, those things have to go."

In his last days as a steady employee at Digital Dreamers, Cole had been relatively healthy for a man in his thirties who rarely did more than try to climb an indoor rock wall on the weekends. Over the past several months, his exercise regimen had expanded to include running for his life with shapeshifters snapping at his legs or swinging a stick with enough force to drive it through a wall. Muscles newly rediscovered and honed through painful hours of sparring tensed beneath his faded plaid shirt. Not only did he want to choke Jason at that moment, but he knew four different ways to do it. "You're saying I'm dead weight?"

Jason shook his head. "Forget I said dead weight. What I meant was . . ." Abruptly, Jason straightened his back and lifted his chin. "You left us in a jam, Cole. You were supposed to come back months ago, but you didn't. I've known you forever, so I let it slide. Then you decide to stay in Chicago, but you still want your job here. You've given me some great ideas for downloadable Hammer content as well as the start of a new project, so I gave you another chance.

We've got games to make and I've hired plenty of new talent who are willing to actually come here every day and make them."

Choking back what he originally wanted to say, Cole grumbled, "I know, I know."

"You've got talent as well as experience," Jason said, "but you can only do so much on your laptop."

"What about those ideas for that new game with the shapeshifting characters or those new tricks for the Hammer maps?"

"All of that was excellent, Cole. We could take that online and be huge with it. I intended on purchasing the rights from you as soon as possible. Since you're here, I can issue a check. That is, unless you'd reconsider taking a prime spot on one of our dev teams?"

"You'd put me in charge of development?"

"Upper tier," Jason clarified. "You've been out of the loop too long to be in charge."

"It's only been a few months."

"That's a long time in this industry. I don't need to tell you that." Jason crossed his arms and lowered his chin. That meant business. "You and I can put some real good stuff together, but not through e-mail. Whatever you're doing in Chicago must be huge to prevent you from accepting the position I offered a while ago. If you came back, it wouldn't be long before you'd see a raise, a chance to start another project, maybe your own office."

That last part had been a last minute piece of cheese set onto the trap. Cole could tell as much by Jason's expectant grin and the subtle angle of his head. But what was he going to tell him? That while he'd been away from his Seattle desk and keyboard, there was a massacre in Janesville, Wisconsin, and an attempted siege in Kansas City, Missouri? Werewolf activity had been down since then, but that wouldn't last forever. Nymar lived in nearly every city, which wasn't anything new. Skinners had even worse things to keep them busy, and Paige . . .

"What about this Paige you've been mentioning?" Jason asked. Nodding with the certainty of someone who actually paid attention during conversations, he added, "Is she the one keeping you in Chi-Town?"

"Don't call it that."

"Whatever. Is she?"

"The last I heard from her, Paige was headed off to try and hook up with some cop."

"Does anyone say hook up anymore?" Jason mused.

"Fuck! Is that better? She went to fuck some cop because Lord knows she won't fucking touch me!"

With Cole's voice bouncing off the exterior walls, Jason glanced around nervously, as if he expected to be collared by one of his own security guards. "Okay. Calm down. Didn't mean to touch a nerve."

As Cole thought back to that conversation, he drove along a stretch of interstate that cut through a quiet section of Minnesota. Stress pushed against the back of his eyeballs and he did his best to alleviate that situation by digging a CD out from a case on the seat next to him. For most of the ride he'd been content to take his chances with local radio stations, but the tension cinching around his guts demanded a very specific kind of music to ease it.

When the first few raging bars of Black Label Society tore through the air, Cole gripped the steering wheel and snarled along with Zakk Wylde. Rather than rip his throat apart trying to compete with the metal legend, he stared at the road and thought about the rest of his visit to Seattle.

"What about Nora?" Jason had asked as he fed a dollar into one of the break room's soda machines. "She's still here, you know."

"Is she waiting for me?"

Jason snickered, stooped down to get his plastic bottle of diet cola and then twisted off the cap. "Yeah. She's been pining away, knitting your likeness into memorial quilts."

"Smartass."

"She asks about you all the time. Hasn't she been calling?"

"A few times, I guess," Cole admitted. "Just didn't seem

worth going through the motions since that's all either of us would be doing."

"She cares about you," Jason insisted.

"Sure, in a 'I hope he's not dead' kind of way. For all I know, that's shifted to something less tolerant."

"There's nobody else in Chicago?"

"I did intend on seeing this one woman while I was out and about," Cole said. "Her name's Abby."

"Ah, let's hear about her."

"I've only seen pictures of her and talked to her a few times on the phone. We're supposed to meet on my way back to Chicago, but I don't know."

"Christ, Cole. Is this some kind of Internet dating thing?"

"No!" Now it was Cole's turn to glance around nervously. There were plenty of young faces pointed his way, surely chattering back and forth about various reasons why some unshaven, shabbily dressed man with messy hair was talking to one of the biggest executives of the company. "She's someone I've met. That's all."

"Where did you meet her?"

"She works for the Midwestern Ectological Group."

"Ectological? Is that a real word?" Before Cole could fully roll his eyes, Jason snapped his fingers and said, "Wait! You mean those ghost-hunting guys with the cable specials?"

"That's them."

"They've got a new show coming up about all the werewolf stories and monster sightings in the news. I was going to DVR it. Should be . . . interesting."

"Abby's a field investigator. She's on a job in Minnesota."

"How'd you meet her?" When he didn't get an answer to that, Jason gnawed on the inside of his cheek and nodded slowly. "Part of your new Chicago life, huh? By the looks of it, that life may not be so good for you."

"Why do you say that? I'm in better shape than ever."

Jason no longer tried to mask his disapproval. "You smell like you've been sleeping in your car."

That was because of the newest batch of soap Paige had

cooked up. The stuff was supposed to hide their scent from shapeshifters, but it wasn't exactly minty fresh.

"You've got scars and bruises all over the place," Jason continued, pointing to the marks left behind by Cole's sparring sessions and the many times he'd been forced to trade blows with creatures that had recently become Internet celebrities. "I don't even know what to make of this," Jason said as he grabbed Cole's wrist so he could get a look at his hand.

The scars from Cole's weapon crossed his palm. They were thick in some places and stretched thin in others. Thinner layers of scar tissue formed a web pattern on his flesh that reacted like an allergy to shapeshifters and Nymar. It was a good early warning system, but not much of a fashion statement.

"Did you burn yourself?" Jason asked. "Is this from a disease? Drugs? What happened, Cole? Is it from that accident in Canada?"

Cole broke his friend's grip with ease. "I can still type. That's all you need to know."

"Why won't you just tell me what's going on?"

Once his pulse slowed down, Cole asked, "Have you seen the stuff on the Internet about those wild dogs in Kansas City?"

"You mean those videos with the 'werewolves'?" Jason asked while framing his last word in air quotes.

"Yeah. I'm one of the people who kept those things from tearing through Kansas City and probably a few other nearby cities."

It was the complete truth, and it went over as well as a stick of phony dynamite at an airport security check.

"I've held onto your job for as long as I could," Jason said dryly. "We can use your ideas and the designs you've done so far, but only as a jump-off point. Digital Dreamers no longer has the funds to pay for outside consultants when we've got plenty of fresh talent on-site."

"You've sure got the funds for a fancy new break room and a bunch of new programmers," Cole griped.

Jason steeled himself and replied, "Your consulting check is waiting for you downstairs."

"And what if I have some more ideas about that new project?" Cole asked.

"Then you join the team."

"What about Hammer Strike? The people on the forums are crying for more levels."

"If you put something together, I'll consider it. If we use your templates, we can pay you the standard fee. I know the fans will appreciate your input."

Cole nodded as his anger began to dwindle. Oddly enough, relief soon took its place. He hung his head low and chuckled softly. "I've never been fired from anything. This sucks."

"What else can I do? Times—"

"Save it. My check's downstairs?"

Jason nodded. "And there'll be more Hammer royalties coming. That should tide you over while you clean up after those dogs in Kansas."

"Kansas City," Cole said.

"Sure." No matter how many freshly hired faces were watching, none of them were close enough to hear Jason say, "The moment you decide you're finished doing whatever it is you're doing, there'll be a spot for you here. Any one of these kids can carry the torch of our game licenses, but none of them can come up with new stuff as good as yours. Pull your head out of your ass, get it back into the game, and we'll make ourselves richer."

"Our*selves*? As in both of us?"

Jason winked in a way that proved he didn't wink very often and followed up with an awkward nudge. "Wait till you see the check that's waiting for you downstairs. It's got your most recent royalty statements for Hammer Strike and the downloadable content. Not too shabby considering all the griping on the forums."

Now that he got a look at the more familiar Jason beneath the executive mask, Cole said, "I'm sorry I left you in a lurch. Things have come up that are pretty important."

"They must be. When we were starting in this business,

you said this was all you ever wanted. Now, you're willing to let go of the dream. Please tell me it's worth it."

"It is."

"Then I guess that's all there is for now. Are you staying in Seattle long?"

"No," Cole lied. "I just wanted to touch base here and try to sell you on the idea of making me the highest paid independent contractor in the industry. Since that plan tanked, I'm gonna snag some coffee and be on my way."

Cole didn't leave the building right away. He and Jason were sidetracked by an old fighting game collecting dust in a corner away from the newer version that was fresh off the boat from Japan. They played without once discussing anything more important than what perverted uses they'd find for the other's virtual corpse after the next battle.

It was nice.

When it became uncomfortable again, Cole excused himself so he could walk to the HR Department and collect his check. That was even nicer.

"Hot damn," he sighed when he looked at the amount that made him wonder if he wasn't the biggest idiot on the planet for turning down the rest.

He went straight to the bank to deposit his check. After that, he drove past his old apartment building on Yale Avenue, ate at one of his favorite burger joints, drove past the electronics stores he used to frequent, and even swung past Nora's place. She wasn't home, which was probably for the best. It had been a long day, so he checked into a hotel and crawled under the sheets. The next morning, he headed east.

Abby would only be on her assignment for another couple of days, and now that he was so close to meeting her, Seattle faded into mental clutter. Cole covered some serious ground in a short amount of time. After a few strenuous days and several near-misses with maniacal semis, he made it to St. Cloud, Minnesota. Once he realized just how close he was to his exit, he gave Zakk Wylde a rest and checked his hair in the rearview mirror. After fussing with the tussled mess, he swore to buzz it off again as soon as he could get a hold of some shears.

The land on either side of I-94 was thick with trees and took him directly between Middle Spunk Lake and Big Spunk Lake. Cole did a triple check to make sure he'd read the signs correctly, indulged in some juvenile laughter, and checked his GPS. According to the female British voice who'd gotten him this far, he needed to drive for another 1.2 miles and take the next exit. He did just that, followed her prompts along the side roads, and then patted the little monitor lovingly when he realized he would have been irrevocably lost if he'd followed his gut instincts.

"Thank you, Romana," he said, naming the British GPS voice after the companion from a classic *Doctor Who* storyline. "Don't know where I'd be without you."

The restaurant was a little place that took up the first floor of a two-story brick building marked by a single wooden sign. Judging by the frillier curtains and knickknacks in the upper windows, the second floor was someone's residence.

Cole parked along the street and got out, leaving his varnished wooden spear on the floor behind the passenger seat. Having been treated with shapeshifter blood, the weapon was able to change its shape when commanded to do so by its owner. It took a lot of practice to get the spear to twitch, but he was getting the knack of it. One of the most practical tricks he'd recently learned was to make the weapon collapse into a more manageable size so it could be carried and hidden much easier. He always kept the weapon close, but decided it could wait in the car for a change while he lived his life. He walked in front of a large picture window, and before he got to the restaurant's front door, Abby was rushing outside to greet him.

"There you are! It's great to see you in person!" she said excitedly.

Abby wasn't much shorter than Cole's six-feet-and-some-odd inches. Dressed in jeans that wrapped nicely around slender legs and curvy hips, she moved almost fast enough to make smoke appear from the soles of her white sneakers. Despite the fact that it was a warm August day, she wore a thin cotton button-up shirt over a dark brown tee adorned with the logo for the Midwestern Ectological Group. His eyes naturally took in the sight of her smooth, generous figure, but didn't linger. Long hair flowed in a thick wave past her shoulders and swirled around her face thanks to a gentle breeze. Abby batted it away and smiled while using the back of her hand to nudge the boxy plastic frames of her glasses farther up onto the bridge of her nose.

Cole smiled effortlessly at the sight of her. "Yep. Here I am. You look great."

Abby immediately shook her head and pulled her over-shirt closed. "I'm in the field, which means I need to wear dirty clothes and these things," she said, placing both sets of fingertips on the edges of her glasses.

Reaching out to smooth her hair back, Cole told her, "I think the glasses are cute."

"No you don't. Nobody does."

"Did you change the color of your hair?"

"Yeah, I'm going back to the red. Actually, the box says Intense Auburn, but that's a little too dramatic for me."

"Well, it looks nice."

"You're only used to seeing me on a webcam, so you don't know any better," she added, "but thanks. Are you hungry?"

"Starved. All I've been eating is road trip food."

"Burgers and trail mix?"

"More like beef jerky and candy bars," Cole said. "Your road trips sound healthier than mine."

Cole had met Abby through Stu, his regular MEG contact, and chatted with her at any opportunity. Phone conversations and the occasional picture weren't anything like the real thing, however. "We don't have to do this if you'd rather not," she said.

He leaned forward to place a simple kiss on her cheek. Grinning as if the gesture had been more of a playful joke, he said, "Let's just eat."

Chapter 2

Abby's table wasn't tough to spot. It was the only one in the quaint little restaurant that looked like a miniature base camp for a surveillance operation. Her laptop was situated upon a chipped wooden table complete with a wireless signal booster, battery pack, and extra hard drive connected to it. A worn black satchel with MEG BR 40 stenciled on it in white lettering was under her chair. Among all that technology, the cup of iced tea and sandwich looked more like an afterthought.

"So have you seen the latest?" she asked as she sat down and curled a leg beneath her.

Cole moved the other chair at the table around so he could sit closer to her. "I don't know. The latest what?"

Tapping the icon at the bottom of her screen, Abby enlarged a window that filled her screen with a page from the website of a news station local to the Kansas City metropolitan area. One side was filled with photos that had either been taken by locals or leaked from any number of official cameras set up around the city. Unlike the first batch of images he'd seen right after the incident in KC, these were cleaned up enough for the Half Breeds' gnarled teeth, gangly limbs, and knotted muscles to be seen. One of them even managed to catch a fairly good glimpse of a werewolf's intensely wild eyes as it ran across a street.

"No," Cole said. "I haven't seen these."

"The story is a riot. Apparently, some of the carcasses were rounded up and taken in for testing. And here I thought you guys cleaned up after yourselves."

Cole glanced at the other people in the restaurant, who didn't seem too interested in who he was or what he was doing there. While more and more pictures of the Kansas City werewolves were popping up online, most of them were attached to half-assed speculation or outright lies. "We cleaned up what we could. Paige didn't seem too worried about the rest."

"Well, read on and see for yourself."

Skipping the editorial comments on the chaos surrounding an "urban riot that was all too indicative of troubled times," Cole found a definite lack of scientific jargon. He scrolled through the story again and said, "This only mentions some tests done on animal remains and hair samples."

The way Abby leaned toward him was promising, but she only said, "They've concluded the remains are canine and that's about it. Supposedly, those canines were too messed up after the cops shot them to pieces or ran them over with their patrol cars for them to find any more than that."

"Didn't they find any blood? There was plenty of it flowing that night from human and werewolf alike."

That caught the attention of a skinny lady behind the counter who smirked and then whispered something to a bearded, barrel-chested man sitting on one of the stools at the counter. When Cole turned back toward Abby, he accidentally got a face full of her hair. It wasn't an unpleasant experience, but ended quickly when she gathered it up and tied it back using a band that appeared like a cheater's ace from out of nowhere.

"Sure they did, but it was a mix of human and canine," she explained. "They're writing that off to contaminated evidence at the scene. There's still plenty of crackpot stories floating around, but the official word coming from the police and Humane Society is that those animals were a breed of large dog suffering from an exotic disease. Once that was released, most of the bigger news affiliates have been focusing on the possibility of an outbreak. Some are even saying that disease got passed from the sick dogs on to us as this Mud Flu thing. They're wrong about that right?"

Cole nodded. "They can only spread their disease when they're alive, and it sure as hell isn't the flu."

The barrel-chested man swiveled around to ask, "You know that for certain, do ya?"

"That's what I read."

"You a doctor?"

"No."

"My granddaughter caught that damned Mud Flu, so it ain't no joke."

When Cole fumbled through a quick apology, the man's gray eyebrows clumped together to make it clear that Santa had found a new name for his naughty list. Grumbling something about another bunch of know-it-alls, he swiveled back around to scoop up some more of his Salisbury steak.

"So," Abby whispered. "Do ya really know that for certain?"

"Yes," Cole assured her. "If Half Breeds could strengthen their numbers through anything as simple as a bite or some sort of airborne disease, there would be a whole lot more of them running around. Have there been any more dog attacks lately?"

Abby shook her head and pecked away at her keyboard. "There have been a few sightings of weird animals digging up backyards in a KC suburb, but that sounds more like people just being nervous. If you want the full details, you should watch our new cable special. It'll be on next month."

"I'd be nervous living in KC too," the bearded man at the counter grunted. "Buncha damn fools runnin' around lootin' and givin' the cops hell while some rabid dogs tear loose."

"I heard it wasn't dogs at all," the woman behind the counter said. "I read somewhere that it was some sort of new tiger that was bred at a private zoo." Leaning across the counter as if she'd just seen Cole, she asked, "Can I get you something, hon?"

"How's your chili?"

"Ain't it too warm for chili?"

Pointing to the metal pot behind her, he replied, "Then it should be too warm for coffee."

The woman looked back, conceded the point with a shrug and lifted the lid to one of the larger pots next to the coffee machine. "How about some beef stew?"

"Close enough," Cole said.

It didn't take long for the stew to be ladled onto a plate over a few slices of white bread, but it was more than enough time for Abby to collect her things and pack them into her satchel.

"So tell me," she said after Cole's stew had been placed in front of him. "How's everything with you and Paige? I heard she was hurt in KC."

"Her arm's still in a sling. At least, it was the last time I checked. She had to go back there to wrap up a few things."

That was the short story.

The long version was that Kansas City had been handed over to the group of shapeshifters that helped rid the city of its werewolf infestation. Mongrels were a long way from human, but they were easier to deal with than Half Breeds, and not as powerful as Full Bloods. Paige was supposed to check in on them to make sure they were settling in and not tearing through anything on two legs. Mongrels seemed to prefer living underground, which was why Cole hadn't flinched at the story about something digging up a yard or two. As for Paige's injury, he tried not to think about that. Doing so only made him feel like an ass for tooling around in a rental car while his partner was on the mend. Then again, Paige wouldn't have responded well to coddling.

Now that her things were packed, Abby sipped some tea and swirled the ice cubes in her glass. "So how was Seattle? Did you get that sweet deal you were after? The one with your new game idea?"

"Yeah, I picked up a royalty check. Caught up with a friend of mine. Got fired."

Abby froze with the edge of the glass perched on her lip. "Did you say fired?"

Thanks to the echo effect the glass gave to her voice, the F word didn't seem so bad. "More or less. I'll still get royalties, though, and Jason will probably throw some freelance work my way."

Setting down her glass, Abby studied him for a moment and then said, "You don't sound too broken up about it."

"You know something? I'm really not. I drove all around Seattle, hitting the old spots . . ."

"I do that when I go home to Michigan," Abby told him. "I call it taking the tour."

"On my way out there, I thought it would be this nice, welcoming thing. Like maybe Seattle would just reach out for me and make me feel at home again." Cole used his spoon to shove a chunk of potato around to clear a path through his watery gravy and nudged a few peas out of the way. When he bumped against the slab of white bread, he set his fork down. "But I just felt like I didn't belong there."

"You don't. You've moved on. Don't you live in Chicago now?"

"Yeah."

"And don't you have a new job?" Lowering her chin and raising her eyebrows, she whispered, "A much more exciting job?"

"It's not just Seattle. It's everything. All of it felt like it was just from . . . before."

"Before?"

Before he was attacked by a Full Blood. Before he was introduced to Paige Strobel. Before he knew monsters were real. Before "Skinner" was something other than a name in a psychology textbook. But he didn't want to say all of that in the restaurant, so he settled on, "It's not part of me anymore."

Abby scooted even closer, wrapped an arm around Cole's shoulders and softly told him, "I heard about what you did in KC and read about lots of other stuff you did *before* that. Everything that's a part of you now seems pretty great."

Cole looked over to her and got a quick nod along with a tight-lipped smile. More than anything, he wanted to kiss her. The only thing holding him back was the fact that they were still technically in the early stages of their first real meeting. And before he could think of another excuse of why he shouldn't do something, he just did it.

Abby's lips were rigid and hesitant at first, but she quickly leaned into him and relaxed. Just as Cole pulled away, he felt a little breath escape from her mouth. She'd only just closed her eyes, but quickly opened them amid a flutter of naturally long lashes. Before he could get much of a look at those eyes, she pointed them in another direction.

"When you're done with that, I've got some business to take care of," she quickly announced.

"I wasn't quite done, but . . . oh, you mean the food." Pushing the plate away, Cole said, "I'm done with that."

"Then take it outside," Santa grumbled.

When Cole started to fish his wallet from his pocket, Abby stopped him with a hand that lingered a bit longer than necessary upon his wrist. "If you're willing to help me with my business, then lunch is on MEG."

"What kind of business are you talking about?"

"You ever hear of a Chupacabra?"

Less than half an hour later Cole was once again in his car. Instead of being led by Romana, he followed the taillights of a cute redhead with thick glasses while holding his cell phone. He poked the newly redesignated second speed-dial button and waited to hear an answer from a contact that had become only slightly less important than his parents.

It took twice the normal amount of rings, but the call was eventually answered.

"Hello?"

"Hey, Paige. I think I might have found a Chupacabra!"

"Are you at a truck stop, Cole? Is this going to be a repeat of the Jackalope incident?"

"No," he said. "This isn't about a fake trophy mounted next to a fire hydrant. I'm talking about a real Chupacabra."

"Just call them Chupes," Paige said. "That's how I'll know when you're talking about the real ones."

"You feel like taking a drive up to Minnesota to track one down?"

She let out a strained sigh. "No, Cole. I'm busy."

"Still in Kansas City with Officer Stanze?"

"No," she snapped. "That's done."

"Done? Why? What happened?"

"It just is. I'm back in Chicago and I don't feel like going anywhere else."

"How's your arm?"

When Paige didn't answer right away, he knew he'd hit a nerve. A few seconds later she grumbled, "It's the same as it was. Maybe it'd be better if I cut the fucking thing off."

"Don't talk like—"

"You've got your MEG girl there with you?"

"I'm following her to the spot where this Chupacabra is supposed to be."

"Damn it. MEG's supposed to stay away from the real things and keep chasing their ghosts around. If just one of them gets killed, the rest will be too scared to answer our calls."

Rather than stick up for Abby, Stu, or the rest of MEG, Cole chalked up Paige's words to a foul mood and a whole lot of pain from a wound that had been inflicted by one of her own concoctions. "They've investigated other things way before we met them," he reminded her.

"Sure, but crop circles and Bigfoot tracks don't bite back." After struggling to open a noisy bag of chips, she asked, "Are you sure this is even a real Chupe lead? MEG jumps at just about everything. But if you're just trying to get her alone in a field somewhere . . ."

"She says she's got a lead. Supposedly, several people from the same area have called in about a strange monster killing pets and other animals. MEG was out here to photograph an apparition in another house when the team decided to check on the pet attacks. Abby says they only found pieces of a few dogs and cats."

"And you're sure it's not a Half Breed?"

"Yeah. All the witness accounts say it's hairless, runs on two legs, and has hands. The evidence matched bits and pieces from some other Chupe case files, including a few from Rico and my own little triumph in Indiana not too long ago."

"You flushed out one little heel-biter and chased it for three hours. That's different than fighting a big one toe-to-toe." She finally got the chip bag open with a frustrated grunt. When she spoke again, Paige sounded as if she'd jogged a mile since her last sentence. "You'll find two kinds of Chupacabras in most witness accounts. There's a two-legged little asshole from a bad movie, and a four-legged one that looks like a dog or some mangy cat."

"Which is the real one?"

"They're both the same thing. The younger ones run on all fours, and sometimes the older ones run that way to change their tracks, but they normally walk upright. They can climb. They can bite. They can scratch and they can *move*."

"Are they dangerous?"

"Those dogs and cats probably didn't fall apart on their own."

"Got any advice?" Cole asked.

"They're not usually pack animals, but Chupes are fast enough to hit you like a small group, and they've made biting and scratching into an art form. I wouldn't suggest taking one on by yourself, but you've already faced a whole lot worse. Abby might drag you down, though. Do you have the shotgun?"

"Yes," he replied as he reflexively glanced at the bundle wrapped in a dark blanket on the floor behind the passenger seat. The Mossberg Model 535 Tactical still had that new gun smell, since its predecessor had been blown apart thanks to his first attempt at crafting his own shells. His spear was in the bundle as well, putting both weapons within easy reach. "I warned Abby about the danger, but she countered that by quoting half a dozen case numbers where Skinners took MEG members out to get a look at Chupes and a few Bigfoots. Are there seriously Bigfoots? Or is it Bigfeet?"

"They're just a different breed of Yeti," Paige said dismissively. "Will it just be you two?"

"The rest of the team moved on to one of the other haunted houses. They aren't exactly in the loop as far as Skinners go."

"Fine, I guess," she said. "She's read the reports. She

knows the risks. Just try to keep her safe, Cole. You might not want to give her a gun. Pepper spray works great on Chupes. Spray it in the eyes, mouth, or ears, and that should do the trick. If you see anything that's too much for her to handle, get her out of there."

"What's too much?"

"We don't take tour groups anywhere near shapeshifters if we can help it, and we don't introduce them to Nymar."

"But MEG already knows about the Nymar," Cole pointed out.

"From a distance. It may only be a matter of time before a Nymar weasels its way into MEG and tries to mess up the deal we've got going, but there's no reason to speed up the process. On the rating system for supernatural flora and fauna, Chupes rank a rung or two above a rat."

"Thanks for the advice, Paige. I'll keep Abby safe. Besides, this will hopefully just be a chance for me to get alone with her for a while."

"That's what I thought. Watch your back."

Tucking his phone into his pocket, he watched Abby's signal blink before her car turned onto a side road marked by a sign that seemed to have been constructed and placed for the express purpose of being overlooked. The road quickly degenerated into a pair of dirty ruts leading to an old bridge. Loose boards thumped beneath Cole's tires in a heartbeat pattern for a few seconds before being replaced by the crunch of gravel.

Abby came to a stop in a clear patch just off the road and had her door open before Cole had a chance to park. By the time he fished his weapons from the backseat, she'd already connected her laptop to a power source and was typing away. "I won't get very good Wi-Fi out here, but I can pull up the files so you can take a look," she announced.

Cole slipped into a harness that was made to hold his spear on his back, angled to be drawn with a quick reach over his shoulder. Pumping the shotgun for maximum effect, he said, "Just tell me how many there are and where to find 'em."

She looked at him, pushed some of her hair behind one

ear and nodded. "You're going for the rugged hunter meets serial killer look, huh? Very nice."

"You said rugged, so I'll ignore the rest. The shotgun's for you, if you want it."

"Oh, I don't know about that. The reports say old-fashioned pepper spray does just fine," Abby said. "And it's from one of you, so it must be accurate, right?"

Cole nodded in what he hoped was an assuring manner. "Right. I just thought you might want something heavier."

"We're not out to kill it. I just want pictures. Maybe a sample of hair or something like that. You know what would be great? Audio recordings! Do they howl? Any kind of weird noise from a Chupacabra would play well on the website. All we need is something the other paranormal and cryptozoological websites don't have."

Looking around at the unpaved road flanked on either side by a dense wooded area, he asked, "So this is where it's supposed to be?"

"There are a couple houses a few miles from here on a large section of property that all backs onto this area. According to witness reports and some tracks that were found, our Goat Sucker should be in this neck of the woods." Seeing the perplexed look on Cole's face, Abby said, "That's what Chupacabra translates to. Goat Sucker."

"You're sure you want to do this?" he asked.

She clipped a nylon belt around her waist. From the stiffness of the pockets and the shininess of the pepper spray cans within them, he wouldn't have been surprised to find a price tag dangling from the black and green mesh. "This is why I joined MEG in the first place! Throw in a UFO sighting and I may become giddy."

"All right," Cole said as he stuck the shotgun along with some supplies into a flexible case. "Let's get moving."

Chapter 3

The spear strapped to Cole's back had the dull sheen of a table leg that had been polished after being pulled from a fire. Having whittled the spear from a sapling, he and it had become attached both physically as well as sentimentally. Not only did the weapon have his blood soaked into it right along with the shape-changing mixture, but it had saved his life on more than one occasion. The thorns sprouting from the handle matched the scars on his palms, and the pain they caused when they pierced his skin was as familiar to him as the twinge he got from his bad knee when the weather changed. He didn't have to apply much of the blood-infused varnish any longer. The Skinner concoction was soaked all the way through, making the wood as light as it was durable.

Cole reached over one shoulder, grabbed the weapon and pulled against the snaps holding it in place. Since there was no immediate threat, his fingers fell into place between the thorns in a loose grip that kept the thorns pressed upon his palm without breaking the skin. Even though Abby was watching, he resisted the urge to do anything fancy before lowering the forked end into the tall grass that grew alongside the trail. He waggled the spear, shaking the grass in quick bursts. "They hate this," he told her expertly.

"Hate it, or confuse it for the movement of a smaller

animal?" Abby asked. "And before you answer, remember I've read the reports."

"If you know so much about it, why don't you take the lead in this investigation?" he asked with just enough of a smirk to let her know he was only needling her.

Abby bumped him with her hip as she walked by. "Maybe I will. You could always wait in the car. So, is it true you can make your weapons change into other shapes?"

Cole stopped and faced her while keeping the forked end of his weapon in the weeds. They were too far away from I-94 for the sounds of cars to reach their ears, but it wasn't exactly quiet. Insects buzzed in the trees surrounding the access road that cut south through the woods, their flight paths swerving due to the same wind that rustled dozens of overhead branches. The rattle of Cole's spear was like one spastic set of drumsticks in an otherwise respectable percussion section.

"Haven't you read my file?" he asked.

Abby fixed her eyes on him and gently prodded his chest with a finger as she said, "You haven't filed any reports, no matter how many times we've asked for them."

"So you want to know more about me?"

"Maybe," she said softly. "You guys are mysterious. Anyone in MEG would like to know more."

"Rugged *and* mysterious? You're making me sound pretty cool."

"*Skinners* are mysterious. Cole Warnecki is anything but. He's a video game geek who tries to be a smooth talker, without a lot of success."

Cole scowled and asked, "My smooth talk isn't working?"

"I suppose it is a little bit. You're also not a bad kisser."

When he put his free hand on the worn denim covering Abby's hip, Cole had no trouble reeling her in. She not only allowed herself to be pulled closer, but helped him out by flicking her head back to get some hair out of her face. All of his training had taught him to watch his opponent's eyes. Hers were very promising. When he moved in for the kill, something landed heavily on the end of the spear that was still in the tall weeds. If the weapon had been made of normal, untreated wood, it would have snapped as a little wild-eyed Chupacabra scrambled toward Cole's shoulder.

The creature stood just over three feet tall upon legs that looked like burnt tree limbs covered in old sap. Its feet and hands resembled something from a preschooler's sketch pad. Long, bony toes and only slightly longer fingers stuck out at strange angles, which made them perfectly suited for wrapping around the spear and holding it in a tight grip. Its head was thin, narrow, and chiseled down to a point that wasn't so much of a beak as it was a solid wedge. The lower portion of that wedge hung down to display several teeth that could very well have been old roofing nails.

Cole took all of this in because it was the only thing he could do during the first few seconds of the attack. It was too late to duck, and impossible to take a swing at the gangly little bugger that perched upon the spear while raking its fingers across his chin and neck. As soon as the creature spotted the first trickle of blood, it let out a hacking croak.

Snarling under his breath, Cole twisted around to shake the creature off. Its stick fingers ripped into his shirt, while its toes maintained a solid hold on the spear. Grabbing its arms was a struggle, simply because they weren't in the right spot. One arm was positioned at about the right height on its frame and less than an inch away from a droopy right breast. The other was about six inches lower and disturbingly close to a festering little wormhole that must have been its navel. Because of this, the creature looked as if it was standing perpetually sideways. Not quite a match to the other Chupes he'd seen, but close enough.

As it wrestled to pull out of Cole's grip, the Chupe swung large clumpy strands of hair that could have easily been mistaken for freshly unearthed roots. Each tug brought another grunting breath that was sucked in through slits on either side of its wedge-shaped head and let out through its mouth. Dark yellow eyes rattled nervously within deep sockets, reminding Cole of pennies trapped within dollops of amber.

Not wanting to prolong the stalemate, he let go of its arms and grabbed it by the neck. His attempt to close a fist around the fleshy tube supporting its head caused the thing to yelp and break away from him. It twisted in midair, swung its head around and deflected Cole's spear with a petulant swat.

Since he'd missed with the first swing, Cole allowed his weapon to keep moving until he could drive the forked end straight at the creature. The smaller spearheads caught the Chupe in the meaty portion of its body a few inches below its neck. As soon as it hit the ground, it rolled into the weeds and was gone.

"Was that a Chupacabra?" Abby cried.

Cole felt as if he'd been twisted into a knot. Once he steadied his feet and raised his spear, he took a moment for his head to stop spinning. "Yeah. That was a Chupacabra. One of the biggest I've seen, but that's a Chupe all right."

"Oh my God, you're bleeding!" She rushed over to him with a tissue that she'd fished from one of her pockets and went to dab his forehead.

"Give me some room," he snapped.

Abby pulled her hand away, but nearly jumped from her hiking boots when the single sharpened end of Cole's weapon moved in her direction. The grass around her feet was rustling, but it was difficult to say if it was being brushed by the wind or being jostled by a little freak with misaligned arms. Cole's scars wouldn't warn him of another attack since they reacted only to Nymar and shapeshifters. A Chupacabra was neither, but it was too big to stay hidden in the grass for long.

"I see it," he whispered. "Get that spray ready." He took a small amount of comfort from the ripping crackle of new Velcro as Abby opened a pouch on her belt for a thin can of Mugger-B-Gone.

The top of the Chupe's head bobbled within the grass around them. It stopped moving half a second before the creature made another charge. All Cole could think about was that Paige hadn't been kidding. The little bastard could move even faster than the four-legged one he'd chased in Indiana. Its scurrying steps kicked up a cloud of dirt, but he managed to trip it with a low sweep of his spear. The

Chupe's arms were placed so it could catch and right itself before falling onto its ugly face. As soon as it was upright again, it scrambled behind Cole and climbed up the back of his leg.

"Son of a bitch," he growled while reaching around to try and grab hold of it.

Even though the Chupe was too quick to be snagged by the arms or neck, its hair was long enough for Cole to pull the thing off his back. The instant the Chupe's body hit the dirt, he brought his spear down to trap it between the sharpened points of the forked end. He wasn't fast enough to catch the wiry beastie on his first attempt, so he brought his foot down for a second. He caught one of the Chupe's legs under his heel, but the creature quickly sank its nails and teeth into his shoe through the upper layer of leather and laces.

Cole swung his free leg in and around for a kick to the Chupe's ribs, but was blocked by a knobby elbow and cut with a raking swipe of jagged claws across his shin. He planted his kicking foot and lifted the other, along with the creature, off the ground. The Chupe let go and rolled away just as he was about to launch it into the trees. It kept rolling in an erratic pattern to dodge a storm of incoming strikes from the spear. Once it got a few yards away, the Chupe dropped to all fours and tore into the surrounding greenery. It seemed even smaller and ganglier as it streaked back between Cole's legs and grabbed onto the seat of his pants. From there, it climbed up to hold onto his shoulders so it could scratch and bite at his scalp and neck.

"Stay back!" Cole said when he saw Abby come toward him with her spray can held in an outstretched hand.

He gritted his teeth through the pain of the Chupe's flailing attack, hoping the serum in his blood would be up to healing all those painful little wounds. Grabbing onto his spear down toward the forked end, he shifted it into a bowed shape and then swung it around his back so it partially encircled him and the gnawing little creature. Its thorny handle dug into the Chupe's flesh with a wet crunch, followed by a grating squeal from the creature once Cole began sawing the weapon back and forth.

"Yeah!" he growled. "Doesn't feel too good, does it?"

Rather than let go or try to get away, the Chupe dug its nails and teeth in even deeper. Its mouth was close enough to Cole's ear for him to hear what sounded like garbled vulgarities in some strange, guttural language.

Cole twisted his head around to look over both shoulders. "How about this?" he asked as he jogged backward toward a tree. Although the impact must have driven the spikes from the handle deeper into the Chupe's back, the weapon itself absorbed a good amount of the blow. The Chupe was about to rip Cole's ear off, so he stepped forward, pulled the spear away, and backed into the tree again. Now, instead of the foreign swearing being spat into his ear, Cole could hear a wheezing grunt.

"There ya go!" He slammed into the tree one more time and felt the grip on his back start to loosen. When the bony tip of the Chupe's nose scraped against the back of Cole's neck, he snapped his head back to try and convince it to let go. All he managed to do was knock his head against a tree as the creature dropped to the ground and scampered away.

Head-butting a tree made Cole dizzy for a second, but it hurt even worse to be showed up by a wiry little shit that couldn't even grow proper arms. To make matters worse, he could swear the Chupe was laughing at him as it rose up to two feet and raced through the weeds.

"Watch my back, huh?" he grumbled while remembering Paige's final warning. "Guess I should have taken that more literally."

Abby wanted to run after the Chupacabra, but stopped before venturing too far from the trail. "I can see him, Cole! He's headed straight that way."

Already looking where Abby was pointing, Cole rubbed his head and got a proper grip on his spear. "I see him," he said as he made a fist that drove the spikes from the handle deeper into his palm. No matter how many times he'd done that, it still hurt. Part of the weapon's varnish healed the wounds inflicted upon the bearer, but nerves never died. The pain lit a fire in his gut that was channeled into his legs as he tore after the ugly little bastard.

The Chupe must have been hurt because it couldn't drop to all fours and gain any real speed. Even though it was easier to see while upright, it was still fast.

Before long, Cole had built up a good head of steam. The grass was tall, but wasn't thick enough to fully hide the rocks or fallen logs that could trip him up. If he paid close attention to when the Chupe hopped, sped up, or slowed down, he could get an even better idea of how the terrain was laid out in front of him.

Suddenly, the Chupe twisted its head around, causing the tangle of rootlike hair to swirl from its face. Greasy yellow eyes darted downward as the twisted semblance of a grin cut through the lower portion of its face.

Cole followed the thing's line of sight for as long as his pace would allow. There was a pile of sticks in front of him, which he was able to clear with a short jump. If the Chupe had somehow hoped to trip him up, it was out of luck. If it intended to lead him to the pit that had been dug just past those sticks and was obscured by a layer of branches, however, it did a hell of a good job.

"Oh shit!" he grunted as he skidded toward the hole.

Once his heel slid over the edge, his foot dropped through empty air.

Cole's momentum carried him into the gaping opening while his body pitched downward. He stretched out to grab onto something with his left hand, but it only slapped against the farthest edge of the hole. His right hand was still wrapped around his weapon, which he drove into the ground directly in front of him. The weight of his body dragged the spear through the last bits of grass hanging off the edge and came to a stop when it snagged against a rock or something just as solid buried in the earth.

Gritting his teeth, he sent a desperate command to his weapon. The spear creaked and extended deeper into the ground, far enough to keep him from dropping any farther. The sides of the pit were fairly straight and textured by claw marks that looked like a close fit to the nails sprouting from the Chupe's fingertips. Just as he started to wonder how far down the pit went, his feet bumped against a pile of large rocks that was about the size of a large dining room table. Cole placed his feet on the rocks and immediately slipped off. His grip on the spear held up, and without it he would have been lucky to only break one leg in the fall.

"Freaking little . . . asshole . . . son of a bitch," Cole growled as he pressed his face against the dirt and pushed up from the rocks. When he tried to grab a handful of grass for leverage, hard little nails scraped at the top of his hand.

He hadn't heard the Chupacabra approach him, but the little thing squatted down less than a foot away to scratch at his flesh. Its mouth hung open and its wedge-shaped head rattled with hacking laughter. Before he lost a hand, Cole grabbed the Chupe's wrist, shifted his weight and dragged the little creep into the hole.

Dangling less than a foot above the rocks, the Chupe stretched all four limbs to grab onto the pit's textured sides. After scrambling up and onto solid ground, Cole plucked his spear from the dirt and drove the largest point straight into the hole. The Chupe was quick enough to turn so the spearhead only glanced along its ribs.

"Don't kill it, Cole!" Abby said as she rushed up behind him.

"What?"

"It's just an animal. You don't have to kill it, do you? Just let me take some pictures."

"It almost ripped my face off!"

"Just let me—" Before she could say another word, Abby was knocked backward by the flailing Chupe as it jumped out of the hole and wrapped all four limbs around her.

Before it could sink its toes into her shirt or its fingers into her jugular, Cole pulled the Chupe off and threw it away. It hit the ground and rolled for less than a second before Cole could make another move. Crab-walking toward a pair of old stumps, it squeezed in between them while grunting its foul language at the humans.

"Perfect," Abby said as she approached the stumps with a camera in one hand and the pepper spray in the other. "I can get a picture while it's stuck."

The Chupe shifted and squirmed between the thick

wooden barriers, glaring out at her with eyes that looked like wet spots smeared onto the bark.

"Abby, don't," Cole warned.

"I'm not getting close enough to threaten it. This picture will be perfect!"

Before he could say anything else, the Chupe's arms emerged from between the stumps like a pair of five-headed snakes. Since they were misaligned on its torso, the skinny limbs had plenty of room to maneuver while their owner stayed in where it was safe.

Cole lunged forward to bring his spear straight down in front of Abby. She let out a surprised scream and jumped back while the Chupe reeled its arms in. Unwilling to sit still any longer, it grabbed the edges of the stumps and launched itself out to grab Cole's head and belt.

"Hold still, Cole!" Abby said as she rushed around him. "I've got it!"

Abruptly, the Chupe shifted its hands so it could rake Cole's eyes. When he twisted away from the spiky, probing nails, the Chupe twisted its head to look straight down the nozzle of Abby's spray can while squawking in a way that sounded awfully close to laughter. Before she could douse him with the pepper spray, Cole slapped the can from her hand and pushed her away. Now that she was clear, he reached over his shoulder to grab the Chupe by its hair.

The wiry creature kicked and slashed at Cole as he swung it in a short arc that ended by heavily slamming its back against the ground. It tried to tear at Cole's wrists, but wasn't quick enough to make him let go before it was lifted up and slammed against the closest stump. For the first time since the tussle started, the creature seemed to be truly dazed. Cole pinned it to the ground with one boot and drove the business end of his weapon straight through its chest.

The Chupe's heels thrashed against the earth and its hands clawed at the spear. All the while, it snarled and spat at the Skinner holding the weapon in place.

"There you go," Cole said. "How's that for a photo opportunity?"

Abby didn't take a picture. She was too stunned to do much of anything but watch as the Chupacabra weakened and finally let out its final cough. "You killed it," she said. "Did you have to kill it?"

"No, I could have let it tear us both to pieces. Would that have looked better on your website?"

"No."

At her meek tone, he unclenched his fists, which allowed the blood to trickle from between his palm and the thorny handle of his spear.

"You're bleeding," she said. Shifting her eyes up, she got a better look at the bloody scratches on his neck, scalp, and shoulders. "You're really bleeding. I've got a medical kit in my car. Come on."

Wiping a hand on his shirt, Cole said, "Let's see your camera." She handed it to him and he took a few pictures of the Chupacabra, cropping the shots so a minimum of gore or anatomical details could be seen. That way, there was plenty of room for speculation when the pictures made it to the Internet. "Didn't want you to leave empty-handed."

"I'm more worried about you. We've got to stop that bleeding."

The wounds on his palm were already closing, but the others were still leaking. "Why don't you find that kit and I'll be right there."

Abby was more than happy to get away from that spot, and once she was out of sight, Cole squatted down beside the grimy little stick figure. He felt for a pulse, but wasn't certain he was feeling in the right spot, so he satisfied himself by poking at the body with his spear. When it didn't move, he figured it was dead. He got his cell phone, hoping to check if Paige had any need for some slightly used Chupe parts. There was just enough of a signal for him to dial the number and listen to it ring once before the call was dropped. He had plenty of choice words to mutter as he hefted the Chupe over his shoulder and carried it all the way back to his car. It gave off the odor of old trees and overripe fruit, which was a lot better than he'd anticipated.

Abby rooted through her backseat when Cole spread a

plastic tarp on the inside of his trunk and then dropped the Chupe onto it.

"Don't even ask," he warned her before closing the trunk and walking over to her.

The rear seats of her car had been removed, making room for plenty of silver cases, satchels, equipment bags, and boxes of folders. He sat down with his back against the rear bumper and stretched his legs out. Soon, Abby was cross-legged in front of him and dabbing at the gashes around his ear with a towel moistened by water she'd poured from a plastic squeeze bottle.

"Those look worse than they are," he said.

"I know. Scalp wounds bleed a lot."

"How many staplers did you throw at Stu to learn that?"

She laughed and splashed some bottled water onto a towel. "Only about seven or eight, and they were gushers. So . . . that stuff in the woods was pretty weird, huh?"

"It sure was," Cole chuckled. "But it was the most fun I've had in a long time."

"Fun?"

"Keep in mind, I've been driving for days and got fired by my best friend. Before that was Kansas City, so yeah, this was fun."

Trading the wet towel for a packet of bandages, she told him, "It was amazing to see something like that Chupacabra up close. After that, I was terrified."

"I felt the same way when I first saw a Full Blood."

"They're a lot worse than that thing in your trunk, right?"

Cole couldn't answer that question right away because he was too busy laughing. When he caught a breath, he told her, "If a Full Blood was within two hundred miles of this place, that little bastard in my trunk wouldn't have poked its head out of its hole. Come to think of it, does MEG always get a lot of calls about Chupacabra sightings?"

"Not like this one. Usually there are a few slaughtered chickens on a farm or a couple missing hound dogs, but this one was picking off small animals for weeks. I really would have liked to learn more about it. I brought a tracker and everything. We could have tagged it and followed it from here. Over the course of a few months, we might have learned its migration patterns or possibly even found a whole nest of them. I really wish you would have given me a chance to do my job."

"Your job?" Cole asked as he climbed to his feet. "You seriously wanted to watch it move on a computer screen like just another blip?"

Abby stood up and looked at him as if she wasn't sure she'd heard him correctly. "That's why we came here. That's what we do. MEG finds these things so we can prove they exist."

"And then what? Clip something into its hair, go back to your office and take notes as it runs from one spot to another? And when the blip stays in one spot for a while, do you flip a coin to decide whether it's sleeping or digging a pit trap to cripple anyone or anything that comes along?"

"You almost fell into a hole," she said. "Let's not blow that out of proportion. If you'd twisted your ankle, would you have blamed that on an animal too?"

"I almost fell into a trap, not just a hole. Either those rocks at the bottom were put there on purpose or they're from the smallest cave-in I've ever heard of. And that creature led me straight to it! When I fell in, it circled back to get me. Weren't you watching when this happened?"

Anger flashed across Abby's face, quickly followed by uncertainty and nervousness. "I've never seen anything like this, Cole. Some pretty weird things happen on our investigations, but I've never had an entity crawl onto my back and try to rip off a piece of me to save for later."

Cole placed his hands on her arms to rub them comfortingly. "I know what you mean. I haven't been at this for long, but the Skinner training program just runs at a faster pace than MEG's. Also, things have been kind of crazy lately."

"I know," Abby said. "I've seen the pictures. One video that was supposed to have been taken by someone's cell phone is of a big thing on four legs running down an interstate." Letting out a tired laugh, she added, "Just goes to show how far some people will go to ride upon such strange coattails."

"Actually," Cole sighed, "that one's probably real."

The color that had started to return to Abby's face drained away. "It was?"

"Was it a big, dark brown, wolf-bear-looking thing with a short brunette hanging onto it?"

"Yes."

"That's a Full Blood. He took Paige for a tour of the Kansas City metropolitan area."

For a second, he thought Abby was going to cry. She wilted against him and then quickly pulled away. No tears streamed from her eyes but she was definitely not the same woman he'd met over a plate of beef stew.

"You did great," he assured her. "You were right there with your pepper spray, and you followed me instead of running for the car. Just think of this thing as a big ugly possum. Would you let a possum go if it killed the neighborhood dogs and came at you like that?"

"No."

"You're right about it being an animal. It was hunting and meant to take us down."

"But you drew it here. Maybe it wouldn't have done anything if we hadn't—"

Cole stopped her with a few shakes of his head. Holding onto her shoulders, he looked her in the eyes and said, "It was attracted to the rustling sound because it sounded like a small animal or something else moving through the grass. Now, if it didn't come to us, it would have gone to the next thing that walked through those weeds. Could have been another dog. Could have been a kid. Harmless animals do their own thing and avoid people. Predators come at you like a whirlwind. Big difference."

Abby nodded. "Yeah. You're right. Big difference."

"Do you want to take any more pictures for the MEG site?"

She nodded again.

"How about some Chupacabra hair? I bet Stu would be jealous." When he caught the first hint of a grin, Cole added, "I could pose by that pit for you. It'd make a nice commemorative collage to go along with the other pictures."

Her full smile arrived after that bit of coaxing, but it was tired. "Maybe just a few more pictures."

Cole held his trunk open so she could get a clear shot. He considered posing for one of them anyway, but decided against it. There were already enough grainy photos of him in KC. Shooting the old finger pistols next to a dead Chupacabra for the MEG site was pushing it.

"So," he said while closing the trunk, "we should get together again sometime. And no more running. I'm thinking of a nice, regular dinner somewhere with actual waiters and food that isn't ladled over white bread."

She smiled sweetly at him and replied, "I don't think so."

"Why?"

"I had fun, Cole, don't get me wrong," she assured him, albeit unconvincingly. "Next time we're both available we can get together and see what happens, but as friends, you know?" In response to his slow nod, she added, "I hope you don't think I asked you to come out here just so I could get these pictures."

"No, I don't think that at all."

She smiled almost to the point of beaming. "Cool." With that, Abby did the worst thing possible and kissed him on the lips with just enough passion to let him know what he was missing. Some women thought this was a good way to let a man down easy.

Those women were wrong.

Chapter 4

Cole parked in the alley next to the dirty remains of a once average restaurant on South Laramie Avenue. The windows were boarded up, the paint was peeling, and all that remained of a sign were some random letters spelling RASA HILL painted near the front door. He still hadn't gotten around to looking up the restaurant's full name, but at this point it didn't matter. When he was in Chicago, Rasa Hill was home.

He popped the trunk, dug out the smelly plastic bundle, hefted it over one shoulder and carried his spear in his free hand. Standing in front of a metal door that had recently been reinforced, he kicked at it and listened to the echo roll through the building. When he didn't get an answer, he balanced the Chupe on his shoulder so he could dig out his keys and unlock the door. Before he could take a full step inside, the metallic clack of a shotgun slide filled his ears.

"My day was great," Cole said cheerfully as he stepped in. "How was yours?"

Even after she saw who was coming inside, Paige didn't lower her shotgun. "What are you bringing in here?"

"The Chupe."

"What do you want me to do with it?"

"I heard they were good eatin'."

Cole used his hip to push the door shut and then walked through a large storeroom. Stopping well before reaching the kitchen, he dropped the plastic bundle and began working the kinks from his arms and legs. "I tried calling you a few times to see if you could use anything from this guy, but you never answered so I just brought the whole thing home."

The storeroom was illuminated by a single bare bulb hanging from the ceiling, making Paige's hair look more like an inky mess, while giving her sweatshirt and jeans a dingy quality. Studying her carefully, Cole reached out for the other two light switches on the wall. When the rest of the bulbs came on, he said, "You look like hell."

Paige not only kept her shotgun against her shoulder, but seemed ready to use it. "And you're home a day early. Your date must have gone *real* well."

Nodding at what seemed like a fair jab in response to his own comment, Cole said, "I scared her away, but it's not the first time I've had that effect on a woman."

"And it won't be the last."

"Okay, okay. Sorry I said you look like hell. We're even."

Paige shifted the shotgun to her left hand and let it hang at her side. Now that the bulky weapon was out of the way, Cole could see the paleness of her face. Her black hair didn't just look like a greasy mess. It was a greasy mess. Normally, she tied it back or wore a Cubs cap to keep it in check, but now it seemed just as worn-out as the rest of her. His eyes were drawn to her right arm, which was wrapped up in bandages and held tight against her torso by a sling. Although she'd been able to grip the shotgun and put her finger on the trigger, her hand remained in that position, like a claw that slowly curled into a fist.

"How's your arm?" he asked.

"Fucked up. Next question."

She stormed into the kitchen and Cole followed. "Did Daniels take a look at it?"

"Yes, Cole."

"Let me see it."

"No."

She'd led him through the kitchen and was on her way to her room. Before she could get there and shut her door, Cole ran ahead of her. "Let me see it," he demanded.

Paige was easily more than a foot shorter, but glared at Cole as if she was about to squash him under her sneakered foot. Eventually she let out a terse breath and shifted so her right side was a little closer to him. Cole was genuinely surprised she'd caved in so quickly.

Reaching out tentatively, he placed one hand on the sling and slipped the other inside it. On the surface, Paige's arm was smooth and finely toned. Her skin was on the cool side, but wasn't as clammy as the rest of her body. Considering the heat of any given night in Chicago during the summer, clamminess wasn't much of a shock. Since she hadn't budged at his initial moves, he pressed his hand down a bit more.

"Does that hurt?"

"No," she replied evenly.

Beneath the skin, her arm felt more petrified than stiff. It reminded him of the process that had turned a sapling into the lightweight, almost unbreakable spear that was his now first line of defense against anything supernatural. He gently ran his fingers along her arm, watching her face for any reaction. The source of her injury was a smeared, jagged line that looked as if it had been left by a felt-tip pen. The mass beneath it felt like a thick piece of wire embedded in her flesh.

"Can you move it?" he asked.

"You had your look, Cole. Just give it a rest."

"You need to move it. And don't look at me like that!" His fingers probed away from the line that had been tattooed into her skin and quickly found more grisly reminders of their time in Kansas City. The Full Blood's claws and teeth had left scars that marred her flesh like a key would mar the paint on a car door.

"All right," she said. "That's enough."

"Does it hurt?"

"No. I can barely feel anything."

"Then move it." When she tried to pull away, he tightened his grip on her wrist and said, "Can you just move your hand?"

She set her jaw into a firm line, pulled in a deep breath and let it out in a hiss. He could see the pain in her eyes, but didn't bother asking her about it. Thanks to the healing serums she'd already mixed and administered, Paige could have recovered from wounds bad enough to make the toughest soldier scream in agony. But healing wasn't enough. Skinners had to chew through regular pain and go in for seconds.

And thirds.

And possibly tenths.

The sheen on Paige's brow grew into several trickles of sweat as she forced her arm to rise up from where it rested within its sling. Her shirt was already soaked, which told Cole she'd probably been working at this for some time before he arrived. When her arm was about an inch and a half above the bottom of the sling, she bared her teeth and extended her hand like a ponderous mechanism that had been forged from rusted steel and bent at joints dipped in cold glue. While letting out another breath, she lifted her arm some more and uncurled her middle finger.

"You flipped me off a little quicker this time," Cole said.

After allowing her arm to drop back down, she swatted him away impatiently and headed for the fridge. "So your MEG girl didn't pan out, huh?"

Cole sat on one of the two stools in the large room and slapped his hands on the stainless steel countertop. "Abby's great, but I don't think she was ready for the whole Chupacabra thing."

"The package in the storeroom says that you handled it, though. Good job."

Catching the can of pop she tossed to him, Cole said, "Thanks. It really tore after me too! Remember how long we had to shake the grass in Indiana before that little one came sniffing?"

"Chupes grow differently wherever they live. All it takes is one generation for them to sprout another ear to hear past loud farm equipment, or longer toes to grab onto a certain kind of tree. Did you know I saw one that literally had an eye in the back of its head? That's what makes them so tough to track." Opening her own can of fully caffeinated soda, Paige took a sip and sat down on the stool directly across the counter from him.

He couldn't help noticing that they were in the same spots they'd been in during his very first visit to Rasa Hill. It was less than a year ago, but felt closer than his desk job and old apartment.

"I didn't need to do much tracking with this one," he told her.

"Chupes aren't usually so aggressive. At least, not with humans. They tend to go for smaller game like dogs or something slow like a cow."

"Or goats," Cole pointed out. "Chupacabra means Goat Sucker."

That got a smile from Paige that wasn't tired and wasn't forced. It went a long way in making her beautiful despite the run-down state she was in. "Or goats," she conceded. "I think you just got lucky with that one and caught it when it was hungry or possibly defending something."

"It ran me into a trap."

Scrunching her eyebrows together, she asked, "Are you sure about that?"

Cole nodded and drank some more pop. "It dug a pit, put rocks at the bottom, and partially hid it with branches."

"Could have just been a hole in the ground."

"Nope. It ran right past it without a stumble like it knew it was there. If I would have fallen in without catching myself, I would have broken something or at least been too hurt to crawl right back out again. It circled back after I fell, and when I tossed it down the same hole, it knew right where to grab to keep from hitting those rocks."

"That is strange," she said. "Good thing you took it out. If a Chupe was getting that ballsy, it wouldn't have been long before it started going after more people."

"Thank you! Abby acted like I was a monster for putting that thing down."

"There's a reason why we only use MEG for communications," Paige told him. "They're watchers. They like to listen for noises and try to figure out what's being said. Skinners listen for noises so they know which door to kick in. Every now and then someone from MEG wants to tag along and see everything we do. If this one was so squeamish, it's good that you took the wind out of her sails. No offense."

Cole rattled his pop can on the counter and watched the light bounce off the rounded edge. "It sucks that she had to be so nice. And cute. And fun."

"You did great. It turned out to be a perfect training run."

"Speaking of training, when are we going to spar again?"

She shifted her right arm within its sling and said, "I'm not in any condition to spar. I don't even know when this will heal."

"What if something happens and we're not ready for it?"

"Nothing's going to happen. The Mongrels are so entrenched in KC that they'll chase away any shapeshifter within four hundred miles, bring them in, or tear them up. On top of that, the cops are on the lookout for anything suspicious on four legs. Did you hear about all the dog fighting rings that have been broken up recently?"

"No. Does that have anything to do with werewolves?"

"Not at all. It just shows we're not the only ones cracking down. If another Half Breed shows itself anywhere near Kansas City, it'll get blasted to pieces by a SWAT team."

"So what happened to all those Half Breeds anyway?" Cole asked. "They were running wild through the streets and now they're all gone. I know we had some help from the Mongrels, but we couldn't have gotten all of them."

"Officer Stanze had some things to say about that."

Cole waggled his eyebrows and asked, "So you did spend some time with him, huh?"

"He said there's been a lot of dead Half Breeds turning up all over the place," she replied, while ignoring the suggestive tone in Cole's voice. "KC seems pretty clear, but after all the stuff that's been on the news or plastered all over Home-BrewTV.com, most of the country considers the KCPD to be the authorities on freaky looking dogs."

"Are a lot of them turning up outside of KC?"

"Yeah. Turning up dead. Even if half of the reports are just misidentified road kill, Stanze says there are still plenty more coming in that are similar to the ones from KC. He's been pretty helpful, but I doubt even he knows how much footage the cops are sitting on so they can try and figure it out. A Full Blood smashed one of their cruisers. Somebody had to have gotten evidence of that." Paige rubbed her sore arm and finished her drink. Finally, she crumpled the can in her good hand, missed a three-point shot at the trash can, and stood up. "Everyone's all worked up about this Mud Flu thing, so maybe that'll be enough to distract the public eye from KC for a little while."

"I heard that flu's actually kind of bad," Cole said. "You throw up, get this gunk in your throat, and there are even some reports of people getting some kind of dementia."

"Has anyone died from it?"

"I don't think so."

"Then it's just another kind of sick," she said. "The press always has to get worked up about something, so at least they're not yammering about us. Right now, I just want to go to bed."

"Are we sparring tomorrow?"

"Spar on your own."

"You can tighten that sling and go a few rounds. Come on!"

"You heard me," she shouted while marching from the kitchen.

Cole followed her and said, "I thought you were recovering. What happened to that?"

Paige's bedroom was messier than usual and, despite the soap she'd made to mask her scent, still carried the fragrance of her skin and the shampoo she treated herself to when she didn't expect to go out hunting.

"I think you're forgetting something pretty important here," he told her.

She squared her shoulders in a way that told him he was very close to regretting having stepped foot into her room. "What did I forget?"

"Your experiment worked. Sure, it may have backfired a little, but you threw down with a Full Blood. That thing should have torn your arm off, but it didn't. It couldn't even bite down to the bone! You may be wounded, but you can still fight."

"Apart from allowing myself to become a chew toy, what the hell am I supposed to do against anything anymore?"

"So that's it, huh?" he asked. "You're pissed because you realized you can't walk through fire after all. Join the rest of us measly humans."

Paige lunged to grab his shirt. Having already been grabbed, hit, punched, swept, and generally knocked around during countless sparring matches, he knew what to expect. What he didn't expect was for the impact of her fist against his chest to hit him like an aluminum baseball bat.

"I know all too well that I'm human," she snarled. "That's been made perfectly clear to me in more ways than you can imagine. How about you shove your analysis up your ass right along with your goddamn pity!"

"Hey Paige. Look down."

Her scowl deepened as if her opponent had just tried to tell her that her shoelace was untied. When Cole nodded and looked down first, she followed suit.

The hand she'd used to grab his shirt was her right one, and she'd gotten it to move faster than she'd been able to in days. Her fingers were locked around a clump of his shirt and the sling dangled from her arm as if supported by her rather than the other way around.

"Oh my God," she breathed.

"You're shaken up, out of your element, and not feeling too good right now," he said while patting the dead weight of her fist. "Believe me, I know all about that sort of thing."

No longer trying to get away from him, Paige slowly flexed her arm as if the muscles had been packed in ice, then lowered it into the sling.

"You could always just twist that arm around and slap it where it needs to go," Cole offered. "You know, like that constable in *Young Frankenstein* with the wooden hand?"

The sight of her trying to keep a straight face was one

of the prettiest he had seen in a long time. She let her head droop so it bumped against his chest. "God damn it," she groaned. "I've messed up before, but why did I have to mess up like *this*?"

He wrapped Paige up in his arms and ran his fingers through the tangled, unkempt mess of her hair. "Look at the bright side," he told her. "If we ever need a light, we can set the tip of your finger on fire. Or if there's a door we can't open, we can use you as a battering ram."

"I get it. You can stop now."

A heavy knock thumped through the room.

"That's enough, Cole. No need for sound effects."

"I didn't do that," he said. "Someone's knocking on our door."

Another couple of thumps rolled through the restaurant. Paige stepped away and looked down at his feet. "You weren't stomping on the floor?" she asked.

"No."

She whipped around so quickly that she almost knocked Cole onto his butt in her haste to get to the panel on the wall next to her door. Once there, she poked at a set of buttons with her left hand. "Someone's at the front door," she said while reaching around to take a little .32 caliber revolver from where it had been tucked at the small of her back. "Take this."

"You really don't like salesmen, do you?"

Scowling in a familiar *Do what I say and be quick about it* way, she hurried into the kitchen, where her shotgun was propped against a wall. Cole got a feel for the weight of the pistol and then flipped the cylinder open to double-check that the gun was loaded. He didn't have time to check what sort of rounds they were, but they all came out of the barrel fast enough to damage human and monster alike.

The windows at the front of the restaurant were boarded up. The main door was latched, bolted, and held shut with steel posts. He stepped up to a slit in one of the windows, which allowed him to get a look outside at the solitary figure standing at the door and a cab that tore out of the parking lot as if the driver had just been tipped off about a shipment of drunk tourists arriving at O'Hare.

"We're closed," Cole said through the door.

The voice that came from the other side was strained to the point of cracking. "I need to talk to you."

Cole's scars itched, alerting him to the presence of Nymar. Even if the man outside was the only Nymar in the vicinity, he knew there should have been more of a reaction than that. Since Paige hadn't said anything about the Nymar before, she must not have felt much of anything either. Cole found her in the shadows on the other side of the door with her shotgun aimed at the entrance.

"What do you want?" he asked the visitor.

"I have to talk to the Skinners," the man replied. "If you're one, then you've got to open this door!"

Cole glanced at Paige again and got a single nod from her. Whatever was on the other side of that door, she was ready for it.

After removing the iron bar from its bracket in the floor and pulling back the bolts, Cole twisted the knob to unlock one of the more traditional mechanisms. When he finally pulled the door open a few inches, he held it there with the side of his foot, as if that could keep out a rowdy drunk, not to mention anything farther away from the human end of the spectrum.

The man outside was dressed in dark cargo pants and boots that could have come off the shelf of any army surplus store. His tattered flannel shirt was open to reveal a bare chest covered in black markings that looked like a massive tribal tattoo. Unlike a tattoo, however, the Nymar's markings trembled beneath his flesh as the spore attached to the vampire's heart shifted within its shell. He had a young, slender face with a minimum of whiskers protruding from his chin, and greasy, light-colored hair that hung down to his shoulders. His cheeks were shallow, but not sunken, and his eyes were wide with barely contained panic.

Cole held the .32 out where it could be seen before having to shove it into the other man's face. "What do you want?"

"Are you Cole?" the Nymar asked. "I need to talk to Cole or Paige. I was told they're here. I need to talk to them."

"Who are you?"

Although he appeared to be looking around while self-consciously pulling his shirt closed, it was obvious that his eyes were twitching as much as the tendrils beneath his skin. "Stephanie told me the Skinners were here."

"Damn it. I'm Cole."

Even when she wasn't anywhere in sight, the head of Chicago's Nymar skin trade still found ways to make things difficult. If the shaky man was sent by Stephanie, he could be anything from an annoying junkie to a suicide bomber.

When the Nymar reached out for him, Cole brought the .32 up and tightened his finger around the trigger almost enough to drop the hammer. "Stay where you are!"

The man pressed one hand against the door and the other against its frame. Leaning forward caused his shirt to fall open and his long hair to drop like a set of light brown curtains on either side of his face.

"I said stay put," Cole warned as he extended an arm to keep him from crossing the threshold.

The man outside gripped the door and frame with enough strength to break them both. His entire body convulsed and pink foam spilled from his mouth with a gurgling heave. Tendrils pressed outward to become swollen ridges upon the Nymar's torso. When they tore completely through the visitor's chest, Cole pulled his trigger while jumping back to give Paige a clear shot. Even as the shotgun roared, he doubted it would be enough to do the job.

Chapter 5

The Nymar straightened up, threw his head back and would have screamed if his throat wasn't already filled with the black appendages that began at his heart and now frantically grasped for something else. Cole's bullets punched into him but did as much damage as they would to a bowl of pudding. Paige's shotgun blast hit the Nymar before he could take one step into the restaurant, opening a hole for more tendrils to explode from his chest. Thinner strings poked out of the Nymar's mouth, followed by larger ones emerging through his neck and wrists.

"Jesus!" Cole shouted as he sent the Nymar staggering backward with a straight kick to his center of mass.

The tendrils looked like eels that had been left out to dry, but felt more like solid muscle as they tried to grab Cole's ankle and snake their way up his leg. They stretched toward the doorway and then grasped at empty air in a futile attempt to find something to latch on to. The Nymar's back hit the ground and he stared up at the cloud-smeared sky, pulling one last gulp of humid air into tattered lungs. The tendrils stretched out in all directions before wilting like dozens of legs sprouting from a dead spider.

Once the Nymar stopped moving, sounds from the street pressed harder against Cole's ears. It was late, but not late enough for them to have complete privacy so close to Laramie Avenue. "Let's get him inside," Paige said. "Actually, you get him inside."

"Is that you acting helpless again?"

"No, it's me pulling rank on you. Get him inside."

There wasn't any way to argue with that, so Cole tucked the .32 in his belt, grabbed the Nymar's ankles and dragged it through the front door. Every step of the way, Paige kept the shotgun pointed at the mess of tendrils. The barrel rested upon her right arm, her left hand wrapped around the grip. It wasn't the safest way to carry a loaded gun, but it would suffice for the few steps required to get away from prying eyes.

The Nymar's arms dangled uselessly and his head wobbled from side to side as Cole pulled him into Rasa Hill. Tendrils hung from his mouth like dark strings of phlegm. The thicker ones sprouting from his chest were almost solid enough to be the tentacles of a sea creature that had died while coming up for air. All the other filaments merely dangled from their various escape routes like wet strings.

After shutting and locking the front door, Paige settled over the Nymar with her shotgun pointed at its heart. "Did you do anything to him?" she asked.

Cole looked up at her as if she'd suddenly become the most unbelievable thing in the room. "Did I do something to him?!"

"Well I've never seen anything like that!"

"He said Steph sent him."

After handing Cole the shotgun, Paige sat at one of the tables and dug her phone out of her pocket. "Hi, Steph," she said after dialing. "Were you expecting my call?"

While Paige tore into one of the leading members of Chicago's Nymar community, Cole took a closer look at the one on the floor. He gathered just enough courage to reach down and poke at one of the tentacles protruding from the corpse's chest. Even though he hadn't seen many of them outside of a body, Nymar tendrils all seemed to have a fluid, almost delicate quality to them. These were tough, leathery, and becoming coarser by the second. Instead of its spore absorbing every last bit of blood or moisture in its host's body before crumbling away, this one had been turned into something resembling a tangle of old tree roots.

"Yeah?" Paige said sharply into her phone. "Well if you don't know who he is, then how the hell are we supposed to find out?"

That was a good question. When Cole heard it, he came up with a solution that seemed way too easy to work. Since he didn't have anything better to do at the moment, he reached through the drooping tentacles to pat the dead Nymar's pockets.

"His name's Peter Walsh," he announced.

Paige nodded to shut him up and kept talking to the Nymar who ran Chicago's lucrative Blood Parlors.

Snapping his fingers at Paige because he knew it annoyed the hell out of her, Cole caught her attention and held it. "This guy's name is Peter Walsh," he repeated.

"Are you sure?"

"Pretty sure," he replied while showing her the dead Nymar's wallet.

When Paige held out a hand, Cole slapped the wallet into it.

"So," she said into her phone while looking over the Nymar's driver's license, "this guy Peter comes all the way from St. Louis and you send him straight to me? What made you do a thing like that?" After a few seconds she smirked and added, "Of course he's really here. He said you sent him. Anything else you want to tell me about this guy?"

The only other things in the dead Nymar's pockets were keys, some money, and a rumpled piece of paper. Cole examined each in turn while Paige continued to send some grief through the digital connection to Rush Street.

"Your Blood Parlors are only open because we allow them to stay that way," she reminded her. "If Cole and I have to come down there again . . . Oh you heard I was hurt, did you? Why don't I just drive on down there and show you how badly I'm hurt? You want to bank on me being too wounded to pull a trigger?" Paige smiled again. If her other arm wasn't in a sling, she would have put it to work patting herself on the back. "All right, then. I'm listening."

Cole took the wallet from her and sifted through it. Peter Walsh didn't have any objections to the intrusion and he didn't have anything interesting in his wallet. Although, Cole did find it somewhat interesting that a vampire needed a driver's license, auto insurance, and memberships to several different retail discount clubs.

"Don't worry," Paige said definitively, "I will. 'Bye." She ended the call and stuck her phone back into her pocket. "Steph says this guy just showed up earlier tonight and asked about where he could find the Skinners."

"Do you believe her?"

"No, because there are Skinners in St. Louis. At least there were the last time I checked." A twitch showed on Paige's face, which betrayed the slightest bit of concern. "Maybe I should check again. Steph kept to her story well enough, and with her Blood Parlors doing such good business, she's got no reason to make a move against us."

"And if she did, she would just send a bunch of goth kids with guns," Cole offered. "That's more her style. Maybe Peter didn't want to talk to the Skinners in St. Louis. Maybe he only wanted to see us. He did ask for us by name."

"Steph gave him our names along with our address. She said the guy seemed desperate and he looked sick, so she wanted to make sure he got here quick enough to make a mess. Her words."

And Cole knew that was just the sort of thing Stephanie would say. He was familiar enough with the Nymar madam to know that driving to Rush Street just to kick in her door would be more trouble than it was worth. If the Chicago Nymar wanted to clean out Rasa Hill, they would have sent a much clearer message.

Paige walked over to Peter's body and started prodding the various tendrils that had emerged from his wrist and mouth. "Steph was right. He did seem desperate and he certainly was sick. These tendrils are almost solid. They should be squishier. More like a jellyfish." She was in trainer mode. Her voice took on a calmer quality when she was showing Cole the ropes.

"Do they normally get that big?" he asked.

Shifting her attention to the tentacles hanging out of Peter's chest, she took hold of one and waggled it as if shaking a dog's paw. "Yeah, but they don't become so solid. They need to move around inside a body, not fill it up completely. The spore like to curl up and stay warm, not . . . this."

"So what happened?"

Paige stood up and shrugged her shoulders. "Hell if I know. Maybe that's what he wanted to tell us. I honestly don't think Steph knows anything either, but we could go talk to her to be sure."

"He's from St. Louis," Cole pointed out. "You said there are Skinners there?"

"Ned Post. He's been there ever since Rico and I left. To be honest, Ned's mostly a night watchman but maybe he—"

Suddenly, the Nymar braced himself with both hands against the floor, propped himself up and got to his feet. "It's in *my* blood!" he said, his mouth covered in a greasy sludge and the tendrils that had come out of him no longer moving. After hacking up more of the sludge, Peter added, "They're part of it. They *gotta* be part of it!"

"What's in your blood?" Cole asked.

Although Peter tried to breathe, the air merely leaked out through his chest.

When the Nymar looked down at his own mutilated torso, Cole took hold of his chin and forced him to look up again. "Look at me, Peter. A part of what? Who are you talking about?"

Peter drew some resolve from whatever was keeping him going and said, "The nymphs. They're part of the infection that's in me. It'll kill all of us!"

"All of you?" Paige asked. "All Nymar?"

Peter shook his head and looked in every direction but where she was standing. Unable to pinpoint where her voice was coming from, he settled for addressing the air around him. "Pestilence. It'll kill all of us. All of us. Just like the Good Book says. JustliketheGoodBooksays. Justlike . . ." He arched his back and grabbed the floor as the tendrils from his wrists fluttered and dissolved into a dark fluid much like the stuff around his mouth. The tentacles coming from his chest finally collapsed to lay like flattened tubes against his body.

Sensing that things were only going to get worse from there, Cole held onto Peter's face so his hands could act as a set of blinders. "What are you talking about?" he demanded.

"Pestilence!"

"You mean a disease?" Paige asked. "A disease in your blood?"

Peter nodded as best he could. "Just like . . . the Good Book says." The tentacles sprouting from his chest had turned into something else. They were no longer leathery, but dry and shriveled, as if the wooden slats of the floor had attempted to reach up and claim the Nymar's remains.

"What," Cole gasped as he set Peter down and stepped away, "the *hell* was that?"

Paige stared down at the mess, watching as the tentacles became even more brittle. She bent down to take a closer look at Peter's face and dipped her finger into the sludge pasted to his mouth.

Cole grabbed her wrist and snapped, "He just said he was sick! Why would you touch that stuff? Awww, *man*! It's all over me!"

"If he's sick and this stuff carries it, we're way past washing our hands now."

She was right about that. The gunk was spattered all over the front of their clothes, arms, and several spots of exposed skin. Calmly pulling out of Cole's grip, Paige studied her hand and rubbed her fingers together. "There's some kind of film in this stuff. I think it's the membrane that held the tendrils together."

"Hey," Cole said as he examined the dark substance that clung to his shirt. "Do you think this has anything to do with the Mud Flu?"

"This crap does look kind of muddy, but I doubt any Nymar disease could affect humans. The organs we use to process food and circulate blood are just padding and ductwork to them. Still, we should check it out just to be safe. He was pretty intent on getting here and talking to us, so we might as well see it through. You get something under that body to stop it leaking on the floor and I'll call Daniels. Maybe he can make sense of this."

"And what was all that talk about nymphs? Did he mean the same one Prophet found at that strip bar?"

Paige bared her teeth in a little snarl. "I knew I shouldn't have given that tramp a pass. If she's spreading some kind of new disease, then I'll clip her little fairy wings and wring Prophet's neck for sticking up for her."

Grabbing Peter's wallet, Cole went through all the slips of paper and receipts one more time. "What was the name of that place in Wisconsin where we met Tristan?"

"Shimmy's. Did you find something from there?"

"No," he said as he removed a bright red ticket from the wallet and handed it to Paige. "But we may have another delightful field trip in store for us."

The ticket was a voucher for a free drink that could only be redeemed at Bunn's Lounge in Sauget, Illinois.

Chapter 6

Daniels walked through the front door dressed in a brown and red checked bowling shirt and baggy pants. "I'm not at your beck and call, you know. I've got a lot going on. I just got things back together with my girlfriend, the Chicago Nymar have finally worked out a deal to quiet things down, and I finally got my online collectibles acquisition business up and running!"

"What deal with the Nymar?" Paige asked.

Cole chimed in with, "What kind of collectibles?"

Daniels pointed to Paige and replied, "Aphrodisiacs for Steph's Blood Parlor, which aren't much more than sugar water." To Cole, he said, "Action figures from any series you can name. Get me a prototype for one of the new Hammer Strike figurines and I'll see about a discount on whatever you like." Back to Paige. "You were supposed to come over so I could take another sample from you. Did something come up?"

Fresh from a quick shower and change of clothes, she kicked the putrid bundle encased in plastic tarp and told him, "You're looking at it."

Daniels was a squat fellow with an ample gut that didn't quite hang over his belt. What little hair he had on his head was in a short ring that went from the back of one ear and around to the other. While most Nymar markings were in the spots with the highest blood circulation like the neck or wrists, Daniels's tendrils were mostly clustered on his scalp like a supernatural toupee. Stopping several tables away from the bundle, he set down the metal case he'd brought with him and grinned, displaying some fangs that drooped lazily down from his gums. "I put together that list you wanted, Cole."

Cole was freshly scrubbed as well, but brightened up even more when he heard that. "Great. Where is it?"

"Got it right here," Daniels replied while digging into his shirt pocket.

"What list?" Paige asked.

Daniels glanced up at her and then closed his sausage fingers around the piece of paper he'd taken from his shirt pocket. "Nothing."

"It's just a list of some other concoctions he's made along with some ingredients," Cole explained.

"Nothing that could really cause any trouble if it got out," Daniels assured her. "Just some things to give him some ideas for the game he's working on. Like power-ups that are different than your typical fare."

Cole winced, knowing that assurances like those were worse than whatever else Daniels had been afraid of saying.

"Game?" Paige growled. "What game?"

"I need something to stay afloat if I'm ever going to get any sort of job back at Digital Dreamers," Cole told her. "Also I thought making a game with some dog-type monsters could deflect some of the heat from the whole Kansas City thing. You know, like that special MEG's going to air about the werewolf sightings."

"How is any of that going to help with that?" she asked.

Daniels shrugged and said, "Makes sense to me. If you want to discredit something like that, don't cover it up and give ammunition to the conspiracy buffs. Trot it right out for everyone to see. Remember that alien autopsy show that was on like ten years ago? They showed a grainy, supposedly classified video on TV and had one of the actors from *Star Trek* host it."

"So that was real?" Paige asked.

"I don't know," Daniels replied. "But if it was, that was the perfect way to make it look fake. You already doctored some of that legitimate Kansas City footage so it looked like a hoax and released it, right?"

Cole nodded proudly. "Yes, and it was brilliant."

"Well, combine that with some cable special hosted by MEG, and your average person will be more willing to believe they're just watching another show, as opposed to anything truly world-changing. Did you hear about those Mongrels that were spotted in Crown Center? The pictures of them skulking under some cars were written off as fakes before they could cause any commotion. People are more ready to accept this Mud Flu as a genuine concern than werewolves."

"You're not putting Mongrels in any game, Cole," Paige said. "That just draws attention to them while they're trying to lay low. If they get backed into a corner, they could get violent, and then we'll have to go back there and wipe them out. That would go against the promise I made to leave them be."

"Those Mongrels are freaky little things, if you ask me." Daniels shuddered. "Not as bad as Half Breeds, but nobody's seen any of them since KC. I mean *nobody*."

As Cole slipped the list into his pocket, Paige said, "Will you just take a look at this mess on the floor?"

Daniels had been doing a good job of distracting himself so far, but he got twitchy as he approached the bulky, misshapen corpse beneath the plastic sheet. As he became increasingly nervous, the Nymar loosened his already baggy shirt by tugging on his collar. His eyes bugged a little, which gave him something of a Rodney Dangerfield quality.

Once he got past the initial reaction to seeing what was left of Peter Walsh, however, Daniels circled the body and took notes in a progressively more frenetic pace. The only time he stopped was to run out to his car and retrieve a case that reminded Cole of a kit used by forensic investigators on TV. The contents of the Nymar's baggage were a collection of test tubes, racks for the tubes, and slips of different kinds of paper to put into the tubes. Once it was all set up,

Daniels pulled on some plastic gloves and got to work. He snipped pieces from different tentacles and took samples of sludge from various spots on Peter's face, wrists, and neck. It didn't take long for Cole to realize why that portion of the investigation was always sped up in a montage for those forensics shows.

A few exceedingly boring hours later Daniels announced, "I've only done a quick once-over, but I can already tell you this man's spore was poisoned."

· "Just his spore?" Paige asked.

"That's right. I can run some more tests—at least the tests I'm equipped for—but his human tissue seems fairly healthy."

Cole let out a single laugh and said, "Except for the tissue that was ripped open like a bag of Jiffy Pop."

"Yes," Daniels muttered. "Obviously. But what's most interesting is this." Taking a pen from his shirt pocket, he used it to poke one of the thickest tentacles that had emerged from Peter Walsh's chest. "Were these always so brittle?"

"No. They were more like muscle before. Now they just look shriveled."

"Could that be because they're outside instead of in?" Paige asked.

Nodding, Daniels said, "Partially. I've done extensive research on myself, and I can tell you that when any part of a spore is taken from its resting place, it maintains a certain . . ."

"Squishiness?" Paige offered.

"I was going to say viscosity, but yes. How long ago did this man die?"

"A few minutes before I called you," she replied.

"If a Nymar has been feeding well enough for its spore to be this large, it would take considerably longer to dry out. But it's impossible for him to have had these tentacles in his chest cavity anyway. As you can see, most of his organs are more or less intact. See the stretch marks on the inner tissue? They're relatively fresh. These thicker protrusions were made this way fairly quickly, maybe even occurring spontaneously as a reaction to some sort of imbalance or foreign substance. Again, this is all based on initial observations, but I can tell you this is as much a Nymar as a Half Breed is a human being. The base materials are there, but they've been warped beyond recognition."

"What warped it?" Paige asked.

"Whatever is tainting this spore, it's not a standard narcotic or any prescription medication," Daniels explained as he pointed to a short rack of test tubes. Each tube had just enough of the sludge to fill the bottom with a different strip of material soaking in it. "Granted, there are a lot of other tests I can run with enough time, but my preliminary findings are that this toxin is natural."

Grateful to look at test tubes instead of the corpse, Cole asked, "What do you mean natural?"

"It's not shapeshifter or Nymar in origin, but it could very well be something from one of the lesser known races."

"What about nymphs?" Paige said.

"That's a possibility," Daniels replied with a nod.

"I thought you said natural," Cole reminded them.

"Yes," Daniels stated. "Shapeshifters, nymphs, even Nymar occur naturally. They're the products of some unusual evolution, but they're certainly not man-made."

Just when Cole thought he'd redefined his world enough, another little corner of it got swept clean of his preconceptions. "Before he died, Peter said something about the nymphs having diseased blood," he said.

Tapping his pen against one of his drooping fangs, Daniels said, "I've read texts written by other Nymar that theorize about a connection between them and nymphs that goes back several hundred years."

"What connection?" Cole asked.

After some uncomfortable squirming, Daniels finally spat out the words he so rarely forced from his mouth. "I . . . don't know much more than that."

"Can you look into it?" Paige asked.

"Definitely," the chemist said as he dove straight back into his comfort zone. "I've had my eye on some old books I found online, but haven't had the money to buy them. It would sure be nice if I had a little help with that."

"We'll float you a loan," Paige said. Before Daniels could grouse about it, she added, "And if your information actually helps us, you can consider them a gift."

"There are a few other books that might be of some use . . ." Seeing the scowl taking shape on Paige's face, Daniels added, " . . . but they can wait."

"Have you ever heard of Pestilence?" Cole asked.

Daniels blinked as if the subject change had been sudden enough to rattle his eyeballs. Then he let his lids drop and recited, " 'They shall be wasted with hunger, devoured by pestilence and bitter destruction; I will also send against them the teeth of beasts, with the poison of serpents in the dust.' " Opening his eyes and taking in the perplexed expressions worn by both Skinners, he said, "Deuteronomy 32:24. I'm certain pestilence is mentioned a few other times in the Bible, but that was the first one to come to mind. That's also supposed to be one of the Four Horsemen of the Apocalypse."

"No, it's something else Peter said while he was talking about the nymphs and diseased blood. You don't think we're all sick now too, do you?"

Looking at his gloved hand, Daniels said, "Nymar don't catch airborne or contact viruses. If this is infectious, I would have had to ingest it somehow, and," he added with a snorting laugh, "I didn't exactly drink any of this stuff."

"Great. So it may just be us."

"Let me keep doing my tests before you get all riled up."

"Here's how it's gonna go," Paige announced. "Get to work on seeing what made this Nymar stop ticking. Pestilence is the name for whatever did this to him, so drop whatever else you're working on and figure out what that is. We'll do the same."

"But," Daniels protested, "the other project I'm working on is the cure for your arm."

"And how's that coming along?"

"I think I may have something . . . but I'll need some more tissue samples to be sure."

"Forget it," she said. "Pestilence is more important, so just focus on that for now. You've got my cell number. If I don't hear from you at least twice a day, I'll call, and if you don't answer—"

"Wait," Daniels cut in. "Where are you going?"

"We need to go to St. Louis. That's where this guy came from."

"But your arm won't get any better on its own," Daniels protested. "And the longer I go without treating it, the less likely it will be that it can be treated!"

"Forget about it. My arm, my problem."

Although Paige tried to leave the room, Daniels reminded her that he wasn't quite human when he actually managed to get in front of her and say, "Whether you administered that mixture prematurely or not, I was still the one who made it, and I intend on fixing it."

"I'm fine," Paige said as she lifted her arm from its sling and strained to flex her fingers. "See?"

Daniels was not impressed. "I'm coming with you," he insisted.

Paige looked at him and shook her head. "Not this time. There's someone in St. Louis who might be able to give us some insight as to what's going on."

"Is this contact a Nymar?"

"No."

"Then they're not as qualified to examine this specimen." Before she could rebut that statement, Daniels added, "If this contact has enough space for me to work in a protected environment, I could move my investigation along much faster."

She narrowed her eyes and stood toe-to-toe with the dumpy Nymar. "Wouldn't the lab in your apartments be a good enough place to work? Or here? You can have the run of this place while we're away. And what about that collectibles thing you started?"

"Actually," Daniels groaned, "my girlfriend's got a whole shopping trip planned to refurnish my second floor apartment. There's colors to look at, patterns to choose, then she'll want me to move furniture. It's a whole, involved process. If I was to come along with you, I wouldn't have anything else to do other than work."

"How is Sally?" Cole asked.

Brightening at the mention of her name, Daniels replied, "Great. After those animals tore through the building the last time you were there, she's decided to move in with me."

"Hey! Congrats."

"How long will it take for you to finish with Peter?" Paige asked.

"Another day should be sufficient. There's plenty of tests to run, but that would be enough time for me to check out a few—"

"You've got until tomorrow," she cut in. "Then Cole and I head out to St. Louis with or without you. Also, you're driving your own car and paying for your own gas."

Daniels obviously wasn't happy about that, but nodded tersely rather than concede. "Fine."

"And you," she said to Cole as she followed him toward the kitchen. "If the wrong stuff from that list shows up in one of your games, you'll see how much I can do with this gimpy arm of mine."

"Yes, ma'am. Nice to have you back, by the way. When you stop feeling sorry for yourself, you become the Paige I've always known."

"You haven't really known me that long," she pointed out.

Cole let go of the heavy door they'd installed. "Hey!" she scolded as she caught it.

Reaching out to push the door back, Cole noticed that she'd been quick and strong enough to hold it open using her right arm. "Sometimes a wounded little bird just needs to be pushed out of the nest," he mused.

Paige strode ahead and grumbled, "I got yer bird right here."

Chapter 7

Coming from Seattle, Cole had needed some time to adjust to the heat of a Chicago summer. He hadn't been away from Washington for very long, so he was still getting used to it. Coming from Chicago, however, the heat in St. Louis was something special. They'd left Rasa Hill after a breakfast consisting of three different kinds of meat, eggs, and cheese sandwiched between bagels or English muffins. Once they got onto the open road, they were able to drive at their leisure. Too bad it felt as if the Cavalier's tires were melting to the pavement.

"Why couldn't we have taken the rental car?" Cole asked. "At least that had air-conditioning."

"Stop whining. If Daniels is going to drain our spare cash to buy books, we can't afford to rent a car. Hang your head out the window. That helped in KC."

"KC was seasonally warm. This feels like a damn blast furnace."

"You'll get used to it," Paige said as she tuned the radio to an alternative rock station and cranked the volume just high enough to discourage more conversation.

It was early evening when they skirted downtown St. Louis and caught their first glimpse of the Gateway Arch.

Having trailed behind them this far, Daniels blinked the headlights of his SUV to let them know he was splitting off to try and make contact with some of the local Nymar. Cole watched the scenery go by as the tall, shining buildings in that area gave way to crumbling apartments and warehouses that looked as if they'd all been scorched by the same fire. Within a fair amount of time, the architecture shifted once again to that of St. Louis University.

Paige sat in the driver's seat as always. Despite the fact that she steered from the sling, she knew the area well enough to be an asset behind the wheel. Her navigation came in very handy since, no matter how much Cole itched to use his new GPS, there was so much construction that the little box would have probably started smoking after chugging through too many recalculations.

Letting his eyes wander along the scenery, he asked, "You used to live here, right?"

"Yep."

"Isn't this where you did your training?"

"That's right," she replied.

"What's his name? Rico. You worked with him here, didn't you?"

"Sure did."

Cole drew a deep breath and hung his arm out the window. When they were flying down Highway 40 at seventy miles an hour, the breeze actually felt pretty good. "Rrrrico," he said, making sure to roll the R off his tongue. "I'm picturing some baby-face little pretty boy with a bandanna and no shirt under a leather jacket."

"Are you? Well, whatever floats your boat."

"You know. Because of that song from the eighties. Rrrrr-rico."

Paige nodded. "Be sure to mention that when you meet him. He loves that joke."

"Is he still here?"

She looked over at him while gunning her engine to get around a Mustang lingering in the right lane. "Ned Post is the resident Skinner around here, but he isn't exactly up to that sort of thing anymore. Rico came by to lend him a hand."

"Sure would have been nice for him to lend us a hand in KC."

"Rico was stomping through the Rockies after some domestic Yetis. Once he gets wrapped up in a hunt like that, he doesn't resurface until it's done."

Paige exited at Kingshighway Boulevard and drove past a large park. Normally, Cole would have enjoyed the greenery, but he'd become all too familiar with the kinds of things that live in wooded areas, whether they were in a city or not. He and Paige both kept their eyes pointed forward.

"This town seems pretty quiet," he said.

"Then you must be deaf."

As if to prove her point, tires squealed at the intersection in front of them and four people started screaming at the white pickup that had stuck its front end out where it didn't belong. Two of those screamers weren't even remotely involved in the averted accident.

Cole made loose fists to rub his fingertips against his palms. "No, I mean quiet in the . . . wait," he said as a fiery pain touched his hands. His scars' reaction to shapeshifters felt like a match being dragged across his skin. "I guess this place isn't as quiet as I thought."

"Rico told me he cleared out all the Half Breeds."

"When did you talk to him?"

"While you were helping Daniels load that body into his backseat."

As they continued down Kingshighway, the pain grew stronger. It wasn't the deep tissue burn caused by a Full Blood, and it wasn't the prickly sensation set off by a Half Breed. When Paige turned onto McPherson Avenue, Cole put a name to the pain. "Mongrels," he said. "And they must be close."

Paige gunned the Cav's engine so she could skid into a parking spot against the curb a split second ahead of the black four-door that had been waiting for it with its blinker ticking. "Damn," she said. "I am one hell of a good teacher."

The black car held its ground, and when Cole got out, a man with a meticulously trimmed goatee stuck his head through the driver's side window and screamed, "That's my spot, asshole!"

Cole took his harness from the backseat but tried to keep it out of sight. Even though the spear was collapsed down to about half the size of a baseball bat, he didn't quite succeed in keeping it under wraps.

"Oh, you wanna go?" the man with the goatee blustered as he kicked his door open.

Paige exited the Cav, walked up to the four-door, ripped the sling from her shoulder and dropped her right arm down onto the hood of the loudmouth's car like a hammer. "Find another spot, dickless!"

The other guy froze half in and half out of his car. Grumbling to himself, he eased all the way in and drove off. Only when he was a safe distance away did he shout back at her.

Paige nodded at the people walking along the sidewalk and then to Cole. "I needed that." She rubbed her forearm and tossed her sling into the Cav before leading the way toward Euclid Avenue.

The sun hadn't set too long ago, and there were plenty of people walking on either side of the street. Cars drifted up and down paths of cracked concrete, passing buildings that were mostly two or three stories tall and made from similar dark red brick. Other structures were lighter in color, but all of them had a flair that made the entire area look as if it had been pieced together with care instead of churned out by a massive corporate construction project. Plants hung down from windows of homes and stores alike. Bright awnings extended over the sidewalks and painted iron trellises framed several windows. Even the people ambling from building to building seemed well maintained. Most of them looked like college students or aiming for that age bracket in the way they dressed. The couple standing between a pair of trees guarded by a little fence near the intersection of McPherson and Euclid would have blended in perfectly if they hadn't been caught staring directly at Paige and Cole.

He returned the stare and started walking toward them. "I think I spotted them, Paige."

The man wore khaki shorts and a baseball cap. He eased one slender, hairy leg back, while his female companion in a jeans skirt bent her knees slightly. Their movements didn't stick out too much amid all the activity around them, but when Cole saw the subtle way they lowered their heads and raised their shoulders, something in his gut told him they were about to pounce.

Paige stooped down to take the baton from her boot holster. "Try to get them across the street to that little garage."

The structure looked like a small cottage with one large door, and was positioned directly across from the fenced-in trees. It was at the mouth of a narrow side street that wasn't half as busy as Euclid Avenue. "Got it," he said as he drove the thorns from his weapon's handle into his scarred palms.

The instant blood welled up from his hands, both of the people he'd spotted picked up on it. Their nostrils flared as they crouched down and prepared to strike.

Cole and Paige ran at them, scattering a group of four pedestrians along the way.

Apparently, Paige wasn't the only one who'd scoped out the little garage, because the Mongrels darted across Euclid and disappeared down that very side street. The movement wasn't spectacular enough to draw more than a few excited voices from the onlookers, but it got the Mongrels out of plain sight. Cole and Paige followed them as the groups of pedestrians went back to their own little worlds.

Having lost sight of the couple, Cole continued down the narrow lane that led past the garage. Paige was directly beside him. Keeping her back against the brick wall of the building directly across from the garage, she looked at Cole and nodded down the side street. The Mongrels were close, which meant they were probably lurking somewhere within the shadows between the buildings.

There was a Dumpster to Cole's left and smaller, one-car garages farther down on the right. He was just about to step forward when something moved within the shadowy space between the Dumpster and a tall wooden fence. By the time he realized the shadow was actually a constricted mass of black fur, the Mongrel had already exploded from its corner.

Mongrels had abilities that varied as much as their appearance. Some were sleek and beautiful, while others were freakish. This one had short, mangy fur that was thicker in the spots that would need more protection. Coarse patches over its back thinned out along the sides of its squat head and the middle of its bony legs. Having squeezed behind the Dumpster so quickly, its main ability seemed to include twisting itself into more shapes than a balloon animal. Curved claws dug into the pavement as it opened its mouth to display a set of thin pointed teeth with a barely audible hiss.

Cole brought his spear up, angled it diagonally across his body and pushed it forward to stop the Mongrel in midjump. The creature's chest thumped against the middle of the weapon, but its arms stretched out enough to scrape one side of Cole's head with slender claws. His back was against the brick garage so nothing could get behind him. After shoving the Mongrel back, it slunk in a tight circle and then reared up on its hind legs directly in front of him. Scraping the forked end against cement, Cole snagged one of the Mongrel's feet and swept its legs out from under it.

The Mongrel huffed as its ribs hit the ground, and then flopped to get all four of its legs beneath it. As it wriggled, the tattered remains of khaki shorts could be seen around its waist. Cole checked on his partner, hoping the second shapeshifter wasn't more than she could handle.

Paige let out a breath that bordered on a snarl as she backhanded the other Mongrel, using her hardened right arm. The impact wasn't as loud as when she'd dented the loudmouth's car, but it spun the shapeshifter around and sent a spray of bloody saliva through the air. Despite the complications that had arisen, that kind of strength was why she'd thought up the ink and tattooed herself in the first place. The idea was to inject supernatural qualities into a human in such small doses that they would only affect a part of them for a short amount of time. One out of two wasn't bad.

If Cole's opponent was a man-sized were–alley cat;

Paige's was closer to a were-leopard. The female's head was wider, giving her room for thicker teeth. Dark gray fur clung to her like paint that was still wet after having been freshly spattered onto her skin. The only noise she made was a low growl as she dropped down to all fours and tensed for another lunge.

Fixing her eyes upon the Mongrel, Paige slashed with the weapon in her left hand, which had shifted from a thick baton to a single, curved sickle blade attached to a thin handle. When the Mongrel popped onto its hind legs to clear a path for the weapon, it was caught with a follow-up blow from the one in Paige's right hand. Compared to the sickle, the other weapon was awkward and poorly shaped. The same mixture that had forced Paige's arm into a sling also marred her ability to change the weapon's shape. The best she could manage was a crude machete. It didn't look like much, but it could get the job done. Sparks flew from the machete's edge as it scraped against the ground where the Mongrel had just been.

Ducking just quickly enough to keep from getting impaled by the sickle, the leopard growled, "Sssskinner."

Hearing that word caused the first Mongrel to snarl hungrily. It had been pacing in front of Cole for the last few seconds, but now raced at him with its belly less than an inch above the ground.

Cole hopped into the middle of the narrow side street with his spear in both hands and the largest point angled downward. He jabbed at the smaller Mongrel defensively but didn't make contact. The were-cat stepped on the spear to push it down and clear the way for it to swipe at Cole with its other front paw.

Claws sliced through the air so close to his face that Cole could feel them brush against his nose. The thorns in his weapon's handle dragged through his flesh, but he maintained his grip so he could will the spear to grow a set of barbs that popped out from its middle section to puncture the pads on the Mongrel's paw.

Twisting away from him, the oversized alley cat let out a high-pitched yelp and limped away. It lifted its nose toward the second floor windows of a building farther down the side street, where several lithe shapes crawled along the ledge and stretched into four-legged forms anywhere from five to six feet in length.

Cole and Paige put their backs to a wall as the first two Mongrels regrouped. While the alley cat scraped at the concrete and twitched its eyes between the two Skinners, the leopard shifted back into the woman Cole had spotted from the street when they'd first arrived. Her body was lean, muscular, and on display, since all but a pair of skimpy boxer briefs had been shredded during her initial transformation.

Standing tall and unmindful of her partial nudity, the Mongrel said, "The old man hasn't killed enough of us on his own, so he called in more of you?"

Cole checked the street to find a few people trying to get a look at the small gathering. They were either being held back somehow or had already lost interest since the fighting had abated.

"What are you talking about?" Paige demanded as she twirled her left-handed weapon. "You're the ones who jumped us!"

"We don't need more Skinners here! And we won't allow more of our kind to be poisoned. Tell the old man we know what he's doing and that his tricks will only get more humans killed."

"What tricks? Who the hell are you anyway?"

Squinting in a way that made her eyes seem like clear, flawless glass orbs, the Mongrel replied, "You have not met the old man yet. His stench is near, but it's not on you."

The alley cat looked up at the female Mongrel and shifted back into a mostly human form. His tattered shorts were now wrapped around a sinewy frame, and he didn't even bother lifting himself up from all fours as he said, "They're Skinners! We kill them and any others that come onto our—"

"Don't you say it," Paige snarled.

The sound of her voice was enough to make every Mongrel on the ledges bare their teeth and claws.

"This isn't your city," Paige continued. "This isn't your

territory. This isn't even your street! Mongrels don't get to roll into this place and stake a claim."

"Tell that to the pack in Kansas City," the leopard woman said.

Raising her machete as if it was a rifle and she was sighting along the top of its barrel, Paige said, "The only reason Kayla got to bring her pack into KC is because *we* allowed it."

Hearing the leader of another Mongrel pack mentioned by name sent a ripple of half voices and growls through the shapeshifters. Cole tightened his grip on his spear and prepared for the worst. He took a quick look over his shoulder, but didn't see anything trying to creep up on them from behind. In fact, there were now no people at all watching from the street.

"Kayla's pack bled for what they got," Paige continued. "They stood toe-to-toe with a Full Blood and earned their place. What the hell have you done?"

"We know all about the Full Blood in Kayla's possession." The leopard woman's clear eyes widened as she added, "But it seems you are surprised to hear about this. Did you think they disposed of Liam when he may be the link between us and immortality?"

Cole groaned under his breath as he thought back to the last moments in the Kansas City siege. The Full Blood who led that charge had claimed that Mongrels could be changed into his kind in a manner similar to how humans were changed into Half Breeds. A few moments after that, the burrowers among the Mongrels had dragged the wounded Full Blood underground, where they claimed they would imprison him if, as was the popular belief, the werewolf couldn't be killed by tooth or claw.

"There's no Full Blood in Kansas City," Paige said. "I checked."

Even as she shifted into something that was more leopard than human, the Mongrel woman didn't lose her condescending tone as she said, "Of course. I'm probably just mistaken."

"You can tell all the tales you want," Paige snapped as she

brought both weapons up. "I helped clean this city out and I won't let a bunch of Mongrel squatters come in and mess it up again. If you want to live here, you'll need to stay quiet and out of sight. If you want to talk shit, you'd damn well be ready to back it up."

The male hopped onto a Dumpster and changed into his alley cat form so quickly that his claws sparked against the metal. He gripped the edge in preparation to fling himself at Cole, but was stopped by a sharp snarl from the leader. As she turned, the female dropped to all fours and allowed her leopard fur to explode from her pores. The snarl turned into a lingering growl as she craned her neck to sweep a warning glare at all the other Mongrels. By the time she'd fixed her gaze back onto the alley cat, her sleek body had gained enough muscle to make her the largest creature in that alley.

Several of the Mongrels on the ledge above gripped the dirty bricks with their front paws and tensed the muscles in their legs. Before they could jump down, a bottle flew up to smash against the side of the building.

"Hey pussies! You gonna hide up there or come down to rub against my leg? I may even have a rubber mouse for you to chase."

The man who shouted up at the ledge was the one who'd thrown the bottle. Walking in a confident gait that caused his heavy black boots to knock loudly against the pavement, he stepped into the light cast from a bulb connected to one of the single-car garages. He was a few inches taller than Cole, had wide shoulders and a thick torso wrapped inside a jacket that looked as if it had been stitched together from mismatched pieces of material. Despite the size of his body, his head looked just a little too big for it. Gray stubble sprang from his face and scalp, as though he'd used the same shears to trim his chin and dome. A wide smile displayed a set of blocky, uneven teeth as he reached under his jacket to produce a handgun that Cole recognized as a Sig Sauer P220. Slowly raising the .45 caliber handgun, the big ugly man said, "Find somewhere else to be or I start making some real noise."

A low growl rolled through the shadows, coming from the combined throats of all the Mongrels gathered there. Cole could see several sets of glittering eyes surveying their surroundings. After another snarl that sounded like an exhalation from the earth itself, the Mongrels on the ledge scaled the wall, hopped onto the roof and disappeared. Only one remained for a few extra seconds. Its head drooped down and loosely swung from its neck as it gazed upon the alley from its perch upon the ledge. Panting in what sounded like a rambling mutter, it leapt out of sight.

Keeping low against the ground, the were–alley cat backed nervously toward the garage nearest to the street. The leader was in full leopard form, and she paced in a tight line, back and forth, clawing at the pavement. Finally, she stopped and let out a noise that didn't sound like a growl, snarl, or anything else a mundane animal would make. Once that signal was given, both of the remaining Mongrels scaled the closest wall and were gone.

Extending his arms as if he'd forgotten about the shapeshifters as well as the gun in his hand, the man in the leather jacket said, "That's my Bloodhound! Barely off the road and already stirring up the shit."

Paige not only smiled at the big guy, but she did so in a way that made her look like someone who was completely incapable of knocking a werewolf down and gutting it. "Hello, Rico."

Draping an arm around the back of Paige's shoulders, Rico replied, "So that'd make you Cole?"

"That's me. I've heard some good stories about you, Rico. Or should I say, Rrrrrico."

Gripping Cole's hand, Rico shook it as if about to yank it loose and hang it from his rearview mirror. "Don't ever say my name like that again."

If Cole could have pulled his hand away from the other man's grip, he would have. Instead, he did his best to maintain his dignity and sputtered, "Paige . . . uh . . . said you'd think that was funny."

Rico tightened his grip just enough to scrape Cole's bones

together. "Real nice partner you got here," he said to Paige. "First sign of trouble and he throws you under the bus."

"No, I did put him up to it," she said. "I like to see him squirm. As for you," she added while slapping Rico's stomach, "there's a little more puddin' in the bowl, but I wouldn't call you a bus just yet."

Finally releasing Cole's hand, Rico said, "She really knows how to build a man up, don't she? I got some stories that might knock her down a few pegs." Holstering his .45 and using that hand to point back toward Euclid Avenue, he added, "They'll have to wait, though. I think we're in trouble."

Standing at the mouth of the side street was a skinny man of average height wearing a plain white cotton shirt hanging loosely over the waistband of a pair of faded olive drab fatigues. Unkempt silver hair and a pair of dark sunglasses made him look like someone who'd been out partying since before most of the nearby college crowd was born. To add another disjointed layer to his overall fashion statement, the old man carried a thick cane with a simple curved handle. A thin gray mustache looked as if it had been sketched above a tight frown. The scowl only deepened when a few kids wearing University of Missouri T-shirts tried to get a look down the side street.

"Dude!" one of the college kids protested as he was nudged by the old man's cane.

Not only did the cane remain where it was, but the disheveled man connected to it pushed the kid away with as much effort as he would use to prevent a child from toddling into a busy street. "Move along," he said.

The defiance on the young men's faces was just a cheap mask, and all of them ambled along.

"The rest of you," the older man said to the Skinners, "come with me."

Chapter 8

Dressel's was a pub in every sense of the word. Everything from the uneven wooden planks on the floor to the dartboards on the walls made the place feel like it had been lifted from the moors and placed into the Central West End. Cole followed everyone inside through a narrow door and was immediately greeted by the sight of a square bar surrounding an island of whiskey bottles populated by the barkeep and an old tape player spouting Celtic music. Tables and chairs were practically knocking into each other in the confined space of the dimly lit room, most of which were either occupied or being shuffled around by bustling waitresses dressed in T-shirts and jeans.

"Maybe there's more room up there," he said, pointing toward a narrow set of stairs that led to a second floor.

"I already got a table," the old man replied. He didn't wait to discuss the matter, and when he sat down, he glared at the empty seats until they were filled.

Paige took the spot next to the old man, so Rico and Cole settled in across from them. Rico sat with his back against the wall and his legs pointed diagonally toward the front door, which meant Cole barely had any room for his feet beneath the worn wooden table.

Although he tried to be discreet, there was no easy way to get out of his harness. His weapon had already been shrunken down to its compact form, but it still caught the eye of one woman at another table, who watched him for a few seconds before losing interest. "So," he mused, "is this some sort of Skinner bar? Do we all meet here because we're welcomed or protected somehow?"

"No," the old man replied. "We meet here because they make their own potato chips. They're good. Also, the Central West End is normally quiet. This whole city used to be quiet until that mess in KC."

Rico gave Cole a nudge and a thumbs-up to go along with it, which he ignored.

"You," the old man said as he jabbed a finger at the big guy, "are damn lucky I was able to keep people away from that scene you created."

"I created?" Rico said. "I was only there to pull these two out of the fire."

"These two didn't know any better. You do." Dropping his voice to a quiet snarl, he added, "And what the hell were you thinking drawing a gun in public? Anyone could have seen you."

Rico shrugged. "I got a permit for that."

"Do you have a permit for being stupid?"

Cole chuckled at that while putting his weapon on the floor with his foot on top of it.

When he pointed at Cole, Rico's hand made a pistol shape that was almost as big as the real thing. "Don't get cocky, new guy. You ain't earned your stripes with me yet."

Before the conversation could get any more awkward, the waitress showed up. "What can I get for you guys?" she asked.

Paige and the old man agreed to split a pitcher of domestic draft. Rico ordered a Guinness, and Cole gambled by pointing to one of the coasters on the table that advertised Newcastle Brown Ale. Before the young woman got away, the old man warmly asked her about the specials.

"The stockpot special is a Wellington beef stew, plus we also serve clam chowder. Our dinner special is an open-faced turkey sandwich."

"Does that come with potato chips?"

"It does if you like," the waitress replied with a grin.

"Sold. Bring another basket of chips for the table."

"Will do, hon."

As soon as the waitress left, the old man's snarl returned. "How did the fracas in that alley get started?" he asked.

Paige told him the short version, but the more he heard, the deeper the old man's frown became. When she was through, he shook his head and grumbled, "It's truly shocking that either of you made it out of Kansas City."

"Yeah?" Cole asked as he fought to get comfortable in the straight-backed, uneven wooden chair. "And just who the hell are you?"

"Sorry," Paige said. "This is Ned Post. He's the resident Skinner for St. Louis. Ned, this is Cole Warnecki. He came to me after Gerald and Brad were killed. I'm training him."

"Doing a hell of a job too," Cole said as he offered his hand.

Ned grabbed Cole's hand and used his thumb to feel the scars on his palm as if he was sampling the texture of cheap fabric. Now that he was closer to him, Cole could see the deep red lines in the coarse and chalky skin around Ned's eyes. That damaged section of his face, combined with the man's wandering gaze, made it clear why he needed the cane and dark glasses. It didn't take long for Ned to let go and grunt, "Still feels like you fear the thorns too much. I hear you're responsible for some of those werewolf pictures on the Internet?"

"Just the ones that got people saying they're all fake," Cole replied.

"Fat lot of good it did," Ned snorted. "Whatever happened to keeping things like that quiet for the common good?"

"That's kind of tough to do when everybody's got a camera in their pocket and are being videotaped crossing the street," Cole said. The waitress stopped by to drop off their drinks and appetizer. When he sipped his Newcastle, he was immediately grateful to whoever had placed that blessed little cardboard advertisement on the table. "Internet rumors are like little bits of leaves and dirt on top of a pool," he said. "They clump together and look really bad, but then they all drift apart and become nothing. Are those the potato chips you talked about?" The basket on the table was filled with thin, darkened slices of potato that still glistened with hot grease. He snagged one, popped it into his mouth and said, "Damn, those *are* good."

"New guy's right," Rico said as he took a handful of chips and washed them down with some Guinness. "I've seen stuff about KC and Janesville on the Net, pictures on websites, even spots on the news, but it's all just the same half-assed explanations. Diseased dogs, exotic pets, that kind of thing."

"Policemen were killed. You think they'll let this just go away?"

"We were there, Ned," Paige assured him. "We covered our tracks as best we could, and the carcasses that were left behind won't be any help to anyone. Whatever tests are done on them will just cause a whole lot of heads to be scratched."

"You did what you could?" Ned groused. He took some chips, ate them, and clumsily poured some beer into his glass. "Does that include handing an entire city over to the Mongrels? Or perhaps you wanted to hand it over to the Nymar just like you did with Chicago?"

"Screw you, Ned," Paige said.

"Hey now," Rico warned. "Let's keep this friendly."

Ned waved off everyone else at the table and drank his beer. He couldn't seem to get enough down to blunt his senses, so he grabbed the pitcher to refill his glass. "City's been quiet for years but now we got Mongrels in the Central West End and Nymar just across the river. What's next, huh?"

Rico put an elbow on the table, leaned forward and dropped the tip of his finger between the beer pitcher and the chips to punctuate his next statement. "Those Mongrels were testing us. That's all that was."

"How do you know?" Ned asked.

"We can have all the technology we want, but humans are still part of nature's system," Rico explained. "Things may have been fucked up between us, the Nymar, and the shapeshifters, but that's pretty much the way it's been for a real long time. All the shit that's been happening lately has fucked things up a whole different way. Janesville and KC threw the whole system out of whack. Bloodhound knows what I'm talkin' about."

Having made an island of ketchup on the edge of a potato chip continent, Paige occupied herself by dipping, eating, and subsequently cleaning off her chin. "You go on ahead," she said while spraying some chewed bits into the air. "Very eloquent."

Rico nodded in appreciation of the backhanded compliment. "The Full Bloods have been around for centuries. We may not feel it all the time," he said while holding up a palm to show enough scar tissue to divvy up between a dozen cage fighters, "but you can bet that everything else out there has a real good idea the big boys are out and about."

"We've got a pretty good idea where the Full Bloods are," Ned said.

"Yeah, but there's a big difference between being pretty sure I got a gun under my jacket." Grabbing hold of his jacket as if he meant to open it and flash his goods to the entire bar, Rico raised an eyebrow and added, "And then there's being *really* sure."

Rico's jacket was a mix of some sort of heavy canvas stitched to large strips of leather that were tanned and treated to the point of being nearly black. A few grommets were positioned on his shoulders and under his arms, and thin leather cords laced up both sides. When he'd first seen the garment, Cole wrote it off as a biker's jacket. Up close and in better light, however, the leather strips had a texture that reminded him of the Half Breed skins Paige used as protective lining for her body armor rigs.

When the heavy material rustled against the .45, Ned looked at him and hissed, "Don't create another scene!"

"Throttle back, Ned," Rico said as he let his jacket fall back into place. "Just makin' a point." He snatched some more chips, shoved them into his mouth, smearing grease into the gray stubble on his chin, and washed it all down with half a mug of Guinness. "What I'm sayin' is that these

Mongrels and whatever else is out there can probably feel the Full Bloods the same way a buncha deer know the wolves are roaming the woods. Now, according to Paige, we're down a few Full Bloods."

When Ned glanced over to her, Paige nodded. "One was taken down in KC and we don't know where Henry is."

"Liam," Cole said as a way to interject something useful into the mix. "The Full Blood from KC was named Liam."

"And Henry is the Full Blood that was tainted by the Nymar?" Ned asked.

"That's right," Paige replied. "We haven't heard from him since Wisconsin."

"You mean the Janesville Massacre?" the old man sneered.

"That's just what some of the tabloids were calling it," Cole said. "Some news channels did a bunch of stories about it for a while, but the case has been closed. The cops saw enough Nymar waving their guns around for the whole thing to be written off as some sort of gang fight or drug deal gone wrong."

"And I haven't heard about it for months," Rico said. "That's because people like to sweep their garbage where they can't see it and go about their day like there ain't nothin' wrong. Animals ain't like that. They know when something's wrong with the natural order, and right now there's a big vacancy at the top of the food chain. When that happens, all the residents of the lower rungs climb up to fill it. Ain't that right, Bloodhound?"

Now fully absorbed in her chips, Paige only nodded.

"All the Mongrels are sniffing around across the country, poking their heads out to make sure there's not a Full Blood around to bite it off," Rico continued as he ticked his points off on his fingers. "I've heard from a bunch of places that Nymar are getting braver too. Even little rodents that are only spotted every now and then when they pick off a dog or slaughter some cattle are overstepping their bounds."

"I was nearly killed by a Chupacabra," Cole offered.

Rico pointed at him and said, "I wouldn't exactly brag about that, but it proves my point." Then he shifted his focus back to Ned. "One Full Blood can stake out a territory that may cover a third of this country. They're powerful enough to enforce their claim and fast enough to patrol it. Take even one out of the mix and it throws things off, just like when too many wolves are killed in a patch of forest. All the other animals spread out and make themselves comfortable. In our case, you get Mongrels challenging us in the open. I know you've been content to sit back and keep the peace ever since we took St. Louis for ourselves, but we can't do that anymore. If anything comes sniffing around looking for a new territory to claim, we gotta kick its teeth in."

"Law of the jungle," Cole said as he carefully selected the burnt chips from the basket.

"Damn right," Rico said while leaning back into his seat. "Law of the jungle."

Ned pulled in a deep breath and let it seep out through his nostrils. He drank some beer, ate some chips, and then looked over at Paige.

"And before you come down too hard on us for stirring up those Mongrels," she said, "you should know that their problem wasn't with us. It's with you."

"What?"

"Oh yeah!" Cole said. "They told us . . . what was it?"

Paige seemed only too happy to reply. "The Mongrels told us to tell the old man that they know what he's doing and that your tricks will only get more humans killed."

"Tricks?" Ned snapped. "What the hell are you talking about?"

"Not me," Paige said. "Them. That's the message the Mongrels gave us."

"And was the leader a tall woman who looked like a panther?"

"I thought she was more of a leopard," Cole replied, "but yeah. She had some guy with her who changed into something that had been eating out of garbage cans most of its life."

"The woman's name is Malia," Ned said. "And the mangy one is Allen. Those two have stayed mostly out of sight and haven't been a problem."

"Until now," Rico said. "When I showed up, things were about to get pretty damn problematic."

"Because you provoked them!"

"What could they be talking about?" Paige asked in a softer tone. "Could it have anything to do with something called Pestilence?"

She laid out the details of Peter Walsh's visit to Rasa Hill and didn't pause until the waitress came by to refill their drinks. By the time she relayed everything Daniels had said, the waitress was returning with the rest of their food. Not surprisingly, the most disgusting of the details hadn't put a dent into anyone's appetite.

When the story was over, Ned asked, "And who studied that dead body? The Nymar you work with?"

"That's right. Daniels does plenty of work for me, so don't give me any grief for bringing him along."

"You brought him along?" Rico asked. Glancing nervously at the old man, he lifted his mug to Paige and said, "Ballsy."

Surprisingly enough, Ned merely shrugged and cut into his open face sandwich. "I don't object to putting a few of them to work for us. Giving them free rein over an entire city is something else. What did he tell you about this Pestilence?"

"Daniels just said it wasn't any sort of drug that he knew about," she replied. "At least, nothing he could pick up on with his first batch of tests, but he'll keep studying it while he's here."

"That still leaves a wide range of toxins from flower petals all the way up to animal venoms."

"Right," Paige said. "That's why he's still running his tests."

"And where will we able to find him?" Ned asked.

"I was hoping he could stay with us."

"No wait," Rico said as he tapped his mug against Paige's. "*That* was ballsy."

Again, despite his previous grumpiness, Ned just shrugged and took another bite of his dinner. "If you trust this Nymar, then he can stay with us. At least that way we can keep an eye him. Where is he now?"

"Driving around the city to see if he can find some more Nymar."

Rico laughed into his beer. "Good luck with that."

"The Nymar who came to Chicago was from here," Cole pointed out. "He's the one who called Pestilence by name and said it was in the nymphs' blood. Also," he added as he put the piece of paper he'd taken from Peter Walsh's body on the table. "He was carrying a free drink voucher from a place called Bunn's Lounge in Sauget."

"I know the place. It's right across the river in Illinois," Rico said. "Prophet was there last month."

Ned tapped the ticket and then pushed it toward Cole. "Right. His purple A-frame theory. I think that man is just trying to frequent strip clubs and call it research so we'll pay him for it. You think this is something we should really check out?"

Cole took another drink of Newcastle and then realized Ned had aimed that question at him. "Oh, well yeah. Peter came a long way to find us and tell us about Pestilence, so it's probably important. If there's any more Nymar in the area, we figured Daniels would be able to find them to see what they know."

"How is he contacting them?" Rico asked as he leaned across the table. "Knowing how the bloodsuckers find each other could be a big help."

Rather than let Cole field the question, Paige stepped in. "Daniels wouldn't say and we wouldn't press him on it. He does a lot for us, but he's not about to hand over all of his kind like that."

"Helping Skinners ain't exactly healthy for Nymar," Rico pointed out.

"Maybe it's splitting hairs, but Daniels won't go that far. He works with me because he knows I only go after the Nymar that overstep their bounds."

"Here we go again," Ned grumbled.

"And," Paige continued as she stared the old man down, "he comes through when we need him, so if he says he can save us some time by helping us get in touch with local Nymar, then I'll let him."

Ned patted her rigid right arm and said, "Yes, I can see your Nymar chemist truly does take good care of you."

"This wasn't Daniels's fault. He mixed up the ink, but I'm the one who used it before he said it was ready. Even so, it worked damn well. Have you ever had a Full Blood chew on your arm before?"

For the first time that night Ned backed down with a simple, "Can't say as I have."

"Well I did, and the only reason my arm is still attached is because Daniels got that ink to work. It's not perfect, but he's still working on it, and if you don't like it, then you don't have to use it when it's ready. And if it makes you feel any better," she added while patting Ned's hand as if comforting an invalid, "you can take me to all of the Nymar locations you've found since you've been assigned to babysit a supposedly empty city."

The old man pulled his arm away and hunkered over his meal.

"So I guess that leaves you and me to check out Bunn's," Cole said to Rico. "The last nymph I met at a strip club was Tristan. She was something else."

"So we've heard," Rico grunted. "Word got sent out that we're not supposed to lay a hand on her."

"Not unless you pay to get into the VIP room," Ned grumbled. After taking a few more huge bites of his sandwich, he pushed the rest aside. "I suppose I'll check to see if the police are circling the neighborhood after your little scuffle. I'll head home from there. You remember where the house is?"

"Yes," Paige said. "I remember."

"Come by when you're ready, and," Ned added as he slapped some money onto the table, "drinks are on me."

"Don't be silly, Ned," Rico protested. "After all the trouble we stirred up in your quiet little neighborhood, the least I can do is spring for the brew."

Looking older than he had just a few seconds ago, Ned stood up and left.

Once he was gone, Rico said, "Something's gotta be done about him. It was fine to have him here when nothing was going on, but with Mongrels and whatever else sniffing around, we need someone who can handle themselves."

"Ned can handle himself," Paige said.

"Sure. Would you want him fighting alongside you if this place turned into another KC?"

She didn't have an answer to that and seemed vaguely ashamed of it.

"And what was that the Mongrels said about him?" Rico continued. "What tricks is he supposed to be pulling?"

"Ned doesn't do anything more than what any of us would do," Paige said. "And if he did, he would have told us about it. I'll trust that before I trust what some Mongrel in an alley says to me."

"If Ned knew those Mongrels by name, he should know where to find them, right?" Cole asked.

Nodding, Rico fixed his eyes on Paige and said, "Maybe. Even if we did find 'em, we can be safe knowing we got little bits of the Blood Blade to throw at them. Why the hell would you destroy a weapon like that?" he snarled. "We can't exactly make another one! I still can't believe you left a Blood Blade with some goddamn Nymar."

Those words landed like an unexpected punch in the gut. Fortunately, Paige was tough enough to handle a whole lot worse. She leaned across the table and made a point to use her right hand to poke Rico in the chest as she said, "Daniels was right there when KC turned into a bloodbath while you were hiking down some scenic mountain trail. What've you got to say to that?"

Rico rolled his eyes as he settled the bill and led the way outside. Even after all three of them were walking back to the Cav, he knew he wasn't going to be let off that easily. Finally, he sucked it up and told her, "I feel like shit for not bein' there. I didn't know you put the call out until after I got back."

Feeling like he'd missed a step, Cole asked, "You called for help, Paige?"

"Yeah, but now you see why I haven't gotten you into that habit." She walked briskly down the street, shoving through a noisy group of frat boys who were dispersed by Cole and Rico before they could get their feathers ruffled.

Jogging to catch up with her, Rico said, "You know you can't rely on outside help. None of us can. As for the crack about your Nymar buddy, you gotta admit we could have used that Blood Blade."

"We are using it," Cole assured him. "Granted, we thought we'd have a bit more of it in one piece, but I've got an idea about a way to give all of our weapons a boost instead of having just one knife to pass around."

The other two stopped and Paige was the first to ask, "What idea?"

"So glad you asked." Cole rubbed his hands together and lowered his voice so it didn't carry to any of the small groups walking up and down Euclid Avenue. "You know that list Daniels made for me?"

"Yeah."

"A lot of it was just different ingredients that could be added to one or two bases to make different things. It's a lot like making power-ups for *Hammer Strike* or any other game."

"Oh Christ," Rico groaned. "You really weren't kidding about this video game crap."

"Let him finish," Paige said. "This stuff usually starts off dumb, but goes somewhere much better."

Taking the not-too-subtle hint, Cole skipped to the important part of what he'd intended to say. "What I wanted to do with my next game was to make it so players could make their own power-ups by adding different things to the same base. When was the last time anyone's added something to the stuff we use to treat our weapons?"

That caught both of the other two off their guard.

Grinning excitedly, Cole said, "Those Blood Blade chips are made to be melted down, so why not just melt them down into the varnish for our weapons?"

"You can't just add whatever you want into that stuff, boy," Rico said. "It's a recipe that's been honed for years. I may not use them sticks as much as I used to, but plenty of folks live and die by those weapons. Screwing around with that ain't a very good idea. No offense, Bloodhound, but you don't exactly need somethin' else makin' it harder for you to defend yerself."

Paige raised an eyebrow and watched Cole expectantly.

Looking more at her than Rico, Cole explained, "We don't need to mess with the whole recipe. Warriors used to dip their arrows and spears into poison. Why can't we add a little bit of the Blood Blade to the edges of our weapons? A little extra kick when fighting a werewolf would come in handy, don't ya think?"

Slowly, Paige's mouth curled into a barely perceptible smile as she nodded and replied, "Yes. I do think. If we dilute it enough, we could even make it a part of the weapon itself so we'd only need to treat them a few times. That way the technique could be passed around to more Skinners."

"We may even be able to make our own Blood Blades," Cole said. "I'm just tossing out ideas, but there's a lot of places to go with this! With four Skinners and a guy like Daniels in the same place, we should be able to come up with something, right?"

"Come to think of it," Rico said thoughtfully, "Ned might be a big help with that. He's got some ingredients that could make all the difference."

"What kind of ingredients?" Paige asked.

"Nothing we could get arrested for, but there are a few mythological beasts that are missing some vital parts. Speaking of vital body parts," he added with a lurid grin, "me and the new guy are headed to Sauget."

"So that means me and the old guy will wait for Daniels to show up." Nodding toward Cole, she said, "Try to keep your tongue in your mouth this time."

Shaking his head, Cole grumbled, "I got kicked out of one strip club. Will you ever let me live that down?"

"Not a chance."

Chapter 9

The hotel was just off of I-55 and Lindbergh Boulevard on a twisted road that wound between a Target, a few chain restaurants, and an electronics store. A mat of dirty cement cut from a broken sidewalk covered the entrance to an underground labyrinth that was guarded by the lanky alley cat Mongrel who'd confronted Cole and Paige earlier that night.

Still wearing his khaki shorts, Allen had replaced his shredded shirt with a new wife beater. The streets around him were a tangled mess and almost always blocked by an endless series of construction sites. One such project had been started the previous year and was abandoned in the last few months. It wasn't clear whether the job had been delayed or if the site was forgotten by the city, but there was nothing on the small mounds of dirt to draw any interest. Beneath those mounds, however, were tunnels that twisted around the foundations of the nearby stores and even poked into a few basements. Allen paced upon the concrete square and jammed a cell phone against the side of his face as if getting ready to eat it.

"No, I didn't find the old man," he snarled into the phone. "Two more Skinners showed up . . . Yes, that's on top of the ones that are already here. I think it was those two from Chicago you told me about, the bitch with the dark hair and the guy with the spear . . . No, you don't need to talk to Malia! Just come here to help us clear these bastards out of our city!" After a pause, he slapped his phone shut and stuffed it into the pocket of his shorts.

Malia approached him in a form that was ninety-nine percent human. She could walk through a mall without frightening anyone, but her perfectly smooth dark skin and large milky eyes would certainly attract some interested stares. She was tall enough to stand out in a fashion model kind of way as long as she didn't smile to display her rounded, needle-sharp teeth. Although she was technically clothed, the oversized button-up shirt hung open so that nothing much was left to the imagination.

"What did Kayla have to say?" she asked.

Allen twitched toward the sound of a siren moving along Lindbergh Boulevard and clenched his long, narrow fists. "Ever since she's curled up in Kansas City, that tunneling little whore thinks she's some kind of queen."

Placing a hand on his shoulder, Malia stroked his neck with nails that slid easily out from the tips of her fingers. "She did a good thing in getting the Skinners to trust her, Allen. Don't forget that."

He looked up at her and muttered, "She wanted to talk to you, not me."

"You'll call her back and she'll talk to you," Malia said. "Kayla needs to be shown she doesn't get to tell the rest of us how to behave. If she wants to lord it over Mongrels, she'll find she won't have many friends outside of the dregs left behind by the Full Bloods. Did you tell her about our little problem?"

"I didn't get a chance. But," Allen added with a twisted smile, "she's got problems of her own. I heard that six more dead Half Breeds were found in KC and St. Joseph. Half killed humans and the rest swept through some of Kayla's own pack. The cops are calling them animal attacks, like the ones that happened during the riot, but some are just being called violent crimes."

"You're sure of this?"

Allen nodded. "The scout I sent to KC sniffed them out

herself. She says a few of the Half Breeds crawled away to their dens before they died, so they weren't found. If that's the case, then there's no telling how many deaths are truly being caused by those beasts."

Letting out a long breath, Malia barely moved her lips as she said, "Half Breeds are bad enough without being driven into this frenzy. The Skinners would be the first to go to such lengths to kill our kind, but Pestilence is something far worse than I could have guessed. The Mind Singer's voice is stronger than ever. It comes and goes like the wind, and all it speaks of is this new plague. We've lost enough of our pack to that foul poison, but the Skinners are the only ones who don't reek of it. Once they know one of their own created something that has killed so many humans, they will put an end to it."

Crawling halfway down the tunnel so only his upper body protruded from the sidewalk, Allen asked, "Do you truly think Skinners will be so charitable?"

"All they need to do is point us toward the source of Pestilence and they will have served their purpose," Malia replied. Then, crouching down so her creamy naked breasts could brush against her knees, she whispered, "Once they stumble upon those filthy, desperate Nymar, our territory will be cleared of more than one plague."

Shifting into his mangy alley cat form, Allen lowered himself all the way into the shadows so he could spread the news to the others. There were preparations to make.

The GPS still gave directions in a kindly British accent, but the Cav had a completely different feel, thanks to the man in the passenger seat who continually shifted his weight along with the gun strapped under his arm. Lights from downtown St. Louis faded behind them as they crossed a wide rusty bridge into Illinois.

"So you think that Nymar who found you came from here?" Rico asked.

"That's what his driver's license said." When he heard Rico laugh under his breath, Cole asked, "Why's that so hard to believe?"

"Because there are no Nymar in St. Louis. Paige and I cleaned them out years ago."

"Just the two of you?"

Rico nodded and looked out the window as if remembering a particularly succulent Thanksgiving feast. "It started out as a training exercise and turned into a rout. Of course, the Nymar around here were a bunch of pussies who got off on flashing their fangs to the ladies and having contests to see who could sulk more. One of them even cried when my little protégé jabbed her sickle through his frilly shirt. It was so much fun that I almost felt bad when it was over." With a wide, square-toothed grin, he added, "Almost, but not quite."

"I wish all of the fanged crowd was like that," Cole mused. "Any time we deal with the Nymar on Rush Street, we have to be ready to catch some hell."

"That's Chicago. I don't think any of the other Nymar were too surprised to hear the pantywaists around here got wiped off the earth. Probably glad to be rid of 'em."

"So you're telling me there's no Nymar anywhere around St. Louis?"

"Not the last time I checked. It's been a while, so there could be more of 'em that drifted in thinking they could lay low. I haven't felt much of anything, though. What about you?"

Cole brushed his fingertips along the scars in his palm as if they somehow needed to be activated. By now it was a reflex along the lines of drooling when he drove too close to a pizza joint. "No, I haven't felt anything since those Mongrels came along."

"Well now I'm feelin' somethin', but that's just because it's been a long time since I've been to a good strip bar."

"Try not to get too excited in the car."

Rico rolled down the window and hung his elbow out. It was getting close to two in the morning, so traffic was light along I-55. It was even lighter once Cole turned onto a smaller road that took him into Sauget, Illinois. From there, the scenery was dominated by trees on either side of the road, interrupted by a few strip malls and the occasional gas station. Before the GPS even mentioned they were drawing close to their next turn, he could see the glow of pastel neon in the distance that was either a strip club or a UFO from the tackiest planet in the universe. A stoplight gave him a moment to get a look at the place before entering the parking lot. "I'll be damned," he whispered.

"What's the matter? You never seen a big wiggling ass made out of neon?"

An illuminated sign like that was hard to miss, but Cole's attention was drawn to the structure itself. "That's a purple A-frame."

"You mean like the ones Prophet's been going on about?" Rico stuck his head out the window and then dropped back into his seat while Cole parked as close to the building as he could. "His theory is that there's something going on with all the clubs that're shaped like this?"

"Shape and color. According to him, all the clubs that are purple A-frames have nymphs working at them."

"You let that one skate in Wisconsin, so they're all creeping in. It probably don't matter what the building looks like."

"Yeah, but still . . ."

"Well, make a call," Rico said.

"Call Prophet?"

"No. Call MEG. Those guys love research projects."

Cole bristled at that, but only because he hadn't come up with the idea first. After dialing MEG's number into his phone, he had to listen to it ring over the thump of music coming from inside the club.

"MEG Branch 40, this is Stu. Oh, hey Cole! I heard you had an eventful date with Abby."

"Yeah, I've got a job for you."

Cole could hear the distinctive rattle and creak of feet being swept off a table and a body leaning forward in an office chair. "A job?" Stu asked. "A job like hunting Chupacabras?"

"Nothing like that. It's research."

If expectations made any noise when they shattered, Cole would have heard it over the muffled thump of Warrant's

"Cherry Pie." "Oh," Stu groaned. "What's the matter? Your Internet access get cut off?"

"No. I just thought you'd have better luck and more resources than me." Sensing that flattery truly wasn't getting him anywhere, Cole added, "It's about a hunt I'm on right now."

"Really?"

"Yeah. I need you to see what you can find about a connection between purple A-frames, nymphs, and . . ." Gazing up at the giant wiggling butt outlined in red and purple neon, Cole decided not to make Stu's job any harder. It was already close to impossible to search for anything online without dredging up some sort of pornography, but opening that door on purpose would have made Stu's job unmanageable. "And that's it."

"Purple A-frames, huh? I ran a quick search on that while you were talking and didn't come up with anything interesting."

"Have him try connecting it to temples," Rico said. When Cole looked over at him with a questioning frown, he added, "Temples, shrines, structural stuff like that. Nymphs are into that sort of thing."

"All right," Cole said. "Stu, add in—"

"I heard," Stu chirped through the digital connection. "That's got the juices flowing . . . so to speak. Wow. I just found a site that makes some pretty strange connections between nature spirits and different colors. I'll send you a link, but don't open it around Paige. Or anyone under eighteen for that matter. Or while you're in public."

"Got it. When you find something *useful*, let me know."

"Will do."

Rico was out of the car and heading for the club before Cole could get his phone back into his pocket. There was something he wanted to ask the other man, or possibly tell him, but he couldn't remember what it was. The unformed words hung at the front of his mind, overpowered by the rush of testosterone coursing through his veins. He barely paused long enough to take the keys from the ignition before racing to catch up with Rico. Memories of the last nymph he'd met were simply too vivid to ignore.

Tristan was like something out of a dream, and she'd played a starring role in many of Cole's dreams since he'd met her. Even though he knew she probably wouldn't be at this club, the very idea of finding someone in her league made him want to kick down the front door of Bunn's Lounge. Fortunately, Rico was just ahead of him and had already pulled it open. When the bigger man stepped inside, Cole remembered what it was he'd meant to say to him. Unfortunately, it was just a little late.

A dim purple glow filled the small room where cover charges were collected, which was accented by a brighter red light flashing in time to a piercing alarm. Before Rico could take another step, he was pushed out by two guys wearing jackets that didn't hide their shoulder holsters half as well as Rico's.

"What're you carrying under there?" Bouncer #1 asked as his partner slapped a hand under Rico's arm.

Rico knocked the hand away without taking his eyes away from the next door in his path.

"No guns allowed inside," Bouncer #2 warned. "Leave it with us or we'll call the cops."

Before either of the Skinners could say anything, they were being herded back to the parking lot. Bouncer #1 shouted, "James! Mikey! We got someone else trying to bust in!"

The reinforcements didn't come from inside. They rushed around the corner of the building, skirted the edge of the parking lot, and charged toward the front door. One of them looked to be somewhere in his early twenties, had the buzzed hair of an infantry recruit and the build of a linebacker. He even lowered his shoulder and bared his teeth as if in preparation to level some poor bastard who'd dared to cross the line of scrimmage. He would have taken Rico off his feet, but was merely deflected into Guard #2 by a quick pivot.

The other man who'd come to help the bouncers at the front door was older and carried his weight evenly distributed upon his arms, gut, shoulders, and chest. He waded into the ensuing brawl as if it was his natural habitat.

Just as Cole was about to try and explain himself, he felt a reaction in his scars that drew his attention toward a pair of skinny figures that had hurdled a row of bushes separating the club from the empty lot next door. A few cars were parked over there, among some stacks of empty crates.

Backing away from the bouncers, Rico balled his fists as if he felt the same itch in his scars. "You fellas expecting someone?"

College Boy whipped around and jogged toward the corner of the building, while the olive-skinned bruiser lowered himself into a fighting stance and squared his shoulders to both Rico and Cole.

"It's more of those freaks, Mikey," College Boy said.

Mikey backed away but didn't take his eyes off of his two targets. "You two stay put." Without waiting to see if his order was obeyed, the olive-skinned guard backpedaled toward the parking lot and then snagged a phone from his pocket so he could start chattering into it.

Seconds later the front door opened and a bouncer from inside emerged with a matching phone held to his ear. An electronic chirp sounded before he asked, "You sure about that?"

"Yeah," Mikey said through the speaker. "They're already in and—"

The crash of metal against brick clanged through the air, followed by two voices: one screaming and the other snarling.

Cole ran for the Cav but was stopped by the end of a baseball bat jabbed into his stomach.

"You were told to stay put, asshole," said the guard who'd steamrolled both him and Rico out of the club's outer lobby. Suddenly Rico was there, pulling the guard back with enough force to knock him straight over the leg he'd positioned behind his ankles.

"Check out what's goin' on over there," Rico said to Cole after forcing the guard to the ground. "I'll cover you from this side."

Cole passed the Cav as he ran toward the corner of the building where the screams were coming from. Even if he'd had the steam that was taken from him by the bat's sharp jab, he still wouldn't have rounded the corner fast enough to make a difference. The side door was made of thick metal and had been pulled from its top hinge. Dim light spilled from inside the club and was obscured by several figures blocking it at the source.

A few steps before he got through the door, he was nearly flattened by a Nymar wearing nothing but tattered pants and a sleeveless T-shirt that still reeked of the garbage pile from which it had been taken. Long, greasy hair made it difficult for him to decide if it was a man or woman, but the faded, grayish color of the tendrils shaking under its skin told him that the Nymar was starved to the point of panic.

When the Nymar took its next step, Cole reached out to grab the front of its shirt. Its eyes were clouded by thinner tendrils that crept up along the inside of its face as it bared all three sets of fangs. When the Nymar's own momentum bounced it against the door frame, yellow fluid sprayed from the curved fangs that fit in beside its thicker feeding teeth. Not a stranger to being spit at by those things, Cole turned his face away and didn't concern himself with the spatter of venom against the side of his neck.

Another Nymar snapped its head forward to sink its teeth into Cole's forearm. This one had the slender build and fuller lips of a woman, but her skin was every bit as filthy as her companion's. Frayed denim shorts and a camouflage tank top were draped over her emaciated figure like they were still on a hanger. She strained her eyes to watch Cole as she used every muscle in her jaw to try and dig her teeth even deeper into his arm.

The feeding fangs had cut through first, digging into Cole's flesh to make way for the curved, snakelike set of teeth that would deliver enough venom to knock him out. He was hesitant to twist his arm away until he felt the third set of shorter, thicker fangs scrape against his skin. Those came up from the Nymar's lower jaw, and he knew if they sank in, he would have better luck hacking his arm off at the shoulder than pulling away from her.

He knocked the heel of his palm against the woman's forehead to loosen her bite enough for him to wrench his arm from her mouth. Blood sprayed across her face and dripped onto her tongue, making the tendrils under her skin quiver with excitement. The intense rush of pain Cole felt was quickly replaced by cold as the healing serum in his system kicked in to repair the damage. He drove his knee squarely into the center of the Nymar's mass, sending her backward and into another woman with red hair who cowered in a corner directly across from the door.

The redhead had the smoothest skin Cole had ever seen, and her hair spilled over naked shoulders in a series of gentle, wavy lines. When she looked at him with tears streaming down her face, everything became quiet enough for him to hear her voice above everything else.

"They want to hurt me," she said.

Cole couldn't let that happen. He grabbed the closest Nymar and balled up his fist with every intention of punching a hole straight through the back of its head. That's when a third person rushed forward to spur all the Nymar into action. One bony elbow hit Cole in the back and another set of hands shoved him to the floor. He scrambled to his feet but was too late to keep the first two Nymar from grabbing the redhead and carrying her out of the club.

Farther inside the building, women screamed, men shouted, and a DJ used the sound system to beg everyone to stay in their seats while security handled the matter. Cole put all of that behind him so he could chase the Nymar and the redhead. As soon as he set foot in the parking lot, a gunshot exploded through the air. The redhead screamed as she was stuffed into a rust bucket Dodge and all of the Nymar piled in with her. Rico was the one behind the gunfire, and his next bullet sent the long-haired Nymar face-first to the ground.

The expression on Rico's face didn't shift in the slightest as he walked forward to pump another couple of rounds into the vampire. Since there was no acidic hiss coming from the wounds, Cole knew the bullets weren't treated with the antidote made to poison the Nymar spore. The rounds were more than just lead, however, because when the fallen Nymar arched his back, he revealed a pair of rough holes that had been punched all the way through him and into the pavement. Apparently, the spore didn't need to be poisoned if the heart was all but liquefied. When either of those things happened, the rest of the Nymar's body dried up faster than hamburger under a heat lamp.

Cole was in the Cav before the fallen Nymar stopped moving. "Get in!" he shouted to Rico as the Nymar's Dodge lurched from its space.

At that moment, a Nymar with short, bleached blond hair leaned out through the Dodge's passenger window to point a shotgun at Rico. It was a double-barreled model with a pistol grip intended to make the weapon compact and easy to hide. It was also illegal to carry a weapon modified that way, but not as illegal as it was to fire that weapon at someone in a parking lot. None of those things stopped the blond Nymar from pulling his trigger and blasting Rico where he stood.

Cole saw it all happen but didn't have time to do anything about it. Before he could warn the other Skinner, thunder filled his ears and Rico was bouncing off the Cav amid a flutter of material that had been shredded from his jacket. As the Dodge sped away from the club, Rico clawed at the ground next to the Nymar he'd put down.

"Holy shit!" Cole shouted while slamming the Cav into park. Even before the Cav stopped moving, the passenger door was being pulled open.

"Okay," Rico said as he hauled himself onto the passenger seat. "I guess I had that one comin'." Noticing the look on Cole's face, he twisted around to display a tattered section of his jacket that still smoked from the impact of the shotgun blast. The patches of canvas were completely blown away, but the leather beneath them remained. The thicker leather patches were barely scratched. "Let me guess," he said. "Paige still uses those harnesses instead of stitching together a proper piece of body armor?"

"That's Half Breed skin?" Cole asked as he cautiously poked the jacket.

Rubbing at a bloody spot at the back of his neck where some of the blast had slipped past his collar, Rico said, "More like five Half Breed skins. Now are you gonna admire my stitching or are you gonna get this heap moving?"

Cole strapped himself in and hit the gas. The Cav was a heap but it took corners well, which made a huge difference in chasing the Nymar through the sleeping town of Sauget. All he had to do to zero in on the other car was roll his window down and listen for the sound of screeching tires and an engine that wheezed more than an asthmatic at a horse show. Between the noise of the Dodge and the honking of the occasional car it ran off the road, he managed to catch up to it before the Nymar reached the highway. Once the gap was closed to a few car lengths, the Dodge tried to lose him by jumping a few curbs. Cole took those turns without an ounce of worry, even as various lights on the dash started blinking. The sound of the car's underbelly scraping against concrete didn't bother him, since the damn thing bottomed out on just about every speed bump anyway.

"They're almost to the interstate," Rico said as he swung his .45 to point to a sign on the side of the road. "Just get as close as you can and give me a steady shot."

When one of the Nymar emerged through the Dodge's side window, Cole braced for another shotgun blast. Instead, it crawled all the way out and jumped at the Cav.

Cole twisted the wheel hard to the right but couldn't go any farther without taking out a cement bench next to a bus stop. His quick thinking and hesitant maneuvering only caused the airborne Nymar to crash into the driver's half of the windshield instead of the passenger's side.

"Get it off!" Cole shouted.

Rico hauled himself out through his own window and sat on the frame with the seat belt wrapped around his left hand and his .45 in the other. The Nymar digging its fingers into the front of the Cav was the female with the short hair and sunken face who'd dragged the redhead from Bunn's. She had thick black markings snaking up along the sides of her neck toward the edges of her mouth. Scraping her nails into the upper edge of the windshield, she scrambled across the front of the Cav while screaming something that was lost amid the engine noise and squealing of tires. Cole cranked the wheel in the opposite direction, which was almost enough to send the Nymar flying. She found something to hang onto, however, allowing her to reach out and grab the edge of Rico's window.

"That's it," Rico said as he jammed the Sig Sauer's barrel against the Nymar's forehead. "Come to daddy."

The car in front of him wasn't trying to get away, so the driver must have expected his partner to make a return flight. Those expectations were blown away, along with a healthy portion of the Nymar woman's skull, when Rico pulled his trigger.

"Jesus Christ!" Cole shouted in response to the gunshot and the spray of oily blood that coated his windshield like a batch of poorly mixed red and black paints.

Despite losing so much of its skull, the Nymar held on and even kept trying to grab Rico by the throat. One of the Nymar's eyes was gone, but the other was fixed intently upon its target. Flipping the switch for the wipers, Cole managed to clear a path through the gore that was just wide enough to see the Dodge and a small section of the road in front of him.

Rico shouted incoherently and used the .45 to drill several more holes through the Nymar's torso. Not only didn't the thing slow down, but more tendrils emerged from the holes in its head and body like probing fingers curling around the edges of the bullet wounds to pull them shut. Tendrils even tugged at the Nymar's face, stretching its scalp over the grievous wound like a cheap throw rug on a stained floor. One of Rico's bullets finally punched through the spore attached to its heart, causing every one of the Nymar's tendrils to slap against the windshield and its hands to lock upon the Cav.

The Dodge swerved to miss a city bus that ambled across an oncoming intersection, and Cole pounded his foot against the brake. Twisting the wheel so Rico would be forced back into his seat instead of out the window, he prayed that Rico wouldn't wind up as a messy street stain on a driver's safety video. The Cav spun across the intersection, resulting in a loud slapping crunch as its driver's side pounded into the side of the bus. Both men in the car lurched to that side while the clothes and dehydrated remains of the Nymar scattered across the dented hood.

As the roar died in his ears and the windshield wipers continued to smear more black-stained blood across cracked glass, Cole gripped the steering wheel hard enough to leave a fresh set of grooves in the plastic.

"Damn!" Rico howled from where he was crumpled in his seat. "That was some fucking brilliant driving! You hurt?"

"I don't think so," Cole said in disbelief.

"Then come on." With that, Rico pushed his door open and climbed outside.

Cole's door was being held shut by a massive chunk of municipal steel, so he fished his spear from the backseat and flopped out through the passenger side. Although the Nymar in the Dodge had avoided the bus, they'd done so just long enough to wrap their car around a parked minivan.

"You assholes better pray that redhead's all right!" Rico shouted.

Slowly, the Nymar dragged themselves from the car. The first one to hit the street was a female with straw-colored hair pulled into a tail that hung askew behind one ear. She staggered for a few sideways steps and dropped to all fours. Next was the beefy guy with the bleached hair. He wore rumpled brown pants and a blue work shirt with the name "Jerry" stitched into the left pocket.

"So the old man finally called for backup, huh?" Jerry asked as multiple scrapes and gashes from the crash were closed by his tendrils. Judging by the wear and tear that remained on his face, he looked to have been somewhere in his forties when he was turned. At the moment he was too stunned to raise the shotgun he carried.

"Where's the redhead?" Rico asked.

"I asked you a question, Skinner!"

Extending his arm to point the .45 at Jerry's chest, Rico said, "And unless you had a chance to reload that shotgun, my question outranks yours."

Cole stood as steady as he could while the cold rush of healing serum put out the painful fires in his body. The pretty redhead pulled herself from the wreck. Unlike the Nymar or Skinners, she didn't even show a bruise after having been in the crash. In fact, she was still looking fine in her filmy dancing attire, which became transparent under the stark white streetlights. She was obviously disoriented, but even her staggers were more graceful than a pirouette. Settling against the closest light pole like a feather drifting to rest upon the surface of a lake, she traced a hand across her cheek to completely wipe away a minuscule trickle of blood that ran down the length of her face.

"This is your lucky day," Rico said to Jerry. "Since the woman's all right, you get the chance to hobble away from here."

Cole tightened his grip on the spear. As the thorns sunk into his flesh, he caught sight of a wide-eyed bus driver running around to inspect the front of his vehicle. Sirens blared from down the street, closing in on the intersection from at least two different directions.

"The nymph is coming with us!" Jerry announced as he dropped the shotgun and stretched his fingers out like talons. "We didn't go through all of this to run away again." The Nymar looked like he was wearing gloves, but the black on his hands was a thick mass of tendrils beneath his skin, pushing out through his fingers to form short black claws at their tips.

"Go ahead and take her," Rico said over the top of his Sig Sauer. "Let's see how far you get."

Jerry and the other surviving Nymar launched themselves at the Skinners with their arms outstretched. Cole braced himself to impale whichever got to him first, but Rico unleashed a quick series of shots that caught the straw-haired Nymar before she got within the spear's range. The bullet ripped through her upper torso, spinning her around to land awkwardly on her side.

"Oh my Lord!" the bus driver said amid the thunder of gunfire.

A police car rounded a corner, prompting the Nymar to

scatter. Even the straw-haired one clamped a hand over her bullet wound and left Jerry on the street behind her. Rico took aim at him, but Jerry sprang up and twisted around so he could land on the soles of his stained shoes and rush forward.

"Oh my . . ." It was all the bus driver could get out before Jerry darted past him in a hissing blur. ". . . Lord!"

Cole reacted out of pure instinct, charging at Jerry before Rico could be cut by those claws. His spear ground against Jerry's shoulder blade, but it didn't keep the Nymar from twisting around to swipe at his neck. After deflecting the attack, Cole raked the forked end of his weapon up along Jerry's midsection. The Nymar recoiled from the spear and bolted for the same alley his straw-haired partner had used for an escape route.

With Jerry gone, Cole was left with nothing but his aching bones and a big pointed stick. He stood in the growing glow of red and blue police lights next to an ugly guy with a gun, a terrified bus driver, and the most attractive redhead he'd ever laid eyes on. The bus was banged up but seemed ready to be driven away. The Cav, however, wasn't in very good shape.

"We gotta get out of here!" Cole said frantically. "The car's engine is still running, so maybe we could drive it away."

Rico tossed his gun through the shattered rear window and said, "Great. You think we can get moving fast enough to outrun those cops?"

The police car was already slowing down to approach the intersection.

"Maybe if you can hold them off, I could get her rolling again," Cole offered.

"You want me to shoot to kill or should I just hit their tires before they drop us both?" Rico asked.

"God damn it, you're the one that started shooting!"

"Yeah, but I'm not about to shoot a cop."

"We heard gunfire!" one of the officers said as he exited his vehicle and approached the Cav with his hand on his pistol. "What happened here?"

Cole's eyes immediately went to the remains of the Cav's

windshield. The Nymar's oily blood was still there, but it had already hardened into a thick crust.

"That big one . . . he's got . . . got a gun," the bus driver stammered. "I saw him toss it into that car."

"I got a license for that," Rico calmly announced.

The cop keyed the radio clipped to his shoulder and requested backup. Then he asked, "Is anyone hurt?"

"He shot someone," the bus driver said. "I saw it!"

That brought the cop's gun from his holster. "Shot who? Sir? Who was shot?"

The bus driver took a step forward, but stopped when he got a look at the policeman's weapon. "He was right there but . . . he ran away. There was another one that was stabbed with that stick, but he . . . ran . . . he ran away too."

Looking back to Cole, the officer said, "Sir, put the stick down."

Cole's head was spinning. That condition became worse when he realized he was now the cop's main target.

"Better do what he says," Rico whispered.

"Sir, put the stick down right now!"

The lights from the police cruiser washed over the accident, painting the scene as well as everyone present in bright primary colors.

Sirens from the cop's backup were now approaching from different parts of town.

The disintegrated remains of a vampire lay on the hood of his car, and blood from another creature was splattered across the street.

"Oh my Lord," the bus driver sighed.

"Yeah," Cole groaned as he dropped his spear and raised his hands. "You got that right."

Chapter 10

An hour earlier

"So," Daniels said as he stepped into the two-story house on Kensington Avenue, "not all Skinners live like squatters?"

Ned's house was covered in faded siding and a new roof. The lawn surrounding it was due for a mow, but wasn't long enough to hide the old rainbow-shaped sprinkler connected to a vinyl hose. Inside, it smelled like dusty books and coffee. Some nice hardwood covered the floor, but was partially obscured by a collection of rugs that may very well have been collected from yard sales spanning the last several decades. The only place Daniels could look without seeing a bookshelf was straight up, but he couldn't do that because of his chronic bouts of mild dizziness. He dragged several cases inside while perusing the shelves set up in the entryway.

"You don't like my house?" Ned snapped.

Daniels shook his head and bent down to look at a complete series of demonic encyclopedias. "On the contrary! It beats the daylights out of an abandoned restaurant in Chicago."

By the time Ned turned to look at Paige, she was already waiting for the inevitable. And, like a good piece of clockwork, Ned asked, "You're still living in that restaurant?"

"Yes, Ned."

"Don't you know that Gerald only picked that spot as a

place for an emergency? It was supposed to be a weapons store, nothing more than that."

"I know," Paige said. "But it's got so much closet space and my very own industrial fridge. Do you know how many pizza boxes I can fit in there?"

The old man shook his head and shuffled through the living room to a staircase. "You got chemicals to work on?"

"Yes," Daniels replied. "And a body to dissect. It's in the car."

Eager to get away for a moment, Paige chimed in with, "I'll get it."

"What are these?" Daniels asked as he pointed toward a set of symbols etched into the door frame. While examining one set of symbols, he found even more that were angular and precisely drawn around the door, with only the occasional break between them. "Is it some sort of language?"

"No," Ned replied. "Don't worry about those. And don't mess with those jars. Just don't open anything unless I say it's all right. That goes for everyone!"

But Daniels couldn't help following the symbols all the way around the door, along the ceiling, and eventually around a window frame.

Standing at the base of the stairs, Ned said, "I'm not working on your schedule, Nymar."

Responding to the tone in the old man's voice like a kid who'd just been called by his first, middle, and last name, Daniels hustled to follow Ned upstairs. He was taken to a small bedroom on the second floor that was at the opposite end of the hall from two larger rooms. Even though most of the room was taken up by several minifridges and narrow tables of equipment ranging from paint mixers to heat lamps, there was still a set of bookshelves wedged in on the wall adjacent to the door.

"There's some plastic tarp in the closet," Ned explained. "Throw that down before you drag any body in here. You're not bringing anything toxic in here are you?"

"If there is anything contagious to be found, it's way too late to worry about infection now," Daniels said. "Are you equipped to run tests on biological material?"

"I've done plenty of work for Barnes-Jewish Hospital, so if there's anything you need that I don't have, just let me know and I'll make some calls."

"How about access to a portable CT scanner?"

"Do you really need that?"

"No," Daniels chuckled as he displayed a droopy fang in a wide grin. "I was just pulling your leg."

"Hilarious," Ned grumbled.

The front door squeaked open and slammed shut. Those noises were followed by the thump of heavy footsteps and the groan of old stairs. Before long Paige stepped past the old man with the body of Peter Walsh wrapped in plastic draped over both shoulders in a fireman's carry.

"Where do you want this?" she asked.

"On the plastic," Ned replied. When nobody moved, he turned toward Daniels and raised both eyebrows expectantly.

Lurching toward the closet, Daniels scanned the shelves until he found a pile of neatly folded tarps. "I'll lay these out. Also, I could use another sample from you, Paige."

"I've had a long day and I don't want to get cut up right now. Didn't you contact those other Nymar?"

"Yes, but they didn't tell me much. That gives us some time to—"

"Gives me some time to rest," Paige cut in. "Now if you'll excuse me, there was a rocking chair downstairs with my name on it."

After Paige left, Ned asked, "What sample were you talking about?"

"A sample from her arm," Daniels replied. "I'm trying to put together a treatment."

"Skin sample?"

"And tissue," the Nymar said with a wince. "From as deep as you can get."

The old man nodded and left the room. He headed downstairs, where he found Paige settling into an old rocker situated next to an older couch in front of a surprisingly new television. She acknowledged his entrance with, "Finally got rid of the set with the bunny ears, huh?"

"Had to, with the switch to digital."

"Oh, right."

Ned went over to one of the many bookshelves in that room. Not only were there more shelves than in the rest of the house, but they were decorated with knickknacks of all shapes and sizes. Pennywhistles and antique Howdy Doody figurines were scattered among volumes of mythology and folklore texts. An African thumb harp sat on top of a row of white witchcraft cookbooks propped against a chipped cement frog that sat with its crossed legs dangling over the edge of the shelf. Ned reached below the frog's feet to a stack of flat leather cases arranged in front of some medical texts. After patting the frog on the head, he unzipped the case to fish out a small scalpel.

"Why don't you tell me how you messed up your arm?"

Paige flinched as if the words had snuck up and smacked her on the back of the head. Since she was too comfortable to escape, she sighed. "The idea was to bond shapeshifter blood to human tissue so we could borrow some of their powers for a little while. The only thing I know that can bond to a shapeshifter other than a person is a Blood Blade. When I got my hands on one, I gave Daniels a piece of it and he came up with a substance that acted as a bonding agent."

"You mean a colloid."

"Right. I couldn't inject the mixture directly into my veins without the chance of being turned, but I thought it could be attached to a buffer and pumped directly into the muscle groups I wanted to enhance."

"That's how you came up with the idea of using the mixture as tattoo ink?"

"Pretty much."

Ned nodded and pulled up a stool made from wicker and tanned leather. "Not bad."

"That," Paige said as she held up her wounded arm, "is where you're wrong. I injected some before Daniels was through testing it so I could toughen up my arm for a fight against a Full Blood. It worked for a while, but didn't wear off like it was supposed to and turned my arm into a hunk of rock."

"Mind if I take a look?" When Paige shrugged, Ned reached out to examine her arm. As he poked and prodded her, he lifted his chin as if listening to music or feeling a breeze move past his face. After he was through, he asked, "You're certain your Nymar friend mixed the ink correctly?"

"We've already been through this," she sighed.

Picking up the scalpel and placing the blade within a centimeter of her forearm, Ned said, "Since you trust him so much, you should give Daniels the sample he asked for. It may sting."

"Carve it up, carve it off," Paige muttered. "I don't care anymore."

As Ned's hands moved to feel her arm for a place to make the first incision, Paige studied the ugly chipped frog reflected in his glasses. Placing one finger along the top of the blade, he pressed the edge upon the meatiest portion of her arm and started cutting.

She looked away from what he was doing and repressed the instinct to pull her arm away. The pain wasn't overwhelming, but it cut through the numbness in her deadened skin just enough to trigger a healthy squirm factor. A few beads of sweat pushed out from her forehead as he sliced a section of her flesh that was smaller than a dime. The skin was so tough that even shaving off that little piece proved to be a lot harder than he'd expected. To make matters worse, his blade got stuck if he stopped moving it for so much as a second. "Something's bothering you, Paige. Want to talk about it?"

Her face not only regained some color but flushed a bit as she snapped, "What's bothering me? How about the vampires knocking on my door and exploding? Or what about the werewolves that are being turned into an invading army? That stuff bothers me."

"I know," Ned assured her. "But that's not what I meant. We've all seen enough to drive most people way past their limits, and just when we think we can relax or take a breath, something else comes along to try and spill our guts onto the floor. You've been living with that sort of thing for a while, though."

She sighed and looked down at her arm. The knife was still making its way beneath a thin flap of skin, but wasn't able to slice it completely off. "Every day, I half expect Cole to come to his senses and buy a plane ticket to anywhere but where I am so he doesn't have to waste his life in a fucking nightmare. It's too late for me, but . . ."

Tightening his grip on her arm, Ned angled the blade in a little deeper and worked as if he was sawing through a tree branch.

The squirm factor returned, but Paige handled it. "Cole already accused me of not doing enough to get my arm working again."

Ned was making progress, but only through a lot of effort. He soon fell into a rhythm where his entire upper body rocked from side to side as he shaved off the coin-sized section of Paige's arm that was now covered in an ugly bruise. When he removed that little piece of her, her arm barely had a chance to bleed before the serum in her system got to work sealing the wound. "I think you're doing all right considering the extent of what happened," he said. "I *also* think you're letting your injury get to you. Maybe that's what Cole's picking up on."

"I've been trying to get through it. Trying to find a way to fix it."

"That's all well and good, but it's not the point." Getting up from the stool, he walked over to the medical kit and sifted through it. "I may not be able to see much, but I've noticed the way you hold that arm. When you bring it in close, you're not coddling it or working out a kink. You're hiding it. I saw that same thing after a buddy of mine came back from the army with a gimp leg. He hated people staring at it more than he hated his physical therapist. And if anyone acted like they felt sorry for him . . . hoooo boy!"

Once the sample was in a little plastic bag, Ned walked over to the rocker and stopped its motion with a well-placed hand on its back. "I know what it's like to be injured and I know what it's like to be pitied. You and I don't take either very well. If there's one more thing I can teach you, it's that you shouldn't be ashamed of getting hurt. Even if it was your fault, groaning about it won't do anyone any good."

Paige stood up and rubbed her arm. The spot where Ned cut her was hurting, but pain was a lot better than numbness. As she massaged the hardened flesh and wiggled her fingers, she realized she could feel her hand on her forearm a little more than she could a few hours ago.

"Take this up to your friend Daniels. If you trust him, then let him work. Otherwise, kindly escort him out of my house."

"Gotcha. Thanks, old man."

He nodded and handed her the Baggie.

It was one thing to watch him operate on her as if he was carving a ham, but Paige had a hard time holding the chunk of flesh he'd taken. She tried to imagine it was a piece of lunch meat, which lasted until she was about two steps from the door to the upstairs room where Daniels was setting up shop. Tossing him the sample, she asked, "Where are those Nymar?"

He'd already laid Peter's body on both layers of plastic and was currently organizing his test tube racks. "They don't seem very organized," Daniels told her. "I tried contacting them through the usual channels but they seemed distracted. They're supposed to call me back any time, though."

"I think I'll head out on my own for a while. I need to get out of here."

"Take my car. Just don't mess it up."

"You sure about that?" she asked.

Daniels had already fished his keys from his pocket, and now handed them over. "If it'll get you away long enough for me to work, then yes, I'm sure."

Rather than argue with the Nymar, Paige took his keys so she could do some hunting the old fashioned way.

St. Louis was a sprawling tangle of old and new structures, streets that changed names depending on where they led and a constant flow of traffic that never let up no matter how late it was. Driving through it all, Paige either felt exhilarated or aggravated, depending on how slow the other cars were moving.

Every so often a subtle twinge rippled through the scars left behind by her weapons, to let her know there was something lurking nearby. Traces of Nymar could be felt as she got closer to downtown, and shapeshifters of some kind were scattered farther north in University City. None of the traces, however, were strong enough for her to follow to a source. Either the locals knew more Skinners were in town or they were roaming too quickly to be tracked.

Paige had just turned off of Delmar Boulevard onto North Hanley Road when her phone rang. She went through the wriggling dance of getting it out of her pocket while driving, looked at the number displayed on the screen and let out a relieved breath. Making sure no trace of emotion came through in her voice, she hit the button and asked, "What is it Cole?"

"How much cash did you bring with you?"

"Fine, Cole. And how are you?"

"I'm serious. I need you to come down here and bail me out."

Steering into the first parking lot she could find, Paige wound up in front of a little white building with a sign that read AMERICAN CLEANERS. Now that she wasn't a moving violation waiting to happen, she asked, "Bail you out? You'd better be kidding."

"I don't have a lot of time to explain it to you, but I *seriously* need to get bailed out!"

"What happened?"

"Rico and I got into some trouble." Not only had his voice dropped to an insistent hiss, but he must have also cupped his hand over the phone because the background noise became muddled as well. "We made it to that club, but found some people with some familiar black tattoos."

Knowing he was talking about Nymar, Paige nodded and started thinking through a dozen different angles at once. "How'd you wind up in jail?"

"We got into an accident and . . . there was a bus . . . and

Rico . . ." She could tell that Cole was having trouble coming up with an effective way to get his point across without saying anything to make things worse, then he snarled, "Just get me out of here and I'll explain it in person. If you don't have enough to bail us both out, that's fine. This psycho friend of yours could use some alone time."

"What police station are you at?"

"We were in Sauget, driving away from that club."

"What station?"

"I don't know! Is there more than one around here? We got handcuffed, tossed into a car, and driven to a big room with a fucking cage. Did you want me to write down directions?" Another voice from the background barked at Cole and was muffled completely as he covered the phone receiver. After a few seconds of garbled arguing, he said, "I gotta go, but the officer will tell you where we're at. Just bring some cash out here quick, all right?"

"Umm . . . I don't have the money to bail you out."

"What? What happened to those funds from . . . all the traveling money and . . . ?" Considering his surroundings, Paige thought, he didn't want to mention the fact that they had a psychic bounty hunter feeding Skinners the occasional winning bunch of lottery numbers, or a group of investors who tossed money their way to thank the people who got them out of any number of supernatural binds.

She had to give him credit for keeping his mouth shut. "We've got bills to pay, Cole. Times are hard."

"On top of everything else, I've got to hear *that* shit again? Maybe I can hang myself from my shoelaces." The muffled voice in the background didn't like that too much.

"Is Rico there?" Paige asked.

"Yes, but they're only letting one of us make a call."

"So you're both all right?"

"Yes," Cole said in a somewhat calmer tone. "We're all right. There's something going on at that club, though. Our tattooed buddies came out of nowhere to grab one of the dancers. I think they were just waiting for a chance to rush the place."

"Sit tight," Paige told him. "I don't have much money,

but I should be able to arrange for bail. If anything comes up and you have to call me quickly, just say you're calling your lawyer, and odds are better you'll get to use the phone again."

"Oh. Okay," Cole said as the muffled voice in the background said a few words of its own. They must have been good because Cole swiftly added, "I have to go. 'Bye."

The connection was broken and Paige saved the number to her phone. She then sifted through her contacts to make another call. It was answered in one ring.

"Hey, Prophet. It's Paige Strobel. I need a big favor."

Chapter 11

After spending some time in the cell without incident, Cole was starting to relax. In fact, the cage was bigger than his first apartment, and its television had better reception. On the other hand, that television was bolted to the upper corner of an open room that contained three short, steel benches, a pair of miniature toilets, and seven other inmates. Three of the inmates were asleep against the cement walls. Two occupied one of the benches. One paced along the iron bars, and the last one waged a losing war against his most recent meal upon one of the toilets. Since that toilet wasn't far from the TV or the benches, he didn't have much choice but to watch.

"Why don't you take a load off?" Rico asked from his bench.

"I think those two want the benches."

Rico twisted around to look at the pair of inmates sitting nearby. They were so dirty that it was tough to determine what they might look like beneath the grime. Rico greeted them with a curt nod and they scowled back at him just as they'd scowled at Cole.

"They're fine," Rico said with an off-handed wave. "Sit down."

Lowering himself onto the bench, Cole took a position that allowed him to keep his eye on as many of the inmates as possible. The pacer was impossible to watch all the time, and the guy on the crapper was impossible to miss. Leaning over to Rico, he whispered, "This is my first time in prison."

"No shit."

"What about you?"

"First off, this ain't prison. It ain't even jail. It's a holding cell. Three very different animals. I actually got fond memories of jail. There was a place up in North Dakota where I spent a few nights with some friends of mine. Served the best franks and beans you ever had. And no, that ain't slang for a hot date."

Cole laughed uneasily and said, "Beat me to the punch."

"After eight weeks there, I got transferred to a real joint in Illinois."

"What did you do to earn all that?"

"It was a bullshit RICO case that's been following me around for too long."

"Did you just start referring to yourself in the third person or did they name the case after you?" Cole asked.

"More like I was named after the case. It's the Racketeer Influenced and Corrupt Organizations Act. When Ned introduced me to Paige, she only knew me as the RICO guy. Name stuck and so did that goddamn case. Pulled my ass out of a cushy jail cell like this one and tossed it into a goddamn hole that served slop for every meal on every day but Thursday." Before Cole could ask, Rico added fondly, "Taco day."

"So you're some big-time mob guy?" one of the two bench warmers asked.

Rico straddled his seat and locked eyes with the inmate who'd just spoken up. "You conducting interviews now?" he snarled. "So what's that make you? Barbara fucking Walters?" Shifting his gaze to the darker-skinned of the two, he added, "That'd make you Star fucking Jones?"

"You'd best chill," Star said. "I'm just sittin' here."

"All right then," Rico said with a nod. "What about you, Barbara? If you want *The View*, I can give you a good one of the inside of a shit bowl when I pull your face off and flush it down that toilet."

Barbara did his best to keep his chin up, but had to maintain a delicate balance between not wanting to back down and not wanting Rico to make good on his offer. Since there didn't seem to be a third, more desirable choice, he backed down.

Rico turned around and said, "I served some time in Pekin, but that was only medium security. Before I got transferred to a max security hole, someone convinced a judge that I wasn't supposed to be there."

"Who?" Cole asked.

Rico leaned over and told him, "Some connected guys were having trouble with a bunch of Nymar encroaching on their drug routes. I put the bloodsuckers down before getting arrested and was mistaken for a professional contractor. When I turned up in the system again, one of my new connected buddies stepped in to make it right. Even after all that, they still owe me a few favors." Straightening up and allowing his voice to go back to its normal volume, he said, "Sometimes it's good to do right by the wrong people. Remember that."

"So should I get used to this sort of thing?" Cole asked.

"Being locked up? Probably not if you're with Paige. She can sniff out cops pretty good."

"Is that why you call her Bloodhound?"

Rico gazed up at the television and smirked. "Not exactly."

When Cole looked up to see what might have caught Rico's attention, he found a rerun of the nightly news from St. Louis. An attractive brunette with short hair and a cute, round face was speaking next to a picture of a sidewalk labeled as North Skinker Boulevard. Several cops and an ambulance were gathered around what looked like a pile of charred garbage partially propped against a building. The moment he spotted the gnarled, leathery tentacles extending from the pile, Cole jumped up and approached the television.

"Sit the fuck down!" Star said. "I'm watching that!"

Cole reached up to the corner where the television was bolted, causing a guard from down the hall to shout, "You break that and you're paying for it!"

Looking along the top of the cell, Cole quickly found the pair of surveillance cameras protected by little steel boxes mounted on the ceiling. He looked at one of the cameras and said, "I just want to turn it up! I need to hear it."

"Then shut up and listen!" the guard shouted.

Since the guard wasn't about to hand him a remote, Cole looked up and watched the rest of the broadcast.

"As of this time, there is no indication of whose remains these are, but this death is presumed to be linked to the triple homicide earlier this evening," the cute brunette said. "Police found evidence of a forceful entry at that earlier scene along with signs of a brutal struggle that left all three victims completely drained of blood. Authorities are not releasing an official statement about this newest gruesome discovery. Please be warned that the images you are about to see are graphic and may be unsettling." After that disclaimer was given, the picture was enlarged to fill the entire screen, with police officers forming a ring around a mess of arms, legs, and thick leathery tentacles.

"Pestilence," Cole said. "That's what Peter looked like after he . . . popped."

Barbara chuckled from his bench, muttering about something of Cole's he'd want to pop.

"Things may be going crazy, but this isn't like anything I've seen or heard about from Kansas City or anywhere," said a man identified by a strip of text along the bottom of the television screen as Patrolman Nick Hencke. "Some of it looks human enough, but the rest . . . well . . ." The uniformed police officer turned away from the camera to where a group of people were wrapping the corpse up so it could be lifted into the back of the ambulance. "For all we know," Nick continued, "this could just be some sort of joke."

The picture shrank down to fill a quarter of the screen so the cute brunette reporter could conclude with: "While there have been reports of several dog attacks possibly stemming from the disease that affected so many animals in Kansas City last month, police sources have declined to say if this could be a new strain that has mutated to affect people. If the situation changes, this station will update you immediately."

"Thank you, Katherine," the brunette's partner said while shifting in his seat to properly address the camera.

"That's what Peter came to warn me and Paige about," Cole said as he spun around to look at Rico. "It's Pestilence. What if it starts affecting people instead of just Nymar? Aw hell! I got it on me! What if I get sick?"

Rico stood up. With his patchwork jacket seized and nothing but a gray thermal shirt covering his thick chest, he looked like a cement wall separating Cole from the rest of the cell. He squared his shoulders, hung his head like an oversized vulture and said, "Paige is getting us out of here, so you need to calm down."

"What if Pestilence is spreading?"

"Then we tell Paige and Ned, not every goddamn drunk in this tank."

Barbara and Star were on their bench, enthralled by the weather report. Pacer was still pacing. Crapper was still crapping. Two of the guys were still sleeping against the wall, but one was watching him intently from his corner directly beneath the television. Although Cole had noticed the lanky guy before, he'd been so quiet that he'd practically blended in with the drab, sour-milk-colored walls.

"I don't think these guys are our big concern," he said. "Maybe I can get another phone call."

"You were lucky to get your first one," Rico pointed out. "It ain't as much of a requirement as you might think."

"But it's been hours since I called her!"

"And we'll probably be in here for hours more before she scrapes together enough money to spring us both. Maybe she won't scrape the money together at all." Seeing the strained expression on Cole's face, Rico shrugged and sat back down. "Just bein' realistic. Let's think this through before we waste a call."

As Cole turned away from the TV, he noticed the guy in the corner was still staring at him. The inmate may have had some muscle under his faded Rams T-shirt and cutoff sweatpants, but not enough to make him imposing. His arms were covered in wiry hair and greasy sweat, but the legs protruding from his shorts were encased in a muddy crust. Plain white canvas shoes were held together with dozens of rubber bands that had probably been stolen from an entire neighborhood's supply of rolled-up newspapers.

Watching Cole with bloodshot eyes that were pinched at the corners, the man squatted down to claw at the floor while mouthing random syllables with cracked lips. He cocked his head to one side and let out a slow, grating breath.

"You need something?" Cole asked in his best attempt at a threatening tone.

"Pestilence?" the man asked.

"Yeah?"

"Pestilence is the Lord's way of cleaning His house."

Cole took a step back and then shot a glance back to Rico.

"I guess that's one way of putting it," Rico said.

Since the only other sound within the cell was a teaser for the sports report and the strained grunting from the man on the toilet, Cole walked away from the filthy guy in the shorts. He didn't get far before hearing the shuffle of wet rubber soles and the scraping of fingernails on the floor.

The Rams fan scrambled out of his corner on all fours and then jumped to his feet so he could grab Cole's shirt. "Pestilence is the Lord's way of cleaning His house! Pestilence is the Lord's way of cleaningHishouse. PestilenceistheLord's wayofcleaning Hishouse!"

Rico got back to his feet and stood behind Cole. "You wanna do something about this or should I?"

But Cole wasn't interested in his place within the cell's pecking order. There was something all too familiar about the pattern of the rambling man's voice.

I remember you too, Skinner.

Although he heard the voice of the filthy man in front of him, Cole didn't see the guy's lips move. He couldn't even be sure if the voice was coming from his ears or inside his head. "Did you hear that, Rico?"

"He's just repeating the same bullshit," Rico said.

"Not that."

You took the worms out of me. You and the pretty one cut me.

"That! Did you hear that?"

Now Rico looked at Cole as if the crazy population within the cell had just increased by one.

I smell you but can't see you.

Suddenly, the filthy man snapped his head to the side as if he'd been cracked across the face with an invisible club. His mouth gaped open but no sound came out. Cole pushed him away and stepped back as the man flexed his dirty fingers and doubled over as if to mimic the prisoner who continued to empty his guts into the toilet. He snapped his head to the side again and again. Each time, the crackle of bones became sharper and more pronounced. When the loudest, juiciest crunch filled the air, the man's head drooped to one side and dangled loosely against his shoulder. In stark contrast to that, the rest of his body straightened up.

"I remember you, Skinner," he said out loud.

As Cole backed up, the picture on the television screen flickered, became distorted, and then faded into a dull glow. The lights set into the wall closest to the man's head went black. Cole looked up to the surveillance cameras, but the little red lights on them had already been extinguished.

When the filthy man peeled his eyes open, he shifted to get a good look at Cole from the peculiar angle of his head. Nothing should have worked in that face. The eyes were clouded and clear at the same time, almost like a crystal ball before the witch got her vision of the future.

"Henry?" Cole asked.

Every muscle in the man's neck strained to pull his head up, but he couldn't get enough height to nod. "I remember you too. You and the pretty one. The pretty one cut me. Shecutmeeeee."

The two inmates who had been dozing against other sections of the wall lifted their heads and slowly stood up. Star and Barbara hopped off their bench and rushed to the bars. "Hey!" Barbara shouted. "The lights are goin' off! Something's wrong in here!"

"Settle down," the cop shouted from his station at the far end of the hall. "It's just something with the power."

Rico pulled Cole back and asked, "Is he the Henry from

Paige's journal? The one that tore through Chicago and Wisconsin with that Nymar Misonyk?"

"I think so," Cole replied.

"Why didn't you spot him before?"

"Because he was never human before! After Paige cut the Nymar spore out of him, he turned into a pure Full Blood and ran away."

Staring at Henry's wide eyes and dangling head, Rico said, "I don't think he's exactly human, and he can't be a Full Blood. We'd have felt it. No matter what he is, we may need something more than what we got to put him down."

Although he seemed to have been mesmerized by Cole's face, Henry snapped his eyes toward Rico and said, "You won't hurt me again! Won'thurtmeagain! Dr. Lancroft promised me."

"Dr. Lancroft?" Cole asked. "You mean Misonyk?"

Henry shook his head, which looked more like a tether ball being nudged by a strong breeze. "Misonyk is dead. The Nymar are all dead. He promised that too. He promised and it is so. Hepromised and it is so. Hepromisedanditisso!"

"Shut up in there!" the cop yelled. Cole couldn't see anyone past his bars, but he could recognize the sound of someone frantically trying to tear apart electronics when he heard it. Since the cell doors worked on an electronic system, that was probably the cop's first priority.

Now there are more of me than you. The Skinners are everywhere and they dragged me down and cut me up but now there will ALWAYS be more of me than you! MOREof-MEthanYOU! MoreofmeTHANYOU!

Henry's lips were moving but were out of sync with the words that tore through Cole's brain. "Pestilence will cleanse us," he said with a trembling mouth and tears welling up in his eyes. "I'm a foul, sinning creature and need to be cleansed. I don't deserve to run free. Idon'tdeservetorunfree! I've tried looking into the eye of the Lord, but He doesn't see foul sinners like me. Not unless we repent."

"What the fuck is he saying?" Star shrieked.

Cole positioned himself between Henry and the rest of the cell. "Keep everyone back, Rico. I think I can talk to Henry. We know each other. Isn't that right, Henry?"

When Henry took half a step forward, the remaining lights in the cell began to flicker.

One of the other two who'd been slouched against the wall jumped up and ran to the toilet in a flurry of skinny legs and flailing arms. His hand slapped against the face of the man upon that throne and knocked the back of his head against the wall. Rico tried to help the guy on the crapper, but the first attack had been too fast to prevent. When Rico took a swing at him, the attacker hissed and crouched over the incontinent prisoner as if he was guarding a prize. The hissing man glistened in what little light made it through the bars from the hallway. The moisture on his face could have been sweat mixing with dirt, but now it looked a lot like mud. Despite being in one of the most uncompromising positions known to man, the guy on the toilet did a fair job of fighting back. He kicked with both legs tangled in his pants and swung with one hand while using the other to hike them up.

"What the hell's wrong with this guy?" Rico snarled as he tried to get a grip on the mud-faced prisoner.

Cole went to help him but was quickly wrapped up in Henry's bony arms. "The Lord brought you to me and there's nothing you can do. Nothingyoucando!"

"All right, that's enough!" the cop from down the hall shouted. Judging by the rumble of stomping feet, he wasn't approaching the cell alone.

Barbara and Star had their hands full with the third man, who'd been slouched against the wall. That one opened his mouth to let out a wail that came from the depths of his throat and sent a spray of muddy bile along with it.

Grabbing onto Henry's wrist, Cole twisted down and around in a forward throw that he'd learned through countless sparring sessions with Paige. Henry was lifted up off his feet, swung over Cole's shoulder, and dropped onto the floor. His hands became tangled in Cole's shirt and his fingers crackled as a few of them popped out of joint, but he still hung on.

"You can't kill me, Skinner!" Henry declared. "I destroyed your Blood Blade!" A shaky smile flickered across Henry's face, and his eyes widened into orbs that looked as if they were filled with water from the bottom of a septic tank.

Caught between Rico and the guy on the toilet, the first muddy figure was quickly brought down. He didn't give up the fight, however. Instead, he clawed at whatever he could reach and even sunk his teeth into Rico's ankle.

"Son of a bitch!" Rico growled as he knocked his other foot into the mud man's jaw.

The cell door came open amid a series of creaks and metallic rattles, allowing a small group of cops to wade into the brawl. A few more stood outside the cell, which meant they could only watch as Henry sprang up from the floor to charge at the first officer he saw.

"You won't cover me with the bag again!" Henry cried. The moment he got a hold of the officer's neck, he sank his jagged fingernails in and pounded his head against the cop's face. "I did what you told me!"

The cop on the receiving end of the assault struggled to pull him off while his partners slammed their nightsticks against Henry's ribs without making a dent. Bones cracked and blood flew, but Henry didn't seem to feel any of it. Cole managed to snake an arm around Henry's throat from behind and pull him away, but the cop in front of him saw something that shook him right down to the core.

Henry's mouth opened wide and his eyes bulged from their sockets. What came out of him wasn't so much a scream as it was a hungry, bleating howl. Filthy hands clawed at the cop while several other officers fired their Tasers into the wild man's chest. Electricity pulsed through Henry's body, forcing Cole to let go and trip backward over one of the benches.

The sickening thump of skull against steel rattled through the cell as Rico slammed the first muddy man's forehead into the toilet.

Star and Barbara weren't doing too well against their opponent, but a pair of cops tipped that balance. Nightsticks pounded against another mud man's torso, tearing flesh away to reveal a surface that glistened wetly in the dim light. More electrodes were fired into the exposed areas, causing the man's back to arch and his arms to stretch out to either side.

Several uniforms filed into the hallway, aiming guns into the cell and screaming for everyone to hold up their hands and lay on the floor. Cole barely heard those commands through the raging tirade streaming through his mind. The officers in the cell did their best to force Henry down, but only received more punishment as their reward.

"I didn't plan on hurting them!" Henry shouted as clubs, fists, and boots pummeled his body. "Those children tried to hide from me! I just want to sit in my corner!"

The Lord has no forgiveness for those who don't know their place. TheLordhasnoforgiveness but now they will do what I say and allwillbeforgiven.

"Go to your corner, Henry," Cole said as he inched toward the man who refused to sit still no matter how much of a beating he was given. When he heard those words, Henry dropped the officer whose face he'd been chewing and knelt amid some other cops that were hurt too badly to get up. Even as he was warned to stay back, Cole approached Henry and said, "Misonyk is dead. Remember?"

Henry looked at Cole and then back to the cops. His head swung at the end of his neck like a pendulum and his eyes struggled to compensate for the peculiar motion. With his shoulders slumped forward and his hands pressed flat against the floor, he reminded Cole of the Henry that had been a twisted beast at the end of Misonyk's leash, writing nightmares into the heads of other monsters.

"You were quiet before," Cole said. "Just go back to your corner and be quiet again. Nobody has to hurt anyone."

Henry turned his head, which seemed impossible considering his circumstances. Catching sight of the encroaching cops, he reared up and bowed his chest out as the muscle tissue began to swell inside of him.

Cole knew all too well what kind of damage a Full Blood could do. They were the most dangerous werewolves in existence, but only if they were allowed to transform all the way out of their human skin. Praying his hypothesis was correct, he threw himself at Henry, wrapped both arms around him and grounded the wailing creature before it could launch itself at the police officers.

Everyone else in the cell responded instinctively to the escalation of the fight. Cops swarmed in to fill the cage, swinging their nightsticks, firing their Tasers and aiming their guns at anything that moved. One of them grabbed Cole by the wrist and dragged him down so his arms could be cuffed behind his back, and the prisoners swung at anyone they could reach, whether the other man was in a police uniform or not.

"I can help you!" Cole said. "You don't know what he is!"

Henry's skin stretched to its limit as his scream was cut short by a clubbing blow delivered straight to his temple. His head snapped to the side as the broken ends of his backbone scraped against each other, but at least he dropped. After that, the police officers were able to sort out the mess.

Cole and Rico's hands were stuck through different sections of the front wall of the cell and cuffed in place. Barbara and Star were similarly restrained, and all of them were placed so none of the prisoners could get to one another. Cole watched as wounded prisoners were escorted away and others were scraped up off the floor.

All of the mud men were covered in sweat and gave off a putrid, pungent stench that must have come from the viscous fluid coating their skin. The one who'd gotten his head cracked against the toilet lay splayed upon the floor. Underneath the flap of torn scalp was a slick surface that looked like the side of a wet tree stump.

Henry lay on the floor, gazing at the bars with clearer eyes. The murkiness was gone and there was no trace of blood within the white surrounding his dilated pupils. When the paramedics arrived, one of them checked Henry's pulse and examined his waggling head before announcing, "This one's dead. His neck's broken clean through. Looks like he also sustained some massive trauma to the face."

"He sure did," one of the cops said. "Bastard tried to kill us with his bare hands."

The paramedic motioned for gurneys to be brought in so Henry, toilet guy, and the more seriously wounded men could be taken away.

Rico turned to Cole and made himself comfortable against the bars. "Since it seems like we'll be here for a while, how about you tell me about this Pestilence crap again."

Chapter 12

The next morning, Paige woke to the smell of burning Nymar and the piercing shriek of her cell phone. Although the ring tone became more tolerable once she got her wits about her, the smell only got worse. She rolled out from under the covers of her twin-sized bed and reacquainted herself with her unfamiliar surroundings. It was a guest room only because of the bed, but was mostly filled with books that were either waiting to be shelved or sold to a secondhand dealer. Volumes in all conditions were piled throughout the room, giving it an overall smell of pulp and cardboard.

She'd fallen asleep after taking off no more than her boots and socks, so she poked her head outside to find traces of light and movement coming from Daniels's makeshift lab. Smoke drifted through that door, but she didn't exactly want to know what parts of Peter Walsh might be burning. And despite all of these halfhearted distractions, her phone stubbornly refused to stop ringing.

Paige didn't recognize the caller information on her phone's screen, so she jabbed the annoying device and squawked, "What?"

"Miss Strobel?"

"Yes."

"This is Stanley Velasco of Liberty Bail Bonds. Walter Nash said you have some friends that require our services."

Forcing her fingers through her thick black hair, she winced as she discovered a series of knots created during her tossing and turning in a twin bed that doubled as a book pedestal. By the time she stormed across her room to pull open the heavy curtains covering the window, her brain had woken up enough to remind her that Walter Nash was Prophet's real name and that he'd told her to expect a call from Liberty Bail Bonds. "You were supposed to call last night," she said.

The man on the other end of the line spoke in a voice that was deep in tone, but had an underlying wheeze that made it sound as if he was forcing each word through a chest clogged with bacon grease. "What's the matter?" Stanley asked. "Your friends not locked up anymore?"

"Can you get them out or not?"

While shuffling through some papers on his end, Stanley said, "Fortunately for you, I've done some work in St. Louis and the surrounding area. Also, Prophet spoke highly of you, so I'll handle your case personally. Looks like your buddies had a fun night. We got charges of reckless driving, failure to yield, destruction of city property . . ."

"What's the bottom line?"

Continuing as if he was talking to himself, Stanley droned, "Criminal mischief in regards to use of a firearm, a few more traffic violations, and illegal dumping of noxious substances."

"What was that last one?"

As the paper shuffling stopped, Stanley said, "It seems your friends didn't stop partying once they got locked up either. There was some trouble at the lockup and the cops don't want to give them up just yet."

"What kind of trouble?"

"A fight, but the two you want me to bail out weren't the instigators. I should be able to get them out sometime today. Tonight at the latest."

"Call me as soon as you can post their bail." Now for the part she was dreading. "How much is this going to set me back?"

"We've got plenty of payment options, but it depends on

how much the actual bail amount is set for. Seeing as how your friends are still in the middle of their own little—"

"How much?"

Shifting into a more candid tone, he told her, "I'll get it down as low as I can. For right now, don't worry about it."

Paige squinted as if she could study the other man through the cellular connection. "What's the catch?"

"The catch is that some vampires have been sniffing around looking for Prophet and a few of my other bondsmen." He let that sink in while slurping from a drink. "And since you didn't tell me I'm a lunatic just now, I think you're just the help I need. Walter's told me about you people, Miss Strobel. I heard what happened in Wisconsin and I also heard about the shit that went down in KC. I'm guessing the noxious substance was the remains of a vampire or . . . what do you call them? Nyman?"

"Did you say vampires?"

"Uh-huh. Maybe you've seen them. Kinda pale, lots of pointy teeth, all marked up with black tattoos, spitting nasty crap that makes you dizzy. Any of this ringing a bell?"

Paige gripped the phone a little tighter, imagining all the unpleasant ways she could convince Prophet to keep his mouth shut the next time she got her hands on him. "They're Ny*mar*," she sighed. "Not Nyman."

"Right. Does this new crop of legal trouble have something to do with the rabid dogs and riots in KC?" Stanley asked.

"What makes you think I was even in Kansas City?"

"Because weirdness tends to stick to the same people."

Stanley definitely had a point there.

His voice reflected a sloppy grin as he told her, "Look, I'm no blackmailer. I don't want to hang anything over yer head, but you folks can't make ends meet by just relying on Prophet's lottery picks."

"He told you about the lottery picks too?" she asked.

"Actually he gave some to me here and there to pay off advances on his salary."

One of the more practical uses for a man who claimed to dream visions of the future was to ask him for lottery numbers. When they panned out, the winnings were divided among Skinners across the country. For the other seventy to eighty percent of the time, the tickets might be worth enough to pay for a few meals or a tank of gas. It wasn't a perfect system, but it had its advantages. One of those was supposed to be a quiet way to pull in some untraceable funds.

Quiet.

That was the key word.

"Do you know where Walter is?" she asked.

Stanley didn't have to be psychic to pick up on the tension in her voice. "Before you start planning any funerals, let me assure you he didn't spell out anything vital for me. What little I pieced together about you or those tattooed freaks I did on my own, and I want the credit for it. If you want to blame anyone for spilling the beans about any overly weird shit going on, blame the little pricks who tried to scare away some of my bondsmen by draining one of them close to death."

"Where did this happen?"

"In Helena about six months ago."

She didn't say as much, but Paige recognized that sort of reckless behavior from Rocky Mountain Nymar. There was a theory floating around that the high altitude or thinner air made them skittish and hungrier than normal. Skittish, hungry Nymar were not pleasant to be around and they didn't care about making messes.

"I've got some major interests throughout Montana all the way down to Colorado," Stanley continued, "and I can't let them go just because some punks with long teeth spit on my men. Word of that gets around and I might as well invite all my clients to become fugitives."

"So what do you want from me?"

"The only time I ever saw these tattooed jackasses get nervous was when they crossed paths with Walter. I kept an eye on him and it turned out he was meeting up with you and some old guy."

That would have been Gerald Keeley. Almost everything Paige knew about cracking skulls and killing monsters had been taught to her by Rico. Anything on the subtler end of the spectrum, such as tracking or using her head as something other than a battering ram, she'd picked up from Gerald. Thanks to a surprise attack from a Full Blood, Gerald and a promising kid named Brad were both dead. On a brighter note, Gerald's last act had been to send Cole her way.

The way Stanley's voice strained, Paige had an easy time picturing him leaning back and swinging his feet up onto a desk as he said, "I figure the next time you're in the area, maybe you can talk some sense into these pricks."

"We're not enforcers," Paige fibbed.

"Would it make a difference if I told you some of my guys found these assholes feeding in public?"

Even though Skinners didn't hunt down and destroy every vampire out there, they drew the line at public feedings. Every Nymar should have known that, but not every guy who worked at a bail bonds office would be privy to that information. The sigh Paige let out slowly shifted into something close to a growl.

"All right," Stanley admitted. "Maybe Walter told me a little more about you Skinners than what I originally said. But that was only after I found out a good chunk on my own."

"We're still not hired muscle."

"I wouldn't imagine putting you in that category! All I'm saying is that you folks must be in need of some legitimate income. Now that I know what to look for, I've realized several of my clients may be strange for reasons other than the normal ones. In fact, a whole crew that's wanted for vice-related shit is marked up with those same tats. They're harder than hell for my guys to track, and if I could get some specialized assistance in that regard, I'd be more than happy to pay my normal bounty hunter fee."

Paige let her finger drift along the edge of her phone, lingering close to the button that would put an end to the whole conversation. The only thing that stopped her was the fact that Nymar did tend to be attracted to the seedier side of life. Some were upstanding citizens who dealt with their problem. Others were kinky, but law-aiding. Then there were the ones who wore their infection with pride. They not only wallowed in certain perversions that hooked up biters with bitees, but created new ones with a considerably less happy ending.

Being in a business where he got hung up on a lot, Stanley no doubt could feel it coming and quickly interjected, "I'll raise my fee for this case. After all, specialists shouldn't get paid the same as the rank and file, right?"

"Get Cole and Rico out of that jail cell and we'll talk."

"How about I go one better? I'm only a two hour drive away. I could go down there and spring them personally in exchange for a guaranteed business meeting within the next week."

"Done."

Paige swore she could hear Stanley smiling through the phone.

"You won't regret this," he said.

"I'd better not," she told him. "Otherwise, the Nymar may get a few phone calls telling them just how much you want to see them gone. And when they come a'knocking, you'll be on your own to answer the door."

"I'm looking forward to meeting you, Paige. Seems like we think along the same lines. You have a nice voice too. Why don't we take our meeting over a nice din—"

She cut him short by finally allowing her finger to hit the magic button. Too bad every interaction wasn't as easy to end.

Chapter 13

Daniels was engrossed in his work, but he stuck his head out of his room long enough to deliver some good news. Whatever feelers he'd put out to the local Nymar came up with a vague location of where they could be found. Paige cleaned up, threw on some fresh clothes, and headed out as quickly as she could. Even so, she wasn't fast enough to get past Ned. The old man insisted on coming along and wouldn't be talked out of it. He settled into the passenger seat of Daniels's SUV with a cracked leather briefcase between his feet and started fiddling with the radio dials.

Their first stop was a fast food place to pick up a sack full of breakfast sandwiches. She handed one over to Ned and unwrapped the other to set it upon her knee. A cup of coffee fit nicely along with a deep-fried hash brown oval on top of her right arm like a baby cradled within her sling. Her right hand was aching and stiff, but it made a fine cup holder. She drove onto Highway 40 and headed for the Poplar Street Bridge.

"Are you going to tell me where we're going?" he asked.

"East St. Louis. Daniels says the local Nymar are holed up near a community college." She looked over at him whenever she could, but didn't see much more than the highway reflected in his sunglasses.

Finally he grumbled, "What's the matter? Am I cramping your style?"

"No. I was just wondering if you intended on letting me know where you went last night."

"I was out looking for more Mongrels."

"You can—"

"Yes," Ned snapped. "Even though most of you all think I'm just some blind man who can't do anything more than sit in an empty city and answer phone calls, I can still do my job."

"So . . . does that mean your eyesight's getting better?"

"One eye's doing pretty good. I can only make out a few blobs or lights in the other."

Paige drove through downtown. The Gateway Arch made for some nice scenery, but she was in no mood to enjoy it.

Ned removed the glasses and rubbed the reddened, wrinkled skin around eyes that were so cloudy they appeared to be made from solid balls of rusted iron. "I'm disappointed in you, Paige."

"What? Why?"

"Because you haven't done any training since you got here."

She chuckled and reached down to the radio to switch to an alternative rock station. "I do more than enough training to whip your ass, old man."

"Maybe you should pick up another fighting style. I've been telling you that for years, though, and you never listen. Are you still using those sickles?"

"They're more than just sickles," she grumbled.

"And what happens if you lose that arm?"

Paige snapped her head around quickly enough to swat her ponytail against the side of her face. Turning to flip her hair into place again, she said, "I'm not going to lose my arm."

"You think I assumed I'd lose my eyesight when I tested out my little innovation? When it happened, I was just as stubborn as you. The first time a Nymar crept back onto Lindbergh Avenue, the damn thing nearly had me for supper. And it was just some smartass little bastard who thought the coast was clear."

"You handled him, right?"

"Sure," Ned grunted. "Shot him half a dozen times and

then had to convince four different sets of cops that the little jerk was trying to rob me. The only thing that kept me out of prison was that there was no body to be found and the right people felt sorry for me. I think I'm still on some watch lists, though."

"Just as long as everything turned out all right." When the inevitable grumble came, Paige added, "I'll figure something out. Right now I just want to track down those Nymar that attacked Cole and Rico."

Ned smiled and lifted his chin proudly. "I've got just the thing for that."

"What is it?"

"For Christ's sake," Ned growled. "Nobody reads the journal entries I file."

Paige slammed her foot on the gas and steered for her exit. "No, Ned. Why don't you pull them out of your little briefcase and start reading them to me? We've got a few days to spare."

His lips curled again, but into a grin. "That's the Bloodhound I remember. Take my word for it, Paige. You can't let your fire get too low because it's damn hard to stoke again."

Cocking her head at a warning angle that she knew was pronounced enough for Ned to see, she pulled off of the highway and onto Eighth Street.

"Do you at least remember the Squamatosapiens?" he asked.

"Those were the lizard men that you were chasing when you could still see, right?"

"Yes. They were spotted more and more throughout the Everglades and—"

"Wasn't the Dover Demon one of those?" Paige cut in.

"Close, but no. Anyway, it turned out the Squamatosapiens were—"

"Could you just call them Lizard Men?" To fill the silence that followed, she added, "It would speed things up."

"You know what would speed things up? If I could speak without being interrupted."

"Okay. Sorry."

"So, it turned out that the Lizard Men were hunting Nymar. To this day I still don't know why. It wasn't for blood or even the spore. When they caught one, they ate the meat and left the rest behind. Sometimes they only took the teeth and fingernails. Anyway, apart from being fast and agile, the . . . I can't say Lizard Men. That's just stupid."

"How about Squams?" Paige offered.

"Fine. The Squams were more than just nocturnal. They could see in almost total darkness, but were exceptionally good at tracking Nymar. That led me to believe they had some sort of adaptation that made them suited for the task."

"Possibly a gland that secreted something onto their eyes?"

Ned snapped his fingers and said, "Exactly!"

Before he could get too worked up, she said, "I just remembered your journal entry."

He kept talking as if Paige hadn't opened her mouth. "I only caught one of the Squams, but that was enough to verify my theory. There *was* an extra gland in their eye sockets and it *did* excrete a substance that allowed them to see in the dark. It's a fluid that interacts with the rods and cones in a way that—"

"In a way that can blind a human who tries to use the stuff on themselves," Paige said.

"I'm not completely blind," Ned snapped. "And the fluid can be used in human eyes now that I've refined it and diluted the compound. It's not like there's been much of anything else for me to do in the years since you and Rico embarked on that reign of terror he called a training exercise."

"First of all," she said while holding up a finger. The nice one. "Those Nymar had to be put down before they gave all the other ones any ideas. Second," she added while uncurling another finger. It wasn't the nice one, but lost its edge since the first one was still up. "That eye stuff isn't safe to use."

Ned was quiet until Paige came to a complete stop at a traffic light. They were only a few blocks away from the East St. Louis Community College Center. The blood in his eyes was the color of rusty water, and his pupils were more like corroded black disks that were chipped around the edges.

"Ned, I didn't mean to—"

"*No!* You listen to me, missy. I discovered those Squam-atosapiens. I tracked them down. I figured out what they ate and how they hunted." Reaching into one of the many pockets stitched into his cotton fishing vest, Ned removed a plastic eye dropper bottle that still had the Visine label stuck on it. "I took what those things gave us and made it into something we could all use. That's what Skinners do. You want to see some real horror stories? Read the history about how our modern medical practices came to be. That's some shit that will give you nightmares, but it was the best way those doctors knew how to test their medicines and surgical practices. The FDA doesn't fund our research, so we gotta do it the old-fashioned way. I read your journal entries and I couldn't be prouder about that whole ink idea of yours. It's rough, but it'll be great with a little more work. So you hurt yourself when you used it the first time? Well join the goddamn club. You know what makes it all worthwhile?"

"What?" Paige squeaked.

"When someone can take what you created and put it to use." Ned grabbed her hand and slapped the little plastic bottle into it. "Here. If you don't have the guts to risk getting hurt again, then you got no place as a Skinner."

Those last words made Paige realize she'd been slumping behind the wheel. She closed her fist around the bottle and straightened up again. "Where do you think we should start looking?"

Without missing a beat, Ned replied, "How the hell should I know? I'm blind!"

The short drive to a parking spot along Railroad Avenue was a whole lot easier than the drive from the city. Paige and Ned shared a much needed laugh while she parked Daniels's SUV within sight of a tall billboard and a long, two-story brick building. There wasn't much to see in the immediate area apart from that building and a whole lot of drab road. The itch in her scars was stronger there than anywhere else along the way, so Paige got out and started walking. Ned fell into step beside her. As much as she wanted to take the old man's arm and lead him, she knew that would be a real good way to get acquainted with his wooden cane.

At the next intersection, they spotted a taller building that looked like it could either be an old factory or an older hospital. A low fence surrounded a wide, flat lawn, giving the whole area the feel of a prison exercise yard. Traffic flowed along Railroad Avenue that was tame compared to St. Louis and barely a trickle compared to the motorized suicide parades in Chicago. Paige walked along the street for about five seconds before digging into her pocket.

"What now?" Ned asked.

"I'm calling Daniels. Maybe he can narrow it down for us a little more."

"Wouldn't he have told you as much before we left?"

"Probably," she replied, "but we're not getting anywhere by just wandering."

Ned tapped his cane against the ground and said, "That's right. And we don't make phone calls when there's hunting to do."

"You're really enjoying this, aren't you?"

"Aren't you?" Too excited to wait for an answer, Ned said, "Put those drops in and we'll find out all we need to know. Since we're close enough to feel those bloodsuckers, we should be able to see where they're congregating or which direction we need to go."

"This stuff can tell us that much?"

"And more. Don't be squeamish. Maddy tested some that was watered down and she said it worked like a charm. You remember Maddy, don't you?"

"The crazy woman from Jersey? Yeah, I remember her."

"Well she was able to track down a group of the slickest Nymar she's ever seen thanks to my innovation."

"It doesn't take much to slip one past her," Paige grumbled.

"That's funny. She didn't have much good to say about you either."

Paige stood on the curb, knowing all too well that Ned was using one of the simplest baiting tricks around other than a triple dog dare. What grated on her nerves even more was how well it worked. "Fine," she said as she opened the bottle.

"You don't know how much this means to me," Ned told her. "The fact that you trust me enough to—"

"Yeah, yeah," she said as she opened the bottle and held it under her nose. The fluid inside didn't smell bad, but it didn't smell like rose petals either. It was the color of seawater, complete with all the wonderful little particles that reminded you just how many animals lived, breathed, and excreted in there. When she swirled the fluid around, a lot of it clung to the side of the bottle and slid right down again.

"What did Maddy say about this stuff?" Paige asked.

"That it allowed her to see scents."

"You sure she wasn't sniffing something else?"

Ned clucked his tongue and stepped back as a row of cars sped down the street. "You know she wouldn't do anything to endanger another Skinner."

"Yeah, I know." Steeling herself as best she could, Paige tipped her head back, opened her eyes wide and held the dropper over the left one. In the end she figured that was the one she'd prefer losing. "How much should I use?"

"Just enough for an even coat. The Squamatosapiens' gland excreted—" Seeing the glare on her face, Ned skipped ahead to, "Two drops in each eye should do it."

Before she could convince herself to do otherwise, Paige squirted a few drops onto her left eye. She'd never been good at giving herself eye drops, so a good portion of the stuff splattered on her eyelid and brow. Rather than use any more, she blinked and rolled her eye under the lid. When she reflexively tried to rub it in, she felt a strong hand on her forearm.

"Don't," Ned warned. "Just let it soak. How does it feel?"

"Warm. No . . . cold. It's cold now, but it was warm a second ago."

"Open your eyes."

Paige opened her eyes and looked around. Almost immediately, panic set in. "Everything's blurry. I think my vision is screwed up. The light's glaring so much."

"Just give it a second."

A second didn't help.

The next few seconds after that, however, allowed the glare around every light source or reflective surface to fade. "It's still a little fuzzy."

"That's because you're in direct sunlight. What else do you see?"

Feeling like she was going to lose her footing, Paige focused on the ugly factory or hospital in the distance. At least that gave her something to concentrate on other than the slick layer of goo clinging to her eyeball and the tingling chill slowly filling the entire socket. When she looked at the street again, she saw ghostly waves of different colors drifting on currents of wind like cartoon squiggles denoting a particularly stinky mess.

"I think I see what you were talking about," she said. "But, it's kind of hard to pin down. It's coming and going."

"That's because you only put the drops in one eye. Do the other one."

She took a breath, held up the bottle and reminded herself that she already had one foot in this particular pool. How bad could it be to step in and swim? Ignoring the weight of her arm hanging from her shoulder, which reminded her of her last bad swim, she treated her other eye.

The same mix of warm and cold flooded across the middle of her face, where it connected to the chill in her other eye. Staring out at a street that was now filled with a smeared jumble of moving blobs and colorful waves, Paige asked, "Right before you went blind, did it feel like your eyeballs had frozen into little round ice cubes?"

"I'm not completely blind," Ned told her, "but yes."

"Great."

"Blink, but don't rub it in. The rest will pass."

It only took a few seconds for him to be proven right. Her vision cleared to the point where she felt like she needed glasses to see beyond a distance of about twenty or thirty yards. The waves of color, on the other hand, remained. When traffic thinned out, the waves became less like smears hanging in the air and more like smoke that held together without the cars breaking it apart. Most of the colors were dull and stagnant, but there was one particular shade of red that caught her attention.

"You say those Squams hunted Nymar?" she asked.

"Sure did."

"There's some sort of trace in the air, but it's not the same color as the rest." Lifting her head like a dog that had just caught a whiff of something cooking in a nearby kitchen, she added, "This one's bright red with some . . . yellow? Yeah, I guess yellow or orange is about right."

"That's it."

"There's a scent coming off of you, Ned. It's got some dark blue and black in it."

"Maddy said those came from the antidote used to kill that Nymar."

"Yeah? Well I'd have to agree because those colors are also coming from you."

Ned patted his pockets and removed a few small syringes containing the antidote that meant instant death to any Nymar who got it injected into their bloodstream. "You still see it?" he asked.

"Oh yeah," she replied as she studied the waves rolling off the thin little cylinders. "But it's also coming from you. Not the syringes. You." Twitching toward the sound of an approaching engine, Paige was able to pick out a subtle glow emanating from the car's windows. She hurried down the sidewalk and soon felt a familiar itch within the scars on her hands. "There's Nymar in that car," she said. "I could see them before I could feel them."

"So the drops really do work," Ned sighed. "I knew it."

"They're weird, but they work. I might have to place an order before I leave."

"It'll be a while before I can fill it. That is, unless you've spotted any Squamatosapiens recently."

Resisting the urge to rub her eyes again, Paige tapped Ned's shoulder as she hurried toward the car. "Which way is the club?"

"A few miles south of here."

"Some of the traces lead back that way, so I guess that's the direction they came from." She pointed past a barely visible cloud of red that only she could see. "If we get moving quickly, I should be able to follow them."

Ned grabbed her arm with one hand and his cane in the other. "Excellent. Can you drive?"

"I can separate the smells from the stoplights . . . mostly. How long does this stuff last anyway?"

"Maybe an hour or two. It evaporates fairly quickly, but I'm putting together some wraparound sunglasses to prolong the effect. Conversely, you can let it dissipate so the effect wears off a little sooner."

He went on about more options for shades, but Paige was too busy rushing to the SUV to listen. Although she was able to see a little better now that she'd adjusted to the constant flow of color drifting around her, it still required some concentration. She simply didn't realize how many smells were out there until she could see them. Fortunately, the Lizard Men were literally focused on Nymar, so those scents stood out like neon amid a background of forty watt bulbs.

After nearly taking a black hatchback out of its misery while trying to make a U-turn from her parking spot, Paige sped to where she'd first picked up the scent and caught it just as the red waves were dissipating. Driving directly through the scent only disrupted it more, so she kept her eyes glued to the traces in front of her.

"Look out!" Ned screamed.

Getting a warning like that from a man who was nearly blind was not a good sign. Paige swerved around a motorcycle in her lane and tried to watch the road as well as the scents. Her task became a lot easier when she caught up to the Nymar's vehicle on East Broadway. Her scars reacted to the Nymar presence and her eyes could see their bright red scent billowing out of their vehicle through partially rolled-down windows. They turned onto Sixth Street and headed into a part of town that, depending on whether someone's glass was half empty or full, could be described as "run-down" or "in development."

The buildings on either side of her were drab but clean. Parking lots were mostly empty, and there were no angry people baring fangs at her from the sidewalk. So far she didn't mind the neighborhood one bit. "Have you ever been to this part of town, Ned?"

"I don't get much past the Central West End anymore."

Tracking the Nymar through one more turn before they pulled to a stop at a curb, she said, "Well we're right around Sixth and . . . Missouri Avenue."

"Still doesn't sound familiar."

Although the Nymar parked in front of a two-story building made from dark red and light brown bricks, none of the three that got out of the car entered the place. Paige stopped along the curb at the intersection, just shy of making the final turn. She sat there, fighting the urge to scoot down in her seat as the Nymar checked their surroundings. Keeping her head pointed forward, she put on the bored expression of someone who was waiting for someone else.

"I can feel them nearby," Ned said.

"Yeah, they're just down the street."

"Do they know we're here?"

"I'm not sure yet." When a fourth Nymar stepped out of the car, he joined the others in lining up along the curb. They talked to each other and studied a building across the street covered in white stucco. Red, white, and green striped awnings hung over the two second floor windows, and a larger one shaded a first floor window in a pattern that resembled a giant simplistic face on that side of the building.

The guy who'd come out of the car last was the biggest of the group and had short, bleached blond hair. He stood with his arm draped around a lanky girl with sunken cheeks and Asian features. Although she wrapped an arm around the blond guy's waist, the gesture seemed more out of habit than anything else. The other two were skin and bones, shifted like little dogs that had to be taken for a walk, and were dressed in clothes from Goodwill's reject pile. The male half of that couple had the scrawny build of a lifelong junkie, and the girl had skin that even looked pasty on a vampire. Their black markings stood out in the sun's glow as they turned around to walk toward a different two-story brick building on the same corner where Paige had parked. This structure didn't have a single window that wasn't boarded up, and judging by the dirty scorch marks on the walls, the glass had probably melted from the panes in a very impressive fire.

"All right," Paige said as she plucked the keys from the ignition. "I'm going to introduce myself before they spot us."

Ned hopped out first, gripping his cane tight enough for the thorns in its handle to dig into his palms. "I'm coming with you."

Since she knew that arguing with him would be a lost cause, Paige strode across the street and met the Nymar's glances with open arms and a beaming smile. "What's the matter with you guys?" she asked. "Can't you afford a nicer hideout?"

The big guy with the blond hair stood in front of the burnt building, wearing the same work shirt he'd had on the previous night. It hung open, so Paige had to wait for the wind to catch it just right before she could read the stitching on its pocket. "You lost or something?" Jerry asked.

The moment Ned stepped onto the curb beside Paige, the junkie beside Jerry bared his teeth in a hiss that would have been more threatening if he wasn't missing most of his human teeth along with a few of his fangs. There was enough ferocity on the guy's darkly tanned face, however, to make up for his oral deficiencies.

Jerry narrowed his eyes and nodded slowly. "I get it. The Skinner from St. Louis finally got some backup."

"He doesn't need backup," Paige said casually. "I'm here to send you Peter Walsh's regards."

She'd been hoping the name would elicit a reaction and wasn't disappointed. The Asian girl with her hand on Jerry's hip looked up at him awaiting her next command. The pasty chick with stringy hair took a spot next to the Nymar with the missing teeth and set her sights squarely on Ned. "I've been waiting for an excuse to bury this tosser," she said in a British accent that was either from a grungy corner of the realm or had been picked up after watching too many Monty Python movies.

Paige stood on the curb with her back straight and her chin held high. Waiting for a few cars to pass behind her, she said, "Do yourself a favor, Gums. Keep the girlfriend on a leash."

Curling his lips over his incomplete set of teeth as if the nickname got to him more than an insult to his pasty companion, Gums seemed relieved when he felt Jerry slap him on the shoulder.

"How do you know Peter?" Jerry asked.

"He found me and my partner in Chicago," Paige said.

"So this one's spending time in Chicago now?" Jerry asked as he nodded toward Ned.

"No, my partner's nearby. Can't have all my cards showing, right?"

Even though "nearby" for her partner meant "locked up in a jail cell," Paige didn't feel the need to share that with the Nymar. And since Jerry took a casual glance at the nearby rooftops and windows, he obviously didn't know any better. "Is Pete with you?"

"No. He's dead."

The Asian woman showed Paige half a snarl that was more menacing than Gums's full show. "Made a bad choice coming here and saying that, Skinner."

"Easy, Sonya," Jerry said. Watching Paige carefully, he asked, "Did you kill him?"

She shook her head. "He was mostly dead by the time he got to us. Something was wrong with him, but I guess you might already know that. Some," she added while looking at the pasty British girl, "may know better than others. See the way her tendrils are pale and can't stop shaking? That's how Peter looked right before his spore exploded through his chest."

"Oh God," the pasty girl said. "I told you I was sick! It was that kid we—"

"How about we take this inside?" Jerry cut in. He grabbed the pasty girl by the back of the neck and shoved her toward the charred building on the corner. Sonya followed, but Gums stayed behind to snarl some more at Paige and Ned.

"So you already know about Pestilence," Ned said as he stepped through the door.

The inside of the building was exactly what the outside advertised. Everything from the floor to the ceiling was either scorched or warped from excessive water damage. Thick layers of ash had become engrained into every surface and hung in the air like gritty fog. Between that and the thick cloud of red mist the drops were showing her, Paige had a hard time keeping her eyes open.

It seemed the room had been furnished by whatever the Nymar could steal from poorly supervised garage sales and a few garbage piles. Considering how well the Nymar in and around St. Louis had been set up before she and Rico cleaned them out, Paige found the contrast particularly jarring. She followed a dim trace of red to a figure curled up in a corner under a thick comforter with stuffing hanging out of several rips in the fabric. "What's wrong with her?"

"She's sick," Jerry said as he leaned against the wall next to a window. "Just like Pete was sick and like all of us are probably sick."

"Pestilence?"

All of the Nymar glanced around at each other before staring intently at Paige and Ned. Creeping forward, Gums asked, "What do you know about it?"

Even though the Skinners made sure to stay close to the door, they were far from secure within the filthy building. Any place a Nymar called home could be hollowed out to hold everything from secret rooms and escape hatches to feeding chambers that held humans as snacks for later.

"I know about it because it was one of the last words out of Peter's mouth," she replied. "And since I made the drive all the way down here, I'd like you to tell me how he got so sick."

"We were hoping you'd be able to tell us that," Jerry said.

Ned shifted his gaze from one Nymar to another as if he could see each of them perfectly well. "We think Peter wasn't the only one to catch this bug."

"This ain't just a case of the sniffles, old man. This is poison, and unless someone stops what he started, you're gonna have a war on your hands."

Paige swung her left hand down to pluck the club from her boot. By the time she brought it up to Gums's neck, the sickle blade had formed just beneath the Nymar's chin. "When did you assholes start working with Mongrels?"

"Wh-What?" Gums stammered.

"Someone else gave me a similar message intended for the old man, and it wasn't one of you. It was a Mongrel leopard leading a bunch of strays."

"Malia is her name," Ned explained. "Surely you know her."

"Yeah, I know Malia," Jerry said. "And why wouldn't she have a beef with the old man?" When he looked at Ned, he chuckled in the most condescending way possible. "But it's probably not *this* old man she's got the problem with. That is, unless he's doing more than selling pencils these days."

Using her sickle to slice just far enough into Gums's neck to draw blood, Paige snarled, "Considering the St. Louis Nymar got their asses kicked so hard that they're still walking funny, you probably shouldn't be talking so tough."

"We're too tired to fight you," Jerry said. "Fact is, I'm the one that told Peter to track you down."

"And why would you do something like that?"

"This Pestilence shit is real Black Plague stuff, but it's the sort of thing that Skinners might know about."

"Or something a Skinner would have made," Gums croaked.

Sitting down on an old lawn chair made from strips of green and white plastic, Jerry said, "Pete wanted to talk to a real Skinner, so I told him about my girl Stephanie running the Blood Parlors in Chicago."

"You didn't know where to find me in St. Louis?" Ned asked.

Jerry looked at him as if he'd just found the source of a particularly nasty stench. "Sure I know, but Pete wanted to talk to a *real* Skinner. Not some blind man phoning in reports to the wrecking crew."

Even though she was a member of that crew, Paige didn't know what Jerry was talking about. She rarely spoke to Ned, and Skinners certainly didn't phone in reports with any real regularity. Still, it didn't hurt to let paranoid Nymar build the Skinners up into a more threatening force. "Pete didn't make it more than a few steps through our door before . . . well, I'm sure you know what happened to him."

"Yeah," Jerry grunted. "I also know what'll happen if you don't ease up off my boy there."

With a thought and a subtle relaxing of her grip around the handle, the sickle blade retracted, allowing Gums to move away without slitting his own throat. "We're not here to start anything with you guys. Just tell us what you can about Pestilence."

"Oh you started plenty with us back when you and that other fucker started killing my kind like you had a goddamn hunting license. But since Pestilence turned out to be just as bad for humans as it is for us, I suppose it couldn't hurt to talk for a few minutes."

Allowing the Nymar to save face with his friends, Paige kept her mouth shut and let Jerry continue at his own pace.

"None of us know exactly how it started," he explained, "but the first Nymar popped open about a week ago in Philadelphia. Let's just say word spread pretty quick once a perfectly good spore decided to come out of its shell."

It seemed Jerry wasn't going to part with the Nymar communication system any more than Daniels.

"It's those nymph sluts working the strip bars," Sonya said.

"They're infected with Pestilence?"

"Nah, but they're working with the old man, because wherever he shows up, there's always a few of those sweet-ass bitches nearby."

"What old man?" Ned asked.

"He hangs out at Bunn's," Jerry said. "From what we heard, he's been on a road trip making appearances from Philly, all through Texas and back up here. He's about my height, got a short white beard, carries a big stick. Plenty of Nymar seen a guy that fits the description in plenty of other clubs. Some say he's been kidnapping our kind for years, injecting them with some kind of weird shit and lettin' 'em go."

"And you just assume he's a Skinner?" Paige snapped. "I know most of the Skinners working in this country and I sure haven't heard of anyone with a catch and release injection program."

Jerry nodded. "He's a Skinner all right. Either that or he just happened to find a magic stick that changes shapes and can sprout blades."

Paige and Ned glanced at each other just long enough for

Ned to shake his head. It seemed no Skinner came to his mind either.

The pasty girl with Gums dabbed her finger into the smudge of blood on her boyfriend's neck and licked it up before saying, "That old man . . . he came after me too! He caught me . . . touched me . . . even stuck me with needles."

"See, that doesn't sound like a Skinner to me," Paige mused. "Because we're usually a little more aggressive than that. Especially when we're dealing with someone who busted into a strip club, kidnapped some dancer, and then tried to kill two of our friends after a car chase."

All four Nymar froze. Even the pasty girl left the tip of her tongue less than an inch from her snack.

Paige nodded in the same smug fashion that Jerry had a few moments ago. "That's right. We know about that. So you'll excuse us if we're not ready to kick back and just lap up everything you feed us."

Jerry stood up and let his arms hang from his sides. "Ain't no problem," he said as the oily black claws eased out from beneath his fingernails. "We weren't there to do anything more than get our hands on one of those nymphs."

"Let me guess," Paige said sarcastically. "A rescue mission?"

"No. Them girls got a special kind of honey flowin' through their veins. Does a body real good, you know what I mean? We need anything we can get to help cure our kind, because this Pestilence shit is spreading fast on its own now. Maybe you heard of the Mud Flu?"

"I don't know what books you've been reading, but Pestilence means something a little worse than a flu," Ned said.

"Pete thought he had a flu," Jerry told him. Waving toward the Nymar curled up on the floor in the back of the room, he added, "So did Lara. She never fed on anyone outside of our regular neighborhood and sure as hell never saw a nymph. Only thing I know for sure is that the old man has been seen in all the spots where the Mud Flu's been the worst. And wherever that Mud Flu is, Pestilence gets into our kind to spill our guts onto the sidewalk. That sure seems like the twisted shit that would come out of a Skinner's mind, but why don't you just go down to Bunn's and see for yourself? The old man's been hanging out there real steady since about a week or so before the flu hit St. Louis."

"This had better not be bullshit," Paige warned.

Holding out his hands as if they were supposed to look nonthreatening with claws sticking out of his fingers, Jerry said, "Pete dragged himself all the way to Chicago because it'd take a Skinner to get anywhere near that club anymore. The old man is there, along with a bunch of nymphs. You already came this far, why not check out my story? If I'm wrong, at least your grampa here can see some bare titties."

"Have you tried approaching this old man yourselves?" Ned asked.

Smiling in a way that showed too many fangs to be friendly, Jerry said, "Them and our kind have a long history. We can't exactly pay our money and just walk into any of them clubs."

"Is that why you kidnapped the dancer?" Ned asked.

"That's our business, blind man, which ain't none'a yours."

"Forget about him. What about the Mind Singer?"

"That's enough, Cass!" Jerry snapped.

Paige stepped toward the pasty girl and spoke in a voice that managed to be both comforting and assertive. "No, let her talk."

When Jerry moved to intercept Paige, Ned's cane lifted to bar his way. Despite the Nymar's attempt to get past the simple wooden barrier, Jerry couldn't budge it more than an inch. And before he could gather himself to make a better attempt, the end of the wooden stick flowed into a sharpened edge that cut the hand Jerry used to try and push it aside.

"Let the girl speak," Ned demanded.

Willing the sickle back into a club, Paige dropped it into the holster on her boot. "It's okay. Just say what you wanted to say."

Cass's eyes darted nervously between Paige and Jerry, which only sped her voice into a quick spray of words. "The Mind Singer started talking to us not too long ago, when Misonyk wanted to gather reinforcements."

"Misonyk's dead," Paige assured her.

"And since then the Mind Singer only got louder. He quieted down for a little bit, but now he won't shut up about how Pestilence will wipe away all of the creatures who haven't looked into the eye of the Lord."

Looking to Jerry, Ned asked, "Is that true?"

The bleach-blond Nymar pulled in a deep breath and closed his eyes before letting it out. "You know what's worse than some religious freak screaming at you? Having a religious freak scream his crap straight into your brain. I don't even know what religion it is! Just a bunch of crazy talk about the Lord's eye and words scratched on the walls."

"All that matters is that Henry believes," Cass said. "He spoke about Pestilence and how Skinners would be the only ones left standing. He—"

"Wait," Paige cut in. "Did you say Henry?"

Cass nodded. "He grew into a Full Blood at Lancroft Reformatory and tried to go back there when you and some other man came to get him. He's dreamt about it for weeks, and when the Mind Singer dreams, we all see it."

"Yeah," Jerry grumbled. "Religious crazy talk and crazy dreams. With that to look forward to every damn day, risking our necks to taste some nymph blood ain't such a bad deal. We'll either get the high of our lives or killed along the way. Any way you slice it, we get some fucking peace and quiet."

Even though she was looking at the reason that Cole and Rico were in jail after getting attacked and nearly killed in a car wreck, Paige was more interested in what Cass had to say. "What did Henry tell you about Pestilence?"

"He doesn't tell us anything," Cass replied. "He screams in his sleep. He has thoughts and wishes and fears and we all get to hear them."

"Do you hear it now?" Ned asked. "What's he saying?"

All of the Nymar closed their eyes until Cass finally shook her head. "I can hear his voice, but it's far away."

"It's background noise," Jerry said. "Like hearing some dickhead blast their music every day. You don't really know what every song is. But when it's loud, it's enough to drive us freaking insane. Finding the nymphs at that strip bar was a blessing. They're the only things that got what it takes to make all the other noise quiet down for a while."

"You know something?" Paige asked. "I may feel for you a little more if you hadn't smashed a door in, kidnapped a defenseless girl, and then tried to kill anyone who got in your way."

Jerry stomped forward, but not close enough to Paige to trigger a fight. "You and another Skinner wiped out damn near every Nymar in St. Louis. Me and the other survivors are scraping by here, but just barely. Now, another one of you cooks up Pestilence to wipe us out, along with shapeshifters, while also infecting a couple hundred humans! Could be thousands by now. If a Skinner gets in my way anymore, I figure I'm more than justified in getting him before he gets me."

Paige tested the waters with, "Does that include us?"

The only response Jerry gave to that was a noncommittal shrug. "You ain't gotten in my way yet."

"If we do go over to that club," Paige warned, "you've got to give us some room to maneuver. Stay away from that place."

Jerry looked around at the others in the squalid room and then shifted his eyes back to Paige. "Normally, I'd agree. But it ain't often Nymar find that many nymphs in one place."

"Fine," Paige snapped. "It's been nice talking to you, but you're on your own. Let's go, Ned." She pushed the door open and kept every muscle tensed in anticipation of fending off an attack.

The hairs on the back of her neck stood up, but that turned out to be empty paranoia. Nobody rushed them, jumped at them, or even threw a piece of garbage at the front door. Considering how many empty food containers, cigarette packs, and beer bottles were laying around, that last part was a very pleasant surprise.

All of the Nymar scowled at the door after Paige and Ned left. When it became clear they weren't coming back, all eyes shifted toward Jerry.

"Yeah, you go on and get the fuck outta our place," he snarled to the closed door. "It ain't often so many Skinners are in one place either. And we ain't the only ones that'll want to know where they're headed."

Chapter 14

Strip bars always looked a lot different in the light of day. At night they exuded a comforting glow that was easy on the eyes, while the thrumming beat of music soothed the ears. They even had a smell all their own, which was an effective mixture of body spray, beer, and hormones. Under the rays of the sun, however, things took a drastic turn. The neon wasn't lit. The music wasn't playing, and the strongest smell was car exhaust from the nearby street.

Bunn's Lounge reminded Paige of a few other places she'd seen. One was a club in Wisconsin called Shimmy's, which employed a nymph who was real good at separating customers from their money. She knew better than to assume all those customers were men, however. One taste of Tristan's supernatural talents had almost been enough to get Paige to fold a few dollars in half and slip them beneath a lacy garter.

"Damn," she said as she shaded her eyes and looked at the building in front of her. "That is one big, purple A-frame."

"Is that all you see?" Ned asked.

She squinted and blinked to stir up the solution that clung to her eyeballs. "I can see Nymar scent around one side of the building, which is where Cole said that redhead was taken from. There's also something like . . . a light green? It's tough to nail it down, but I haven't seen it until now. Other than that it's just a whole lot of purple."

She'd parked within spitting distance of the front door, due to the fact that there was only one other car in the lot. It was a newer model Hyundai from the "I have kids but I'm still cool" line. As she walked toward the red mist, Ned followed behind her. Around the corner, several garbage cans, crates, and trash bags were piled against the building. The mist took her away from the structure and through some thorny bushes.

"The Nymar were right here," she said from the other side of the shrubs. "Looks like they waited around here for a good long while."

"How can you tell? Is the trail a different color? Is there a different intensity?"

Picking her way back through the bushes, she said, "Nope. There's a ton of cigarette butts, pop cans, and beer bottles piled up back there."

When the side door creaked open, Ned tightened his grip on the top of his cane and turned toward the building. Only the sharpest eyes would have caught the subtle shift as the cane's lowest end sharpened to a point.

"What's goin' on out here?" asked a muscular, olive-skinned man wearing a T-shirt that was so tight it may have been colored onto him with Magic Marker. His short black hair wasn't slicked back, but was combed and styled into perfect shape.

"Do you work here?" Paige asked.

Although the guard in the T-shirt wore a standard, menacing snarl, he softened up a bit when he saw her. "Yeah," he said. "What are you doing back there?"

"I heard there was some trouble last night. Is there anyone I can talk to about that?"

The guard's brow furrowed. "You a cop?"

"No."

"Reporter?" he asked with a hint of curiosity.

"We're the ones who know what kind of dancers you've got inside," she said. "And we're also the only ones who might be able to help you with the problem you've been having with fanged, tattooed freaks harassing your girls."

Paige wasn't dressed in anything too revealing, but her

navy blue shirt and jeans hugged her figure just enough to possibly give her some leverage with a man. While the guard was definitely a man, he worked around naked women often enough to have no trouble keeping his line of sight above her neck. While that would normally have been a refreshing change, Paige couldn't help but wonder if she was losing her touch.

"What do you know about those freaks?" he asked.

Ned cleared his throat and said, "We know one of your girls was dragged away from here. I trust she made it back safely?"

"Yeah," the guard said. "Kate's all right."

"That's because of two friends of ours. One had a leather jacket, and they're both in jail after helping send Kate home."

"She did mention something about those two lending a hand. Come on in and I'll see if Christov wants to talk to you."

The guard stepped aside and held the door open for both Ned and Paige while making sure they could see the gun holstered under his arm. The door led directly into a short hallway cluttered with a few crooked bar stools, a couple broken tables, and stacks of other things that must have been taken from the main room. After two sharp turns, the hall ran the length of the entire building. There were a few doors on the left and one to the immediate right next to a large window that looked out to where the real action took place. As the guard took them to the end of the hall, one of the doors on the left opened up.

Even before the blonde stepped into view, Ned perked up. His head snapped toward her as if his sight had miraculously returned. Paige almost hoped that was the case because no man would have wanted to miss seeing her glide out of the frilly dressing room. The best way Paige could describe her was a pinup model carved out of living candy, appealing to every sensory nerve wired into a human body.

Patting the guard on the cheek, the blonde said, "Hi, Mikey."

Even while giving her half a smirk, Mikey somehow managed to keep his eyes from wandering along the blonde's impressive body, which was barely covered by a half shirt and low-ride Capri jeans. "Hello, Shae."

Shae's breasts moved just right and hung just low enough to be real.

There were no visible roots to be found within hair that dangled past her shoulders in a flowing wave. Either that hair was a naturally occurring miracle or it was cared for at a salon that cost more per visit than Paige had ever spent on a car.

She was tall without the benefit of heels.

Her smile was not only genuine, but also gorgeous without a hint of makeup.

What Paige noticed most of all, however, was the cool green waves that flowed from Shae's skin like a naturally occurring veil.

"These two know the men that helped Kate last night," Mikey said.

When Shae looked at Paige again, she did so as if she'd just found an old friend that had been presumed dead. "What are those guys' names?" she asked.

For some reason, giving Rico's nickname seemed like a snub to Shae, so she replied, "Terrance. And Cole."

Extending a hand to Paige, she grasped it and held on earnestly. "Those two were so brave. If there's anything they need, just let us know. And if anyone here refuses you, tell them to answer to me. That goes for both of you."

Paige smiled, pleasantly surprised to find someone like Shae who ranked so low on the Bitch Meter.

Reaching into a purse tucked under her left arm, Shae pulled out a little case that was a miniature version of the purse. It opened like a compact and held two different styles of business cards. "Here," she said as she handed one to Paige. "This is my personal phone number, and I'll always answer it when I'm away from here. I'll be around for a while, though." Her pale blue eyes dropped and then flicked back up again. Leaning in closer, she added, "I love those boots. They'd really come in handy fending off the drunks that waddle through this place."

Not only had Shae managed to ease right onto Paige's good side, but she'd also noticed the batons that were hidden well enough to get through most security checks.

And then she was gone. She walked through the door beside the large window and headed straight across the main room to see to her own business. Mikey continued down the hall and motioned for the Skinners to follow him.

The house lights were on, which allowed Paige to see straight through the tinted glass and into the main room. Without those lights, the window would most likely be a one-way mirror reflecting three large stages, brass poles, and several tables and chairs scattered throughout the central part of the club. While she expected the floors to be covered in spilled beer and God only knew what else, everything out there appeared spotless. A few dancers in street clothes clustered on the main stage, talking among themselves and pulling on a shiny brass pole to test how well it was anchored to the floor and ceiling. While all of the dancers were pretty, only one was in Shae's league, and she also gave off the cool green scent. The only other source of the scent was a redhead sitting at the bar in the opposite corner of the room adjacent to the main entrance. Shae walked over to rub the redhead's back and point toward the glass.

"Hi!" the redhead shouted just loud enough to be heard.

Ned looked toward the sound and asked, "Who's that?"

"Kate," Mikey replied. "She'll want to talk to you, but let's check in with Christov first." He led them down the hallway, past the dressing rooms and to a narrow door marked PRIVATE. He knocked, waited for a few seconds, and then opened it.

The first thing that caught her attention was a man wearing a pale silk shirt sitting behind a cluttered desk. His clean-shaven, sharply angled face was just as smooth as his bald, polished scalp.

"Christov, these two say they know the guys who chased those freaks away last night," Mikey explained.

By now Paige's eyes had adjusted well enough for her to get a feel for the rest of the room. It could very well have been the security office of a small casino. Christov's desktop was buried beneath a computer and several stacks of papers. The wall behind him was adorned with various certifications and commercial licenses, but the two largest walls were covered with monitors showing various sections of Bunn's Lounge from different angles in crisp black and white. Watching the dancers was obviously not the priority, since the cameras were pointed at the bar, the edges of the stages, the tables throughout the room, and an area filled with overstuffed couches and armchairs sectioned off by a thick velvet curtain. After tapping a button that dimmed the glow from his computer monitor, Christov rolled along the edge of his desk in a cheap office chair. He studied Paige and Ned while flaring the wide nostrils of his thin, hooked nose. "What am I supposed to do with them?" he asked in an accent that could have been European, Asian, or possibly African.

"They say they also know something about the . . . uh . . ." Finding himself at a loss for words, Mikey used two fingers to tap the spot on his mouth where a Nymar's feeding fangs would be.

"Yeah. I just bet you know all about them," Christov said as he stood up to model a crisp pair of suit pants and a thin leather belt. "That'd make you Skinners?"

"Yes sir," Ned replied. "You're familiar with us?"

"The girls I have working for me, they're more than just pretty, you know? They tell me about the ones like you. Between the old man and your two buddies from last night distracting my security, my girls wouldn't be in so much trouble."

"My friends are behind bars right now and your girl is sipping daiquiris in the next room," Paige said.

Christov's movement was either a shrug or a way to adjust the shirt upon his shoulders. "Don't mistake me. I do appreciate their help."

"Then return the favor by answering some questions. First of all, what old man are you talking about?"

While studying her carefully, Christov bumped a folded newspaper lying near his computer monitor to reveal the handle of a gun. Although the bump was hardly an accident, he didn't make a move toward the pistol. "He comes in to talk to the girls. The *special* ones, you know? He pays well and always buys drinks." Nodding toward Ned, he added, "Carries a stick with thorns like that cane of yours. Shae, Jordan, Kate, and the ones like them told me about Skinners because this old man is one. He didn't lift a finger to help with those tattooed freaks, though."

"Have you ever spoken to him?" Ned asked.

"I approached him once. He seemed quiet, so I leave him be."

"Does the name Peter Walsh ring any bells?"

"No."

Having dealt with Nymar for several years, Paige had become very skilled in picking out lies. Nothing about Christov—from the way he carried himself to the tone in his voice—set off any alarms. When she reached for her phone, Christov tensed but still didn't go for his gun. Ned, on the other hand, swung his cane up to slap it against Mikey's arm before the bouncer could reach his shoulder holster.

Paige took out her phone and held it up for everyone to see. "I've got a picture. Maybe you recognize him."

Christov nodded once to calm Mikey down and then held out his hand.

Pulling up a photo of Peter's face, she turned it toward Christov and showed it to him the way a cop would display a badge.

After studying the display for less than a second, Christov snapped his fingers. "That asshole stormed my place. He got in because none of my men ever saw him before, but he's one of those . . ."

Before Christov started pantomiming a scene from Dracula, Ned told him, "They're called Nymar. How long have they been stalking you?"

"Not stalking me. My girls. Those freaks hang out in the bushes, lurking in the shadows like ghouls. I had to close down during lunch hours because I couldn't afford to pay for security when the only customers are businessmen and old timers who wander in to stare at tits." Placing his hand upon the pistol lying in front of him, Christov fumed, "Those tattooed assholes harass my girls every chance they get. When

I call the cops on them, they scatter. I pay to arm my men, but those shit stains don't fear guns. Jordan missed her last shift, so who knows what they did to her. They have fangs. All of them. Especially that one," he added while pointing to the picture on Paige's glowing phone display. "He was the boldest of them all. Last week he walks right in through the front door and makes it all the way to VIP room. When Blake tried to get rid of him, he sprouted enough fangs to fill his whole mouth and spits in his face."

"Yeah?" Paige asked.

"Mikey, send Blake in here."

When Blake walked into the office, Paige was surprised the room could hold him. He stood well over six feet tall and seemed almost that wide. His stout body made it uncomfortable for him to lower his arms all the way, and his skin looked like heavy canvas that had been scorched to a deep black. Regarding each of the people in turn, Blake let out a haggard sigh.

"You see?" Christov asked. "That man in your picture spit into *his* face."

Blake's eyes rolled toward the top of his head at the indignity of having to wedge himself into such a cramped space just to relive that particular memory.

"Tell them what happened after he spit on you."

"I . . . I don't see what . . ." Blake stammered in a voice that was so low it practically rumbled beneath the floor. Seeing the insistent scowl on Christov's face, he said, "I almost passed out. *Almost.*"

Looking around at all the monitors, Paige said, "Something tells me we can see all of this for ourselves."

Christov dropped into his chair and filled the office with wailing squeaks as he rolled to a small table weighed down by a stack of VCRs and tapes. "I expected the cops might be poking around, so I had this ready." Picking up a remote and jabbing a button, he added, "I think you'll see more than the cops anyway."

One of the monitors on the wall showed a view looking down into what must have been the VIP room. Separated from the rest of the club by a thick curtain, the room was a silky, padded cave lit by a few recessed bulbs tastefully covered to look like glowing moons in a velvety sky. More curtains lined the walls, and plush couches interspersed with wide, heavily padded chairs were filled with customers that must have paid through the nose to be escorted into their excessively comfortable seats. The time stamp at the bottom of the screen was from a Friday night about a week and a half ago.

Shae was only one of many dancers grinding in laps in impressive displays of erotic contortionism. Some of the guys were a bit too excited, but were kept in line with a few polite wags of their girl's finger. "All right," Christov said, having already seen the movie. "Here comes the good part."

As promised, a young man wearing torn jeans and a Black Sabbath T-shirt lunged into the frame and grabbed the blond nymph. She struggled to pull her wrist from his grip but was unable to pull free. There was no sound on the tape, but it was obvious that the guy in the T-shirt wasn't screaming compliments about the upholstery or curtains. Paige stood up and walked over to the screen, which only made the picture seem worse. She took a step back until the pixilation wasn't so bad, studying the man dragging the dancer by the wrist.

"Is that Peter Walsh?" she asked after catching a glimpse of the black markings on the young guy's neck.

Christov nodded. "That's the guy from the picture you showed me."

The image was close enough for Paige to sit down, but it was a far cry from the image in her head of the sweating, sickly Nymar who'd showed up at Rasa Hill.

On the video, Blake and Mikey rushed into the room and knocked the Nymar against a wall. Peter fought back just enough to shove the bouncers away, but it allowed Shae to wriggle free and seek refuge between a couch and chair. Peter got within inches of her before Mikey grabbed him by the back of the neck and pulled him away again. Tearing free with enough force to send both men staggering into separate pieces of furniture, Peter jumped onto a couch and showed them all three sets of fangs.

The bouncers kept their composure, even when dark froth began trickling from the corners of another customer's mouth. Looking like some random guy in his forties, the customer went from pressing himself against a wall to throwing himself at the nearest bouncer. From out of frame another person with a mud-smeared face grabbed Blake and started pounding both fists against his chest and stomach.

"Who are these guys with the dirty faces?" Paige asked.

"Don't know," Blake replied. "They didn't have fangs or tats. One of 'em's been coming to the club for a few weeks without any problem. That night he flipped out."

Not all of the customers joined the fray. Some scrambled to get out, while the dancers still trapped in the room did their best to put as much furniture as possible between themselves and all those swinging fists. The moment Peter started to get overwhelmed, he backed away from the bouncers and found the guy in his forties with the muddy face. It was a standard tactic for cornered Nymar to get an extra dose of strength by feeding on anyone in sight. Peter clamped his mouth onto the patron's shoulder, drank what he could, then discarded the man like an empty juice box.

When the next wave of bouncers appeared, they were brandishing pistols. Peter took a few powerful swings at them, which were followed by a quick series of muzzle flashes. The blood was too fresh in his system for the gunshots to do much against him, so he refocused on Shae. The next bullet caught him in the back, and the wound was closed by a black tangle of threadlike tendrils. When Blake tried to get to Shae, Peter spat a wad of venom into his face. The hulking bouncer staggered, Peter knocked him down, and Shae leapt from the room. Finally, Peter clutched his chest and dropped to his knees with a severe case of dry heaves. Before Mikey and another bouncer could grab him, Peter darted away in a flicker that looked more like a glitch in the VCR.

"Didn't see him again after that," Christov said.

Still squinting at the monitor, Paige asked, "And you never saw anyone with that stuff on their face before?"

"Hell no! Nobody looking like that would be allowed in

my club." Staring at his bouncers, Christov added, "Would they?"

The bouncers couldn't shake their heads fast enough.

Grateful to look away from the screen after straining his good eye for so long, Ned asked, "Did you call the police?"

"No," Christov replied sternly. "We handle ourselves when there's a fight. Other clubs have been shut down for less than this. Besides, the police would only make me piss into a test jar if I told them vampires were storming my place to try and kidnap a nymph. And with all this talk of the Mud Flu, if a video or even rumor of something like this gets out, I'll be lucky if the government doesn't burn my club down to the foundation."

"What do you know about Pestilence?" Paige asked.

"Never heard of it."

"I doubt that very much," Ned stated. "You and your men seem accustomed to the presence of Nymar. You know the nymphs on a first-name basis. You even know about Skinners. The odds that you don't know about something like Pestilence are pretty damn remote."

Mikey positioned himself behind Ned, and Blake draped his thick, steaklike hands on Paige's shoulders. She wasn't helpless, but she doubted she could put the massive bodyguard down quick enough for both her and Ned to get away.

"I have dealt with many different monsters to get where I am," Christov hissed. "Just because you help one of my girls doesn't give you the right to come in here and make demands."

"Dealt with monsters," Ned repeated. "So the Nymar approached you before?"

After nodding to his guards so they eased toward the back of the room, Christov said, "When I first opened this club, they came to me and asked to use it for their own. Before I had a chance to get worried about it, they disappeared. I hadn't heard from them again until the last few weeks."

"Are they the same ones who've been stalking your dancers?"

"No. Different faces. Same tattoos."

"Let me guess," Paige said. "The first Nymar were

tall, dressed in fancy clothes, and threw a lot of money around?"

Christov nodded. "They offered to buy in to my business, but threatened me when I wouldn't sell."

Paige didn't have to say a word to Ned on the matter. That was a picture-perfect description of the Nymar that had resided in St. Louis prior to her and Rico's infamous "training exercise."

"These new ones," Christov grunted as he settled back into his chair and rolled behind his desk. "They're filthy. They reek of cheap beer and act like punks off the street. At least those other ones bathed. These are crazy. They sniff around my new girls, waiting for them to leave. Jerry, the leader, he even followed me home and offered to buy one of them from me! Every time I tell one of them to go to hell, they all get bolder. Just when I think I'm rid of them," he added while waving at the monitor displaying the frozen image of what Peter left behind, "they charge my club like a pack of wolves."

Paige pulled up another picture from her phone and held it up. "If that's Peter's Before picture, take a look at the After one."

Christov's eyes widened at the sight of the dead Nymar lying on the floor of Rasa Hill with the petrified tentacles emerging from his chest. Even in the darkened room it was obvious he'd gotten a whole lot paler. "I've heard someone mention Pestilence, but I don't know who."

"Could you point him out to us?" Ned asked.

"I don't know. It's . . . a bunch of people. Just random customers at the bar, they babble about crazy things including this Pestilence." Waving a hand to his guards, Christov added, "They know the voice I mean!"

"It's like folks whisper all this stuff as they wander around," Blake said. "Then they just start talking normal again."

Mikey listened to all of this, but seemed ready to jump out of his shoes. Focusing on him, Paige said, "You've heard this too."

The bouncer rubbed his hand over a layer of hair thin

enough to be a single coat of paint on his scalp as Christov muttered to himself in another language. Mikey was
about to say something, but stopped as the faint scent of
lavender drifted into the room. The brunette who appeared
in the office doorway was several inches taller than Paige,
had straight black hair that formed a single wave down to
the middle of her back, and a perfectly upturned nose. She
smiled at Christov and his men while saying, "I believe I can
take it from here."

"Well now," Paige said. "You're a long way from Wisconsin. What was your name? Trinity?"

"Tristan," the brunette corrected. "Who's your new
friend?"

Even with one eye damaged beyond repair and the other
one not quite what it used to be, Ned could still enjoy the
sight of the statuesque nymph. He introduced himself and
was promptly led out of the office by her. When Paige went
to follow them, the men in the office seemed more than
happy to be rid of them both.

Tristan moved with natural grace. Although she wore a
plain white tank top and not-too-tight jeans, she still managed to be a work of art. Falling into step between Paige and
Ned, she draped her arms across their shoulders and moved
with them like a shared thought. Her hair smelled of fresh,
airy mornings that only happened in coffee commercials.
"Christov is just protecting his interests. Come back tonight
and he won't be so snippy."

"Paige never told me she had such interesting acquain-
tances," Ned said.

"Prophet was watching Tristan at a club in Wisconsin,"
Paige replied, "and my partner got to know her in a more
professional manner."

"How is Cole?" Tristan asked.

"Locked up."

"Well he couldn't control himself very well the last time
we met, but he had the stench of Nymar venom on him. I
heard you mention Pestilence. When you come back tonight,
I'll be able to help you with that."

"How about you help us with it now?" Paige asked.

Tristan smiled and shook her head in a way that was decisive without being arrogant or condescending. "There's a regular you'll want to meet."

"Is he the old man we've heard about?" Ned asked.

"He gets here a few hours before closing, so if you come back around midnight or one, I should be able to introduce you. Don't think too hard about it. Just come back then and I'll tell you everything you need to know."

"We're here now," Ned said. "Why not just tell us what you can?"

"Because if I mention too much, you'll be thinking about it when you leave. You may not try to think about it, but the names and information will be rattling around in your heads and it'll all be used against you when you return." Having taken them past the window looking out at the main room, Tristan grabbed the handle of the door that opened near the largest stage. "You did a favor for me that has paid off in more ways than you could know, Paige. I owe you. I assume you're here about the Nymar. They are a nuisance, but they're not the real threat and they're not the ones who took my sisters. Come back tonight and I'll show you the man you're after," she said with a smirk that was equal parts naughty and nice. "We can mask you from the Mind Singer, but only if you're here. You'll need to prepare to fight a murderer. Bring whatever weapons you need. I promise nobody will stop you at the door. Just remember there will be customers here as well. I can't warn them away without making our mutual friend suspicious."

Before she knew it, Paige had another escort on her way to the front door. Kate was dressed in green shorts and a matching top that made her red hair look ridiculously attractive. She started to wave at the Skinners, but backed off when she saw the quick shake of Tristan's head.

"You've got to give us something," Paige insisted. "How are we supposed to prepare if we don't know what we're up against?"

Arriving at a decision by the time she arrived at the main entrance, Tristan said, "The Mind Singer may be able to read anyone's thoughts if they're not properly guarded. If I say anything more, you could be at risk of allowing a trap to be set."

"Didn't you see what happened to the Nymar who attacked one of your girls in the back room?" Paige asked. "This place isn't as safe as you think it is."

Tristan had only been leading the two of them by entwining her arms in theirs as if the trio was simply walking down the Yellow Brick Road. When she let them go, the Skinners still didn't drift too far from her side. Reluctantly, she nodded.

"You may be infected with the same thing that's been killing Nymar," Paige explained. "The one who attacked Shae was infected and now he's dead. Other people are dead too, and this mud crap is showing up all over the country."

"My kind cannot be sick," Tristan said. "It's just impossible."

"Then they're the lucky ones. There's a whole lot of people out there who don't have it so good."

"This infection has been around for a long time, but never amounted to anything until recently."

"What's that supposed to mean?"

Smiling as if she was gently breaking bad news to a child, Tristan said, "Humans are always infected with something. There are plagues, poisons, diseases, and any number of things that come from any number of places. For every one that's fatal, there are hundreds that you don't even know about. This particular affliction first struck your kind in other parts of the world a very long time ago. Now, something has caused it to blossom into something worse. Some call it the Mud Flu, while one man has named it Pestilence."

"Now I really want to meet this old bastard," Paige snarled.

"Come back tonight and you will." With that, Tristan turned her gorgeous back to them and headed for the bar.

Paige looked over there but couldn't see anyone else apart from the tender. The guy tossed them a friendly wave and continued unpacking a box of bottles and placing them upon the shelf behind him. Since the club seemed to have dried up for the time being, she and Ned walked out. Both of them climbed into the SUV, but Paige made a call before driving away.

"Hey," Prophet said once the connection had been made. "I just talked to Stanley, and your boys should be out by tonight. It's taking a little extra pull thanks to the big guy's record, but—"

"That's not why I'm calling. Have you still been chasing down those nymphs working at purple A-frames?"

"Yeah."

"You remember that brunette we saw in Wisconsin?"

"Tristan," Prophet said wistfully. "Her and that buffet put Shimmy's on the map for me. She's working at the place I'm staking out right now. At least she was the last time I was there."

"When was that?" Paige asked.

"About an hour ago. Usually the places that never close are on the nasty side, but this one bucks that trend."

Paige turned the key in the ignition, wishing she had Cole's GPS to tell her how to get to wherever the bounty hunter was located. "Where are you?"

"About fifteen minutes north of Albany."

"Albany . . . Missouri?"

"There's an Albany, Missouri? I'm in Albany, New York. You heard of that one?"

Paige's hand dropped away from the steering wheel. "How long ago did you say Tristan was there?"

"About an hour, give or take ten minutes. Why?"

"And you're sure it was her?"

"I wish I lived in a world that was filled with women who could be mistaken for her. Trust me. It was Tristan." Just to be thorough, Prophet described what Tristan had been wearing. If the Tristan in Bunn's was a twin of the one in Albany, both women had also coordinated their wardrobe.

Chapter 15

The rest of the day went by in a rush. Paige used her phone's Internet connection to put together a list of other strip clubs in the area so she and Ned could take a quick tour. There wasn't a purple A-frame in the bunch. They also didn't get the slightest itch from their scars. They hit Jack in the Box for lunch, and although she had a hankering for fried tacos, Paige ordered a burger and curly fries instead. Indulging in that particular brand of spicy delight without Cole just seemed like the culinary equivalent of adultery.

Upon arriving back at Ned's place, she went upstairs to check on Daniels. The Nymar looked up from his burner and hot plate to give her a quick wave as he announced, "I think I've made a breakthrough!"

"It's already been a long day. Don't make me guess."

The Nymar used a pair of tongs to pick up a metal bowl from atop the hot plate and swirled its contents around. "I've come up with a brilliant switch in ideologies where your ink is concerned. Instead of trying to inhibit the natural tendencies of the reaction between the Blood Blade chips, colloid intermediaries, and the receiver's own plasma, I think the shapeshifter enzymes should be allowed to run their course."

"But that defeats the whole purpose," Paige said. "That ink is supposed to give someone *part* of a shapeshifter's power without turning them into a shapeshifter. That's why it's put under the skin instead of in the blood."

"The ink will work," Daniels said as he continued to mix, "but just not like you thought it would. Instead of trying to concentrate it so heavily, a diluted mixture will be used as more of a general enhancement. You should see increased durability, greater speed, and thanks to the Blood Blade, the receiver's blood won't be permanently tainted. Your delivery system into the muscle tissue will dole out the effects over a longer amount of time."

"What about a cure for my arm?"

"That's not so good. Nothing has proven effective on that newest sample. Whatever was done to the metal in the Blood Blade wasn't made to be reversible." He took one of the metallic chips from a Baggie on the counter. "Watering down the ink in the way I suggested will keep what happened to you from happening to anyone else, but it's too late for my holdout plan to even be worth trying."

"And your holdout plan was?"

Without a twitch, Daniels replied, "To physically excise all of the tissue that's currently tainted by the first batch of ink."

"You mean cut off my arm?"

"No! Only about sixty-five percent of it. By the way, do you have any of that first batch of ink left?"

"Yes."

"I'll want that back to dispose of it."

Looking at the metal chips on the counter, she asked, "What about his idea to mix these into the varnish for our weapons?"

"Oh, that's easy," Daniels replied. "The first batch of varnish is in the paint mixer right now. The wood may not be as pliable after the process, but your weapons would be imbued with a good portion of the Blood Blade's potency. It's a classic gaming trade-off," the Nymar added with a snorting laugh. "Power versus speed. Cole would've liked that one. Will he be back soon?"

"He should be released by tonight. Did you already give up on studying Peter Walsh?"

Daniels's eyes widened, but quickly shrank down to their

normal size. "There was something else I wanted to say about the Blood Blade . . . but it . . . escapes me right now."

"Focus, Daniels," Paige said as she snapped her fingers a few inches from the Nymar's sweaty face.

"Oh, right. The uh . . . Walsh remains. His spore was definitely contaminated by some sort of natural chemical. Possibly something from an exotic species of flower or even snake venom. Whatever it was, it wasn't pharmaceutical and it's not in any records that I've been able to locate. Before you ask, I do have other sources looking into it."

"Could it infect humans?"

After thinking it over for less than half a minute, Daniels said, "Not this particular strain, but it could easily mutate into something more virulent. The outer layers of flaky tissue on the tentacles contains a very high concentration of what could very conceivably be a catalyst for . . ." Seeing Paige's eyes glaze over, he sputtered and eventually came up with, "There was a reaction when combined with the substance taken from Peter's mouth. You know, that muddy stuff?"

Paige nodded.

"Typically, I like to mix and match when I have so many different unknown elements to work with. There are occasionally explosions to deal with, but there are other times that prove rather telling." Daniels quickly shifted his attention to the rack of test tubes he'd set up near the table that bore Peter Walsh's body wrapped in several layers of plastic. The fluid inside those tubes ranged from partially cloudy to blacker than black. "For example, when this muddy substance is combined with the substance found *inside* Peter's mouth, its base elements match the toxin's core structure. But when the muddy substance mixes with the Nymar's blood and is eventually introduced to the spore, it forms something that's highly toxic to all Nymar."

"Is it safe for you to be so close to it?"

Daniels looked at the test tubes and waved them off. "Oh sure. It needs to be ingested to do me any harm. The really interesting part was when I tested the ashen substance on the tentacles themselves. It seems to be an ideal carrier for spreading Pestilence among humans."

Hopping back a step, Paige slapped a hand over her mouth. "Jesus! Why didn't you tell me that before?"

"Because you've been breathing this stuff since you first came into contact with this man. Besides, I tested that sample of your arm and there are no toxins whatsoever. I tested Ned as well and he's just as healthy. It seems the healing serum in your system is the best possible immunization you could ask for, which is fortunate since the Mud Flu is a less aggressive strain of Pestilence that has adapted itself quite well to human physiology."

"Will our healing serum work as a cure for everyone as well as it works for us?"

"Doubtful, since Skinners literally have the serum running running through their bloodstream. Peter had some of the Mud Flu substance on his face, which would be peculiar, since it's different than the substance that killed him. Did he come into contact with someone infected with the Mud Flu?"

"One of the guys in the strip club we just came from had that stuff on his face, and Peter fed on him."

"Then we may have found out how Pestilence is being spread!" Daniels declared excitedly. "It's a *binary* compound! Nymar suffering from their own ailment are producing their portion of Pestilence or may even be acquiring some sort of catalyst from somewhere else."

"Those Nymar we found in East St. Louis said another Skinner has been kidnapping Nymar and experimenting on them," Paige offered.

"Were they exposed to chemicals or possibly injected with something?"

"Yes! They were injected with something."

"Then that could be the start of the whole process, but it would take a whole lot of injections to spread the substance as far and wide as the Mud Flu. On the other hand, that does sound like something a Skinner would do."

Paige didn't like hearing that sentiment again after hearing it from Jerry, but she couldn't really dispute it. Settling for nudging the conversation back on track, she asked, "How does Pestilence become Mud Flu? Or is it the other way around?"

"My guess would be that the Nymar were infected first. This other substance on Peter's face, which I had already guessed was the by-product of Mud Flu, has an extreme reaction when it comes into contact with Nymar blood that's been exposed to even the smallest amount of the original toxin."

Pressing her fingers to her temple, Paige let out an exasperated groan as if her head truly was about to explode.

Daniels took the hint and boiled his explanation down even further. "Somehow, the base elements for Pestilence were injected into Nymar, where they fermented and developed into another kind of toxin. That's where the abductions and forced injections on Nymar from your mystery Skinner come in. Given enough time for mutation, when those infected Nymar feed on humans, it's possible for the toxin to mutate again into what we see as the Mud Flu."

"And you've figured all this out with test tubes?" Paige asked.

"Your friend Ned has some remarkable equipment in here," Daniels gasped. "I don't know how he acquired a Mark 7 centrifugal—"

"Okay," she cut in. "You've got more than test tubes. Go on."

"Right, so it starts in Nymar, moves to humans, where it develops into Mud Flu. Although I don't have the hard evidence to back this up completely, my theory is that when a Nymar feeds on someone infected with Mud Flu, it creates some sort of . . ."

"Feedback?" she offered.

He nodded excitedly. "Yes, feedback! Because this toxin is prone to such drastic mutations, I'm sticking to my initial guess that it's based on something that's naturally occurring. Synthetics are rarely so eloquent in their life cycles."

"Wait. That first theory was a guess?"

"Of course," Daniels said with a couple of twitching blinks. "Essentially that's what most theories are. Educated guesses. The scientific process can't start with concrete answers, otherwise there's no need for the process. That is, unless you're starting from an answer and working your way back. Then you could—"

"Paige!" Ned called from the first floor.

Grateful for anything to hit the chemist's pause button, she wiped her hands together like a blackjack dealer passing her table over to the next shift. "I think I've got a good grasp on what you're saying, so let's quit while we're ahead. Will you be able to figure the rest out on your own?"

But Daniels was already engrossed in his next problem. He frantically dug through his equipment before disappearing into the large supply closet. Leaving him to his work, Paige went downstairs to find Ned looking out a window.

"Can you answer a question for me?" he asked.

"As long as it doesn't involve theoretical chemistry."

"Who are all those people staring at my house?"

She went to the window, which looked out onto Kensington Avenue. It was a pleasant neighborhood that was usually quiet because the neighbors kept to themselves. But now Paige spotted three of them standing on the sidewalk in front of the house, staring at it. The more she looked, the more people she found on both sides of the street. None of them spoke or even moved. They'd simply dropped whatever they were doing so they could stare.

Catching herself before she repeated Ned's last question, Paige asked, "How long have they been standing there?"

"A couple minutes now. I noticed one when I came out of the bathroom. I think it's Joey from across the street. Then the others showed up."

"What about those two old ladies down by that red house?"

"Yep, I see 'em," Ned said. "They're new. Maybe they like you."

"What do you mean?"

As Ned did his best to focus on the scene outside his window, the rattle from the air conditioner clanked like two pots banging together. "Before, they all just stared at the house," he told her. "Now, they're staring right at you. Aren't they?"

Paige stepped away from the glass, walked past the front door, and pulled aside the curtains covering the window on that side of the entrance. Apart from the blocky symbols stenciled into the frame, she revealed two thick panes separating her from nine people who stood outside with their arms hanging loosely at their sides. It only took a second or two before they all caught sight of her, shifted their gaze toward her and cocked their heads to one side.

"What . . . the . . . hell?" she whispered.

For the next few seconds the neighbors didn't do anything but stare at Paige's window, and she didn't know what to do but stare back.

The silence was broken by her ringing phone, snapping Paige from the bizarre connection between her and so many strangers. She dug the chirping piece of equipment from her pocket and glanced down at the screen to see the name S. Velasco printed on the illuminated surface. Looking up from there, she found herself less than four inches away from the blank, sunken face of a middle-aged woman with wet mud flowing from her mouth. Having climbed into the bushes growing around Ned's house, the woman leaned forward and rested her forehead against the outer window.

Steam formed on the glass in front of the woman's dirty mouth when she said, "You cut me, Skinner. But I . . . found you."

As Paige backed away from the window, Ned approached her carrying an older model .45.

"You cut me, Skinner," the muddy woman repeated. "But there's more of me now than you." Slapping her hands against the side of the house, she shoved her face close enough to knock her teeth against the glass as she shrieked, "Moreofmethanyou! Moreofmethanyoumoreofmethanyou!"

Paige looked through the peephole to find a young man standing on the porch. He was still watching the window where she'd been, but slowly turned toward her. Features warped by the curving glass were further obscured by streams of mud dripping from his eyes and nose to mingle with the sludge from his mouth. Taking one lunging step forward, the man scraped his fingers against the door like an animal trying to escape a fire.

"They can't get in here," Ned told her confidently. "The runes won't allow it."

More words came out of Ned's mouth, but Paige couldn't hear them. Every sound seemed to be garbled, as if she'd been dunked into a vat of water.

I smell you, Paige, Henry whispered into her mind. *Lick-youfromtheinside.*

Suddenly, she had trouble keeping her head up.

Something filled the spaces in her chest cavity surrounding her heart. As Henry's presence drew closer, a flood of cold swept through her body to wash him away. The healing serum in her system left her a little drained, but not enough to keep Paige from raising her weapons. By the time she collected herself, the face on the other side of the window was gone. The woman had staggered back to join the other neighbors staring at the house. As she watched, Paige noticed a heavyset man walking his little black and white dog farther down the sidewalk. Although the man nervously took in the sight of the people standing in and along Kensington Avenue, his thirteen pound canine snarled without an ounce of fear. The dog walker turned crisply around and pulled his bodyguard along with him.

"They're starting to disperse," Ned announced.

Paige looked at each of the people in turn, all of them filthy from their chins down to their necks. A kid in his early teens locked eyes with her and snapped his neck to one side. What had started as some kind of fit quickly turned into something much worse as the kid violently twisted his head as far as it would go. Paige pulled the door open and bolted outside just in time to hear the loud crunch as the kid's spine gave way.

The sight of the teen standing there with his head dangling from atop its severed spine was enough to freeze Paige in her tracks. His eyes still blinked and his mouth still moved as he spoke into her brain and ears at the same time.

"I can go anywhere I want now," he said. "Dr. Lancroft showed me how."

Without realizing it, Paige angled her head in the same direction as the kid's. "Henry? Is that really you?"

Although he could talk, the teen couldn't nod. He didn't need to. "The fire ain't in you, like it is in a lot of folks."

"What fire?"

"Pestilence."

"Are you doing this to all these people?" she asked.

It was in 'em already.

"Let them go," Paige said as Ned's feet shuffled across the porch behind her. "Henry, let them go or you'll never sit in your room again. Remember your corner at Lancroft Re—"

"Shut yer mouth, bitch! I got somethin' to stick inityou-filthywhore!"

But Paige wasn't about to be frightened by words, whether they were in her brain or in her ears. When the kid took a step toward her, her right hand reflexively drew the club from that boot and willed it to take the only form she could manage. Although still crude in appearance, the machete's edge was more than sharp enough to get the job done. "You don't like hearing about the reformatory?"

Henry's wild, twitching eyes snapped within the boy's sockets as the rest of the muddy neighbors swayed in the stagnant humidity of a calm St. Louis night.

"Or is it Lancroft?" Ned asked. Henry's eyes widened and his mouth dropped open a little more. "Looks that way. You don't like hearing the proper name of that reformatory. Did you ever meet Lancroft?"

"He will heap disasters upon you," the boy said. His mind, however, spewed the words, *Pestilence and the teeth of beasts. Pestilenceandtheteethofbeasts!*

"You know your scripture," Ned replied.

"Then he should also know his history," Paige snapped. "I gutted you once, Henry, but you were too stupid to let it end there. No other Full Bloods are here to help you this time. Is that why the big bad Mind Singer has to crawl around in other people's heads now? You're too afraid to face me alone?"

"I ain't alone no more," Henry croaked through the teen's ravaged windpipe. "I can be anywhere I want." *Anyone I want.*

"Then come and get me," Paige said. "Wherever that ugly Full Blood body of yours is, climb back into it and rip me to shreds."

The teen's face became tranquil, and one by one the muddy neighbors started to drop. "It don't got to be so bad," he said. "These folks ain't got to hurt no more. They just been put out to clean up the leeches and wolves and such."

Ned raced to the old woman who'd been clawing at his window and caught her before she hit the ground. She coughed up more of the mud but didn't have any trouble breathing. Within seconds she and most of the other neighbors were wiping their mouths and looking around in growing confusion.

"See? Doc Lancroft is a good man," Henry said. "He sent Pestilence to devour the wretches and kill them bloodsucking leeches."

"Lancroft is dead," Ned said while tending to the old woman.

Paige wanted to help the others who'd awakened from their muddy sleepwalk, but they were getting up on their own. "Jonah Lancroft made Pestilence? Was that when you were in the reformatory?"

Henry backed onto the curb as a police cruiser rounded the corner from Academy Avenue onto Kensington. Someone must have seen the strange assault on Ned's house or gotten spooked by the swaying crowd because the cruiser hit its flashing lights as it drew closer.

"Lancroft is dead," Paige insisted. "He was a Skinner like us. Whatever he did, it's over now. Whatever you're doing to these people, stop it."

"I am the teeth of beasts," Henry declared, "with the poison of serpents in the dust."

And when the police cruiser rolled up to Ned's house, the teen fell backward into the street. His eyes clouded over in the short time it took him to fall, and when his body thumped against the car, his head twisted around as the rest of him rolled across the hood like the limp, abandoned vessel it was. Standing there gripping her poorly formed machete in an aching fist, watching that kid hit the street in a heap of tangled limbs, Paige had never felt more useless.

Ned tossed his gun into the bushes in front of his house, took Paige's weapon from her and threw it in next while the cop was examining the teen with the broken neck lying near his front tire. In the minutes another police cruiser showed up and was quickly followed by an ambulance.

Statements were taken, questions were asked, hours passed, but the only real incident to be reported was the boy who'd been pronounced dead after throwing himself in front of a moving police car. Even though the rest of the neighbors seemed fine, the paramedics had no trouble spotting the grime on their faces. Talk of delirium stemming from the Mud Flu circulated as a possible explanation for the night's events. All of the neighbors were taken to the hospital, and Ned and Paige were encouraged to do the same.

"Can't be too careful," one of the paramedics told her.

"Yeah," Paige said. "Thanks for the advice." Her eyes remained locked on the first cop, who was still talking to a fellow officer, giving an impassioned statement while gesturing at the mangled front end of his car.

Knowing Paige well enough to read her mind without any supernatural tricks, Ned wrapped an arm around her and led her back to the house. "You can't tell them what happened," he whispered.

"But he didn't kill anyone. He'll have to live with thinking he broke that kid's neck."

"Then we'll have to make sure this gets balanced out in the end. It's what we do, Paige. Little lies need to be told and smaller sufferings need to be felt to keep the bigger ones from causing more damage."

"That doesn't sound right."

"Tough," Ned snapped. "It's been a long day and that's the best I could come up with. Answer your phone."

"What?"

"Your phone's ringing. Answer it."

After digging the phone from her pocket, she jammed her finger against the glowing green button. "What is it?"

Stanley Velasco's voice dripped with self-satisfaction as he said, "Come and get 'em."

Chapter 16

Cole emerged from the Cahokia Police Department, turned around and then looked at the building where he'd spent the better part of the last day. It was a little structure that barely seemed large enough to hold the cell, not to mention the officers guarding it.

Rico, on the other hand, wasn't about to look back. "Another notch on my belt," he said as he strode toward Paige. She tossed him the keys to the nearby SUV, but that didn't stop him from lifting her off the ground in a bear hug. "I knew you'd sniff us out, Bloodhound. That's what you do!"

"You know what else I do? Kick the hell out of big hairy creeps who try to throw me around."

Rico set her down and examined the keys she'd thrown him. "What's this?"

"Your ride home. Me and Cole are taking a cab."

"You sure?"

She nodded and then looked Cole up and down. "Anyone try to molest you, pretty boy?"

"It was just a holding cell. No biggie," he replied with strained nonchalance while running his hands over the top of a head that was greasy on the outside and sore on the inside. With every breath of fresh air he pulled in, the throbbing pain subsided. "Go on and leave without us, Rico. I'll pick up the Cav from the impound lot."

"All right then," he said as he hefted his jacket over one shoulder. "I'll check up on that guy who sprung us, maybe see if there's anything more about those bodies we saw on the news."

"What bodies?" Paige asked.

"Let's get away from here before the cops change their minds."

The village of Cahokia was a flat collection of squat buildings and wide streets. There didn't seem to be much to look at under the best circumstances, and even less to catch the eye once the sun was down. A few streaks of light colored the sky's lower edge, but it wouldn't be long before darkness claimed Missouri. The cab arrived quickly, and when it did, Cole sat with his wallet, spare change, cell phone, and watch wrapped up in a plastic bag on his lap. His spear lay on the seat beside him, still in its harness and labeled with a tag from the police department, which he pulled off and tossed onto the floor. There was a lot to tell Paige, but he didn't want to get too involved with the cab driver less than three feet away. When he looked over to her, she was already showing him a tired half grin.

"I missed you," she said.

"Really? I thought you'd chew me out for getting locked up."

"I will later. Right now, I'm just glad you're out."

"Some guy named Velasco arranged it. He says we owe him big-time, but the cops were glad to be rid of us after what happened while we were in there." Again Cole looked toward the driver's seat and cut himself off before finishing his story. "How's your arm?"

She shrugged. "A little better."

It was a short ride to the impound lot, and when they arrived, Cole was handed the keys to the Cav and a slip of paper that read PAID IN FULL. "Damn," he grumbled. "Looks like we really do owe that Velasco guy."

Once they got to the spot where the Cav was parked, Paige looked the car over from front to back. Her mechanical expertise wasn't extensive enough for her to guess how much repairs might cost, but she'd been with the old rust bucket long enough to know what damage was new and what had been written off as "charming imperfections" long ago. While she completed her inspection, Cole sifted through his plastic bag to make sure all of his stuff was accounted for. Once his phone was turned on, several missed calls and text messages blinked to his attention. Most of the calls had been from the MEG guy, Stu, and all of the voice mails, asking why he wasn't answering his phone. Paige slid in behind the Cav's wheel and prepared to turn the key in the ignition.

"If it doesn't work, can we scrap her and get a new one?" Cole asked.

Paige gritted her teeth, turned the key, and smiled when the engine rattled to life. "No such luck."

After settling into the passenger seat, he pressed redial on his most recent Missed Call notice.

"MEG Branch 40," Stu said after one and a half rings.

"Are you stalking me?" Cole asked.

"Have you been on the trail of something? Is it another Chupacabra? Why did you take Abby on that hunt and not me?"

"Didn't your parents ever give you the Talk?"

"Romance aside, we're on the same team," Stu grumbled.

"What's so important that you had to call me a thousand times?"

"I got somewhere on that research you asked about. Did you open those pics I sent?"

After sifting through the text messages, Cole found the ones with attachments. "Not yet. What are they?"

"Etchings and paintings of various temples found all across the world that share certain structural similarities."

"A-frames?"

"Yep," Stu replied. "Or the ancient equivalent. And they're always described as colorfully painted to match local flowers, the morning sky, or flowing wine."

"So . . . purple."

"Right again. There were always inscriptions along the outer perimeter of the temples, but the stranger thing is that nobody seems to know who these temples were built for. Most of the texts just say they were discovered in good condition and filled with offerings. The only statuary or murals on the walls are of your generic sort of magical creatures and beautiful women. The pics I found are all over the place stylistically. Renaissance, Christian influenced, Hindu, Slavic, you name it."

"What about nymphs?" Cole asked.

Stu groaned. "You can imagine what I found on a Net search for that one. We have access to more specialized libraries, but didn't find much apart from the typical stuff. Nymphs are all very pretty. They like to dance in the forest. Big-time party girls."

"Have you gotten any more reports from other Skinners about them?"

After a few taps on his keyboard, Stu told him, "There were a few recent ones, but they were mainly complaints about how you and Paige let that one go in Wisconsin."

"You mean Tristan."

The mention of that name caused Paige to tap Cole's shoulder. "What about Tristan?" she asked.

Rather than hold a conversation on two fronts, Cole waved impatiently toward the road just beyond the lot's fence. She took the hint and drove for the gate amid a series of loud rattles and screeching belts. Apparently, slapping against the side of a bus didn't do the Cav any favors.

"Is Paige with you?" Stu asked. "Tell her hi. And yeah, it was Tristan. After that first sighting, all the others have been watching her. She's not causing any problems, but she's been moving around quite a bit. She was seen in Boston, Jersey, Wisconsin, Minnesota, Missouri, and several different spots in California. Huh. Our records might be a little off, because it says she was seen in L.A. and Cincinnati on the same day within a span of a few hours."

"Can nymphs really fly or something?"

"Not as far as we know, but most of the paintings and mythological references show them with wings. Even the wingless ones depict nymphs floating through the air."

"Thanks, Stu. You did a great job."

"Be sure to check the base of the next purple A-frame you find. If there's writing or arcane symbols etched close to the earth on an outside wall, you've got yourself a temple. Those symbols, the color, and the shape of the structure are the only constants. One of my books says that the A shape can channel, focus, and disperse energy. I had to do a lot more digging, but these particular structures are tied in to a ton of ancient pagan rituals involving primal energies and mystical power sources. Do you know what lay lines are?"

"No."

"Good, because these aren't the same thing. Abby and I had a big throw-down about that. Lay lines are thought to be sources of natural energy that can be tapped for power. These structures are meant to amplify mystical energies, boost them, and even store it up for later."

"Is there a way to detect that kind of energy?"

As Stu paused to think about that, Paige finished haggling with the attendant of the municipal lot regarding the difference between an impound fee and an additional fine for driving a car that no longer conformed to Missouri safety regulations. Recognizing a losing battle when she was in one, she handed over the money and set the Cav loose upon the world again.

They were tearing toward the highway when Stu said, "If this sort of energy registers on the electromagnetic spectrum, I suppose the meters we use in our ghost hunts could pick it up. We should be able to modify the same equipment to pick it up but I'd need to be there to take the readings. Think you could give me an exclusive?"

"Hold on," Cole said as he gripped the dashboard. "I'm about to get into my second wreck this week and I think Paige is flipping off a Denny's."

"Just relax," Paige said. "You busted out the blinkers on this side so I've got to use hand signals."

"Did you signal that last turn before almost sideswiping that Taurus?"

Lying on her horn in response to the wail from the other car, Paige said, "No."

"Then bring it down a notch!" Once he'd caught his breath, Cole put the phone back to his cheek. "So where does this energy come from?"

"Any number of places. There's rituals and of course mystical creatures or spirits. I wouldn't have more of an answer to that until I knew what sort of energy it was, which is where my proposed field trip comes in. How's this weekend sound?"

"Do you have anything else for me as far as your research goes?"

Stu sighed. "No."

"Then I'll get back to you about the rest." With that, Cole cut the connection. "Where are we going?"

"Somewhere to help you feel better after your jail time," Paige said. "What did the MEG guys have to say?"

As Cole ran down the basics of his conversation, he watched the highway through the cracked windshield. Wind rushed in through the gaping hole where the passenger window used to be, while metal scraped against metal in at least four different spots on the Cav's chassis. And yet, the car didn't have the good sense to give up and die. He had to admire the ugly heap for that. They rattled onto I-55 and headed toward South County with lukewarm night air rushing across their faces. She kept driving south before finally exiting at Lindbergh Boulevard.

Cole's eyebrows perked up when he spotted a row of car dealers lining the busy street. "Do I get to pick out the new Skinnermobile?"

"Not if you're gonna call it that."

"Okay. We'll call it whatever you want."

"Still no."

"But you said you were going to make me feel better." He turned to her and grinned luridly. "Unless you had something a little nastier in mind?"

"No," Paige said as she crossed Tesson Ferry Road. "But your tongue will still be plenty happy."

Chapter 17

Eat Rite was a diner.

It wasn't a restaurant or a bar. It was a diner and didn't try to be anything but. There were less than a dozen tables in the narrow storefront space located between a pawnshop and a paintball supply store. Cole and Paige sat on stools bolted to the floor along a counter that ran from the front of the place all the way to the storage rooms in back. His spear looked harmless enough, if a bit out of place, propped against the counter like a piece of shoddy sporting equipment near Cole's feet. Behind the counter were pyramids of mini cereal boxes, stacks of plastic cups, pastries in a clear case, and a display for locally made oatmeal cookies next to a coffee machine and a milk dispenser.

When she sat down, Paige refused a menu and ordered, "Two coffees. Two slingers, scrambled eggs, sausage, and toast on the side."

The waitress was a cute girl with nice legs and dark hair cut in a bob. Scribbling the order onto a long pad of green and white paper, she asked, "You want onions on those?"

"Of course."

The coffee was some of the best Cole had tasted in recent memory.

A short cook wearing the standard-issue uniform of greasy white T-shirt under greasier white apron put their order together while Paige told Cole about her introduction to Ned's neighbors. When the cook was through, he handed the plates to the waitress so he could disappear through the back door with his pack of cigarettes. The concoction that was placed in front of them was composed of eggs, sausage, chili, cheese, and onions served on a bed of hash browns.

"This looks like a heart attack waiting to happen," Cole mused.

"Say that now," Paige replied. "Thank me later."

Cole didn't know where to start. After taking his first few bites, he didn't know if he'd be able to stop. "Thank you," he said through a mouthful of artery-clogging goodness. "Thank you. Thank you. Thank you."

Paige smiled and shook hot sauce onto the glorious mess occupying her plate. "You weren't inside for long, but I thought you'd be hungry for some real food." She scooped some potatoes and chili onto her fork, jabbed a hunk of egg, stuffed the whole thing into her mouth and asked, "So what happened in there? I heard there was some commotion."

Telling her about his encounter with Henry and even describing the slime oozing from those glassy-eyed inmates wasn't enough to put a dent in Cole's appetite. He finished his story while smearing grape jelly onto his toast. "After the mess was cleaned up and the paramedics left, things were quiet. The cops took it easy on us since Rico and I helped bring those nut jobs down, but it still wasn't easy getting out of there. Whoever that Velasco guy is, he pulled a lot of strings."

"So you're sure it was Henry?" she asked.

Using the side of his fork to cut up his last sausage patty, Cole replied, "He talked like Henry and knew all the stuff Henry would know. He was sure bat-shit crazy as Henry."

"Henry's a Full Blood," Paige reminded him. "He's also the only one who's found a way to get around our early warning system. Maybe he's not so crazy."

Cole looked down at the scars on his left hand. "I didn't feel a twitch from any of those Mud Flu people either, but they seemed to be controlled by him."

"The medics called it the Mud Flu?"

"Yep."

"How bad were they?"

"Apart from the bumps and bruises they got during the fight, those muddy prisoners were fine after Henry was gone. The paramedics said he snapped his neck during a seizure because of the flu, but he snapped it himself. I heard his voice in my head, so maybe he can throw the rest of himself into people's minds now. The whole neck snapping thing may be Henry's way of getting comfortable in a new body. There's no bouncing back from that once he leaves, though." Tapping his fork against his chin, Cole added, "I think I also saw him try to change. He kind of puffed up like he thought he could shift into . . ." There was only one other customer in the place, reading a newspaper at one of the back tables, and neither he nor the waitress were interested in what the Skinners were talking about. Even so, Cole lowered his voice and grunted, "You know."

The waitress loitered at the other end of the counter, washing silverware in a long sink. After circling to refill coffee cups, she started in on the rest of her side work.

"When I spoke to the Nymar, they called Henry the Mind Singer," Paige said. "Maybe this jumping around from one person to another is what separates him from any other telepath."

Cole didn't notice the waitress straightening the cereal boxes nearby when he asked, "Did they know the one whose body they showed on the news?"

"Ew, that was gross," the waitress said. "I think it was some sort of prank, though. Like those fake werewolf pictures from Kansas City."

Cole showed Paige a chili-stained grin at the mention of his handiwork.

Placing two packets of Wet-Naps on the counter, the waitress said, "Be sure to wipe your hands when you're done. Can't be too careful with this Mud Flu going around." She shuddered and washed hers vigorously in the same sink where she'd just cleaned the dishes. "Can I get you two anything else?"

"No, we're fine," Paige said.

"Then I'll run to the back for a smoke. Just holler if you need me."

Cole tore once again into the pile of meat, cheese, and potatoes on his plate. "So, you missed me, huh?"

Stopping her hand a few inches from her mouth, Paige allowed her eggs to slide off and plop onto a mound of chili. "I was stuck with Ned. That sort of trauma will make you say things."

"Well, you made it up to me with this."

"Play your cards right and I may even spring for a lap dance later tonight. We're headed back to Sauget to meet your stripper buddy, Tristan."

"The nymph from Wisconsin? She really gets around."

"You don't know the half of it," she told him. "I called Prophet to see if he'd seen her recently and he had. Only an hour before I did. In Albany, New York."

Cole chewed his next bite thoughtfully. "That's a hell of a long way to go. Even if a plane could make the trip that fast, that barely leaves enough time to get to an airport."

"She's not taking a plane. Those nymphs have something else going on. Either they've got some way of getting from one spot to another in a hurry, or there's more than one Tristan."

"More than one Tristan?" Cole's mind drifted to a happy place filled with blue skies, cool breezes, and multiple copies of a woman who seemed built to stimulate the male psyche.

"You're such a pig," Paige muttered.

"I didn't say anything."

"You didn't have to."

"Just because I—" Cole dropped his fork as if it had come to life and bitten him. Something reacted with his scars that felt like a hot poker scraping against the bones of his hand, causing both him and Paige to look at the front door. "Pay the check and let's get out of here," he said. "If a Full Blood tracked us here, I don't want it leveling this place. The food is too damn good."

She slapped some money onto the counter as Cole picked up his spear. The waitress hurried from the back room as soon as they left their seats, spotted the cash and then sepa-

rated her generous tip from the price of slingers and coffee.
"Come back again!" she implored.

The diner may not have been crowded, but that didn't
hold true for Lindbergh Boulevard. Being one of the main
streets that cut through the entire city meant it was almost
always filled with a steady flow of traffic. The dinner rush
had slacked off several hours ago, and it was a bit too early
for the late night snack crowd, which made Eat Rite a quiet
spot next to the speeding, honking sampling of the St. Louis
population.

Cole's hands were burning when he slid his fingers between the thorns on his spear's handle. "It's close," he said.

Paige effortlessly plucked the baton from her left boot and
then flexed her right hand a few times before drawing that
weapon from its holster. "I'm hoping it's Burkis."

"You want to see Mr. Burkis again?"

"No, but if this isn't him, there's another Full Blood in the
area. That's something we don't need."

The first time Cole had seen Mr. Burkis, he'd watched the
werewolf shred a cabin filled with hunters, hikers, and two
Skinners. The next time, Burkis had tracked him to Daniels's apartment in the Chicago suburbs and proceeded to
tear that building apart before escaping with a chunk of the
Blood Blade embedded in his face. As reassuring as it was to
know a Full Blood could be hurt, Cole was fairly certain the
whole face stabbing thing wouldn't act in his favor.

A low voice rumbled from the storefronts to his left. "You
can lower your weapons. If I meant to feast on your innards,
I wouldn't do so after you've gorged on so much greasy
food."

A solitary figure rounded the corner of the short, run-
down strip mall where Eat Rite was located. The last time
Cole had seen him, Burkis was wearing a cheap suit that
had ripped like wet tissue paper during his transformation
from man to beast. Now, the tall, broad-shouldered werewolf wore baggy sweatpants and a plain white tank top. His
human form was muscular, but not in a way that reeked of
locker rooms and gym memberships. Cold, gray-blue eyes
peered at the Skinners through a loose mane of dark brown

hair. Somehow, those eyes were more brilliant in the shadows than when he stepped into the meager light thrown off by the storefronts.

"Not dressing up for this meeting, huh?" Cole said. Brushing his hand along his cheek, he added, "Suit not match the new face?"

A subtle twitch shifted beneath the scar that ran down the right side of Burkis's face from the bottom of his eye to just above his chin. It wasn't the only scar he bore, but looked more tender than the rest. "I wear my mistakes just like everyone else," he said. "And since you no longer have the blade that did this, I wouldn't be so quick to taunt."

When Cole moved toward the Full Blood, Paige stopped him with an outstretched hand. "All right, Burkis. You found us. Now what?"

"I want to know where the Mind Singer is. You know of whom I speak." Shifting crystalline eyes toward Cole, he added, "You have heard his voice."

"You mean Henry?" Cole asked.

Burkis's nod was nothing more than one slow dip of his chin.

"He paid me a visit when I was in jail along with a bunch of those slimy nut jobs that fight for him. If you want to know where he is, maybe you should try a psycho ward with real thick walls."

Burkis remained silent. Before his pause became awkward, someone stepped out of the pawnshop, climbed into their car and left. Now that the parking lot was all but empty, he said, "Henry's touched in the head. I don't know if that's a cause or effect of his gift."

"Henry was infected by Nymar spore and controlled by one of their kind named Misonyk," Paige explained. "That's how he got his gift. The spores are out of him, but he must have been able to hang on to Misonyk's ability somehow."

Burkis was a large man and he moved like an even larger animal; heavy and powerful. "It doesn't matter how he got his gift. All that matters is how he uses it. Of late, he only speaks of Pestilence. What do you know about that?"

"It's something that's causing Nymar to explode like party

poppers," she said. "When it shows up in humans, it makes them hack up some sort of muddy slop, and I think it paves the way for Henry to control them."

As Burkis studied him and Paige, Cole wasn't sure if the Full Blood was thinking about what they'd been talking about or if he was wondering how many bites it would take to get to the humans' juicy center. "You know more than you say."

"Sure we do," Paige replied.

"Then tell me about Jonah Lancroft."

"I can tell you he's a very popular guy around here, but he's also long dead."

"Pestilence is his creation," Burkis said. "As is the Mind Singer. Both of which are more far-reaching than you know."

"How can you be so sure of that?"

"Because if you knew the true scope of this matter, you would not be stuffing your faces with food as the rest of your country festers under Lancroft's plague. Mud Flu is only the most recent name given to something that has been festering in humans for decades, and within the fangs of the leeches for only slightly longer. Do you even know how this plague affects the Mongrels that you embrace as friends?"

"Why don't you tell me?" Paige snapped.

"Follow me and I'll show you. That is," Burkis added as his eyes narrowed almost imperceptibly, "if you're able."

With that, the Full Blood strode through the parking lot toward Lindbergh Boulevard. He crouched down as if to tie his shoe and then leapt completely over all six lanes of traffic. His arms stretched out and his legs tucked in close to his chest as the transformation rippled throughout the werewolf's entire body. Compared to the form Burkis had taken in Canada or Chicago, this one was leaner and more than seven feet in length. Most of its muscle was packed into the creature's legs, which were strong enough to launch him onto the roof of a squat little dump of a bar across the street from an Olive Garden.

"Shit," Paige growled as she raced to the Cav and fumbled for her keys.

Cole followed her while looking around to see how many people had spotted the Full Blood's inhuman leap. A few cars swerved on Lindbergh and several people pointed toward the bar, aiming their camera phones and clicking frantically. As he dropped into the passenger seat, Cole thought about how he could smooth over this little incident once it made its first appearance on the Internet. After a car screeched to a stop so its driver could hang out the window for a better look, he decided it was already too late for smoothing.

Paige pointed the Cav toward Lindbergh and flipped her blinker on. Burkis crouched upon the roof of the bar, grabbing the edge with both hands and craning his neck to watch the street. Facing the northwest, he pushed off with thick legs that bent backward to accommodate a four-legged gait.

"Aw screw it," she snarled before hitting the gas pedal and driving through a gap barely large enough to fit a car half the Cav's size. Other drivers honked at her, but only a precious few swerved to clear a path. Most of the vehicles seemed ready to plow straight into her just to prove they had the right of way.

"Crazy bastards!" Cole yelled. Turning to Paige he added, "*All* of you!"

"Just buckle up and keep your eyes on Burkis."

Although Paige was driving without any regard for traffic laws or human life, she wasn't doing much to stand out from the rest of the pack vying for lane space. Even the cars that ambled along at a leisurely pace sped up when they were about to be passed. Once she managed to get by them, they slowed as if grudgingly admitting to a loss. Looking for a werewolf amid all of that was a welcome distraction.

They'd just crossed Baptist Church Road when Cole's scars alerted him to the Full Blood's proximity. Straining to see through the stark contrast of lights and shadow on both sides of the street, he caught occasional glimpses of the creature bounding from a rooftop or disappearing behind a billboard. Just when he'd lost sight of the beast, they drove past a large theater illuminated by several sets of colored lights. A glowing white sign close to the street spelled out movie names and times in short black letters. A familiar shape perched upon that sign, dressed in the tattered remnants of a white shirt and dark sweatpants.

"There he is!" Cole said.

Burkis's leaner upright form was better suited for scaling surfaces or balancing on narrow ledges. His limbs were extended past the point where he could pass for some lunatic who'd climbed up onto the marquee, and if there still was any doubt as to what he was, his coat of long, dark brown fur was an even bigger giveaway. When the Cavalier closed in on him, Burkis sniffed the air and jumped off the sign as if he'd been launched by a catapult.

"He's leading us down the street," Cole said while reaching under his seat to grab the little black case containing his GPS. After switching it on, he waited for it to receive a signal from the satellites.

"What the hell are you doing?" Paige asked. "You think you can look up 'werewolf' under Points of Interest?"

"I was just gonna pull up the map and see where this street goes."

"I *know* where it goes," she barked. "I used to live here, remember?"

"Then maybe I can see if there's any traffic or construction up ahead. Does your inborn city-sense get minute-to-minute updates?"

"You can see traffic updates on that thing?"

Cole nodded and rubbed the top of the GPS without smearing the touch screen. "Romana's got the deluxe package. Ah. See? Looks like there's some construction a little further up."

"There's always construction," she snapped. "What about traffic?"

"On the right."

"How bad is it? Should I detour?"

"No!" Cole said as he pointed at his side window as though there was still glass in the frame. "On the right. There he is!"

Paige leaned over the top of the steering wheel and spotted Burkis leaping down from atop a gas station sign to land in the parking lot and shift into his barrel-chested, four-legged form. His ribs were hidden beneath a thick layer of fur and his chest nearly scraped against the cement as he darted across the busy street. Whether out of reflex or as a warning, Burkis snapped at a few cars that honked at him while driving by. To those drivers' credit, they seemed just as annoyed to let him get ahead of them as they'd been when anyone else tried to pass.

Since it was obvious that Burkis wasn't trying to lose them, Paige drove the rest of the way without risking life, limb, or any more police involvement. She remained with the rest of the cars, which put her well above the posted speed limit. The werewolf attracted plenty of attention, but moved too quickly for anyone to get more than a fleeting glimpse. After crossing Watson Road and passing under I-44, they headed north. The large, bounding creature darted from one side of the street to another, sought periodic refuge in the shadows, and finally hunkered down to leap effortlessly into the inky sky. This time, however, Cole couldn't see where Burkis landed.

"Shit," he said as he reflexively looked down at the GPS screen. He looked up twice as fast, hoping he wouldn't catch any more grief from Paige for trying to use the device to spot a landmark that obviously wasn't in the system. "I think he's gone."

Paige settled into her seat. "I don't think so. He could have left us behind at any time, but made sure we were headed this way."

They kept driving, but the heat in Cole's scars cooled at an alarming rate. As they continued north, traffic snarled up thanks to construction that blocked off two of the lanes. Just when he thought he might hop out of the car and try running ahead a few blocks, he felt a jolt of unnatural fire.

"I see him," Paige said as she flicked on her turn signal and veered to the right.

Burkis was in his human form, but his clothes were ripped and barely hanging on his sinewy frame. There were a few other people near him on the sidewalk, but they were too wrapped up in yelling at each other or into their phones to notice the man who watched the street with icy, predator's eyes. Once the car had pulled to a stop along the curb between two others, Cole climbed out and slipped his harness over both shoulders. Thanks to the smaller size of the spear, it didn't make much of a bump under the baggy flannel shirt he tossed on over it.

There was a set of railroad tracks nearby, complete with a station that looked like something from a quaint little toy train set. Most of the other buildings were cast from a similar mold. Cozy houses had been turned into homey shops, giving the area a cute, almost delicate feel. "What should we do if he tries to kill us?" Cole asked.

Paige walked alongside him and flexed her right hand to somewhere near its normal range of motion. "Kill him back."

After crossing the street, they still needed to walk for another half block before finally catching up with Burkis. "All right," she snapped. "Why drag us all the way to Kirkwood?"

Burkis turned away from the train tracks to go down a narrow side street. All of the friendly looking shops were closed for the night, but Cole could hear music and raucous voices coming from what he guessed were a few local bars. Uninterested in two-for-one drafts or Jell-O shots, Burkis headed straight to a gazebo built next to a garden supply store on East Argonne Drive. Between the store and the gazebo were bags of soil stacked near a selection of cement lawn statues that were either not valuable enough to be locked up or too heavy to steal. Behind those things were the bodies of three of the Mongrels that had welcomed Cole and Paige to town outside of Dressel's pub. A fourth lay buried at the bottom of the pile. Unlike the felines that Cole had seen before, the bottom Mongrel had a ratlike tail, two sets of wings evenly spaced along its back, and was covered in a slick layer of mud.

Burkis crouched to grab the base of the Mongrel's right forewing and flipped it over to reveal yet another carcass. This one was a Half Breed. Its lean body and gnarled snout were almost as distinctive as the knotted muscle holding together the skewed, broken bones beneath its pasty flesh.

"This wretch had just fed," Burkis said as he gazed down at the Half Breed. "It's one of the few to make it out of Kansas City, and I've been tracking it to see if it might lead me to any more. Once I was certain there were no dens in this city, I was going to put it down myself. That's when these three descended upon it."

"Didn't anyone else see all of this?" Cole asked as he looked around. Cars drove along the street, but were more concerned with finding a parking space than what was going on behind a garden supply store. Pedestrians stayed on the main walkways and were barely paying enough attention to keep from tripping over cracks in the sidewalk.

"There wasn't much to see," Burkis replied. "The wretch was barely able to keep its head up, and the Mongrels fell over the moment they drew its blood."

"So the Half Breed was dying and the others followed soon after," Paige said. "Sounds like they could have been poisoned."

"Spoken by someone who knows such cowardly tactics all too well," Burkis sneered. "Now look closer." He grabbed the Half Breed's throat with a hand that had suddenly sprouted thick, talonlike claws. Hooking a couple of the claws into a flap of skin on the Half Breed's neck, he pulled it aside to reveal the underlying muscle.

Half Breeds always stank, but the inside of a dead one redefined the term. While Cole turned his head and willed himself not to puke, Paige used a baton to hold its neck open. The specially treated wood creaked in her right hand to form a flat-bladed machete that was a distinct improvement over her last few attempts.

"This looks like wet tree bark," she said as she scraped the tip of the blade against the hardened, leathery surface. "Feels like it too. And there's hardly any blood."

The Half Breed had the mass of a small man, but Burkis lifted it as if it was just another sack of manure from a nearby pile. "Its blood is there."

Cole took his spear from its harness and used it to scrape the muddy sludge caked upon the ground. "This is the same kind of gunk that came out of Peter Walsh," he said. "There were some men in jail across the river who were leaking it from their eyes. So was Henry."

"I doubt that," Burkis huffed. "Henry is a Full Blood, and

we are not affected by Pestilence . . . or War or Famine or even Death. You're too ignorant to have caused such a plague, but there's one Skinner whose hands are particularly muddy."

Gritting her teeth, she said, "Let me guess. Jonah Lancroft?"

"I've heard that name whispered by Mongrels and Henry alike, but neither of those are very reliable sources. Lancroft was a brilliant man, and my guess is that some of his journals have been discovered by an element that would be considered undesirable even by Skinner standards." Dropping the Half Breed onto the pile, he nudged the Mongrels with his toe. "These came from Malia's pack. With Pestilence known to be linked to a Skinner, these deaths may just convince her to even the score at your expense."

"And why would you be so kind as to warn us about that?" Cole asked.

"Because now that Henry has been made aware of his full capabilities, it won't be long before humans, Nymar, and shapeshifters alike will experience death on an epic scale."

Paige lowered her weapons an inch or so but remained on her guard. "So this stuff is activated by Henry?"

"Or any Mind Singer, I would assume. Since there has only been three in the past two hundred and sixty years, Henry should be the only one you need to worry about. But that brings me back to the problem at hand. I have heard the Mind Singer repeatedly since I have come to this city. His voice is strongest here, but his scent is not."

"Maybe he's somewhere else," Cole offered. "What's the range on psychic transmissions anyway?"

"Henry's talent is unfocused," Burkis continued. "He reaches out to all of us with thoughts that are nothing but wild screams. Now, he whispers to unleash this poison among our kind while turning yours into plague-infested rats."

"Full Bloods don't give a shit about Half Breeds," Paige said, "and I seriously doubt you've made a truce with Mongrels. Pestilence has changed from the Mud Flu into Half Breed poison, so you're just worried that you'll be the next one to feel the sting."

Burkis lowered himself to one knee as his entire body shifted into a taller, bulkier form. His face stretched into a long, tapered snout filled with teeth that were angled back like barbs on an arrow. By the time he'd backed into the shadows beneath the gazebo, he was something close to the beast that had almost separated Cole from his head on more than one occasion. He pulled in a deep breath and rolled it around the back of his throat. "The plague is changing. Once it becomes deadly to us, we will have no choice but to kill every carrier we can find. The Mind Singer is the spark, the deliverer and the answer. Since Liam is missing, the responsibility of maintaining this territory falls solely to me."

"Awww," Cole chided. "Poor little werewolf is all alone. Cursed to live through the ages with nobody to play with."

"Wait a second," Paige snapped. "You said Liam, as in the Full Blood from KC?"

Burkis's intense glare was more than enough to confirm that.

"So he's missing. Not dead."

A barely perceptible nod came from the Full Blood.

"I saw him die in Kansas City," Paige insisted. "I punched holes in him myself. Cole knocked him out with a car and the Mongrels ripped him to shreds while they . . ." Her eyes narrowed and she wheeled around to swing her machete straight through one of the support beams of the gazebo. "Son of a bitch!" she shouted, drawing more attention from the pedestrians on the street than the werewolf standing a few paces away. "Why the hell wouldn't those Mongrels finish him off?"

"Perhaps they have taken him somewhere else to feast on him slowly, just as you Skinners would have loved to tear him apart and use the pieces for yourselves." When he said that, Burkis displayed fangs that had thickened into ivory stalagmites. The ones that Paige had knocked out before heading to KC were only slightly shorter than the rest.

"They said they would bury him," Cole reminded them. "They were supposed to suffocate him in the ground or stuff him somewhere he couldn't be found. Is that why you can't find him?"

In a flat tone, Burkis said, "I will find him and that's all any Skinner needs to know. The only reason I'm speaking to you now instead of pulling your bones out through your mouths is because, without your Blood Blade, you are no threat to me. Maintain your territory on your own or I'll be forced to do it for you." The more he spoke, the larger Burkis became. While other animals might raise their hackles or puff their chests to assert their dominance, a Full Blood simply became larger than their opponent like a wall of heavy clouds filling a darkened sky.

Paige stepped forward to declare, "We don't do chores for Full Bloods. You want Henry so bad? You find him. Why would we give a shit if this disease grows strong enough to kill you?"

"Henry's Pestilence has only started taking root," Burkis said. "His voice needs to be silenced before this entire continent is infected. I have already been to both coasts and can tell you the stench of this plague has spread well beyond the cities you protect."

"It's already gotten as far as Chicago?" she asked.

"And farther."

"Henry's a Full Blood too," Paige said. "You don't mind us going after him?"

"He is a Mind Singer," Burkis said. "They have always been trouble. He must be dealt with as quickly as possible. You are given this chance to resolve this situation because I do not wish to see so many humans destroyed."

"No," Cole grunted. "Just the ones who get in your way."

Shifting his gaze toward him, the Full Blood snarled, "Just the ones who don't know their place."

"And what if we find him?" Cole asked. "Should we give you a call or just squeeze a squeak toy a bunch of times?"

Burkis dropped to all fours and shifted into his barrel-chested running form. His eyes narrowed into slits and his teeth grew long enough to pierce through his cheeks. It was the first time during this meeting that he truly seemed ready to kill either of the Skinners.

One leap carried the werewolf to the top of the gardening supply store. Several people on the street pointed at the large shape on the roof, but they lost sight of Burkis after his next bounding step. With nothing left to see, the pointers continued along their way.

"You really shouldn't make doggie jokes when referring to Full Bloods," Paige sighed as her weapons shrank back down so she could holster them in her boots. "They hate that."

Chapter 18

They drove through the city, waiting for a twitch to let them know they'd found Burkis again, but didn't have any luck. Considering that Full Bloods held portions of entire continents as their territories and had the speed to patrol them, trying to chase after one was even more pathetic than a dog running after a speeding car. The Skinners made the effort anyway before heading to Ned's house to regroup.

Daniels had a batch of the new weapon varnish cooking, but it wouldn't be ready for a few hours.

Ned was gone and Rico wasn't about to wait for him to return before setting Cole and Paige both up with .45s. They weren't as nice as his Sig Sauer, but he insisted on trading them for the smaller revolvers Paige carried in her glove compartment.

"I wanna try to make these standard issue," Rico told her. "Since most of us make our own ammunition, it's easier to swap shells if we all pack the same caliber."

"Where's Ned?" Paige asked.

"Checking on something or other downtown. It's just as well because I woulda told him to sit this one out anyways. Last thing we need is a blind man dragging us down at that strip club. Last time I was there, me and Cole got knocked into a bus." Seeing the glare from Paige, Rico quickly amended his statement with, "Sorry. *Half* blind man."

It was too late to mount a search for the house's owner, so they stuffed some extra clips into their pockets and drove out to Bunn's Lounge.

Before the three of them entered the club, Cole examined the outside of the structure at its base for any markings that Stu had mentioned when talking about the A-frame temples. All he had to do was kick away a few tufts of grass to find a chain of strange, curving marks half covered in topsoil.

"Check," he said. "Now let's go in to check for any unusual statuary or depictions of naked women."

"Yeah," Rico grunted. "What're the odds of us finding that kinda stuff in there?"

Tristan was good as her word, leaving instructions with the front door security to let them in through an unmarked entrance with no metal detector. Striding into the club wearing a baggy flannel shirt over his harness and a pistol tucked into a new holster at his hip, Cole couldn't help but grin. If he heard tinny piano music instead of Tone Loc's "Wild Thing" blasting through an expensive sound system, he would have felt like a real gunslinger.

In contrast to the fully lit place with the spotless floors Paige visited earlier that day, the strip club had come alive with pulsing music, obnoxious DJs, strobe lights and the frequent catcall. It was a quarter past one in the morning, which was barely prime time for Bunn's. The dancers on-stage were pretty, but didn't quite know how to fully utilize their groove thangs. A crowd was shaping up, however, and almost all the tables were full.

"So you really think this other Skinner will be here?" Cole asked.

"If he isn't, there'll be a certain nymph getting her pretty ass kicked."

Rico strode through the club wearing his patchwork jacket over his firearms and a wide, ugly smile on his face. "I bet we could charge a hell of a lot for that show," he said. "Besides, it's not like we've got a bunch of other leads to follow."

Either she wasn't about to bite her trainer's head off or she agreed with the statement, because Paige let it slide. Two of the stages were being used, which meant there were several tables and a whole lot of horny guys between her and the other side of the club. One of the tables was occupied by three dudes wearing University of Missouri shirts who barely looked old enough to drink the beers piled in front of them. The closer Paige got to them, the more obnoxious their attempts at charm became.

One of the dudes reached out to snag her, but was shoved straight back down into his seat by Rico. "You don't want none of this, boy," he snarled as another of the Mizzou boys sprang up to face him.

Apparently, that held true for all three of the dudes, and they quickly got back to divvying up their singles.

Pulling a chair up to the table Cole had chosen, Rico dropped into it and declared, "If I don't get something to drink real quick, there's gonna be some trouble."

"The drinks are on me," Paige said, "if you talked to Stanley Velasco like you said you would."

"Oh, I did. We got a nice deal all worked out."

"How bad are we stuck?"

Rico leaned back to tell a waitress what he wanted and then waved off Paige's question. "Don't worry about it. The bill's been paid and we may not live long enough to worry about settling up. Life is good."

The waitress made a good first impression by returning quickly with an oversized mug of beer and tussled his bristly hair when she took his money.

"All right you horn dogs!" the DJ announced. "Point your eyes center stage and keep them there for our lovely Shae!"

"Ooooh," Rico mused.

Shae strutted onto the stage wearing a miniskirt that was more of a silk sweatband around her waist and a matching camisole that had been cut just short enough for the bottoms of her breasts to hang below the thin material. She waved at the Skinners' table and then climbed the brass pole like a cat ascending a carpeted post.

Rico started to say something else, but closed his eyes and let out a breath. Before Cole could brace himself, he was reminded of why the nymphs demanded and received such outrageously high pay for lap dances. As Shae ground her body against the pole, Cole could feel the friction from his chest all the way down to his groin. She leaned back, pumped her hips against the pole and sent that sensation through him as well. And when she playfully pinched her nipple, everyone seated at stage side cleared their chairs.

Paige wasn't immune to the effect, but was the first to get back to business. "Hey!" she said. "Did you do anything useful since you've been out?"

Between the phantom fingers running beneath his clothes and the beer he'd just downed, Rico looked like he didn't know what the hell was going on. "Oh," he said as if he was coming out of a coma. "Yeah. I did a little digging on Jonah Lancroft. I think he's been around a lot longer than we thought. Either that or the old journals are messed up."

Shae was crawling around the edge of the stage, sometimes balancing impossibly upon the narrow bar separating her from the front row admirers. Since they were already hooked and gleefully handing over their money, she no longer projected her sensations to the crowd. Without that distraction, the conversation at Cole's table flowed much quicker.

Settling in with his beer in one hand, Rico said, "There was some con man named Dr. Lancroft traveling around New England around the 1760s. He went from village to village, supposedly slaying vampires. Folks thought he was crazy, but he got results. Sound familiar?"

"There were vampires here in the 1700s?" Cole asked.

"Nymar have been around a lot longer than that. There were some Skinners in the Colonies back then along with Gypsies, trackers, and all sorts of folks who didn't laugh at the whole vampire and werewolf thing. They weren't exactly public figures, but they were smart enough to pool their resources for a good long while. A century later Jonah Lancroft built his reformatory as a place to study the monsters and figure out new ways to cause them grief."

Shae's heels clacked against the stage as she approached her pole. Knowing there wouldn't be much time before the conversation would slow down again, Paige said, "You had a point, Rico. Get to it."

"Skinners are still around," he stated without taking his eyes from the perky nymph. "We may not see eye-to-eye with all the Travelers, but Gypsies are still around too. The reformatory itself may have collapsed, but there's a lot of shit buried under there. Any number of right-thinking lunatics from any number of groups who have survived this long could have gone down there to find Lancroft's journals or research or notes or whatever else."

"Right-thinking lunatics?" Cole chuckled.

"I'd say we qualify for that title," Rico said while raising his ridiculously oversized mug. "And I bet the Cahokia Police Department would agree."

"At least to the lunatic part," Paige grumbled while rubbing her sore arm.

Cole drummed his fingers as something popped into his head. It was one of those things that didn't feel right as a thought and surely wouldn't feel right as a statement. Even so, he decided to let it fly anyway. "What about Henry?"

"What about him?" Paige asked.

"He was in Lancroft Reformatory for God knows how long. He went back there when we were chasing Misonyk out of Chicago. If he's this Mind Singer now, maybe he's cleared his thoughts enough to put together something like Pestilence."

"You mean that psycho with the broken neck who was knocked senseless in the jail cell?" Rico scoffed. "He could barely put together a sentence."

"I agree," Paige said. "Henry may be a lot of things, but he's not a chemist."

Cole felt a warm hand settle upon his shoulder. Tristan moved in behind him and leaned over to run her fingers along his chest. He'd felt her phantom touch before, but the real thing combined with a soft voice in his ear, was enough to make every nerve ending stand up and salute. "Good to see you again, Cole. I never got to finish that lap dance we started in Wisconsin. Although I should warn you," she added as she lowered herself onto his lap, "it's never a good idea to lick the dancers." Once his face was sufficiently flushed, Tristan acknowledged the rest of the table. "Hello again, Paige. Introduce me to your friend."

Rico almost knocked his chair over in his haste to get up and introduce himself.

"Ah," Tristan purred. "Rrrrico."

Unlike when Cole had rolled his R's, Rico seemed positively delighted to hear Tristan make the same reference. "I take it Tristan is just a stage name," he said.

She took a sip of his beer. "A girl's got to have her secrets."

"Girl?" Paige grunted. "You mean nymph. She's a nymph, Rico."

Tristan seemed more perplexed by her tone than anything else. "Aren't you the one who convinced the other Skinners to give us a pass?"

"I convinced them to give *you* a pass, and that was just as a favor to Prophet."

"How is Walter?"

"Fine."

"Well, you still have my thanks," Tristan said earnestly. "And I'll have you know that we haven't abused your concession one bit. In fact, we've been able to get steady work and create a very lucrative business."

"An entire chain of purple A-frames," Cole said.

"Us and IHOP."

"IHOPs aren't temples," he pointed out.

Curling an arm around Cole's head so she could rub his chin, Tristan replied, "That depends on how much you like banana pancakes."

It took every ounce of will, but Cole somehow kept his mind in focus. "These are temples, Tristan. Paige and I checked on our way in here and we saw the runes or glyphs or whatever you want to call the markings along the bottom of the outside walls."

When Tristan looked at him, Rico shrugged and told her, "We did our research."

"What does it matter if these are temples?" the nymph asked. "We're not forcing anyone to come here, we're not preventing them from leaving, and we're not forcing them to worship us. They choose to do all of that on their own."

Judging by the way her hips shifted just perfectly against his lap, Cole didn't have any trouble believing her.

"So why build temples?" Paige asked. "Aren't there already plenty of these dumps all over the country? It's not like any of you would have trouble landing a job at one of them."

Tristan lowered her voice and said, "First of all, our temples amplify our talents. They also allow us to live without being sniffed out by every shapeshifter or Nymar out there."

"They don't seem to work too well in that regard," Rico pointed out. "Otherwise there wouldn't need to be so much extra security around the side door."

"Those leeches didn't find us on their own," Tristan hissed. "You see that man sitting over there?"

Cole and the other two Skinners looked across the club to a section of small round tables scattered in a far corner. It was almost directly between the VIP area Paige had seen in Christov's video and the door marked EMPLOYEES ONLY next to a huge mirror. A few of those tables were occupied by adventurous couples looking to spice up their love lives, but most were taken by men on their own watching the dancers from afar instead of sitting close enough to smell the perfume. Only one of them didn't seem overly enticed by the dancers. In fact, the girls making their rounds asking for private dances completely avoided him. The lighting in the club wasn't very good, but Cole could see the thick, impeccably trimmed whiskers covering the man's face.

"You mean that guy with the beard?" he asked.

"That's the one. Do you recognize him?"

Strobe lights created shadows upon the bearded man's face that shifted in time to the beat of the music. Black lights were absorbed by the coarse texture of his neck and arms. His posture was just straight enough to make him look confident instead of rigid, and he kept one hand flat on the table a few inches away from a glass of what looked to be cola. He wore simple clothes made of thick cotton and the pleasantly neutral expression of someone watching squirrels scamper across a quiet park.

"He look familiar to you, Rico?" Paige asked.

The big man shook his head. "Why should he?"

"Because," Tristan said, "he's one of you."

"He's the Skinner you told us about?"

Maintaining a playful smile and nodding without looking directly at the table, she said, "I saw the scars myself. He even smells like one of you. Tree sap, gun oil, and blood. Those leeches were following him, and when they realized my sisters were here, they started camping outside our door waiting for their chance to get us. If it wasn't for the protection of our temple's glyphs, they would have been able to charge in here and take us by force."

"What do the Nymar have against nymphs?" Rico asked.

Tristan shifted in Cole's lap as if about to float across the table. "We're the reason vampires exist, sweetie."

"Nymar spore are why vampires exist," Paige corrected.

"Yes, but haven't you ever wondered why there aren't Nymar dogs or Nymar snakes? Or I should say, why there aren't Nymar dogs or snakes *anymore*?"

"Yes," Cole said. "I have always wondered that." He shifted to get a look at her face, and Tristan adjusted accordingly. As her body curled in his lap, Cole's hands supported her. "My brain just works like that."

Gazing at him as if she'd found a new favorite student, Tristan said, "Nymar spore used to inhabit whatever bodies they could find. Anything with blood flowing through it was good enough. They'd get inside, lay dormant until their systems adjusted to the animal's body, and then attach to its heart to do what they do. Somewhere along the line, a Nymar got lucky enough to taste the blood of a nymph. One of the stories is that an infected cat curled at the feet of its mistress and lapped up some of her blood when she pricked her finger. After that," she said in a silky voice that rolled through Cole's ear as phantom fingers slid down the front of his entire body, "the Nymar became so infatuated that it climbed out of the cat and into any animal that could get closer to that nymph. It's supposed to have infected her lover, who could get all the alone time he wanted. Her attentions were so wondrous that all Nymar decided to attach to human hearts, just for the chance of getting that close to a nymph again."

When Tristan shifted back into her normal voice, Cole felt a jolt worse than if he'd accidentally stared directly into one of the nearby strobes.

"Some of the more colorful details were probably exaggerated, but the core of it is true," she said. "A Nymar's thirst for human blood above all others stems from that first sip from a nymph. That's why the few of us that are left must protect ourselves, and why the Nymar will not stop once they've found us." Tickling Cole's chin, she added, "Deep down inside, they know we're the sweetest tasting things on this earth."

"I can vouch for that," Cole said before he could stop himself.

Losing the singsong quality of her voice as if she'd flipped a switch, Tristan said, "That Skinner over there brought the Nymar to this club, but it's not why he came. Like those leeches, he came for us."

"Why does he want you?" Rico asked.

Paige locked her eyes on Tristan so she could watch the nymph carefully as she said, "Maybe it has something to do with how this one can be here after being on the other side of the country less than an hour before."

For the first time since they'd met, Tristan looked genuinely stunned. Even so, she recovered with a pretty smile and a cute little upward curl of an eyebrow. "That's part of it. When he arrived, he asked to use us as a way to reach the entire world at once. When we refused, he asked to run some tests on one of my sisters." Grimacing as if the words themselves were fetid upon her tongue, she added, "He wanted samples from them. When we refused that, he kidnapped two of my sisters and threatened to kill them if we didn't do what he asked. Ever since then he comes here every other night and sits there like an arrogant bastard, writing in his notebook and collecting our sweat with cotton swabs."

"Why doesn't Christov do anything about this?" Paige asked.

"Because I didn't tell him the whole story," Tristan replied. "All he'd do is try to send Mikey or one of the others after him, and that would only get my sisters killed. I don't need bouncers. I need Skinners."

Cole's first impulse was to agree to do whatever Tristan wanted. More than anything, he *wanted* to do what she wanted and it didn't matter what it was. But before he could roll with those instincts, he took a moment to question what had put them there. And that one bit of questioning was all it took for him to say, "You were lucky to get that first pass from us. Just because we sat here and listened to you doesn't mean we're just another group of admirers."

"What?" Tristan asked.

"Yeah," Paige said quickly. "What?"

"I haven't done my research on nymphs, but I've seen enough to get the gist of it. You get your way and have a few sexy tricks up your sleeve, which are boosted by this temple or whatever. We're not drones. If you have a proposition to make, then make it. We don't do anything just because you snapped your fingers." Seeing the hurt expression on Tristan's face, Cole couldn't help but add, "Not to be mean or anything, but . . ."

Paige reached over and rubbed his arm. "Valiant effort, young one." To Tristan, she said, "How about we start with what that old guy was so interested in."

Rico pushed away from the table and took his almost empty mug with him. "And I'll start by introducing myself. If this guy is a Skinner, I wanna know about it. If he ain't, then I got a real problem with someone sayin' they are when they ain't. And if he is, no wait . . . I'll be right back."

"Leave the beer," Paige said. "You've had enough."

As he crossed the room to the bearded man's table, Rico couldn't help but notice Shae making her rounds. Very few words were exchanged before the older man got up, grabbed her by the wrist and dragged her toward the employees' entrance. Within seconds after that, Rico was close enough to hear the bearded man say, "Sing for me," to the frightened nymph.

Rico clamped a hand on the old man's shoulder and squeezed with enough force to crush a beer can. "Ain't exactly the best time to get yer rocks off, pops."

Up close, the bearded man had the presence of a washed-out photograph. His skin was rough and leathery and his clothes had the musty smell of the most unpopular section of a library. When he looked at Rico, he seemed more confused than anything else. "You should be helping me. I'm one of you. See?" He swung his other hand up to show a palm that was so scarred, it looked as if it had been stitched together from numerous shreds of torn skin. "These nymphs have a part to play in destroying the filth that have hunted us for too long. Help me."

"Why don't you help yourself by letting her go?"

The bearded man lost his patience in an instant. Pulling Shae closer, he picked up the stick that had been propped against his table and snarled, "Do you know who I am? I made every Skinner what they are today!"

"Lemme guess," Rico chuckled. "You're Jonah Lancroft?"

"Then you do know. Enough damage has been done by those who would sully our craft. Unhand me and help put these Dryad whores to work before it's too late."

Rico blinked and tried to replay the last few sentences in his head to make sure the beer hadn't hit him harder than he'd thought.

"I have no time to waste," the old man said as he shook loose of Rico's grip. "This place will have to be sacrificed along with you. Henry, give the Mongrels what they want."

Rico pressed the barrel of the .45 against the man's elbow and said, "Let go before you lose an arm!"

They're coming, Dr. Lancroft!

The voice rattling inside Rico's head was quickly wiped out by the hacking cry of the waitress who'd brought him his beer. She screamed at him through a mouthful of sludge and tried to pull his gun away as if she'd lost all fear of it going off in her face.

The music faded for a second and was replaced by an updated mix of Van Halen's "Hot for Teacher." Right on cue, Kate strode onto the stage wearing a plaid skirt, glasses, and her red hair tied in pigtails. Strictly speaking, the outfit was more of a "hot for student" sort of thing, but none of the patrons seemed to mind. In fact, their cheers were so loud that nobody could hear the slam of tables being upended through-out the club or guards rushing toward the rowdy customers. Cole had been struggling to catch sight of Rico through the milling crowd and wriggling dancers when he heard a voice that was part scream and part gurgle. More shout-ing followed as people backed away from the instigators of the brawls that had all sprung up at the same time. More and more of the customers and employees showed traces of watery sludge dripping from their eyes or thicker mud flow-ing from their mouths.

Cole jumped to his feet, lifting Tristan up with him. "Shit! Where did they come from?"

"I think they can come from just about anywhere," Paige replied as she stood up and drew the baton from her left boot. "Henry's got to be close."

"He's always close."

At first the fights were treated like any other scuffle in such a deep pool of testosterone. People moved away from those swinging the punches, while others welcomed the chance to dive in and get their hands dirty. That all changed when people looked closer at the groaning faces at the center of the disturbance. Blank faces caked with mud all turned away from Cole and Paige to fix upon the back of the room. Then the people who weren't infected tried to get away from those who were, sparking more and more fights like little fires crackling around an inferno.

"These dudes are sick!" someone yelled.

When someone else shouted, "It's that Mud Flu shit!" dis-temper grew into panic.

Rico didn't want to kill anyone, but he also wasn't about to let himself be overrun by the growing mob converging on him. He fired a shot intended to frighten the Mud People away, but all that did was change panic into a riot.

"God damn it," Paige snarled. "Try to draw some of them over here."

She and Cole screamed at the Mud People, but they wouldn't listen. They closed in on Rico, held back mainly by the uninfected customers who fought to get to the front door. He was a capable enough fighter to stay afloat for years in that kind of a fight, so he craned his neck to try and get a look at his partners. Unable to see them, he settled for being heard.

"That old man grabbed Shae!"

Only a couple minutes had passed since the first punch was thrown. That was enough time for the crowd within the club to get ugly, and more than enough time for a pack of Mongrels to make the run from St. Louis. As soon as Cole felt the burn in his scars, he heard the commotion of people being knocked away from the front door to make room for a group of new arrivals to get inside. Cole recognized one shabbily dressed woman immediately and stood with Tristan behind him. "That's Malia!"

As Mikey led a few other bouncers to greet the Mongrels, more of the shapeshifters forced their way inside.

"We came for them," Malia said, pointing a long finger at the Skinners.

Mikey stepped between the intruders and the rest of the club, but was met by a sharp punch from Allen's bony, human-sized fist. Since the Mongrel's punch did about as much damage as a cat's batting paw, Mikey grinned and grabbed Allen by the front of his shirt to shove him toward the door. The other bouncers fell in behind him, but were soon facing claws instead of fists.

"Damn it," Paige snarled as she headed for the door. "Make this quick, Cole. Get them outside before getting too rough."

But it was too late. The Mongrels knocked the bouncers down like bowling pins. Malia pinned Mikey to the floor and crouched on his chest while slowly shifting into her leopard form. "The Mind Singer was right," she growled. "They're all in one place."

"Yeah," Cole said as he drew his weapon from its harness. "Tough luck for you."

Chapter 19

The spear creaked as it shifted into a weapon that was the size and shape of a longbow. The forked end split apart to form a set of sharpened horns. Paige wielded both of her weapons, but only the one in her left hand changed into the bladed version, while the one in her right remained a simple baton.

"You know better than this," she warned while taking a stand at the front of the club. "Turn back before you make an even bigger mistake."

Malia's eyes had fixed upon Paige's right arm. She pulled in a breath through her nose as if she could smell weakness. Halfway through that breath, her face stretched into a wide snout and all of her muscles gained an extra layer of bulk. The other Mongrels took that as their cue and pressed forward.

"Jesus!" yelped the young guy behind the counter near the front door. His main job was to check IDs or answer the phone, but he also had a panic button hidden near his knee, which he now pressed in a frantic series of taps.

Allen and the other male Mongrel transformed as if they were being crumpled into a ball by invisible hands. They arched their backs as they ran forward, twisting their heads like dogs forced to listen to a wailing car alarm. Their bodies thinned and stretched out, causing their clothes to hang looser on their frames than when they'd been human. By the time he reached Cole, Allen was the wiry alley cat that had been prowling the Central West End.

Malia and the females had a much easier time of it. They shifted from one shape to another with the fluidity of seasoned runway models stepping out of one dress and into a more expensive design. Malia's front paws hit Paige squarely in the chest and her mouth yawned open to show dozens of spiky teeth.

Twisting her upper body to the right, Paige brought up her left hand while snapping that weapon around in a quick semicircle. Although Malia dodged the first lethal swipe of the sickle's blade, the blunt end came back around to crack against her temple. She retreated to shake off whatever cobwebs had been loosened within her skull. As the Mongrel pressed her chest to the floor, the vertical lines of her pupils widened to take in the sight of her prey. Paige knew better than to stare at those eyes for too long because the followup attackers were already coming for her. Another wereleopard sprang to attack from the high road, while one of the gangly males skittered along the low.

Paige met both of them with weapons that were as different from each other as one Mongrel was from the first. The more elegantly shaped sickle came up in a series of quick, looping slashes to tangle up the leopard's paws, while the crude machete in her right hand dropped straight down in a glancing blow against the side of the alley cat's forehead.

Meanwhile, Cole, having avoided Allen's first attack with a well-timed sidestep, held his spear vertically in front of him to catch the first incoming female. The minimal amount of clothing she'd been wearing was now almost completely lost beneath the black and gray striped fur that sprouted from her skin. When she slammed against the spear, Cole snapped both arms straight out and twisted around to push her to the side. A second later she righted herself and clamped her teeth into his shin.

"Son of a *mother!*" he yelped as he drove the main spearhead into her neck. The cooling flow of healing serum rushed through his leg, but that didn't do much against the pain.

The Mongrel's muscle tissue was thick enough to absorb most of the spearhead. She twisted her head to one side so the weapon came loose through a flap of skin instead of driving deeper into her throat for a killing blow.

Cole brought the spear around in a smooth arc to intercept another Mongrel that was about to tear his head off. Her neck became wedged in the forked end of the weapon, but she continued to swipe at him while straining to get close enough to bite. After thinning the light brown fur on her head to reveal a flat, vaguely feline face, she wheezed, "We're not . . . afraid of you."

"Yeah," Cole grunted as he willed the forked end to close around her like a pair of wooden pliers. "Maybe you should be." Using all the muscles in his arms, shoulders, and back to lift the Mongrel off her feet, he slammed her down and kicked at the wiry, oversized alley cat that had been creeping toward him.

His foot caught Allen in the side of the face, but not hard enough to keep him away. Some blood still dripped from Cole's shin and was smeared against the floor as Allen continued to crawl toward him. The Mongrel's eyes were fixed on the bloody leg, and he licked his chops with a long, thin tongue. Before that leg could be torn completely off, Cole shifted his stance so his other leg was in front. Sweeping the weapon in a continuous back-and-forth motion allowed him to punish Allen's scrawny torso and bloody anything else that got close enough to bite or scratch him.

The alley cat Mongrel didn't have anywhere to go but down. After being thumped and cut by the spear, he was shoved against the floor and forced to curl up and protect his head. The striped Mongrel wasn't as passive and she pounced onto Cole's back. Claws ripped through his clothing and sank into his shoulders as her teeth scraped against his ear to bring the words, "All Skinners die."

The music was still thumping through the club's speakers, but wasn't loud enough to cover the excited roar of the customers or the distinctive blast of a gunshot. The weight on Cole's back shifted and the striped Mongrel let out a grunt as a bullet thumped against her side. While he appreciated the effort, Cole knew the bouncer's guns wouldn't put her down. Another shot was fired from farther away, and then he heard a scream that sounded more like a woman's shriek than an animal's roar. The claws came out of Cole's shoulder, so he straightened up and threw the striped Mongrel off. Taking a moment to check where that other shot had come from, he spotted Rico near the second stage with the Sig Sauer in his hand.

Paige was nearby, holding down the second alley cat Mongrel with her boot. Her sickle blade was trapped under its neck, so she pulled it up and out in a single motion that was strong enough to cut all the way down to its spinal cord. Blood sprayed onto the floor and the Mongrel's body went limp. When Malia circled around to try and attack her from the side, she was grazed by a shot from Rico's .45.

Mikey and a younger guy with the build of a football player wrestled with frantic patrons and a few of the human dancers to keep them toward the back of the club as the muddy customers were shoved or knocked aside. The un-infected people close enough to see the Mongrels bolted for an exit, rushed to the bathrooms, or searched for someplace else to hide. The only island of calm in the middle of that tempest was Rico. He stood his ground next to the stage, extended his arm and pulled the trigger. The sight of the gun was enough to get people to move away from him, but the roar of it being fired sent several customers and dancers alike under the closest table they could find. Rico's smile didn't become any prettier when it widened at the sight of his shot hitting its mark.

The bullet struck one of the larger were-leopards that had been circling Paige. Cole had seen shapeshifters hit with all kinds of ammunition, and their reactions usually ranged from mildly amused to somewhat annoyed. Fully automatic fire merely got snagged up within the fur of a Full Blood, while it took several rounds to make a dent in one of the less powerful species. These rounds, however, were doing some real damage.

The leopard that had been stalking Paige didn't move as Rico's bullet drilled through her shoulder and exploded out through a messy hole halfway down her back. Once the delayed reaction hit her, however, she flopped onto her side and struggled to get back up while yelping in pain. Cole looked at the striped Mongrel cowering a few paces away, licking one of the bloody wounds she'd been given. Much like the other leopard, her wound went all the way through.

Holding up the smoking pistol, Rico said, "Snappers!"

Before Cole could ask what the hell that was supposed to mean, a wave of bodies rushed for the front door. With the Mongrels wounded and scattered, the crowd's top priority had become getting away from the big guy with the gun in his hand. Rico turned toward the back of the room to check on Lancroft. The staff in the man's hand, along with the fact that he walked against the tide of people, made him easy to spot as he dragged Shae toward the door marked EMPLOY-EES ONLY. The nymph was putting up a good enough fight to keep Lancroft from reaching his goal during the initial confusion.

Paige stood with her back against Cole's and held her weapons so they ran along her forearms and wouldn't be snagged by any of the civilians stampeding the front door. "Are you all right?" she asked him.

"Yeah!" Cole screamed, to be heard over the cacophony of music, shouting, and pounding footsteps. "Got bit on the leg, but it's already healing. What about you?"

"With my arm so messed up, I've been injecting enough serum to get hit by a car and not feel it."

They readied their weapons when the burning in their scars started to itch. With the club's bouncers preoccupied by the stampeding crowd, the shabbily dressed Nymar were able to force their way in through the front door. The first batch of customers who'd escaped the club were met by four Nymar who carried them back inside like duffel bags full of dirty clothes.

Jerry, Sonya, Gums, and his pasty girlfriend spotted the Skinners right away and bared their fangs. One of the patrons intent on leaving the club was a young athletic guy in a sleeveless shirt and baggy shorts. He knocked Sonya aside and tried shouldering past Gums but underestimated the Nymar's strength. Gums held the guy's arm and sank his fangs deep into his flesh. Although he didn't have the thicker set of lower fangs to keep the athlete from getting away, Sonya did, and she sank them into the guy's neck along with enough venom to drop him to his knees. The remaining crowd filled the club like Ping-Pong balls rattling inside the basket of a lottery drawing, preventing Cole or Paige from reaching the athletic guy before the blood was gulped from his veins.

"There!" Jerry said as he pointed at Tristan.

Even the Nymar that were feeding dropped their meal and jumped over Cole and Paige to claim their prize.

Rico sighted along the top of his .45 but quickly abandoned the hope of hitting any more of the Mongrels. The shape-shifters had either been swallowed up by the frenzied crowd that now flowed out through various wailing fire exits or were fending off the contingent of wildly swinging Mud Flu victims. When a customer fell beneath the wave of flailing arms and trembling bodies, one of the bouncers raced to help him. Since Cole and Paige were both going after the Nymar, Rico spun around to try and find Shae.

The employees' entrance swung open and Christov emerged carrying a shotgun. "Shut those alarms off! *Now,* goddamn it!" he shouted loud enough to send Blake running.

"Where's Shae and that bearded guy?" Rico demanded.

Hesitant to leave the doorway, Christov looked up and down the hallway running behind the large mirror and shouted, "Nobody is here but me."

Rico meant to have a look for himself but was prevented from doing so by another wave of persistent, muddy hands.

Once the door alarms were silenced, the only noise that remained came from wounded customers, hissing Nymar, moaning Mud People, and growling Mongrels. The CD player had been knocked over sometime during the panic, but the strobes continued to flash, which gave the club a hollow, frenetic atmosphere. About half of the crowd re- mained, most of which were covered in a glistening muddy sheen. Still in combat mode, the Nymar pounced on anyone they could reach to gain a boost before going another round with the Skinners.

Gums's pasty girlfriend fed on the young guy working the front counter. The employee was paralyzed and unable to do a damn thing about the hungry woman drinking from the gash in his throat, so Paige buried her machete into the Nymar's back. Strangely enough, that's when she remembered the pasty bitch's name.

Cass.

Didn't matter now. The spore attached to Cass's heart was nearly cleaved in two as the blade sliced all the way to the vampire's center of mass. Gums wasn't far away, and he flew at the Skinner in a rage. Paige's sickle cut through the air on its way to his neck but was slapped away before it could land. Venom dripped from his curved upper fangs, making Gums appear more like a snake than anything that should be walking on two legs. He spat at her, but Paige reflexively turned her head before any of the venom got into her eyes.

Gums took advantage of the momentary distraction and scurried away from her weapons, enabling the young guy at the front counter to crawl back to his post, reach under the counter and find the gun stashed there. Opening his mouth as if to shout something, he only managed to choke on the dark fluid bubbling up from the depths of his throat. His first shot punched into the floor several feet from Cole, and his next one was even wilder, thanks to the way his head snapped violently to one side.

Paige cracked her left arm like a whip, releasing her sickle at the last second to send it flying into the kid's jaw. She'd been aiming for his temple, but he still dropped before winding up like the teen whose neck had been broken by Henry's psychotic essence.

"Are you all right?" she asked a woman on the floor who'd been one of the customers the Nymar forced back into the club.

The woman was stunned, pale and speechless. She covered her mouth, coughed, and wasn't able to keep the mud from running between her fingers.

"Damn it. Cole, more people are getting sick!"

Cole wanted to help her, but half a dozen other customers stood between him and Paige. When he tried to get to her, he was blocked by a fat man with his fist still closed around a wad of singles and a steady trickle of muddy fluid seeping from his tear ducts. More of the pungent gunk dripped from his mouth when he opened it in a wordless series of moans. All of the Mud People in the club screamed in unison, showing teeth that were smeared with slimy residue.

Destroy the Nymar.

Those words hissed within every mind in the club, causing the infected customers to throw themselves at the remaining Nymar, who clawed their way toward the bar where Kate and Tristan were huddled. At opposing corners of the room, Cole could see Sonya climbing up the wall near the large one-way mirror, and Malia perching upon a stack of speakers, eyeing the Skinners hungrily.

"Shae's gone!" Tristan screamed.

Cole and Paige both looked toward the bar. When they ran in that direction, they were swarmed by infected customers. Before he could get to where the nymphs were hiding, Cole was grabbed by at least four sets of filthy hands. They dug their nails into his skin and pulled him in while chattering "Ican'tletyouhurtthem!" again and again in different voices, at different speeds, and in different rhythms, until the words became just another kind of mush spewing from their mouths.

The combination of not wanting to hurt a civilian and thinking he could power through the efforts of a bunch of sick people turned out to be a bad one for Cole. In a matter of seconds he was pulled off balance, and swinging his spear at anything within reach, but the Mud People didn't feel it when they were hit in the face, ribs, or anywhere else.

The Mud People.

Cole recalled that's what Burkis had called them. They weren't the customers they'd been, or innocent people that needed to be protected. They were Mud People now. More important, they were winning. As he tuned out the constant jabber coming from all those sullied mouths, his body went numb from the constant barrage of kicks, punches, and slaps. When the flow of healing serum pulsed through him, he grasped the spear with both hands and prepared to fight back.

It would have been easy to sink a sharpened end into the closest Mud Person's gut. Even as that person spat murky bile onto his face and dug nails into his flesh, Cole couldn't get himself to kill a puppet that regurgitated Henry's words along with their sickness. He took an extra moment to blunt the other end of his weapon so he could fight the Mud People descending upon him without ending their lives. Women and men alike hit and kicked each other in their haste to get to him. Not far away, Paige followed his lead by knocking aside the horde using a pair of mismatched billy clubs.

Cole lowered his head, brought his spear in close and started swinging. The first few impacts were the hardest, simply because they landed flush upon muddy faces without the slightest bit of resistance. After those two people dropped, he was on his way to clearing a path. Just when he'd taken a few steps toward Paige, the first Mud People he'd knocked down jumped up to grab his weapon and hold it in place so the others could scratch, hit, and tear however they liked. Once Cole was wrapped up to the point of being immobilized, all of the people in front of him were knocked aside by a figure clad in a few strips of clothing over a pelt of matted fur.

It was Allen. He bared rows of thin fangs and almost sank them into Cole's shoulder before Mikey threw his considerable bulk at the Mongrel. Turning his focus to the bouncer, Allen slashed Mikey's thick arms and decimated everything above the neck in a quick series of bites. Cole sharpened his spearhead as quickly as he could and then drove it into the Mongrel's side. Once Allen was impaled, he finished him off by willing the spearhead to bend within the Mongrel so it damaged as much as possible when he twisted it. The werecat let out a wailing cry as Cole ripped the spear out and knocked him over with a straight kick.

Mikey was long gone, so Cole stepped over the dead Mongrel to help Paige. She was at the bar, doing her best to drag

Sonya away from Kate while shoving aside all the grasping Mud People. Setting his sights on the Nymar, Cole was ready to swing for the fences to get her away from Paige. Before he could get within the spear's range, however, he nearly tripped over Gums.

"Fuck!" the gap-toothed Nymar grunted as he grabbed Cole's leg. "It burns! Goddamn dirty bitches!" Punctuating his tirade with a high-pitched scream, Gums arched his back as a mess of black tentacles exploded from his rib cage and neck.

Not only was it a gruesome sight, but it made one hell of a mess. Cole barely managed to avoid getting snagged by the flailing tentacles, but didn't fare so well against the mud-covered floor. His heel slipped in a puddle, sending him straight to his back with a thump that knocked the wind from his lungs. Sonya ducked under a swing from the machete in Paige's right hand and bared her fangs triumphantly, so Cole drew his .45 and sighted along the top of the barrel.

A lot of thoughts rushed through his mind in the split second before Paige's blood would flow into Sonya's mouth. Cole hadn't wanted to fire the pistol for the same reason he hadn't wanted to swing a sharpened spear in the middle of a crowd of former civilians. Also, he had his doubts as to how far he should trust his aim with Paige so close to his intended target. In the end, he fell back on instincts that screamed at him to pull his trigger before Paige was bitten. It helped if he imagined the whole nightmare was just another video game.

The .45 bucked in his hand three times, filling the club with thunder that joined a pair of shots from Rico's Sig Sauer. Paige dropped straight down, and Sonya reeled back as two out of three shots drilled through her body. Before Sonya could recover from the wounds, Paige followed up with a quick slash of her sickle that sent the Nymar flopping onto the bar. From there, Sonya was set upon by Mud People who bit and clawed at her in a blind frenzy.

"Get to the back room!" Tristan shouted.

With most of the Mud People converging on Sonya, there was just enough of a gap for the Skinners to escort Tristan

and Kate past the main stage. Rico was in that vicinity, surrounded by the remaining Mud People. Still chanting Henry's words, some of them clawed and swung at him, while
the others latched onto his arms and legs. Henry had made
an appearance as well. Cole could tell as much by the muddy
corpse on the floor that was swollen from an attempted
transformation and left with its head twisted at an unnatural
angle. Behind him, Cole could hear the horrific tearing of
flesh followed by the leathery flow of tentacles as Sonya was
overcome by an overdose of Pestilence that was easily ten
times more than what had killed Peter Walsh.

"The old man got past me!" Rico yelled as soon as he
caught sight of Cole and Paige. "In the back room! *Go!*"

While he may have been inclined to follow that order
under normal circumstances, Cole wasn't about to do so
when Rico was close to being brought down for good. Rico
not only had the Mud People to contend with, but Jerry had
flanked him and was about to blindside the big guy. Cole
ran forward and used his momentum to drive the spear deep
into the Nymar's side, angled toward his heart. Enraged by
the proximity of the nymphs and all the Pestilence in the
air, Jerry turned into something that could no longer even
pass as a person. Cole ground the spear within his chest as
if turning a crank until he felt the point snag upon the spore
attached to the Nymar's heart. Once it was punctured, the
spore sucked all of the moisture from Jerry's body in a futile
attempt to heal. The Nymar's last movement was to reach
out for Kate's arm as she hurried past him.

"*I said move!*" Rico bellowed. This time he enforced his
own decree by pushing Cole toward the employees' door.
Paige tried to protest but was shoved even harder as Malia
scampered along the wall above the one-way mirror to
pounce at the group of Skinners. She was still airborne when
the mirror exploded outward with a deafening roar that sent
hundreds of shards of glass flying into the main room.

Malia was knocked off course, to land on her side upon
one of the few tables that had yet to be overturned. Although
some of her fur was bloodied and singed, the Mongrel wasn't
about to be put down by a single shotgun blast. Christov stood

in the hallway behind the shattered mirror, still grasping the smoking weapon in his hands. "What the fuck's happening here?" he screamed, as though on the verge of tears.

"Come on!" Tristan said as she pulled the employees' door open. Kate rushed through, immediately followed by Paige.

Rico fired his last shot at Malia, sending the Mongrel darting under a different table. "There's a few more of Christov's boys back there," he said to Cole. "Some big black dude and a preppy kid. If that old man's still here, those bouncers will need all the help they can get."

The Mud People shifted their attention back to the Skinners, and several were knocked off their feet as Malia charged through the group. Careful not to bite any of the Mud People, she scurried beneath a table and lunged at Rico. In the time it took for him to reload his .45, his arm was grabbed by two of the mud-faced customers. Both of them were dressed in plain shorts and T-shirts. No more details than that could be seen through the stains smeared into their clothes. More of the diseased customers grabbed Malia, causing the Mongrel to swipe at them with her claws.

One of the Mud People closest to Rico turned to look at him. She was one of the human dancers, but now her face was slick with dark bile. When she opened her mouth, she coughed so violently that it snapped her head to one side, which was followed by the wet crunch of breaking bone. "Pestilence will make the world new again," she said. "Maketheworldnewagainmaketheworldnewagain!"

The other muddied customers may have tried to say those same words, but they couldn't get out more than gurgling croaks since their throats were now full of blackened paste. As one, all of the Mud People shifted their eyes toward the employees' entrance.

When Cole ran to help Rico, he found himself quickly looking down the barrel of the Sig Sauer. "I'm covering *you*, damn it!" Rico barked. "Now do what I fucking told you to do!"

"We're all back there, Rico! How about you move your ass and come with us?"

The bigger man thought about that for as long as it took to crack the side of his pistol against the temple of a Mud Person who tried to close his hands around his throat. As soon as the would-be strangler was down, Rico followed Cole to the door.

No matter how many Mud People had piled onto Malia, there weren't enough to keep her pinned. She slashed her way through them amid a wailing, feral snarl.

"Shit," Rico grunted as he stopped just short of the door, then waited for a clean shot and fired a round that dug a bloody trench down Malia's back.

Pain, desperation, and fury gave Malia the fuel she needed to shake the Mud People loose and charge at the true target of her aggression. "Out of my city!" she snarled through a mouthful of teeth that looked like sharpened icicles.

After everyone had made it through the door, Rico filled up the entrance with his body and lowered his head as Malia ripped into his back. Cole grabbed onto the lapels of his patchwork jacket and tried to pull him in, but Paige shouted, "Leave him!"

A rotund man wearing khaki pants and a flower print shirt stepped through the broken mirror while filling the back hallway with a wet groan. Christov fired another blast from his shotgun, which liquefied the former customer's legs and stopped the rest of the Mud People in their tracks.

"Hang on," Rico growled. "Almost . . . got it." Gripping the door frame as well as the hand Cole offered, he pulled himself into the hallway as the sound of tearing flesh drifted through the air. But the flesh being torn wasn't Rico's. Instead, Malia's teeth had clamped around his jacket, and she tugged at it like a dog trying to claim its end of a knotted sock. Though she shredded a good portion of the protective layers, her teeth didn't make it through the Half Breed body armor.

Using the blunted end of his spear just in case he hit Rico by mistake, Cole reached over the other Skinner's shoulder and cracked the bridge of Malia's nose. She opened her jaws, shook her head wildly and snarled at the clawing Mud People behind her. She must not have liked her odds any longer because she crossed the room in one jump to land upon a partition separating the restrooms from the rest of the club. One more jump took her to the front of the club, where she darted out the front door.

Rico shoved past Cole and slammed the door shut. "Thanks," he said while twisting the lock above the handle.

"Will you be safe in your office?" Paige asked Christov.

"My guys are already in there," the bald man replied.

"Fine. Just dig in and stay there."

Christov didn't need any more coaching before pressing his back to the wall and shuffling past the broken mirror. The Mud People may have seemed mindless, but the sight of the infected customer squirming on the jagged shards of glass after getting his leg blown was enough to make the rest of them hesitant to pass that line. When Christov scooted past the dressing rooms, the hobbled Mud Person snapped his head to one side and pulled himself over the razor-sharp glass.

"Dr. Lancroft don't wanna be interrupted!" Henry said through the Mud Person's slimy lips.

Henry nearly eviscerated himself to crawl over the glass. Kicking frantically at the possessed customer, Christov ran to his office and almost rattled the door off its hinges before the bouncers inside finally let him in.

Paige, Cole, and Rico formed a barrier between the Mud People and the remaining dancers. Somehow, Tristan and Kate had kept their wits about them long enough to bring two of the human girls away from the main room as well.

Cole could hear Shae's screaming, but couldn't quite place where it was coming from.

"Did they get out through the side exit?" Paige asked.

Tristan turned to place her hands flat upon the wall at one end of the hallway. "No," she replied. "They're in here."

Some of the Mud People grew brave enough to crawl over the shell Henry had left behind. The slaps upon the employees' door grew not only in number but in intensity.

"They'll break through before too long," Paige warned.

Rico double-checked his .45 and took steady aim at the broken mirror. "So will the cops."

"Christov won't call the police," Kate said.

Cole stood so everything was in front of him. "Some people got away from here, and they'll sure as hell call somebody!"

Tristan pressed one hand on the wall at waist level and reached up with her other to press a spot just over her head. Both panels clicked at the same time, allowing a portion of the wall to swing inward. She squeezed in through the opening as soon as it was big enough. "Shae!" she shouted.

As soon as Tristan was through, the Skinners and the other girls followed. All Rico had to do was give the secret door half a shove for it to slam shut and seal itself with whatever mechanism kept it from being discovered in the first place.

Lancroft and the blond nymph stood in a room that was a little less than half the size of the VIP area. It was divided by a curtain made of hundreds of strings of beads that hung from the ceiling. As he backed toward the beads, the bearded man held his wooden staff to Shae's neck. "Make her release the energy," he demanded as the weapon creaked to form a narrow blade directly under the blonde's chin, "or I kill this one."

Cole stepped forward with his spear held in front of him. "God damn it, can't you see we're Skinners too?"

"Yes," the old man said. "And you should be grateful for what I've done."

"Taking a woman hostage is nothing to be proud of."

"This isn't a woman," Lancroft said. "She's a thing wrapped in a package that's appealing to human eyes. A carnivorous plant that smells good to flies just so it can lure them in to be eaten. Since fools like you and Miss Strobel are content to hand our world over to the beasts, I've taken steps to rid it of the shapeshifters and Nymar."

"Excuse me?" Paige snapped.

Regarding her with the minimal amount of effort required to move his eyes and form a scowl, the old man said, "My work must be allowed to continue."

"Let her go and we'll talk about it," Cole said.

In the hallway, glass shattered and the Mud People flopped in through the remains of the mirror.

"You know what I want, bitch," Lancroft said through clenched teeth. When his grip around Shae's neck tightened, she closed her eyes and hummed a strangely beautiful tune. Less than a second after that sound drifted through the room, the beads hanging behind her started to glow.

It was then that Cole could see the designs scrawled upon every surface of the room. The ornate symbols looked as if they'd been scrawled by an artistic wild man. They also bore a striking resemblance to the markings he and Paige had found along the base of the outside of the club. Whatever they were, they pulsed with energy that he could feel rippling through his feet like ghostly fingers interrupting a body of smoke.

"You can't have her!" Tristan said as she lunged forward to grab Shae's arm.

Seizing the opportunity, Shae pulled away from the bearded man. When he tried to reclaim her, she spat a sound at him that caused a few of the symbols at his feet to spark like a shorted electrical outlet. And when Lancroft looked down at the spark, all three Skinners rushed him. Cole was closest, so he moved in first with an upward diagonal strike meant to knock the bladed staff from the bearded man's grasp.

Lancroft moved with impressive speed. He spun the staff in a tight circle, batted away Cole's attack, and had enough time to take a quick stab at Rico that would have sliced between his ribs if it hadn't been stopped by one of the leather sections of Rico's jacket. The elongated blade stuck into Half Breed leather and just started to cut through before Rico dropped an arm over the weapon and shifted his weight in an attempt to pull it away from Lancroft.

Once Rico moved to the side, Paige stepped in to swing her machete at the bearded man's shoulder. Lancroft dropped to one knee and cracked the other end of his staff against her wrist. The wood creaked as blood dripped from his palms, and a pair of thin branches snaked out to ensnare Paige's hand. When Rico tried once again to disarm the old man, the staff withered down to a single root that Lancroft easily pulled away.

Rather than focus on the weapon, Cole went straight to the source. He waited for Lancroft to look at one of the others before extending his arms so his spearhead was pressed against the bearded man's throat just beneath his chin. "Whatever you're doing," he warned, "stop it."

Lancroft froze but didn't seem alarmed. "You've made mistakes and been misled, but you're still Skinners. I've made you what you are, so I'm willing to see you through these confusing times."

"Funny how you wanna talk now that you're about to get dropped," Rico said.

With a simple clench of his fists, the old man willed the branches holding Paige to become sharper than razor wire and align with the arteries in her wrist. The other end of his weapon stretched into a single point that curled up to place a spike directly against Rico's jugular. "Do what I asked," the old man calmly said to the women huddled in the far corner, "or I'll kill all three of them."

Cole pressed his spear against the old man's neck. "Not before I give you an instant tracheotomy!"

Shaking his head so his beard brushed against spear, he said, "I've lived since this country was a New World, and have fought terrors that your generation of so-called hunters have dismissed as legend. I won't allow you to threaten me one . . . more . . . time."

And then Tristan started to sing.

She gave voice to a single tone that echoed within the room and through all of the looping symbols carved around her. When Shae lent her voice to the song, the symbols emitted a pulse of wispy green light that bent toward the curtain of beads, to be absorbed by them.

Showing his approval with a single nod, the old man took a step back and was gone.

The beads clattered against each other, shimmering with energy that flowed out to every symbol etched into the walls.

"What happened?" Paige asked. Her wrists were cut, but only in shallow slices that the razor-wire branches had left behind. Cole stood with his spear pointing at the beads, and

Rico wasn't quite ready to lower his chin after the living barb had come so close to impaling his neck. Turning to Tristan, Paige pointed her weapons at the nymph as if she was ready to swing at any target she could find. "What did you do? Where is he?"

"Gone," Tristan sighed.

"What the hell is this place? What happened to that son of a bitch?"

"He was sent away," Tristan replied. "It's an ancient ritual that allows us to cross from one temple to another."

"Why did you give in like that? We almost—"

"You were almost killed," Tristan interrupted. "And if you somehow found a way to hurt that man before he murdered at least two of you, Henry would have found a way to kill my sisters who are still being held captive."

"Then send us to wherever you sent him."

The nymph shook her head. "I can't. It takes energies that need to be replenished."

"Replenish them!"

Tristan placed a hand upon Shae's back and rubbed it soothingly. "It will take time. Go and rest. Come back tomorrow night and I can try to—"

"I don't want to hear *try*," Paige snapped. "Do what you've got to do and then—"

"Ease it back, Bloodhound," Rico said warily. "None of us are about to step into some damn radioactive beads before I know what the hell they are. Are those people outside still gonna knock this wall down?"

Placing her eye to a spot on the wall, Kate shook her head and replied, "The ones in the hall are curled up and . . . puking. Gross."

"Let's see what can be done for these folks," Rico continued. "You and Cole go rest up. I'll stay here and have a chat with these fine ladies because I sure ain't leaving before I know how that disappearing thing worked."

Paige let out a sigh as the adrenaline slowed its pace through her veins and the battering she'd taken over the last few minutes had a chance to seep in. "How long is it going to take to charge your batteries?"

Tristan touched a symbol that caused the door to swing open much smoother than when she'd activated the devices to get in. "I'd say twenty-four hours. That is, if we still have a place to conduct our business."

Cole stepped into the hall and found several people doubled over on the floor or leaning against a wall. Turning toward the bead room, he groaned. "Smells like a swamp exploded out here."

The door at the other end of the hall was pulled open and Blake staggered out. "Cops are on their way. One of the first bunch to bolt outta here must've called them."

Paige sighed. "You'd better call an ambulance too," she said. "Now that Henry's gone, most of these people should be all right, but we can't just send them home."

"You've seen this shit before?" the bouncer gasped.

"Yep. You don't want to know about the details, and," she stressed pointedly, "neither do the cops."

"Hell no, I don't wanna know the details," Blake said. "What the hell do we do with all these people?"

"When the cops and ambulances get here, tell them the truth," Cole said. "That they were infected with the Mud Flu. It's not like you'll be able to hide that part."

Although none of the Skinners could translate Christov's native language, the ferocity in his words made it clear he was ready to eat his own shotgun.

Chapter 20

Three days later

Immediately following their first encounter with the man calling himself Jonah Lancroft, the Skinners fully expected a veritable tsunami of excrement to hit St. Louis. The Mud Flu was already being called an epidemic by news sources that didn't even know the full story, and the occasional dead Nymar showing up in national coverage looking like a pile of burnt calamari didn't help matters. But the tsunami didn't come.

Since Henry had already found Ned's house, the Skinners all but abandoned it. Only Daniels and Ned remained, but they were either engrossed in research or accustomed to coming and going without drawing attention from the neighbors. The windows were all shut, which suited a Nymar and recluse just fine. Rico took it upon himself to act as Tristan's shadow and personal guard, while Cole and Paige settled into a hotel in South County.

After a day and a half, the two of them drove back to the club in Sauget. Windows were boarded, the neon sign was dark, and the front door was nailed shut. Cole ran up to knock, but spared his knuckles when he read the note from the Health Department stapled to the newly placed two-by-fours.

Bunn's Lounge was no more.

Since the markings at the base of the building had faded as if they'd never been there in the first place, Cole figured the room with the beaded curtain had been similarly wiped away. Before breaking the seal along with a ban from the Health Department, he called the man behind Bunn's.

"What the hell happened?" he asked.

"They shut me down!" Christov roared through the cell phone. "When the ambulance came to cart those people away, they see the mud and smell the sickness and see it is that damn flu and they shut me down!"

"I didn't see anything on the news about it yet," Cole offered hopefully.

"That's because there is still investigation," Christov replied. The angrier he got, the thicker his accent became. "One of the ones that died was the one I . . . well . . . you know."

"The one you shot?"

He was shushed so loudly that Cole thought static was pouring through a bad connection. When Christov spoke again, it was in a harsh whisper.

"Those sick people don't remember how that man lost his leg," Christov said. "The cops are blaming it on madness from that flu. They worry about more madness if people hear there was such a big outbreak, so they shut me down and threaten to prosecute me if I incite a panic. Oh dear Lord! I shouldn't have said outbreak on the phone. I should hang up now."

"Wait! What about that secret room? We need to use that place."

"Oh, you need to use that place? I need a *new* place. All that's left in Bunn's is some broken furniture and lots of mud. You need anything else, talk to Tristan. She will know whatever you want. I give you the number where she is." After rattling off the string of digits, he spat, "You call her. Don't call me again."

"Did the cops ask about us? Do they know everything that happened?"

"I don't know."

"Did they get to any of your security tapes?" Paige asked.

"Ah-ah," Christov snapped. "There are no security tapes,

understand? I am grateful for you saving my life, so I destroyed my whole office before any of those tapes are seen. After that, I cannot be bothered with you people any longer. I need to scrape together money to open a new club and times are—"

"Yeah, yeah," Cole sighed as he cut the connection. "Times are hard."

Dialing the new phone number while heading back to the car, he waited through several rings before being connected to a machine. He stuffed the phone into his pocket and told Paige, "The place is called The Emerald. It's not open for a few more hours."

"But it's after six."

"Fine. You wanted to keep a low profile after that fight, but let's forget that, drive down there and bust the door in. That shouldn't draw any attention to us or the nymphs working to pose as employees."

They took a drive down Lindbergh Boulevard, supposedly looking for stray Mongrels. Although they certainly watched the streets and waited for their scars to burn, Paige was too anxious to pay attention to anything. Cole knew there were plenty of things he could be doing on his laptop, many of which might go a long way to mend some bridges in Seattle, but he saw more use in staring out the Cav's broken windows on the off chance that they actually found something. Not only did they come up empty, but St. Louis itself seemed tired and worn-out. Traffic moved as if the heat was melting tires to the pavement, and the wind seemed unable to blow without a Mongrel to stir it. Nightfall helped turn the oppressive heat down from a hot, wet slap of stagnant humidity against his face into a lukewarm slap.

"You hungry?" Paige asked.

"For all we know, Pestilence has infected everyone," he pointed out. "Or, Henry can spread it just by projecting his thoughts or essence or whatever into anyone he chooses."

"Yeah?"

"And the guy behind it is a Skinner who can not only order Henry around, but fight like nobody I've ever seen."

"Yep."

"And you're thinking about food?"

"You know what's better than a good meal that you eat when you're really hungry?"

"What?" Cole sighed.

"A snack at the wrong time that has no redeemable qualities whatsoever." When she caught him looking over at her, Paige asked, "Who wants fried tacos stuffed with mystery meat?"

Half an hour later they were in their hotel room. A bag from Jack in the Box had been ripped open like a gutted deer and a dozen little grease-stained paper envelopes emblazoned with the word TACO lay scattered on the table. Paige sat in a chair with her feet propped upon the edge of the mattress, and Cole hunched over a pile of empty wrappers.

Without bothering to wipe the hot sauce from the corner of her mouth, she flipped open her cell phone and dialed a number. "Hey Rico. It's me. How are the nymphs coming along?" Rolling her eyes at whatever lewd comment Rico gave her, she asked, "Will they be able to help us or not?"

As she listened to Rico's report, Cole tore open another taco and went through a very strict ritual. The wrapper was spread open to form a plate. The fried shells were carefully pulled apart so as not to tear the whole thing in half. Then a hot sauce packet was ripped open at one corner and the bright red fluid was evenly distributed among the innards of the taco. The halves were closed and the good times commenced with a first bite at the lowermost corner. No matter what else was going on in the world, that simple process made everything seem okay.

"Forget about my arm," Paige said. "Have you talked to Daniels? . . . Uh-huh. Really? What's that mean?" She snapped her fingers and pointed to the last taco in the sack. When Cole tossed it to her, she tore open a hot sauce packet with her teeth, squirted some into the shell, and ate it straight out of the paper envelope.

"Barbarian," Cole muttered.

"No, I didn't seal the hotel room . . . Why not? Because that's a bunch of superstitious bullshit, that's why not. Paranormal is one thing. Supernatural is something too. Magic is bullshit . . . No, I don't know how Lancroft teleported, but there's gotta be an explanation. How long before Tristan is ready to go? . . . Tomorrow?" She sighed and flexed her right hand until her fingers were almost opening and closing at normal speed. "No. We're way across town, so you work on that and I'll check later . . . Okay. Yeah . . . Okay. 'Bye." She snapped the phone shut and tossed it onto the bed.

"What did he mean by sealing the room?" Cole asked.

"You remember all that writing on Ned's walls?"

"Yeah."

"There you go," Paige grunted. "It's the same language that was on the walls of Henry's room back at the reformatory. Rico still believes all those charms and runes and whatever else can keep evil at bay."

"Does it work?"

"It sure didn't work when Henry and those Mud People found Ned's house."

"Sure," Cole said, "but did any of them get inside?"

"No, because we kept them out the old-fashioned way."

"No offense, Paige, but we tend to get attacked in a lot of hotel rooms. Me especially. If there's a chance to cut down on that, I'm willing to draw some symbols on the walls."

"It's more than that," she explained. "It's a whole ritual involving paints, a new language, and precise patterns to focus some very unpredictable energies."

"But it works?"

After mulling that over while licking some taco sauce from her fingers, she admitted, "Every now and then. Most of the people who attempt it anymore aren't doing much more than writing 'Keep out' in seven languages on their windowsills. All that does is ruin the paint."

"What did Rico say about your arm?"

"Never mind that. I just need to wrap it up and learn to fight better one-handed."

"Great," Cole said while getting to his feet and brushing the chunks of taco shell off the front of his shirt. "Let's see what you've got for a new fighting style."

"We don't have time for that."

"All we've been doing for the last few days is drive around. How much more time do you need?"

"I fought pretty well at that club," she said. "If that's not enough, then screw it."

Recoiling as if he'd just been popped between the eyes, Cole asked, "What happened to the Paige Strobel that used to put me through my paces four times a day?" Getting nothing more from her than a shrug, he crossed his arms and said, "You want to be punished for screwing up? You got it. You've sentenced yourself to a whole lot of extra training to get back to where you were. Maybe you'll never get all the way back. Maybe you'll get to a whole other place."

"Like you have any fucking idea what you're talking about."

Stepping close enough to grab the arm of her chair and turn it so she was facing him, Cole looked her in the eyes and snarled, "I had a job. A *good* job. A job I loved. Now it's gone. I had a girlfriend. I had a great apartment. I had a god-damn monster-free life and it was fan-fucking-tastic! Well I don't have any of that stuff anymore. Some of it's changed, some is gone for good, and some is better than what I had before."

"It's not the same," she said as she quietly looked away. "I'm not the same. The only reason I got out of that club alive is because I had backup. I'm lucky I can steer a car. What if the next mistake I make kills me? What if it kills you?"

Cole gently placed the edge of his hand beneath her chin and said, "Then don't do that."

"I don't want to become like Ned."

"Then don't."

"It's not always that easy," she said.

"True. But sometimes it is. You want something to happen? Make it happen. If you can't do it right away, find a way. Even if it doesn't happen, at least you didn't just sit around whining about it."

Paige reached up to place both hands on his face. "Pretty third-rate stuff as far as advice goes, but it's nice to hear. Especially from you." Then she pulled him down some more and kissed him on the lips. "Now that you mention it," she said while pushing him back so she could get out of the chair, "there is something I've been meaning to make happen for a while now."

Sliding one hand around Cole's neck, she pressed against him and ran the tip of her tongue up along the base of his neck. He didn't waste a second before wrapping his arms around Paige and lifting her off the ground. Their next kiss was deeper and much longer than the first. All of the aches, pains, and worries that had filled him a few moments ago were forgotten as he allowed himself to do something that he'd imagined more times than he could count. Paige's body felt warmer than he'd anticipated and she hung on tighter than he could have hoped.

Dragging him down to the bed on top of her, she traced the lines of muscle on his shoulders and back that she'd help sculpt through the last several months of sparring. Cole placed one hand at the small of her back and moved the other up into her thick black hair. Paige arched her back, which prompted him to move his mouth down to taste the freckles spattered just above the curve of her breasts. When he tugged at her shirt, she squirmed out from under him and off the bed.

"What's wrong?" Cole asked.

"This heat is making me sweaty," she said while pulling her shirt up and over her head to toss it onto the floor. He'd seen her in a sports bra more than once, but this time his eyes burned trails across her skin.

Turning to face him, Paige unbuttoned her jeans and eased them over rounded hips. Her little black panties rolled down as the denim moved past them, but stopped just short of revealing the Promised Land. Smiling while reading everything going through his mind, she flipped her jeans away with one foot and peeled off her bra. As she began unbuckling his belt, Cole pulled his shirt off and tried to think if he was wearing any boxers that had a pattern or picture dopey enough to blow the mood. Paige bypassed that potential obstacle by pulling his jeans and boxers down at the same time. She then turned her back to him and asked, "Who gets the shower first? You or me?"

Cole kicked the jeans away as if they'd tried to bite his ankles and grabbed her by the hips. "If you think I'm letting you get away this time, you've got a whole other fight on the way."

She placed her hands on his as they eased her panties all the way down. Taking another half step forward, Cole pressed against the curve of her back. He was already hard enough to cut glass, and Paige slowly wriggled against him to see if she could possibly break that record. Before too long she did.

Stepping into a tub that was just large enough to comfortably fit one and a half people, they got a shower going and spent a few minutes beneath a spray of cool water. She twisted the knob to the warmer side as Cole rubbed a little square of complimentary soap against Paige's wet, naked body. When it was her turn, she rubbed the soap over his chest and across his shoulders. Paige rinsed off, handed the foaming bar back to him, and then turned to reach for a miniature plastic bottle of generic shampoo. "I know you're an ass man," she said, "but try to get the rest of me just as clean."

"I can try," he said as he started rubbing her hips. "But it might take a while."

Now that the initial tension had passed, Cole put his hands on Paige's shoulders and started to massage. She let her head roll forward while scrubbing the shampoo through her hair. After rinsing off, she placed her hands on either side of the showerhead and let the water flow down over her entire upper half. "That feels nice," she said.

"No," Cole replied as he pressed against the smooth curve of her backside and reached both hands around to cup her breasts. "*That* feels nice."

Shifting her hips to coax a bit more from his erection, she said, "It most certainly does."

Every inch of her was wet, soft, and warm. As his hands moved up and down her sides, Cole listened to Paige's breaths mingle with the spatter of water against the tub and walls. When he hit a certain little spot near the upper portion of her inner thigh, she let out a giggle that echoed through the bathroom. Her hair hung in two thick sections divided unevenly between her shoulders to expose a soft, rounded divot that Cole had never seen before. As he placed his lips on that impossibly silky skin, he moved his hands to the warmer, even silkier region between her legs.

Suddenly, Paige turned around and planted a kiss on him that drove Cole back against the shower stall. Her feet slipped in the soapy water and she tried to grab hold of his arm, but her right hand couldn't get there fast enough. He caught her just before she took a painful spill and held her while she let out a soft, embarrassed laugh.

When they kissed again, she chewed hungrily on his lower lip and writhed against him as her back was placed against the wall. Cole grasped at her thigh, so she propped that foot up onto the edge of the tub. Just as the hardness between his legs slipped into the softest softness he could imagine, Cole snapped his eyes open and said, "Um, hold on a second."

"What?" Paige breathed. "What, what, *what*?"

"Do you have any . . . protection?"

She pushed her head back to get a look at him. "Are you serious?"

"Yes. I mean . . ."

"Don't worry about that. All those serum injections sterilized us both a long time ago."

"Wh . . . huh?"

"Kidding. I've been fixed. I'm also starting to prune."

Paige reached for a towel as soon as she stepped out of the shower, but Cole wasn't going to let her get away from him. Drops of water trickled down her shoulders, tracing slippery lines between her breasts. He snatched the towel from her hand, threw it away, and let his hands roam freely. It had only been a few seconds, but she felt different to him. The water faded from her bare skin, allowing tight muscles to relax into smooth contours. When he tried to pull her over to the bed, she diverted him with a few playful shoves and then pushed him backward into a chair.

Cole's butt had barely hit the seat before Paige was straddling him. She grabbed onto the back of the chair with her right hand while using her left to explore his chest and stom-

ach. He couldn't decide what he liked more: feeling her or
watching her. The muscles of Paige's finely toned stomach
would have held his interest for hours if he hadn't been distracted by the touch of her hand wrapping around his erection and guiding it into her.

She pulled in a breath, shifted, and then exhaled as she
lowered herself onto him. Before he was all the way inside,
she placed her hand on Cole's shoulder and locked eyes with
him to watch an expectant smile grow into a relieved grin.
Her face showed a hint of surprise when he pushed up into
her a little more after she'd eased all the way down. After
that, Paige grabbed onto the back of the chair with both
hands and rocked back and forth on top of him.

Suddenly, Cole was very grateful for all the time he'd
spent learning how to steady his breathing. Paige's body
was strength in motion. Her muscles rippled beneath her
skin as she glided up and down in his lap. Placing his hands
upon her hips allowed him to slow her down or keep her
completely still as he pumped up into her. Not wanting to
rush to the finish line, he reached up to cup her breasts and
gently teased her rigid nipples as she ground slowly back
and forth.

Paige clenched her eyes shut and moaned appreciatively.
Sliding her hands down so her palms rested flat against his
stomach, she began thrusting her hips in stronger, more insistent motions. She rode him with purpose as sweat rolled
down the front of her naked body.

But Cole wasn't content to just sit there. He found a rhythm
of his own, ebbing when she flowed, pressing forward when
she fell back, until they were pressed tightly against one another. Before he could lift her up and carry her to the bed,
Paige buried her face in the spot where his neck and shoulder met. Her moans caught in her throat and her entire body
clenched around him. As she climaxed, her lips curled back
and she reflexively dug her teeth into his flesh.

It wasn't a hard enough bite to break the skin, but it would
certainly leave a mark. That little jolt of pain, however, was
more than enough to break through the steely discipline
that had allowed Cole to last this long. He stopped holding

back, held onto Paige and allowed her to sweep him over the edge.

When he caught his breath, Cole was glad he hadn't tried picking her up. He doubted he could lift his own ass out of that chair.

They did manage to get some sleep, but not much. When they stirred beneath the tussled sheets, the heavy curtains were drawn tight enough to keep out all but a trickle of lights from the parking lot.

"Are you awake?"

After a pause and a stretch, the response came. "Yeah."

"You don't know how much I needed this."

"I think I do."

"After all that's happened, it's good to have something to look forward to. Is that corny?"

"Yes." They shifted to face each other, arms and legs entangling within the fabric cocoon to draw their bodies closer. "But I know what you mean. Sometimes, you must think I'm just . . . well . . . I want to tell you how great it is that I found you. Or you found me. With all the stuff I've seen—now that *we've* seen—it's good to know there's something better than just more blood and more killing."

"Mmm-hmmm."

"I know it's sappy, but this is the best I've felt in a long time. Everything's different and I'm glad."

"Mmmmm. Me too."

"I think I'll wrap you up in the comforter and dump you out the window."

"Hmmmmm."

"Are you awake?"

This time the deep breaths didn't even try to form a word.

"Fine. Whatever."

Chapter 21

"After last month's events in Kansas City, are any measures too extreme to combat what's recently been called the worst outbreak of rabies in the past two centuries?"

The woman who asked that question did so from behind her anchor desk at a St. Louis television studio. Her short brown air was perfectly maintained and her hands were flattened nicely upon her prop desk. When she addressed the camera, she did so with the same seriousness she would have used to report the next world war.

"According to the Humane Society of Missouri, four dozen animal fatalities have been attributed to what is believed to be deliberate poisoning. Most of these slain animals have been found in or near Kansas City, but nearly half a dozen similar cases have sprouted up in the St. Louis metropolitan area, with several others cropping up around the country. While a few of the animals were similar to the dogs that terrorized Kansas City streets or viciously attacked several people across the nation over the last several weeks, the animals found locally were mostly feline. At this time it is unclear whether these large cats had escaped from a zoo, were part of an exotic private collection, or simply wandered in from the wild."

The camera panned over to a younger woman dressed in a navy blue suit. "Thanks, Katherine. In other news, two more business establishments in Sauget were shut down after reports of possible Mud Flu contagion. Earlier today, authorities issued a statement confirming the discovery of at least forty-six Mud Flu cases at an exotic dance club. Nine more people were treated in a residential section of the Central West End, and eighteen have been checked into hospitals over the last two days. While several people are in critical condition after what are being reported as incidents of panic relating to the flu, all other patients have since been allowed to return to their homes. Stay tuned to this channel for any updates regarding this and other stories."

Ned turned away from the television and took a long pull from his beer. The Keyhole Tavern was closed for the night, but he had become friendly with its owner after putting an end to a group of Nymar who tried using the place as their personal feeding ground. Since then he could stop by when the customers were gone and collect his thoughts amid the neon beer signs, retro video game cabinets, and blinking pinball machines. Headlights from a passing car were narrowed down to slivers thanks to yellowed blinds that had been drawn over the front window. When those same headlights swept over the front door, they cast the shadow of a figure on glass frosted in a way that had been stylish about fifty years ago. The figure on the other side of the door tapped on the glass with the knuckle of one finger.

"You got that?" the bartender asked from the back room.

Ned hauled himself off the stool and made his way to the door. "Yeah, I got it. I can lock up too. My friend and I just want to shoot the breeze."

"Sure. Whatever you like."

Moving fluidly in the near darkness, Ned skirted tables without disturbing any of the chairs stacked on them to flip the latch over the front door and head back to his seat. The man who stepped inside wore a tan jacket that extended an inch past his waist, and he had enough pockets to make a shoplifter drool with envy. He twisted the latch back into place using a scarred hand, walked to the bar in a few quiet strides, and propped the staff he'd been carrying against it.

"What happened, Jonah?" Ned asked. "This was supposed to be a way to clean up the storm that was kicked up in KC, not create a new one."

Lancroft's beard didn't have a single whisker that was too long or out of place. His eyes were cold and calm as he said, "The mess is getting cleaned up. Thanks to the pheromones from the nymphs I've harvested, the Half Breeds have been drawn to the Pestilence carriers quicker than we could have hoped. Even Mongrels drop dead within a few seconds after Pestilence gets into their system."

"And what about the Nymar? Every time one of those things pops, it's a goddamn spectacle."

"I could have spread Pestilence a lot quicker using those temples, but things didn't turn out that way. It's worked out for the better, though. My original creation has mutated like any other virus strain. Its effect on the Nymar has given me some ideas as to how to modify the next batch."

Lowering his voice to a fierce whisper, Ned snarled, "That creature of yours is running wild. It found my home. It killed an innocent boy."

"Henry wasn't after you. He has some history with your student, but he is also a necessary part of the equation. Without the Mind Singer—"

"See, that's what I don't like," Ned snapped as he twisted around to stab a finger in Lancroft's direction. "Right there. Only the shapeshifters call that thing Mind Singer. When I agreed to work with you, it was to make a move that had to be made. I don't give a damn if you're the real Jonah Lancroft or not. The way I see it, any man who does what we do against these monsters has gotta have a screw loose. You wanna be called Lancroft? That's fine. I knew a guy down in Florida who thought he was St. George the Dragon Slayer. He was a hell of a good Skinner, so I called him George and fought alongside him. You came to me with this notion to poison the well, so to speak, and it seemed like a shitty way to fix an even shittier situation. A minimum of folks would get hurt in exchange for Half Breeds to be wiped out."

"And I've held up that end of the bargain," Lancroft pointed out.

"Yes you did. Since the people comin' down with this

Mud Flu seem to be getting better, I can let a lot of this pass. But I will not stand by and let you attack other Skinners. We're all in the same fight here!"

Lancroft reached into one of his pockets for a metal flask and set it on the bar, where an inscription on the flask of flowing symbols caught the glow of tired neon. "If those three had come to me earlier, I could have spoken to them the way I've spoken to you. When they arrived, they'd already been swayed by the nymphs. Your students even took orders from one among them with roots that go much deeper than the other girls."

"From what I hear, you were the one to get the fight rolling."

"They were not in a bargaining frame of mind."

"Well they probably wouldn't have liked your goddamn proposal since it's turned into an epidemic."

"Don't be so dramatic," Lancroft said. "You're starting to sound like those people on the news, crying because they had a sore throat that lasted for a few days. The Mud Flu is messy, but not fatal."

"Not unless you're one of the ones killed by a Half Breed."

Lancroft shrugged and pushed the flask toward Ned. "Some had to be targeted so numerous others could be spared. Because of those sacrifices, there is hardly a Half Breed population anymore, and once I spread the nymph pheromones, the Nymar population will take an even larger hit."

"Those pheromones are too potent. They don't just attract the Nymar like we thought. They whip them into a frenzy. When they get a whiff of that stuff, Nymar don't just feed, they tear people apart. I've seen it. And the Half Breeds are slaughtering more than just the folks that were sprayed with that nymph scent."

"The wretches are strong-willed if nothing else. By any account, it's worth some blood being spilled if it rids our world of such abominations."

"They'll come back," Ned grumbled. "Half Breeds always do, and Nymar are worse. What if they get an immunity to Pestilence? What if they're like cockroaches that can't be poisoned by anything? You ever think of that?"

"By the time they adapt, I will have created a new strain. It's the natural cycle between predator and prey."

Picking up the flask, Ned ran his fingers over the cool metal and held it closer to his good eye. The symbols engraved on it were too large and irregular to be letters, but not detailed enough to be pictures. "What is this?"

"It's called Memory Water. I told you I'd try to do something about your injury in exchange for your help."

Ned set the flask down. "Keep it. We're through."

Smiling warmly through his silver beard, Lancroft signaled to the bartender, who'd just returned, and ordered a dark lager. "You've done more than enough to earn it," he told Ned. "Besides, I'm a man of my word." Leaning over to him, he added, "How do you think I've stayed so healthy for the last couple of hundred years?"

"Did you make this stuff?" Ned asked as he reached out to touch the flask.

"No. It's been around for a long time. Now that your students have grown so close to the nymphs, they'll probably find out about it sooner or later."

Ned shook his head slowly at first, but quickly built up steam. "I been gettin' along fine as I am." He rapped his knuckles against the bar and pointed at a bottle of mid-grade vodka. As the bartender poured some into a shot glass, Ned grumbled, "All I do anymore is stroll around this city and chase off a few Nymar here and there."

"Maybe you should take a more active role. Skinners need to learn from experienced trackers instead of splicing videos for the Internet. Men like us are needed to cut straight to the root of the problem and make sure the next batch does the same."

Ned grunted. "The public barely even knows there is a problem."

Lancroft chuckled and sipped from his pint glass. "True enough, my friend. Back home, all I meet are Skinners who would rather go into business with creatures that don't have a place on God's green earth."

"Where did you say you were from? Philadelphia?"

"That's right. Did you know some Nymar back East want

to become Skinners? They speak with forked tongues while dressing like whores or dandies. Where the hell did these youngsters get the impression devils like that could be trusted?"

Nodding as if he'd just heard his own thoughts put into words, Ned raised his drink and knocked it against Lancroft's glass. "Traditionalist, huh? That's nice to hear. Makes me feel like I ain't the only one anyway.

"The monsters fear us because they don't fully understand us. It's an old strategy, but a very, very good one. We can't pick and choose which prey to hunt either. That decision has already been made for us by the natural order. Working with Nymar, trusting outside groups like those crackpot ghost chasers, those are the sorts of things that will undo us."

"Welcome to the modern world."

"Keep it," Lancroft sighed. "I've had my fill."

Surrounded by the comforting dimness of the bar and the warbly prerecorded voices of pinball machines, Ned savored the slow burn of the vodka easing through his system. "You'd best pull up your stakes and burn whatever's left of Pestilence," he said. "Otherwise, those youngsters of mine will burn you along with it."

Lancroft placed both hands on the bar. "If we're parting ways, let's do it amicably. One more drink to celebrate a fine, albeit short, partnership."

Taking his cue, the bartender waddled over to collect their glasses. He filled them and set them in front of the only two customers in the place.

"After all that's happened," Ned said, "another snort wouldn't be such a bad idea." He took his glass, doffed it like a cap, and knocked it back in one swig. The liquid inside tasted clean and cool. It had the burn of vodka, but a salty sweetness that didn't belong. "This ain't the usual brand."

The bartender took a step back, cocked his head to one side and silently wiped at a dark trickle that ran from the corner of his mouth. In his hand was Lancroft's flask.

"What the hell is this?" Ned snarled while throwing the glass away and reaching for his cane.

"A gift from the fairer sex," Lancroft mused. "Memory Water."

"I told you I didn't want it!" Shifting an angry glare to the bartender, he asked, "What the hell did you do, Tom? Did you spike my drink? Did you?"

The bartender pressed his lips together as if suppressing a laugh. The trickle of dark fluid along his chin turned into a gush when he opened his mouth and violently snapped his head to one side.

"Get out of him!" Ned roared. When he tried to rush around the bar, Lancroft's staff blocked his path like a cement post.

"Henry's learned to do so much with his gift. But only recently has he grasped the notion of subtlety."

Something twitched in Ned's eye that was different than the usual pain. He blinked and resisted the urge to touch his face so he could keep both hands ready to attack or defend. The longer he stood there, the more the bar around him shifted into focus.

"Tastes good, doesn't it?" Lancroft asked. "Makes you feel as strong as you did when you could still be out there fighting the darkness. Back when something as idealistic as that actually seemed possible."

"What's happened to me?" Even as he asked that, Ned looked around at the bar he thought he knew like the back of his hand. Instead of dimming the harsh glare of the outside world, his sunglasses now impeded him. Ripping them off allowed him to discover shapes in the shadows, coasters on the tables, writing on the beer taps, colorful cushions on the chairs. "Is this a healing serum?"

"Not as such. It's essence wrung from the nymphs. Since you helped me find so many of the elusive little whores, it's only fair you taste their nectar."

Ned gripped his cane and looked away from the bartender. It was too late for him now.

"There used to be a time when Skinners opposed all creatures that fell outside the natural order and put whatever gifts they had to proper use," Lancroft said. "Now, they are making deals with Nymar and handing over entire cities to Mongrels! I have restored your vision, just as I can restore the ones who don't bounce back from the Mud Flu."

"The plan was to take out the Half Breeds. That's done. It's over!"

Shaking his head solemnly, Lancroft said, "Are you *still* blind? The Book of Luke told us there would be pestilence, fearful sights and great signs from heaven. We've seen more than our share of fearful sights. We've seen Pestilence. Now we see the great sign. My toxin has evolved into something greater than we could have hoped. It kills Nymar and other shapeshifters alike, and all we need to do is stand back to let it run its course."

"Stop quoting scripture like it means anything to you," Ned snarled. "You just want an excuse from on high to do what you please. Those Half Breeds were mad dogs, and poisoning them was a good way to put 'em down. Not all Nymar are killers!"

"Once the bloodsuckers start feeding on infected people, there won't be any more Nymar. And since I've observed how crazy the scent of nymph blood drives them, I can make them feed on whoever I choose."

"And who will that be? Who will be handed over to be torn apart?"

"Every human that dies from the new strain will take at least one Nymar with them into eternity," Lancroft replied. "There will always be plenty more humans to replenish the species, while Nymar will simply become the myth that everyone already thinks they are."

Blood poured from Ned's hands when he gripped the handle of his cane just as they had when he'd first learned to use his weapon. For years it had barely trickled when the scars were punctured, but now the thorns dug through thick, sensitive flesh.

"So you truly want to end our partnership?" Lancroft asked. "After I restored your sight, I would have thought you'd be convinced of how far my research has come. Today's Skinners have gone astray. The good ones need to be found and the rest need to be flushed away. I have resources and plenty of time to put them to use, but there is only so much I can do on my own."

"Pestilence will purify the fallen," the bartender hissed. "Pestilencewillpurifythefallen."

"Yes, Henry," Lancroft said patiently. "But we're speaking now." Once the bartender crouched low and backed into the nearest corner, Lancroft whispered, "I've been around since the early days when people had their eyes open and noticed things like empty graves, black auras, and shapes prowling the dark. They called me a quack back then, but Skinners maintained their resolve and kept fighting." Slamming his open hand on the bar, he said, "No town was handed over to the Nymar just to make our battle easier! Not even the smallest village would have been given to a pack of Mongrels! Not *ever*! It wasn't long ago that you agreed with me."

Ned's hands were slick with blood and pain flickered across his twitching face as his cane sluggishly gained a sharpened tip. "I agree something needed to be done after what happened in Kansas City. If those Half Breeds had been allowed to spread, they might have swept through the whole country."

"That was from one Full Blood." Holding up a finger to illustrate his point, Lancroft bellowed, "One wild stray. Thanks to us, the only Half Breeds you see on television or anywhere else are dead ones. We have Pestilence to thank for that."

"But humans are the ones that are infected," Ned reminded him.

Lancroft took his flask from Henry and tucked it into one of his jacket pockets. From another pocket, he removed a brass, richly engraved cigar case containing fragrant, hand-rolled cheroots. Lancroft selected one, struck a match against the rough side of the antique case, touched the flame to his cheroot and said, "Those that make the sacrifice will be doing it for the good of their species."

"You're full of shit." Throwing a disgusted look at the bartender's filthy shell, Ned said, "For all the preaching you do about Skinners making deals with monsters, you sure don't seem to mind running with that one."

"He's not my partner. He's a subject. Besides, you'd be amazed how much we can learn from someone like Henry."

Back in his corner, the bartender perked up and watched the other two like a dog who'd just caught a whiff of fresh cold cuts.

"Even a fiend like Misonyk," Lancroft added while puffing the cheroot. "When he was chained and bleeding like the stuck pig he was, he evolved. He forced Henry to evolve. It was really quite a beautiful thing."

Ned blinked several times. So far it had taken an effort to keep from smiling at the glorious sights flooding in through his tingling eyes. "I don't know what you're talking about."

"Maybe you don't. Maybe I'll explain it all to you. That depends on how quickly you hand over the ones who don't uphold their duties as Skinners. The new fellow, Cole, has promise. That woman is an able fighter, but she is too quick to make a deal with the wrong species. Bring them both to me tomorrow. It's the least you can do considering the gift I gave you."

The hatred rolling through Ned's chest wasn't enough to eclipse the divinely subtle shift of light upon the rounded glasses and colored bottles behind the bar. Not even the pain in his hands or his cane's stubborn refusal to shift any faster were enough to sully the joy he tried so desperately to hide. Shoving all of that aside, he forced his will into the sluggish weapon. "Put an end to this Pestilence business. We were wrong to think killing people to take out those Half Breeds was nothing but acceptable losses. Can't you see that?"

Lancroft grabbed his staff as if he had every intention of driving it through the floor. "Don't you dare preach to me, boy! I've killed more unnatural trash than you and everyone you know combined. There are breeds of shapeshifters that are *extinct* because of me."

"Last chance," Ned warned. "Pestilence must have an antidote. Give it to me."

The answer he received was a quick slash from the long, slender blade at the end of Lancroft's staff. Ned blocked the swing with a quickly upraised cane, stopping the other weapon less than an inch from his face.

Nodding, Lancroft said, "That's the spirit I was looking for. Skinners are meant to fight. We don't deal and we don't give one inch of ground to our enemies."

Stepping back into a lower stance, Ned raised his cane. The hook-shaped handle hadn't shifted as much as he would have liked, but it was more than sharp enough to eviscerate the other Skinner. The two weapons rattled against each other in a flurry of blocks and parries that ended with Ned swinging the cane's pointed lower end at the other man's face level.

Lancroft ducked and followed through with a sweeping blow that connected with Ned's ankle. When Ned fell onto his back, Lancroft drove the staff's blade straight down toward his chest.

Pushing off with one foot, Ned rolled away so the incoming blade dug into the floor. He kicked the weapon out from under Lancroft and then rapped his cane against the nerve running down the side of his leg. Lancroft didn't fall, but needed a moment to collect himself. Ned took that opportunity to scramble to his feet. Another of his slashing attempts was knocked away, so he thumped the handle of his cane against the hardened muscle of Lancroft's stomach. By the time Ned brought the cane up toward the other man's jaw, he'd added a row of short spikes to the curved strip of wood.

Lancroft leaned back and away to avoid the potentially disfiguring blow, which wasn't enough to keep one of the spikes from dragging through the side of his chin. He reshaped his weapon into a shorter double-bladed version and swung at Ned's throat. When the cane blocked the upper blade, he bent the staff in the middle like a large stick of rubber so the lower one could slice across Ned's stomach.

Ned grasped his midsection and backed away, angling his cane to cover his retreat. When he looked toward Henry's corner, he found the Mind Singer crouched on all fours, watching intently.

"What's the matter, Ned?" Lancroft asked. "Not feeling the cool rush of serum in your veins? That scratch I gave you isn't closing up like it should?"

It had been a while since Ned had actually been injured in a fight. Even so, the first cuts he'd been dealt shouldn't have remained open so long. There was the possibility that he simply hadn't injected enough serum to maintain the proper level in his body, but he didn't have time to think it over at length. He willed the end of his cane to flatten into a short sword, which he twirled around his body like a propeller.

Lancroft held his staff in the middle and curved its ends around to form a single oval-shaped blade. The new weapon moved like an extension of his arm, meeting every pass of the whirling cane with a burst of sparks. After deflecting a particularly strong assault, Ned leaned in and lowered his weapon so the cane caught Lancroft on the shoulder.

It was a deep cut. Ned's eyesight was good enough to see that much. He could also see the flow of blood lessen to a trickle before being stanched completely. Spotting an unprotected spot near Lancroft's hip, Ned feinted high and then stabbed low. Not only were both attacks defended with ease, but the other man tagged Ned with two quick cuts. One high. One low.

"It's the Memory Water, Ned. That's why I had to modify the stuff for myself. The nymphs call it that because it returns your body to an earlier state, when you were healthier or before illness had a chance to seep in. It brings you back to younger days, before you lost your eyesight or injected all of that serum into your blood."

When Ned lashed out with his cane, Lancroft batted it away and then stepped in to open a deep gash between two of his ribs with a quick horizontal slice. Allowing his hand to slide within the oval, he whipped it around to cut once more through the same wound. Without clothes, skin, or the outer layers of meat in its way, the blade scraped against vertebrae before coming out again.

Ned reacted more to the impact of the hits than the cuts themselves. He stepped back, refusing to lower the cane even though he needed it just to prop him up.

"At least you're a fighter," Lancroft said while knocking aside his trembling final stab. "Rico seems like a fighter as well. Maybe he's the one I need to speak to."

Blood poured from Ned's wound, blurring the vision he'd so recently regained. His skin was becoming cold and clammy. As a Skinner, he'd felt pain, but not such weakness. Not since the first Mongrel—

His thought process was cut short along with his hamstring by the next cut from Lancroft's circular blade. After losing so much blood, he didn't even feel the impact of his body against the floor. Lancroft stepped over him, placed his foot upon Ned's chest and spun his weapon in a quick slash that cut Ned's throat all the way down to the vertebrae.

"Dr. Lancroft, can I eat now?" Henry asked while eyeing Ned's body. "I'm so hungry. Sohungrysohungry."

Stooping to pick up Ned's cane, Lancroft said, "This man died like a Skinner and you won't even think about desecrating him. Understand me?"

The bartender's head bobbed up and down while he backed into a corner.

Chapter 22

The morning news was filled with reports of more rabid dogs turning up dead all across the Midwest. Cole scanned dozens of other headlines and watched video clips on his laptop while Paige went through a new exercise regimen outside the bathroom in the space formerly occupied by luggage racks and a chair.

"See?" he said as he scrolled through a batch of e-mails, none of which had been sent by Jason or anyone else at Digital Dreamers. "All you needed to get going again was some sweet—"

"Hold on," Paige snapped. Wielding a baton in each hand, she stood in a horse stance with her feet planted far apart, squatting as if in a saddle. Cole liked to call it the Groin Pull Special and he avoided it whenever possible. Staring straight ahead while flipping a weapon in a series of swift movements, she said, "Come over here and finish that sentence."

Grateful to hear his phone ring, Cole politely declined the chance to get his newly energized undercarriage batted into his stomach. He picked up the phone, checked the caller ID, and tapped the Answer button using a set of motions that was more deeply engrained than any fighting technique. "What's up, Ned?"

"Not Ned," the voice on the other end squeaked. "It's Daniels."

"Oh, you're just calling from Ned's phone. What's going on?"

"How quickly can you get here? I've got something you'll want to see."

The hotel wasn't the best, but it served free breakfast, and a good one at that. Not only were there bagels and doughnuts, but a small buffet with heated pans of scrambled eggs and sausage patties. Cole and Paige put together a few obscenely large sandwiches, threw lids onto their cups of coffee, and were out the door. They'd dawdled just long enough to avoid getting stuck in traffic and made it to the Central West End in good time. Ned's section of Kensington Avenue was quiet, and the only thing waiting for them was a little business card wedged between the screen door and frame.

Paige plucked the card out, examined it for two seconds, then flipped it around so Cole could see the gold badge embossed next to the name of the detective who'd left it there. "Cops," she groaned. "Probably asking about Henry's visit."

"You should probably call them," Cole said. "Or they'll just keep coming back."

"Great idea. You do it."

Before he could protest, the card was stuffed down the front of his shirt and Paige was knocking on the door.

The steps thumping within the house were so loud that both Skinners reflexively reached for their weapons. Even when Daniels pulled open the door in a huff, neither of them were ready to lower their guard. "You're here!" the Nymar said. "Excellent!"

"Is everything all right?" Paige asked tentatively.

"Of course."

"Where's Ned?"

"He stepped out last night and hasn't come back. He does that a lot."

When Cole walked into the house, he took a breath and immediately regretted it. Although the musty smell of all those bookshelves and old knickknacks had a certain charm, the scent did not blend well with the pungent mix of burnt chemicals, decaying carcass, and body odor. "Could you crack a window before I die?" Cole gasped.

Paige already had her hand over her mouth when she added, "Better yet, take a shower. Ned may be cheap, but he's got running water."

Daniels placed his hand flat on his head and rubbed his scalp nervously. The tendrils beneath his skin went from looking like a toupee parted down the middle to one that was parted along the right side. "I don't like showers."

"Is that some sort of Nymar thing?" Cole asked.

"No," he replied as he lowered his hand and sniffed his fingers. "It's an I don't like to get wet thing. Considering how hard I've been working without any help or a *meal*, you two should be more grateful. Instead, you leave me in this house all by myself."

Working her way around the perimeter of the house to open all the windows she could, Paige sighed, "So what's the big news?"

Racing to a small table next to an overstuffed sofa in the next room, Daniels took something from a familiar case. He approached Cole wearing the same excited grin that practically jumped off his face. "Give me your arm, big man."

Seeing the electric tattooing machine in the Nymar's hand, Cole shook his head fiercely. "Oh no you don't. I thought you abandoned that tattoo project."

"I don't abandon anything. I fix it. Just give me your arm."

"So I can be the first test subject for this new batch of ink? Hell no!"

Holding up his left arm, Daniels showed Cole a design that looked like a small curved T etched a few inches above the crease of his elbow. He then backed into the kitchen and started running. The Nymar's first few steps were as heavy and slow as anyone might expect from a guy his size, but the ones after that sent him past Cole, into the next room, through the kitchen and back again with the speed of a Half Breed that had nearly hit its stride. When he came to a stop, Daniels walked forward to hold out his forearm again. All that remained of the T was a wavy upper bar. "You aren't the first test subject."

"Holy crap!" Paige said as she rushed forward to grab Daniels's arm. "You got it to work?"

"It's not exactly like you imagined, but yes. I broke the shapeshifter enzymes down to their most basic elements and let them flow. While there aren't as many enhancements as we'd hoped for, there's heightened speed and a little bit of strength. With the Blood Blade fragments acting as a colloid, the scaled-back mixture does its job while bonding to the fragments instead of directly to any living tissue."

"So how long does it last?" she asked.

"As long as the ink holds up." Showing the fragment of a design on his forearm, Daniels explained, "This used to be the symbol for pi. I did a few laps around the room before you arrived, which burned most of it off, and what you saw just now almost drained the rest of it. You won't be anywhere near the power of a shapeshifter, but it should pump you up pretty good before a fight."

Paige touched the tattoo fragment tentatively. "I wish you would have told me before you tested this on yourself."

"You would have just told me not to."

"Damn right I would."

Shaking out of the tender moment, Daniels said, "Most of the hard work was done while I was in Kansas City with you two. I took a lot of notes, but there are some pivotal ingredients among Ned's supplies. Hopefully he won't mind me taking some of those."

"So when can we use this stuff?" she asked.

Daniels walked back to the staircase and said, "I made a bunch of small test doses of varying consistencies. Now that I know which one works, I can mix the rest to the proper level and type up a recipe card for your files."

"What about that other thing?" Cole asked.

"You mean the improved varnish for your weapons?" Daniels asked. He ran into the kitchen with just enough of his tattoo left to send him skidding across the linoleum. Despite the near fall, he was beaming proudly when he returned to the dining room to set a glass casserole dish on a square table amid some cereal boxes and a few square metal pans. "Without worrying about living material being damaged or one type of organism infecting another, it was a simple matter of figuring out what would form the best cohesion between the blade fragments and the varnish you use. It turns out that—" Abruptly, Daniels recoiled as if he'd been jabbed in the temple with a knitting needle. He staggered to one side, pressed a hand to his head, and would have fallen over if Cole hadn't rushed to catch him.

"You all right?" he asked.

When Daniels looked around at them, he seemed more embarrassed than dizzy. "It's been a while since I fed."

"Maybe we can bring you something," Paige offered.

"Or someone?" the Nymar asked. "There's always pizza delivery." Too excited to be sidetracked, he pulled himself together and went to the table.

Sensing Cole's empathy with the fellow science geek, Paige looked over to him and explained, "Nymar can go for almost two weeks without feeding. Especially if they're on a diet as steady and consistent as someone who lives with a girl who doesn't mind letting someone nibble on them. By the way, have you had time to call Sally?"

The only way for Daniels to look any guiltier was if his hand was actually trapped within a cookie jar. "Yes."

"And do you honestly need to have one of us take you by the hand and make sure you're feeding in an unobtrusive spot so you won't—"

"No! I'm just a little hungry, okay?"

Paige smiled victoriously and let it drop.

Cole approached the table to get a closer look at the experiment in progress. The large aluminum pan was the kind used for paint, and it currently had a thin layer of a silver-tinted watery substance at the bottom. Instead of a roller, a broken baseball bat lay half in the stuff. "I'm guessing this is either the new Blood Blade varnish or a secret weapon for the Cardinals."

"The former," Daniels replied. "There's still some wrinkles to iron out, but it's ready for you to use."

"You sure?" Paige asked as she extended her aching right arm. "I'm a little weary when it comes to wrinkles."

"If you recall, I never said that first batch of ink was ready to use."

"Fair enough."

Despite its watery appearance, the stuff had the consistency of gelatin. Cole dipped the end of his spear into it and nearly dribbled some onto the table. Judging by the metallic spatters already on the table and wall, Daniels hadn't been so cautious. "Ned's going to kill you when he sees this mess."

"Wait until you see the basement," Daniels groaned. "That's where I test-fired the silver bullets."

Paige's laugh was a quick snort.

"Silver bullets?" Cole asked. Then he looked down at the pan and lit up like the proverbial holiday greenery. "That's perfect! Dip some rounds into this stuff and—"

"And," Daniels cut in, "you get a mess on the walls as the coating flies off at approximately 1,065 feet per second."

"But—"

Silencing Cole with a quickly raised hand, the Nymar said, "It won't stick to lead. I've got a lot of irons in the fire, so I'll work on that one some other time."

"What about Pestilence?" Paige asked calmly. "Please tell me you haven't forgotten about that."

"No, I haven't forgotten. After everything you told me regarding the Mud People at that club," Daniels reported in a voice that quickly built to his previous levels of excitement, "I would say my previous deductions were correct. Since I have the infection, but not the actual flu, I was able to isolate the abnormality in my blood. See, Nymar blood is a very simple solution compared to human plasma." Seeing the impatience building on Paige's face, he skipped to the next section of his presentation. "I'm mostly certain that the bacteria infecting me and, I assume, most Nymar, originated from a fungus native to what is now called Ecuador."

"Now called Ecuador?" Cole said. "So it's in Ecuador."

"Not anymore," Daniels replied. "It's supposed to be extinct. Wiped out by modern contaminants, deforestation, or just died out the way some plants or animals die out. One of Ned's friends from the hospital helped me isolate it, and there was an obscure record of it on one of my normal research—"

"So this fungus causes Mud Flu," Paige cut in.

"Yes, but not as we now know it. There are archived accounts from explorers who'd made contact with descendants of the Mayans who reported seeing members of their party display symptoms like the Mud Flu. I figure that fungus was mixed with another ingredient to produce the Mud Flu as we see it today. This muddy residue is toxic to shapeshifters and can potentially cause a most unpleasant death for Nymar, as demonstrated by our late friend Peter Walsh. Things got really interesting when I tested the substance from one of those neighbors who tried to break in a little while ago."

"When did you get a sample from them?" Paige asked.

The guilty look on Daniels's face returned. "I snuck out when the paramedics were here. There was so much confusion that nobody noticed."

"Go on," she said.

"The mud on those people had something else in it," Daniels said. "It's something I think may even be produced within the human body by glands similar to the ones that produce endorphins or other hormones, but it would take some extraordinary activity in the brain to produce it."

"What about the psychic projection of a crazy Full Blood?" Cole asked.

Looking to be genuinely impressed by the deduction, Daniels said, "Yes! The most dangerous form of the Mud Flu is therefore a *three* part compound with the fungal base, the mud from those who were infected, and the unique hormones resulting from the presence of the entity known as Mind Singer." After saying that, he let out a breath and sat down in one of the chairs next to the square table. He looked as spent as Cole felt after his night with Paige, and almost as happy.

"Did you come up with a cure?" she asked.

The happiness on Daniels's face dropped away. "I came up with all of that and you want *more*? Do you know how little I'm working with here? Do you know how much research I did to connect all of this data with such limited laboratory resources?"

"Ned's got more equipment scattered in this house than some small forensics departments," she said. "And I know you well enough to be pretty sure you've been through every inch of this place whether Ned knew about it or not. Plus," she added with a confident nod, "you're a smart guy. That's why I work with you."

Letting out a ragged breath, Daniels said, "I'll work on it but can't guarantee anything."

"Great, now where the hell is Ned?"

"He never tells me where he goes," Daniels said. "Always in and out with that guy. It's his house, so what was I going to do about it?"

Paige dropped to one knee and pulled open a cabinet that was a facade for a small refrigerator locked with a digital mechanism. "Stubborn old man's probably on patrol," she said while tapping a number onto the fridge's keypad. "Look on the wall near the phone, Cole. That's where he'd leave a note."

Cole made his way across the room to a small alcove that was just big enough to hold one shelf. A phone rested on top of an answering machine that belonged on display with the other antiques. It was a touch-tone made to look like a rotary dial, and no lights were blinking on the machine. When he returned to the kitchen, Paige was taking a plastic eye-drop bottle from the fridge. "Nada," he reported.

"Then I'm calling him," she said while flipping her phone open. The longer it rang, the more she shook her head. Too anxious to bother with voice mail, she asked, "Where's that card?"

"The one from the cops?" Cole asked. "I've got it."

She extended her hand to him and said, "Hand it over. Maybe one of these dumb shits is forcing Ned to answer a bunch of stupid questions."

"Umm, maybe I should call the number," Cole said.

"Then call it! I'll give our weapons a dip in this stuff. Didn't you hear anyone knocking when they left the card, Daniels?"

"Sure. On top of everything else you want me to do, I should answer the door *and* take messages."

Cole was more than happy to hand over his spear just to give Paige something else to do. She piled her weapons on top of his and grabbed a rag to dip into the silvery mixture in the paint pan.

The name on the card was Detective Tracey Shin, and she picked up her phone after one ring.

"Hi, my name's Cole Warnecki. I found one of your cards on my door, so I figured I should call."

Detective Shin spoke in an even, professional tone, sounded somewhere in her late thirties or early forties, and was curt without being rude. "What was the name again?" she asked while flipping through papers on her end of the line.

"Cole Warnecki. I'm a friend of Ned Post's. It was his house where I found your card."

The rummaging stopped. "Oh. When was the last time you saw Mr. Post?"

"A day or two ago. Why?"

"What's your relation to him?"

"I'm a friend." Cole's stomach clenched and a cold sweat threatened to break from his forehead. Paige sat at the table, silently prompting him for details.

"Does Mr. Post have any immediate family?" Detective Shin asked.

"Not that I know of. What's wrong?"

After clearing her throat, Shin said, "I'm sorry, Mr. Warnecki, but Mr. Post is dead."

"Wh-What happened to him?"

"I'd like to talk to you about that in person if I could. Can you come down to the station?"

"Tell me what happened first," Cole insisted.

The detective's voice shifted subtly, which made it seem more like she was an actual person instead of a voice behind a badge. "Mr. Post's remains were found at a bar in U City along with the bar's owner. It's looking like there was a robbery."

"So he's . . . dead?"

Hearing that, Paige jumped up from her chair fast enough to hit the table and splash some of the silver water onto the floor.

"I'd really like you to come and talk to me before I give any more details over the phone. Mr. Post was already in our system due to some minor weapons charges, so we've made an identification, but we'd like you to verify it. There are also some reports that need to be filed, and if there are any immediate family members—"

"Where was he found?" Paige asked.

Covering the phone's speaker, Cole whispered, "Some bar in U City?"

She nodded and left the kitchen.

"How soon can you get here, Mr. Warnecki?" Detective Shin asked.

"I'll leave right now. Where's the station?"

She gave him the address and expressed her condolences, but Cole didn't accept them with more than a few grunts as he scribbled the important information on the closest pad he could find. He hung up, nodded at Daniels's stunned face and went after Paige. He expected to walk into a meltdown, but only found her standing in the living room with her arms crossed and her eyes fixed upon one of the house's many shelves.

"I'll go to the cops and see what they know," Cole offered. "Maybe it's not even him."

"Find out as much as you can, and if you run into any trouble, call me. If they won't let you call me, call Stanley Velasco. You have his number?"

"Yeah. It's in my phone."

"If Rico calls, don't tell him anything. Don't even answer the phone. Let me tell him." She wrapped her fingers around the eyedropper bottle as if she would never let it go. "Ned used to go to a bar in U City called the Keyhole Tavern. I know where it is. Rico and I will check it out."

Now that he'd stood with her for a few moments, Cole could tell she wasn't just staring at the bookshelf. Paige was looking down at the cement frog that sat on the edge with its legs crossed and hanging over the side. It was one of the most putrid pieces of random decoration Cole had ever seen, but seemed perfectly at home among all the dusty books, obscure manuals, and specimen jars. He put his hands on her shoulders and pulled her closer. "Maybe you should stay here. There's probably not much to see."

"We'll check it out."

"The cops said there was a robbery, Paige. It could be that Ned was just in the wrong place at the wrong time."

She turned on him and snapped, "Ned wouldn't have been killed in a robbery. It's just not possible. He could probably take a bullet or get stabbed and not die with all the serum in him."

"The serum didn't help his eye."

"That's different, Cole. God damn it, just trust me! The Nymar Rico and I cleaned out of this city could never have killed Ned. Not on their best day, so there's no fucking way some robber got that lucky. The only Nymar Ned and I saw in Sauget were either killed or too sick to do much of anything. Malia's pack is too scattered to worry about him. That leaves Henry and Lancroft. This could be payback for chasing him out of that club or just something to distract us from coming after him again. I don't give a shit what happened, this can't go unanswered."

Chapter 23

Rico tore up Hanley Road as if he was trying to break the sound barrier. "It was only a matter of time before those gutless fucking Nymar came for payback after getting their asses chased from this town." He parked with one front tire on the curb and jumped out with his Sig Sauer in hand.

"Put that away!" Paige said.

Bits of glass and cigarette butts stuck to the concrete, announcing the Skinners' steps with a muffled crunch. The humid Missouri air hung around the bar, making the Keyhole seem even more isolated from the world of the living.

Rico's eyes were fixed upon the front of the bar and he made it all the way to the entrance without noticing the place was closed. "Or it could be those motherfucking Mud People," he snarled while holstering the .45 so he could pull at the door. "They found him once and they must have found him again. It's not like Ned tried to shake up his routine or anything. He must come here three times a week. I told him not to be so goddamn predictable, but did he listen? Fucking cops probably wrote this place off without even bothering to look for anything."

Paige tipped her head back and put a drop into each eye from the bottle she'd taken from Ned's. "Before you get too worked up, let's see what we can find in here."

There wasn't much to see from the parking lot. Most of

the windows were covered by shades yellowed from age and overexposure to daylight, but a few were uncovered. Looking in at the bar through one of them, Rico didn't see anything but shabby furniture and old arcade cabinets.

"Ned was here," she said as she studied the waves of Skinner scent drifting within the bar. "From what I can see, there were no Nymar."

"Can you be sure about that?"

"No."

"Then keep lookin'."

After letting the drops soak in, Paige picked up even more of the Skinner scent within the place. "I think there may have been another Skinner in there with him."

"What makes you say that?"

She looked at the scent left behind by herself and Rico and compared it to the traces inside. "Because Ned doesn't move around enough to lay down that much scent. Even if he did laps inside of that place, his scent would have had to dissipate by now, right?"

"You're the one with the funky vision," Rico grumbled.

Compared to the fresher scents they had left, the trails drifting inside the bar were like wisps of stubborn cigar smoke. The longer she stared through the window, the more wisps she picked up. "Looks like it's concentrated at the bar. There's so much. My gut's telling me there's too much in there to have been left by just one of us. Did anyone else come here?"

"Any other Skinners? Not that I know of." Rico's expression took on a cold, steely edge. "Hasta be Lancroft. That old fuck got to Ned."

Paige's phone rang. When she answered, Cole immediately told her, "It's him."

"You saw the body?"

"I saw a picture of it. I met with Detective Shin. She had a picture on her laptop, and yeah," he repeated with a sigh, "it's Ned all right."

"Are you alone?"

"Nope," Cole replied in a forced conversational tone.

"What do the cops know about how he was killed?"

"The bar was robbed. They found the owner with a broken neck and Ned's throat was cut. There wasn't much by way of security at that place, so they're going with the robbery."

"Then meet us at The Emerald. You remember the address?"

"I got it."

"Good. Any problems, give me a call." She snapped the phone shut and turned on her heels so she could walk up the sidewalk to Rico. The big man got some amused looks from passersby, thanks to his deathly stare and patchwork leather jacket, but he wasn't concerned with any of that. He clenched a cigarette between his teeth and expelled smoke as if trying to spit it into the world's face.

"You wanna hear something stupid?" he asked.

"I've spent enough time with Cole to make me immune to stupid."

Rico's eyebrows flicked up as one choppy laugh pushed the rest of the smoke out of his throat. "Damn! And here I thought you liked the guy."

She lowered her head and stuffed her hands into her pockets while walking away.

"I knew it," Rico grumbled as he fell into step beside her. "So have you two . . . ?"

"I thought you had something stupid to tell me."

He watched her for another second, took the cigarette from his mouth and said, "I actually thought Ned was safe. Not like I didn't think anything would ever happen to him, but just that so much shit already has. He was the only one to walk out of Miami after all those other Skinners got ripped to shit. We thought we lost him in the Everglades while he was off chasing Lizard Men."

"Squamatosapiens," Paige corrected. "The proper term is Squamatosapiens."

"Right. Then he loses an eye and comes here to watch over an empty city. The old buzzard could handle himself, but he also did a damn good job of laying low. He dealt with the troublemakers and kept everything in line. I mean, I really thought he was safe."

"You're right. That is stupid."

* * *

By the time Cole arrived at The Emerald, the new coat of foul-smelling varnish on his weapon had dried and a citation from the St. Louis Police Department was in the glove compartment. Daniels's SUV was already in the parking lot, and Rico and Paige were leaning against it. "With all the shit going on around here," Cole fumed after climbing out of the Cav, "the cops at that station bust me for not being roadworthy! What the hell does that even mean?"

"It probably means we should get those windows replaced," Paige said.

"We should replace the whole car."

"Do you know how long it takes to get all the secret compartments in the trunk, doors, and glove compartment just right?"

The Emerald wasn't a purple A-frame, but according to the green neon sign out front, it did have Amateur Night every Wednesday. The sun was still a few notches above the horizon, giving the large one-story building a washed-out quality. A few other cars were in the lot, clustered directly in front of the entrance and Mötley Crüe's "Girls, Girls, Girls" was just loud enough to make it through the walls.

Rico walked around to the back of the SUV with his phone pressed against his ear. "Yeah, it's me. We're here. Are you ready for us?" While he listened to the response, he pulled the rear hatch open to expose Daniels to the light. Although the Nymar wasn't about to burst into flames, he didn't seem happy about the interruption as he fidgeted with several boxes of supplies.

"Well how much longer?" Rico growled into his phone. "Fine, we'll be right in . . . What? Why not? It's hot out here!" He sighed, gritted his teeth and flipped the phone shut with almost enough force to crush it. "We're waiting out here until the girls are ready for us. Shouldn't be too long."

"Screw that," Paige snapped as she headed for the main entrance.

Rico grabbed her arm and absorbed the hooking punch to his shoulder that followed. "Tristan's coming out here to talk to us, Paige. If you can't be civil, then keep your damn mouth shut for a change. I put too much hard work into this for you to trash it now."

"What's your hard work consisted of?" she asked. "Lap dances with one girl compared to two?"

"There was lap dancing involved, but not how you think. Do you know why all of these purple A-frame strip clubs have buffets?"

"Who cares?"

"To keep horny guys from leaving long enough to get a burger?" Cole offered.

"Close," Rico told him. "It's because their customers don't *want* to leave. Not even long enough to eat. Turns out nymphs are like muses. They get their power from being worshipped. Suck it right out of the air like a Nymar sucks blood from a vein. That's where the lap dancing comes in. One on one contact like that, staring right into someone's eyes, any one of these ladies can charge ten batteries in that many seconds."

"Ladies, huh?" Paige snorted. "Did they get their hooks into you after one too many freebies?"

Rico took an even sharper tone when he said, "Hey. They haven't done any harm to anyone. A bunch of them have already been taken and may be killed at any second by that Lancroft asshole. Tristan and the others are willing to put their own necks as well as the necks of their sisters on the line to help us. Since they've offered to repay our help on a long-term basis, you should show some respect."

"You're right," she admitted. "I'll keep the attitude in check."

"Good, because Ned wouldn't want us to screw this up. It may be too late to save him, but we can make him proud of us wherever the hell he is. Plus you're really going to like the deal I'm working on."

"All right," Daniels said from the back of the SUV. "I'm all set." He climbed down from the vehicle, picked up a thin vial of black liquid and allowed his jaw to hang down far enough for his drooping fang to slip all the way out of its casing in his gums. When Cole followed Daniels's line of sight to the vision strutting toward them, it was easy to figure out what had stymied the Nymar.

Tristan rushed across the parking lot wrapped in a tan robe that covered her from ankle to neck. Although she held it shut well enough to keep from stopping traffic, a breeze flipped it open to show that all she had on beneath it was a collection of multicolored veils that stuck to her like pastel smoke. Quick to pull the robe shut again, she said, "We're almost ready for you. Since we're not in a proper temple, we've had to gather a lot more energy than normal."

Cole felt a tightness in his chest that he hadn't experienced since the first time he followed Paige on a hunt. "Are we really doing this?" he asked. "This is teleportation. We could never be seen again. We could get some kind of exotic disease. Hell, we could freaking *melt* for all we know!"

Rubbing Cole's face, Tristan purred, "You're cute. Why don't you bring your things and come with me? We'll talk along the way."

As Rico walked with him to an unmarked side entrance, he slapped Cole on the shoulder and said, "Don't get worked up. I checked it out already. Well, as good as I could check it without actually trying it. The theory sounds pretty solid."

If Daniels's loud muttering wasn't enough to get his displeasure across, he made sure to slam his cases shut as loudly as possible before hauling them out of the SUV. Cole went to the Cav and stuck his head in through the broken passenger window so he could pull the GPS unit from the bracket mounted to the dash and stick it in his pocket. Seeing the impatience scrawled across Paige's face, he told her, "This thing's worth more than the damn car."

The club's side door opened into a storeroom that was filled with cases of beer, empty kegs, stacks of coasters and bundles of napkins. Tristan walked through another door that led to the narrow space behind the bar, rubbed the tender's shoulder and skirted the edge of the main room.

It was a short walk that allowed the Skinners to sneak in without attracting much notice. Then again, considering what was going on in the spotlights, a herd of elephants could have ambled through without being noticed. Two large stages were bathed in pulsing light. Shae was on the first one, crawling up to a row of gray-haired gentlemen standing with dollars in their hands. Her miraculously perky body was on display thanks to a pair of shorts that could have easily passed for a rubber band and a wet T-shirt plastered to her breasts. Every move she made was enhanced by a spray of water droplets, and when she brushed them off her skin, everyone in the club could feel it.

Kate was on stage number two in a one-piece swimsuit made of two strips of material that crossed her front and back to form a V on either side of her body. Although Cole could feel her touch running down his stomach, he decided the real magic trick was how she managed to keep the straps of her suit in place.

The free show was over in a matter of seconds as the Skinners were led into another storeroom. This one had been emptied of clutter and supplies so the walls and floor could be marked with the same swirling symbols as the ones in the purple A-frame. As with the previous temple, a beaded curtain hung from the ceiling to separate the front half from the back. "These look kinda like hieroglyphics," Cole said as he extended a hand to touch some of the symbols. "But they don't seem to have a beginning or an end. I can't even tell if one leads into another."

"That's the language of the dance," Tristan said. Looking to Paige, she added, "And I'm not trying to be poetic. That's truly what it is. My sisters and I speak through our bodies. Our gifts flow through our movements. These symbols date back to a time before humans decided to write in straight lines from one side to another. I explained it all to Terrance."

Cole started to say something, but Rico beat him to the punch. "It's still Rico to you, boy."

Holding up his hands, Cole was more than happy to concede the point.

"Most of our gifts use energy that we extract from a person's spirit," Tristan explained. "And most of our talents aren't much use to anyone but our kind. There are some gifts, however, that have made my sisters and I very sought after throughout the years. We are what you might call magical beings."

"Oh, Christ," Paige groaned. "Here we go."

"See!" Rico said as he snapped his fingers. "I *told* you magic was a real thing! I've been telling this one for years, but she never listens."

Paige stepped through the beads and pivoted on the balls of her feet as a crackling force tugged at her hair. "Magic is what people call something they can't explain. It's a term used for something that can't *be* explained. Our weapons, everything we do, and all the things we fight, have an explanation. There is no magic. Even these beads have an explanation. What are they made from?"

"Ceramic," Tristan replied. "Some are glass and some are metal."

"Forged through a specific process?"

"Yes."

"There you go, Rico." Paige nodded to Tristan and said, "Please continue."

"The magical forces my sisters and I produce allow us to create a bridge from one temple to another. With enough power, we can create a passage using only one temple, but it's not very stable."

"So that's why Lancroft took those other nymphs?" Cole asked.

Rico stood with his back to a wall, eyeing the beads as if he was ready to charge through them no matter where they led. "If that asshole is spreading Pestilence around, I can't think of a better method. He could just teleport it into the sky or into the water. Ain't that right?"

Lowering her head, Tristan pulled in a deep breath and let it out while the lids slowly fell down over her eyes. "It shames me to think of it, but I suppose so. With all the other Dryads he's been collecting, he must be doing . . . something else with them."

"Dryads?"

"It's the proper name for our kind, Cole. We're more than the nymphs of human legend. Actually we're more like several of your legends combined."

Tensing up even more, Paige asked, "So can you send us to Lancroft or not?"

"You must understand. The moment we send you any-where or do anything to put you onto this man's trail, my sisters' lives are in jeopardy."

"They're in jeopardy now," Rico told her.

Slowly, Tristan nodded. "You promise you'll help them?"

Paige stepped in front of her and held onto both of Tristan's hands. Looking her directly in the eyes, she said, "There could be thousands of lives at stake if Pestilence isn't stopped. That's our first priority."

"Pestilence may not be anything you can stop. It could be something no human can stop. Ancient Mayan mythol-ogy tells of the Mud People and Wood People. Legends say the gods made several attempts at creating man before they got it right. Among the failures were people made of mud, who were too soft, and people made of wood, who were too brittle. Those beings were discarded once the gods settled on flesh and bone as their materials of choice."

"Ah," Paige sighed. "That makes sense."

But Tristan wasn't put off by Paige's sarcasm. "A lot of mythology and folklore came about as people's way of ex-plaining their world, so this legend could very well have been inspired by a jungle tribe stricken with an early form of Mud Flu. At the very least, that means Pestilence has been around for a very long time. Something that old rarely dies without a fight."

"We're ready for a fight," Paige assured her. "And I swear to you, if there's any way for us to find those other women and free them, any way at all, we'll do it. That may not be exactly what you want to hear, but we're the only ones who stand a chance against this guy."

The Dryad nodded again. This time there was conviction in the gesture instead of merely resignation. "You've already proven to be good to your word." Pulling in a deep breath, Tristan straightened her back and lifted her chin. While she hadn't been slouching before, she seemed to have cast aside her other posture like a dirty coat. Her beauty remained, but there was now something else in her aura. Something regal. "It takes a lot of energy to send a human from one temple to another," she said. "Even more is needed to make a bridge without an active temple on either end. Since we've gotten set up here, we've been dancing for days and have drawn quite a crowd."

"This room isn't exactly as nice as the other one," Paige said.

"Our new hosts have been accommodating, but we'll return to Christov when he's back on his feet again. Let me spread the word for my sisters to prepare for your trip." Striding past the spot where Daniels had set down all of his cases, but stopping with her hand on the door, Tristan said, "There's something else you need to know about the man you're after."

"Now's the time to tell us," Rico said.

"When he first arrived, he wasn't fully shielded by the Mind Singer. Being in our temple allowed us to see more of him than he would have shown. He's more than a Skinner. He is a torturer. He is a murderer. And he is more than three hundred years old."

Chapter 24

It didn't take long for Daniels to get his cases open and prepare the equipment. Grinning at Cole in a way that made him look more like a vampire than usual, he said, "Roll up your sleeve, tough guy. Time to get inked."

"Wh-What?" Cole sputtered. Hearing the grating whine of the electric tattooing machine in Daniels's hand didn't calm him down in the slightest. While it had been modified for portable use and fitted with tubes of ink that slipped in and out like smaller versions of printer cartridges, the equipment still sounded like something from a sadistic dentist's wet dream. "Screw that! No offense, but one backfire with that stuff is enough, don't ya think?"

Rico stepped up beside him and dropped a hand upon Cole's shoulder that felt more like a hammer. "C'mon, boy! All the bugs were worked out. Stop whining and pick your design. I'm thinking of something in the snake or shark territory."

"And if anything goes wrong, I'll be there to help," Daniels said as he took hold of Cole's wrist while revving the machine to get the ink flowing into the needle. "I already have a design in mind. Just hold still or you'll ruin it."

"Where did you learn to tattoo anyone?" Cole asked.

"From a book," Daniels replied. "And I've been practicing on cuts of meat."

"Shouldn't you sterilize that thing first?"

"Listen to this one," Rico said while slapping Cole's back hard enough to shake him and Daniels like rag dolls. "He's about to get shapeshifter blood and exotic metals injected under his skin and he wants to be swabbed first."

Before Cole could request a shot of something from the bar, the electric needle dug into his forearm. It hurt, but not as badly as he'd expected. After the initial sting wore off, it became more of a scraping sensation. "So what's this deal you worked out with Tristan?" he asked as a way to distract himself.

Rico's posture straightened into the pose of an old-fashioned mayor holding onto the lapels of his leather jacket while modeling for a portrait as he proudly declared, "After this job, we'll get to take full advantage of the Strip Club Express."

"We'll be able to teleport to strip bars all across the country, huh?" Paige asked. "Do we still have to pay the cover charge?"

"Laugh all you want, Bloodhound. From what Tristan told me, there are temples all over the world, and we'll be able to go back and forth between them when we want. We hear about some Full Blood in Alaska, and we can get there! Even if there ain't a club in the exact city we need, we'll get close enough to save a hell of a lot of time and travel expenses. We just need to let 'em know we're coming and they'll be ready to zap us where we want to go."

"And I suppose all nymphs get a free pass to go along with it, huh?" Paige grumbled.

"Not nymphs," Cole said. "Dryads."

"Yeah," she said while rooting through one of the cases. "That one bugs me. Nymphs are one thing. They dance around, tempt men into acting like idiots, nothing too bad. The whole invisible touching thing is a neat trick, but that's about it. Dryads are different. They're . . ."

Cole twitched as the needle was dragged through a sensitive spot in his flesh. "They're what?" he grunted. "Magical?"

"Try elemental and ancient. I don't like the thought of

something that powerful being under my nose without being able to sniff it out."

"Rico seems to think we can work with them."

Looking directly at the big man's ugly face, Paige said, "Rico thinks a lot of stuff. When we first met, he was still carrying holy water just in case we met something from a crappy movie."

"I got my methods and you got yours," Rico said. "But this deal ain't just good for us. It'll hold up for all Skinners. Let's hear you bitch about that." When Paige focused even more intently on finding the supplies she was after, he growled, "Didn't think so."

Drops of sweat began trickling down Cole's face, so Paige walked over to him and ran her hand along his forehead. When she said, "Look at me," he was more than happy to comply. Her face was directly in front of him, framed by strands of hair that had come loose from the band she'd used to tie it back. She looked into his eyes and then set them on fire.

"All done," Daniels said.

Cole pulled his arm away from the Nymar and went to rub his burning eyes. Grabbing his wrists before he could, Paige said, "Those are the drops that Ned made. Remember me telling you about them?"

"Yeah, but I don't remember you telling me you were gonna squirt them into my eyes!"

"Just relax. It's hot at first, but cools down. After that you'll be able to see scents given off by Nymar and other things."

Since his eyes had indeed cooled off, Cole stopped trying to rub them. He thought he was blinded at first, but quickly realized the room was filled with a neon fog of light green mist. The rest of the room slowly came into focus, but the green remained. Soon it became apparent the fog was emanating from the symbols etched into the walls and floor. When he looked at Paige again, she was surrounded by the mist and following it with her eyes.

"Cool, isn't it?"

Eventually, Cole admitted, "Yeah. It is."

"Here," she said as she tossed the bottle to Rico, "you know what to do."

"Looks like there's something coming off of you, Paige," Cole said.

"That's Skinner scent," she explained. "Probably a mix of the Nymar and shapeshifter blood in our serum and weapon varnish. Lancroft is a Skinner too, so if Tristan can get us close to him, we should be able to track him down."

"See why we call her Bloodhound?" Rico declared proudly while applying the drops.

The thick green fog and hints of crimson had put Cole into a holiday frame of mind, but Daniels shot it to hell with a splash of alcohol on his arm to ignite a solid jolt of pain that started at his fresh tattoo and lanced all the way into his shoulder.

"So," Daniels said anxiously. "What do you think?"

Beneath the wet layer of alcohol and the redness of Cole's skin was a black design about the size of a silver dollar and in the distinctive pie-with-a-wedge-missing shape of Pac-Man.

"You're a video game guy," the Nymar explained. "I thought you'd like that."

Laughter rolled from Rico like bass from the speakers inside the club. "Oh, man. I needed that."

"That should give you a little extra strength or speed," Daniels said as he packed the tattoo machine into its case. "Think of it like running to your limit and then pushing yourself just a little more. Same thing with strength. Just push a little harder and you'll have a little more to give. Use it sparingly, though. The ink will burn off fairly quickly."

Apart from the pain of the process itself, Cole only felt a slight twitching where the Pac-Man had been placed. A few flexes of his arm seemed to pump whatever was in that ink throughout his body, because more random muscles began twitching every couple of seconds. Stepping away from Daniels, he asked, "Isn't anyone else getting done?" Since the other two Skinners looked away, Cole figured he was the only test subject this time around. "Fine. So what happens when we get to wherever we're going?"

"Lancroft's been using Tristan and Shae to zap him back

and forth a few times," Rico explained. "They don't know exactly where he is, but they can feel where the other girls are, so they'll get us close. I figure Lancroft will have something rigged to let him know that we're there, and he'll definitely know once we get to them Dryads he kidnapped."

Paige twirled her batons to loosen her muscles before zero hour. "He won't need alarms or surveillance with Henry as his watchdog. He's been using other people's bodies all the times we've seen him, but odds are good the real thing is close to Lancroft's place. Just don't forget he's a Full Blood. Cole and I had our weapons treated with the new Blood Blade varnish so we'll take him."

Clamping his teeth on a cigarette, Rico opened his jacket to reveal the double rig shoulder holster. The Sig Sauer rested under his left arm, and an older model .45 hung under the right. "Oh, I got something for Henry." He ejected the clip from the Sig Sauer and flicked the top round loose. "I been workin' on these babies for a long time. They're called Snapper rounds."

The bullet in his hand didn't look remarkable, but the extra magazines in his inner pockets gave off black wisps, as if he'd snatched the bullets from the air after they'd been fired. "What are those in your pocket?" Cole asked.

"Nymar rounds," Rico said while patting them. "Hey, I can see the antidote scent."

Steering Rico back on track, Paige asked, "You used Snappers at the club, right? They did a pretty good job against those Mongrels."

"And they should do a damn good job against any shapeshifter." Rico held the bullet between two fingers and turned it so they could see it from all angles. "Regular rounds just get snagged in their fur. Teflon ammunition can cut through Kevlar body armor and does a good job against some fur, but doesn't pack the punch needed to damage a Mongrel or Half Breed. They'll pass straight through like a laser, and a shapeshifter won't even know they were hit before the wound's healed. Hollow points can mess up a shapeshifter's day real good, but only if they get through the fur. Coating hollow point rounds with Teflon keeps them from flattening properly, but I put together a nice little hybrid that gives the best of both worlds."

Catching the bullet Rico tossed her, Paige studied it carefully.

"Inside," he continued, "there's a little plastic pin that keeps the hollow point from flattening right away. That's what really messed me up, you know. Getting the pin to fit in the round was hard enough. A metal one kept it from flattening at all, but some plastics didn't hold up long enough. I even kicked around the idea of using wood to—"

"We've got a lot to do, professor," Paige scolded.

Unaffected by her prodding, Rico popped another round from the Sig's magazine and cracked it against the floor. As he lifted it up, the front end of the bullet collapsed partly into itself with a sharp *clack*. Judging by the proud grin on Rico's face, he'd just turned lead into gold.

"So what?" Cole asked.

"So, the Teflon coating lets the bullet get through a shapeshifter's fur. The pin inside the bullet is weakened on impact and delays the collapse of the hollow point until it's in good and deep." Beaming proudly, Rico said, "At normal speed, the bullet flattens just past the fur and shreds our shapeshifting friends like a set of claws from the inside out. If we're real lucky," he added with a feral grin, "they don't come out at all."

"And they really do work?" Paige asked.

Rico nodded and loaded the bullet back into its magazine. "You ever seen a Mongrel drop the way they did back at Bunn's?"

"But will they work on a Full Blood?" Cole asked.

"Hard to say. I ain't had a Full Blood to test 'em on yet. Hopefully that'll change tonight."

Flipping her right baton to grip its handle, Paige willed it to form a slightly cleaner version of the machete. "And if those don't have enough snap," she said while the handle narrowed even farther, to reveal the tooth she'd attached while in Kansas City, "we can do things the old-fashioned way."

Cole checked his weapon and saw that the melted chips

of the Blood Blade had added a metallic glint to the largest spearhead. Even after hearing Rico's explanation for his
Snapper rounds, he would have felt more comfortable if the
whole silver bullet thing had worked.

Tristan announced her arrival with a few knocks on the
door. She, Shae, Kate, and a few bars of "Baby Got Back"
drifted in from the main room before the door was closed
again. "Better make this quick," Tristan said. "The regular
girls can keep the crowd busy, but not for long. We've stirred
them up pretty good."

Shae and Kate took positions on either side of the room
and started humming softly. Although it wasn't nearly as
ornate as the proper temple, the room didn't look anything
close to a revamped storage space once the Dryads got
warmed up. The wavy, erratic markings glowed as if they'd
been collecting daylight for centuries just to send it into the
hanging strings of beads at that moment. Entwining lines of
energy curled through the air as they made their way toward
the curtain. When the two Dryads began singing in earnest,
brilliant green bolts created patterns that were pulled from
the same language as the etchings on the walls.

Tristan moved over to Paige and placed something in her
hands. "I want you to take this."

Holding the sickle under her arm to free up her good hand,
she accepted the offering. It was a small flask engraved with
more of the undulating script. "What's this?"

"It's called Memory Water. My sisters and I are the only
ones who can make it. Drink this, and it will make your
body as it was before your arm was hurt."

"This can fix that much damage?"

"It doesn't fix damage," Tristan said. "It restores you to a
point when there was no damage. This should be just enough
to heal your arm."

Paige furrowed her brow and asked, "Why would you give
me this?"

"Haven't you ever gotten an unexpected gift?"

Although her glance in Cole's direction wasn't obvious, it
wasn't slick enough to get past Tristan. "Not really," Paige
said.

"Then think of it as a way of helping my sisters. With your arm restored, you'll be able to fight better. I would have given it to you earlier, but since the raids led by Ponce de Leon, it's been in very short supply. I had to be sure about you." When Paige tucked the flask into her pocket, Tristan stepped back and lent her voice to the song.

Chapter 25

For something as remarkable as teleportation, Cole found his journey to be a little disappointing. He didn't feel his body get disassembled and put back together again. The earth didn't rumble. There wasn't even a glowing tunnel for him to fly through at a thousand miles an hour. The beads clung to him like strings of magnets to a suit of chain mail. A breeze hit him in the face, accompanied by the vague scent of mountain air and freshly cut timber. When his foot touched the floor on the other side of the beads, he, Paige, and Rico were somewhere else. There was a taste in his mouth that felt like it had been rinsed by purified water, and since the others smacked their lips as well, they could have tasted it too. Not exactly a high ranking on the yowza meter.

They were still in a dark room with strange symbols on the walls. A bass line was thumping through the building, but came from a much smaller set of speakers. When he tried to bat at the beads he still felt touching his arms and legs, he only swatted air.

"Don't worry," Paige said nearby. "I still feel them too."

It looked as if they were in a house that had been stripped of everything but shades on the large windows next to the front door and a lamp against one wall. The more Cole looked around, the less he saw. One barren hallway led to a pair of empty rooms. There was no furniture to be seen and the small kitchen at the back of the house was completely gutted. In fact, the entire place barely seemed large enough for more than one person to live there. He stepped up to a picture window framed by the light seeping in from the street. Pulling aside the blind gave him a view of a curb lined by parked cars of all colors and states of repair. Only one of them was running, and it was the source of the thumping music he'd heard since his arrival. Someone emerged from a house across the street, got into the car, and was driven away.

"There's nothing here," Cole said. "We must be in the wrong place."

Paige sighed and took the same tour as he had, which she completed in a matter of seconds. "Where the hell are we?"

After fitting his spear into its harness, Cole took the GPS unit from his pocket and turned it on. While it acquired the satellites needed to pull up a map, Paige looked out the front window. Rico paced the room and quickly worked his way over to the lamp sitting by itself on the floor. He turned it on, but the bulb was only powerful enough to cast a dim glow in one corner. Fortunately, Cole didn't need a light to read the GPS screen. When the map came up, he announced, "We're in Philadelphia. Looks like a neighborhood called Germantown."

Now fascinated by the wall at the back of the room, Rico stood with his face less than two inches from the water-stained plaster. "Tell me you see these symbols."

Cole didn't want to bother with dirty walls when he could get so much more from Romana, so he ignored the request.

"What symbols?" Paige asked.

"The symbols right here. Or they were right here," Rico muttered as he dug into one of the inner pockets of his jacket. When Cole finally looked over at him, Rico was grumbling, his face pressed against the wall, before saying, "*Ha!* Found 'em! That's the trick. Just gotta keep your eye on the ball."

Before Cole could question his sanity, the symbols appeared all around him. Actually, they reappeared. "Wait a minute! I saw those when we got here, but I just . . ."

"Put 'em out of yer mind?" Rico asked. "That's what you're supposed to do. That's what these babies *make* you do. Runes like these give you a splash of discombobulation mixed with a dash of déjà vu. Right, Paige?"

"Huh?"

For once Cole didn't feel like the stupid one.

"These runes!" Rico said. "They're the ones I been trying to get you to learn for years, but you were too stubborn to pay attention."

Now that they'd been seen, the symbols gave off faint trails of black smoke, similar to the scent that had shown up in other Skinner creations, like the ammunition crafted to kill Nymar. Paige followed a line of smoldering symbols etched along the top of the front window, then stepped back and said, "I've seen these before."

"I know," Rico snapped. "I showed 'em to you before."

"No, not from you."

Now that he had a chance to look at them more than a moment, Cole experienced the same kind of frustrated familiarity that was written on Paige's face. The symbols were indecipherable, but in a familiar way. Then it came to him. "These are like the marks on the inside of Henry's cell back at Lancroft Reformatory, but there's something . . . off about them. I can't quite put my finger on it."

Rico squatted down to some of the lower symbols and stretched a hand out behind him. "Paige, got a mirror?"

"Sure, Rico. It's in the bottom of my purse next to the gum and mascara."

"Okay, then. Cole! Gimme that GPS thing."

Reluctantly, he handed Romana over.

Rather than marvel at the improved touch technology or any of the optional extras in the programming package, Rico switched it off and held the device up to the wall so the symbols were reflected on the black screen.

"Hey! Those are exactly like the symbols at the reformatory!"

"The ones in Henry's cell would have been to keep something in," Rico explained. "These are to keep something out. One's written forward and the other one's backward. Nice and easy. If I knew exactly what each of these markings here meant, I could even tell you who this was written for."

"So those runes you taught Paige really work?" Cole asked.

Rico ground his teeth together as if every fiber of his being wanted to say something but he just couldn't get the words out.

"No," Paige said. "They don't."

"She's right," Rico sighed. "The runes I know work okay sometimes, but not like these. It's a lost art. There used to be something else, some other element that really put the zip in these things. It may be something from back in the day when Skinners were friendlier with the Gypsy clans, or it could just be something that got lost in translation over the years. I learned a good chunk of the runic language from books and old journals, but not how to give them that old pep. I'm sure the MEG guys have read every book on ghosts and demons front to back, but that don't mean they can summon or even communicate with 'em."

"Maybe we can call someone who does know," Cole offered. "Like someone from back in the old days?"

"Don't think so," Rico chuckled. "The old days I'm talkin' about are somewhere back in the seventeenth or eighteenth century. But one thing's for sure," he added as he dug a little spiral notepad from his jacket, "these were put here by a Skinner who knows his shit. They're keeping this place sealed off from certain things comin' in, and since we got here without too much trouble, I'd say we ain't the target. Those symbols along that other wall over there are what's screwin' with our perception." Rico removed a pen from the spiral rings of the notebook and tapped it against his chin. "All this stuff is protecting and hiding something, though. Give me a few minutes and I should be able to get us in."

"In where?" Cole asked.

"I don't know, but I bet it's good."

Cole and Paige patrolled the house with their weapons drawn, waiting for someone or something to find them. After searching the cramped, empty house for thirty long minutes, they longed for the distraction of finding someone, even Henry kicking down the front door. But they were still taken by surprise when they found a lumpy figure sitting with his back pressed against the back wall of a closet in the house's only bedroom.

Extending her sickle in one hand while keeping the machete closer to her body, Paige whispered, "Is that you, Daniels?"

"Y-Yes."

When he heard the muffled voice, Cole rushed into the room behind Paige, with his spear at the ready. Sure enough, Daniels sat in the closet with all of his equipment piled around him. "I searched this room when we got here," he said. "I looked in that closet. Where the hell were you?"

"I . . . was hesitant to step through the curtain when you three disappeared," the Nymar told him. "I needed a minute to . . . collect myself."

"Didn't you hear us in the other room?"

Daniels nodded meekly, but pushed himself farther back into the dark. "Oh, God. I'm so sorry."

Paige lowered herself to one knee and watched him carefully. "What's wrong?" she asked. "Why are you sorry?"

"Back in Kansas City . . . I destroyed the Blood Blade."

"That's done," she said with strained patience and a hint of resentment. "You were trying to work on the ink, I was rushing you and—"

"No! I didn't want to break the blade apart like that! I only wanted to take some more samples, but he made me do it! He made me do it and then he made me think I wanted to do it. I sort of knew what was going on, but then I didn't. I just couldn't quite put my finger on it."

Paige dropped her weapons, grabbed the Nymar by the front of the shirt and pulled him sharply to his feet. "Who made you do it?"

"Henry," Daniels squeaked. "The Mind Singer. It's what he does. He spoke to me, whispered into my brain while you were in Kansas City and told me to destroy the Blood Blade. When I was chipping off samples of the blade I just . . . kept going."

"And he didn't tell you to get rid of the pieces?" Cole asked.

Daniels looked over to him, back at Paige, and back again until his movements became an insistent shake of his head. "Once it was done, Henry was happy. I wanted to tell you, but I just couldn't get myself to say the words until now. I wanted to say that he was in my head, but I just couldn't and I don't know why! I'm so sorry! Henry wanted the blade destroyed and then he made me forget about it. I'm so sorry."

"Why haven't you said this before?" Cole asked. "Surely there had to be times when Henry had his guard down."

"I didn't even remember what I did until now!" Daniels insisted.

"And how do we know you're not still talking for him?" Paige added. "We're probably closer to Henry now than we've ever been. It makes sense that he would want to throw us off track."

"It's the runes," Rico said from the doorway of the next room, where he'd been standing in case his partners needed backup. He tucked the Sig Sauer into the holster under his arm and said, "The runes are keeping Henry out of this place. Working with a Mind Singer may come in handy, but Lancroft ain't stupid. If he didn't keep someplace safe from the freak, he wouldn't be the one in charge. Is there a way you can test to see if Henry can hear you or not?"

"Already did," Daniels replied. "If I usually even think about destroying the Blood Blade, I'd forget why I brought it up. I didn't this time, so you must be right."

Wheeling around to return to the room and the wall he'd been studying, Rico said, "Man, I *got* to find out what's in this house."

Daniels shook his head and rubbed his eyes. "There's always been something I wanted to tell you, but I could never put my finger on it."

When Cole charged across the room, it wasn't because of anything he saw or sensed. It was plain, gut-level rage. Leaning into the closet, grabbing hold of Daniels and pulling him out, he slammed the balding little man against the nearest solid surface so there was no escape when he asked, "Did you intentionally screw up the ink Paige used on her arm?"

"Cole, he—"

"I'm not asking you, Paige! I'm asking him!"

She refrained from saying another word. It was one of the few times he'd ever seen her back down so easily.

Daniels tried to clear his windpipe by stretching his neck and craning his chin above Cole's arm before he was choked into unconsciousness. When he tried to speak, his fangs drooped from their sockets and his tongue flicked out to wet his lips. "I wouldn't do a thing like that! Paige . . . she saved my life. More than once, she—"

"Maybe you didn't do it on purpose," Cole interrupted while thumping Daniels solidly against the wall. "Maybe Henry told you to do it. Maybe you remember it now."

"But Henry didn't know details like that. All he asked was basic things like—"

"Like what? Hurt the Skinners? Hurt Paige? Is that basic enough for Henry?"

No longer struggling to breathe, Daniels hung from Cole's arm like a dirty shirt on a clothesline. "I don't remember."

"Try."

From behind him, Paige said, "That's enough, Cole. He told me the ink wasn't ready. I was the one who pushed for it. I was the one who used it, so I'm the one who messed up my arm."

"I already heard that from you, Paige. I want to hear it from him." Narrowing his eyes, Cole glared at Daniels in a way that he'd never looked at another living thing. He didn't see a man who'd helped them out of life and death situations. He didn't see a fellow geek who had the best collection of action figures outside of a museum. He didn't even see a guy in a tough spot who had a girlfriend waiting at home for him. All he saw was someone who wouldn't draw another breath if he didn't choose his next words very, very carefully.

Slowly, Daniels shook his head. "I tried to tell her not to use that stuff. I worked on it day and night."

"Except when you were chipping the Blood Blade into pieces."

Daniels didn't have anything to say to that. He clenched his eyes shut, almost as if he welcomed the pressure of Cole's forearm against his throat.

Touching Cole's shoulder, Paige said, "It's okay. If Daniels wanted to hurt me, he would have given me that stuff way before I took it. Lord knows I would have been stupid enough to inject it."

That didn't make things easier, but it made sense. Plus, the touch Cole felt was from her right hand brushing against the side of his neck. Paige's skin was soft, and the muscles were moving like something other than a clunky prosthetic. Finally, he eased back and allowed Daniels to breathe.

Even after he'd been freed, Daniels didn't move away. "I'm sorry," he said while rubbing his throat. "I don't blame you for not believing me, but if there's anything I can do to—"

"Forget it," Cole said. "I just . . . I had to make sure." He turned away to look out a small window set up high in the wall, as if to overlook something as tall as a dresser. Other than the cheap shades on the window, there were only more runes scrawled in an orderly set of rows along the middle of the wall. Outside, a little woman walked a big dog on one side of a deserted street. The night sky hung over it all like a black canopy faded by the city's glow, and the black scent from the wall hung in front of it.

"Hey!" Rico shouted from the front room. "Let me know if this does anything."

The black trails drifting from the runes tapered into wisps before cutting off completely.

Paige jogged out of the bedroom, anxious for any bit of progress she could get. "I think those runes are weakened. Is that what you meant to do?"

Rico studied a cluster of runes on the wall between the front room and the kitchen. Even though it was at the other end of the house, it was still within spitting distance of the bedroom. Cole emerged from the bedroom and asked, "What's going on?"

"There's a door being covered up by these runes," Rico told him with a scowl. "Whatever Lancroft is protecting has gotta be through there."

When Cole looked at the wall, he could only see more runes. "What door?" he asked.

Screwing his face into a confused grimace, Rico grunted, "Damn! It was just there a second ago."

"Oh for Pete's sake," Paige said as she stomped toward the wall. "Just start wiping these symbols off and let's see what's here."

"You can't just wipe them off," Rico insisted. When Paige tried using the sleeve of her jacket to do just that, she was hit by a jolt comparable to sticking her finger in a socket. "Told ya," he sighed.

Cole watched the street through the front window, saw the little lady with the dog stationed at a patch of grass on the nearby corner. Before he could get too suspicious, the dog squatted.

"What if we break the wall?" Paige asked.

"Tried that while you were in the other room," Rico told her as he turned to show both her and Cole the left side of his jacket. "It didn't work out so well." The heavy canvas had been burnt to ash, and the leather patch on his shoulder was scorched black. "Melted a few layers of skin on my arm, but that's all right," he added with a tired smirk. "Chicks dig the scars. I weakened 'em a little, but you can't just go around busting walls down. Whoever put them there will know if that happens."

"Are you sure?"

"No, Paige! I'm not sure. I've been tryin' to figure these things out through books and old letters since before you came along, but it's like learning how to fix an engine without ever gettin' your hands on one. Just give me a minute to think before you start kicking anything down."

"The runes we saw at Lancroft Reformatory were mostly intact," she said. "But Henry came and went as he pleased. Half Breeds made a den there, and I sure as hell didn't feel any magical barrier."

Squatting down to follow a line of blocky script that turned vertically toward the floor, Rico said, "That whole reformatory was a heap of rubble. You think maybe those runes were deactivated on purpose once Lancroft moved along? Or is it possible they're *why* the reformatory was a rock pile?"

Paige pursed her lips as she thought about that. Unable to come up with an answer that would further her cause, she left Rico alone and joined Cole at the window.

Across the street and two houses down, a door opened and a man with a gut big enough to hang over his boxers stepped onto his stoop. A compact car parked in the middle of the street, and its driver stepped out to join the woman and her dog. All of them turned toward the man in boxers to watch as he repeatedly snapped his head violently to one side.

"Uh, you may want to turn those protection runes back on," Cole announced. "Either this place has a Neighborhood Watch or someone knows we're here."

The first one to come to Cole's side was Daniels. He looked nervously out the window as more people stepped outside. "He's right. These people are displaying some troubling symptoms."

Paige took in the scene with a simple, "Huh. That's strange. Looks like our Rune Master wasn't as careful as he thought."

"How bad is it?" Rico asked.

Boxer Guy's head straightened to a proper angle before twisting viciously to one side. Cole couldn't hear the crunch of breaking bones, but recognized the way the man's body swelled to another shirt size. "It's about to get a whole lot worse."

Henry's thick head swung at the end of his broken neck, but his lips flickered as he spoke in a string of unending syllables. Although Cole couldn't hear the words, a few choppy sounds drifted through the back of his mind like snippets of a song from a poorly received radio station.

Rico looked back and forth from his notepad and frantically examined one symbol after another. "I don't feel a Full Blood anywhere near here!"

"He's in another body," Cole said, "I'm looking right at him."

Rico's hand trembled as he reached out to touch the wall. Finally, he used the tip of his first two fingers to trace the runes in front of him while making a few lines that hadn't been predrawn.

Outside, Henry screamed at the other neighbors who'd gathered around him. When they screamed back, dark viscous fluid poured from their mouths. The only one who wasn't infected was the dog, and it ran away as fast as its four legs could carry it. As the underdressed man in boxers got closer the house, the broken transmissions in Cole's brain became a bit clearer.

. . . s, Skinners . . . see you. I see . . . ou. IseeyouIseeyou-Iseeeeeyoouuu.

At least a couple dozen people had stepped out of their houses or cars to gather in the street. Pestilence must have flowed through Philadelphia a lot worse than it had in St. Louis because there were no clean faces to be seen. They looked at the little house with eyes that oozed black tears. As Henry loped toward the house's front porch, all of the Mud People followed.

Both of Paige's batons flowed into their bladed forms. "Can you get those runes to work or not?" she asked Rico.

"Probably."

"You've got five seconds."

Henry threw himself at the door.

"Make that three seconds!" Paige shouted while she and Cole jumped away from the front of the house.

Henry and the Mud People thumped against the door without budging it. The panes in the windows didn't rattle in their frames and not even a speck of dust was dislodged. Outside, Henry backed away from the porch. The Mud People stared at the house and hacked up mouthfuls of thick paste.

Henry charged the door at full steam. As soon as his feet hit the porch, something flowed from his back like a gust of wind that ruffled his shirt and appeared amid a brief flicker of illuminated dots behind him. When the man's face punched through the door like a bloody battering ram, there was no consciousness in his eyes.

Cole followed the barely noticeable trail of orbs as they flowed back into the broken body that lay halfway across the threshold. Lifting a freshly split head on a cracked neck, Henry moaned, "Dr. Lancroft don't want you here."

Chapter 26

The only thing Cole could think to do was kick Henry back out through the door. Henry skidded onto the porch, but immediately scrambled toward the house on all fours like a wolf in man's clothing. No matter what face he wore, he was still there, leering at the world through bloodshot eyes and screaming through a diseased mouth.

"Got it!" Rico announced.

Half a second after his front end crossed the threshold, Henry was pinned down by a force that Cole saw as a murky wall of black smoke seeping from the Skinner runes. Henry's chest and chin hit first, forcing the air from his lungs along with the very essence that had been controlling him. Orbs scattered from his back, leaving the man behind.

Outside, the Mud People stopped.

They were close enough for Cole to hear their strained breathing.

"That did it, huh?" Rico said proudly.

All of the Mud People set their sights on the front door and jogged toward the house. The fastest among them was a young woman with short blond hair and a slender frame that absorbed a flurry of orbs like water soaking into porous desert rock. Her mouth twisted into a feral snarl and her head snapped to one side. Before her spine gave way, Cole charged outside, pushed through the first wave of Mud People and cracked the side of his spear against her chin.

Despite the monster possessing her, the woman's body was still human, and the blow dropped her to the sidewalk before Henry had a chance to break her.

"If that hidden door is what we're after, then get it open!" Paige shouted.

Rico struggled between flipping through his notebook and tracing the runes. "I don't know how to get it open without shutting the rest of them off, and the runes are the only things keeping Henry out of here!"

When he looked up, all Cole could see was a wave of mud-smeared faces and clawing, desperate hands. They swarmed him from all sides, grabbing and punching and slapping in a wild mess of frenzied attacks. None of them did any real damage, but it was enough to push him down and keep him there. If he lowered his head to protect his face, one of the Mud People clawed the back of his neck. If he pushed some of them away, others would crawl under his guard. The moment they started digging their teeth into him, Cole gave up on defense and focused everything he had on offense.

I remember the golden haired one. She was so soft, but I didn't have enough money for them both.

Cole checked the woman he'd knocked out. She'd gone limp and was bleeding from the mouth, but at least her head was properly attached. He swung an elbow to catch one of the Mud People in the temple, drove his knee into the ribs of another, and then spotted Henry's essence soaking into a small figure walking toward the house.

Several of the Mud People grabbed any piece of Cole they could reach. Willing his spear to blunt on both ends, he backed toward the house while knocking aside as many of them as he could. The figure approaching the door was a small boy whose head was already cocked to one side.

"We can only lower the defenses for a few seconds!" Paige shouted at him. "Run for it!"

Cole shoved through the growing crowd and said, "No. Keep them up." Seeing the hesitation on Paige's face, he shouted, "Do it!"

She turned and said something before a wave of dark

smoke formed in front of her. Judging by the way she wheeled around to tear into Rico, she'd wanted to be on the other side of that barrier when it went up.

The sheer number of Mud People was enough to weigh Cole down. Just keeping his head up and feet moving pushed him to his limit. He pushed just a little bit harder and hoped the ink didn't turn his arm into a useless piece of meat. The patch of skin pinched as if the needle was once again biting into him, but it gave him enough strength to shove past the hands that clutched at his clothes and limbs. After breaking free of the crowd, he scooped the boy into his arms and pushed him face-first into the smoky barrier.

Instead of a quick, powerful jolt, Henry was given a prolonged taste of the runes' power. The kid kicked and fought to get away, but Cole held him in place. Although his body didn't show the first hint of a wound, whatever was inside the boy rattled as if it was being shoved into an electric fence. A few more seconds of that and the orbs flew from the human shell. This time they sped in different directions, causing a single sigh to emerge from every one of the Mud People. The ones that had been on their feet collapsed. The boy, as well as the people who'd been crawling on all fours, merely settled on the ground as if they'd decided to take a nap.

The instant the smoky barrier dissipated, Paige grabbed Cole's arm and pulled him into the house.

Rico stood by a newly revealed door and declared, "I bet you'll *both* study those runes now!"

Looking down to the kid on the porch, Cole asked, "What about him?"

"He's out," Rico said. "Just like the rest of them."

"For how long?"

"Hopefully long enough for us to see what's in this place that's valuable enough to be so heavily protected." With that, Rico opened the simple wooden door he'd worked so hard to uncover.

Paige gave Cole a quick once-over. "Are you okay or do you need a minute?"

"I'll be fine," he replied. The serum in his blood gave him

a slight chill, but nothing was broken. "How long do you think we have until the cops arrive this time?"

"I'd say we're on our own here," Daniels replied as he stepped forward with his cases clutched in his arms and hanging from straps off his shoulders. "Given the number of people that got here on such short notice, it seems a safe bet that this whole neighborhood is infected. Maybe the whole city."

Nodding as he walked toward Rico's door, Cole said, "Good. I've had my fill of cops for a while."

Reaching for the tattoo machine, Daniels feebly asked, "Would you like a touch-up?"

Less than half of the Pac-Man design had faded, so Cole said, "No, but thanks."

"I brought a bunch of healing serum. I'll inject as many of those folks as I can."

"You do that."

No matter how suspicious he was of the Nymar or how angry he'd been a few minutes ago, Cole found it difficult to hang on to all of that when he watched Daniels hurry outside to tend to the sleeping Mud People. He wanted to apologize to the squirrelly Nymar, but also knew what it was like to be hunted by things several rungs higher on the food chain. Daniels didn't need to be coddled. If anything, he needed to keep scurrying and twitching at every sound. Those were survival instincts in motion, and Cole wasn't about to dull them by trying to make nice. Suddenly, Paige's cruel sparring sessions made a whole lot of sense.

On the other side of the hidden door was a stairway leading down to a cramped room that felt like it had been carved from one massive block of subterranean concrete. The only things on the walls were thin cracks and cobwebs lit by a single bulb encased in a recessed metal cage. One door led out of the room, and Rico stopped before pushing it open. "These drops wouldn't have worn off already, right?" he asked.

"They lasted a few hours before," Paige replied as she looked around. "I just don't think there's anything around here to see. What about you Cole?"

"Feels like I'm in a tomb. Could we just move on?"

"Sounds like a plan," Rico grunted as he walked into the next room.

That room was larger than the one at the bottom of the stairwell and was cut from the same cracked cement. Cole considered himself slightly taller than average, but he swore the top of his head was close to brushing against the thick wooden beams crossing the ceiling. A few small rectangular windows were boarded up along the upper portion of the wall, which he assumed opened to ground level at the base of the house. Once the smell of blood and dead meat hit him, he wished all of those windows were open.

Along both sides of the room were long workbenches where carcasses of Half Breeds, Mongrels, and a few smaller creatures in various stages of decomposition were being held by expertly fashioned wooden racks. From what he could tell, the fluids from the bodies had been drained into old baby food jars that were stacked next to a large tool chest in a corner. The chest was as tall as the workbenches, and when Cole pulled open one of its thin drawers, he found teeth organized by size in the spots where drill bits or socket wrenches should have been.

Moving along the other side of the room, Paige examined a set of wire racks bolted to the walls. Everything from tongs, saws, hammers, and drills hung above each bench. If any equipment was missing, its spot was marked by an outline traced on the wall. "Holy crap," she said as she touched the crude shape of a claw hammer within the rack that was its home. "If hell had a version of my dad's garage, this would be it."

Rico lingered in front of a metal locker set up near another door at the far end of the room. The tall, narrow cabinet opened to reveal a collection of weapons including pikes, stakes, and even a small pitchfork. All were carved from similar kinds of wood and each weapon's handle was adorned with short, bloodied thorns. "Whoever this guy is, he's been a Skinner for a hell of a long time."

"The only name we've heard is Jonah Lancroft," Cole said. "Why can't you believe that's the man we've been after?"

"Because Lancroft was a Skinner from the 1700s. We're

lucky if we can make it through our fifties. Three hundred years is a bit of a—" Rico's next words caught in his throat. He reached into the locker, past the pitchfork, and grabbed a cane with a sharpened end and spikes along the handle. "Son of a bitch," he snarled.

"Is that Ned's?" Cole asked.

Rico held the cane so he could get a closer look at the handle. "Yeah. It's his. He put notches on here for every Half Breed den he cleared out. All forty-nine of 'em."

There were plenty of notches on the handle, but Cole didn't need to count them. Paige and Rico had known Ned a lot longer and they recognized the cane all too well.

Something rushed through the next room that sounded as if it had brushed all four walls along the way. A light flickered beneath the thick wooden door to reflect off the metal locker with a soft green glow. Rico set the cane down and grabbed the door handle while drawing a .45 from its holster. Cole and Paige gathered around Rico and nodded for him to open the door. He did, then stepped away so as not to obstruct either of his partners.

If there were lights in the next room, the Skinners didn't need them. The glow given off by the Dryad temple provided more than enough illumination for them. Cole stepped into the room behind Paige. Rico brought up the rear and whispered, "I'll be damned. This place sure looks familiar."

The room was close to triple the size of the one at Bunn's Lounge, but every other detail, from the engravings to the texture of the walls, was identical. Cole approached the still swaying beads and stretched a hand out to feel the crackle of residual energy against his fingertips. The symbols on the walls pulsed with a power that matched the ones Tristan had drawn, but three of the four corners were obscured by something he'd mistaken for shadow. On second glance he picked out the traces of crimson within the black grime hanging in the air. "A Skinner's been through here."

"Yeah," Rico replied as he waved his fingers through the gritty mist. "And one's been writing on the walls." He walked toward one of the corners in the back of the room where the symbols shifted to a more angular script.

Paige made a sharp hissing sound that stopped him in his tracks just before he crossed the beads hanging from the ceiling. "They're still crackling," she warned. "You sure you want to go through those?"

"Good point. I'll cross at the wall. Maybe it's safer if the beads ain't on both sides." After pushing aside some of the hanging strands, Rico slid his shoulder against the wall and moved forward. Once he was past the curtain, he asked, "What have you got over there, Cole?"

"A perfect spot to hide some collectibles."

"What?"

Before Rico could scoff, Paige said, "I know this sounds dumb now, but let him run with it."

Cole grinned and approached the murky spot in the corner on his side of the beads. Even though he couldn't read the Dryad script or Skinner runes, he'd seen enough of them both to tell that both were on that wall. "In games that have exploration levels, you should always look back to make sure you haven't missed any nooks or crannies where something cool might be hidden. If you're ever going to find a bunch of extra ammo, new weapons, or collectible items, you'll find them in places that are meant to be overlooked." Having traced the shape of a door framed in Skinner runes mingled within the Dryad script, Cole triumphantly added, "Like this one right here."

Rico came over and studied the wall. With so much script flowing in so many different directions, it was easy for the eye to get lost. "Hey, you're right," he said while tentatively brushing his fingertips over certain symbols. "I think that's a cloak and alarm combo."

"Can you get us past it?"

"It's not as complicated as the one upstairs. Give me a sec."

Rather than hang over Rico's shoulder, Paige walked to the side wall and shimmied past the beads. Her first cautious step was quickly followed by a hop that took her past the curtain and to the other half of the room. Walking toward the corner that Rico had originally spotted, she asked, "What's over here? I can see where the symbols change again."

Rico continued to work while referencing his notebook.

"Looked like a larger cloak. Not like the others, though, so it's probably not a door. Could just be hiding something else that isn't supposed to be seen." Glancing back at Cole, he added, "Maybe it's an extra life?"

Squaring her shoulders to that corner, Paige rubbed her hands together anxiously. "Can I just reach in there?"

"As long as our homeowner wasn't trying to hide a guard dog, poisonous plant, or open flame, you should be fine."

She stood there for a few seconds before taking one of her batons from where she'd tucked it under an arm. Holding it in her right hand, she shrugged and muttered, "Why turn my arm into a lump if I can't get some use out of it?" Before Cole could offer an opposing opinion on how a wounded arm would still be better than a bloody stump, she reached toward the corner until the baton, her hand, and even her arm up to her elbow disappeared.

Cole nearly walked straight through the hanging beads in his rush to get over to her. Stopping when his nose brushed against the curtain, he hurried around to the side wall and stepped through. "Are you all right?"

Scrunching her face and shifting her weight, Paige grunted, "Yeah. I feel something in here. It's . . . moving."

"Is it furry?" Rico asked.

Under any other circumstances, that may have seemed like an odd question. In a basement filled with mystical runes and a Dryad transporter, it didn't raise an eyebrow.

"No," Paige replied, "and it's not biting me. Wait. It's moving." She pulled her hand back so it was once again visible. After holstering her baton, she reached out with both hands. A few inches from the wall, her arms disappeared.

"Got it!" Rico declared.

"Me too!"

Cole nearly threw his back out trying to look at both ends of the room in such quick succession. Rico stepped away from the wall as the runes re-formed into a single shape. The blocky markings sank in to create a solid arch the size and shape of a door. A second later the hinges, wooden slats, and brass knob could be seen.

Paige dug in with both feet and struggled as if something

wasn't letting her go. Before she was dragged into the hidden section of the room, Cole grabbed her by the waist and pulled. With a little effort, he and Paige hauled a naked woman tied to a chair through the field that had obscured her.

"Whoa," Cole sighed.

The woman had been talking as she was dragged into sight, but her voice couldn't be heard until she was clear of the runes. Her bare skin had a soft, Asian hue and was covered in dewy beads of sweat. Short, lustrous black hair framed a perfectly angled face. Cole couldn't help but admire the smooth slope of her breasts or just how perfectly her inner thighs led up to—

"Hey!" Paige barked as she smacked him on the back of the head. "She's another nymph. Walk it off." Once Cole shook the haze from his skull, he nodded and gave her a tentative thumbs-up. Paige took a folding knife from her pocket and used it to cut the ropes binding the naked brunette. "Are you Jordan?"

"No," she replied as she shook her head in a way that made her bobbed hairstyle waggle attractively. "I'm Elsie. Jordan's in that corner over there."

Cole found the cluster of runes in the adjacent corner and reached into them. He felt a crackle of energy at the plane where his hands disappeared, but otherwise it wasn't much different than stretching out to grab a bottle of ketchup from across the table. His hands brushed against something soft and curvy, so he widened his grasp until he felt shoulders and arms. A bit lower and he felt coils of rope encircling a petite figure. He grabbed the rope, pulled, and produced another naked woman out of thin air. "If only it was that easy when I was in high school," he mused.

This woman was slightly taller than the brunette, had darker skin and light brown hair streaked with chestnut highlights. Before he got too distracted by the rest of her, he turned to Paige and said, "Why don't you untie this one and I'll see what Rico's doing."

She rolled her eyes and flipped the knife in her hand as she walked passed him.

Rico's door was ajar and the room beyond emanated a

harsh, white light. Blocking most of the opening with his bulky frame, the big man said, "Let me guess. Both of them ladies in the chairs are nymphs and you ain't seen either one of 'em before."

"You got it. How'd you know the second part?"

"Each nymph hits you between the eyes like that the first time. It wears off the more you see 'em. Come take a look at what we got in here," he added as he motioned for Cole to follow him into the next room. "It'll sober you up better than a cold shower."

The glare of fluorescent lights came from a set of buzzing overhead tubes encased in plastic. There were symbols etched into the institutional green walls, but no beaded curtains or naked damsels tied to furniture. The room was a little more than a quarter of the size of the temple, but felt much smaller because of everything stuffed into it. A long counter, sink, and several metal cabinets were set up along one side, and the other side was lined by trays of medical equipment stored in towers of racks. A narrow computer desk was set up at the back of the room, but there was no room for a chair due to the large operating table taking up most of the floor space. Even without the panels that extended from each side of the table, it would have been large enough for a professional wrestler to lay flat on his back. The panels extended the width of the table by a foot or so, which still didn't seem like enough to hold the massive body of the creature sprawled on top of it.

The werewolf was in its upright form, so its legs were long enough to hang off the edge of the table. Both arms were draped over the sides, but the table's extensions kept the hands dangling about an inch off the floor. Claws still coated in old, crusted blood sprouted from its fingers, and a thick tail drooped over one side like a length of knotted rags. As he approached the table, Cole could barely make out the runes engraved into the metal surface of the tabletop.

Its chest was cut down the middle in a Y incision and held open by shiny metal pins as thick as Cole's fingers. The skin and several layers of muscle were peeled away to reveal a set of ribs that had been neatly sawed apart, allowing him to gaze down into the yawning cavity. Half of the innards were in the carcass and the rest was divided up among several containers kept within the cabinets Rico was examining.

Tugging at a flap of skin so he could twist it around and show him a patch of tan fur, Rico asked, "You recognize this one?"

Cole tried to steady himself with a deep breath, but only managed to pull in a lungful of air that stank equally of dead meat and industrial strength sanitizers. "Looks like a Full Blood," he choked. "I didn't think anyone could kill one of these."

"This Lancroft guy may be an asshole, but he's one hell of a Skinner."

As horrible as the sight was, Cole couldn't take his eyes away from it. Despite looking as if it had been blown apart by a hand grenade, everything around the carcass was pristine. Not one drop of blood had been spilled onto the dry concrete floor, which Cole now saw bore runes that were mostly filled with dust. Not one stray bit of fur could be found on the table or any of the cabinets. If the sink was used recently, it had been vigorously cleaned. He kept moving along the edge of the table, surveying the body of one of the most fearsome animals ever created. After seeing one Full Blood shake off fully automatic rifle fire and another tear his way through an entire city on a whim, it hardly seemed fair for any human to get close enough to poke one in the face without consequence. "How fresh is this thing?"

"I can smell formaldehyde," Rico grunted as he knelt to get a better look at some of the machinery lined up against the wall. "And most of these units down here could chill this whole room down plenty low enough to keep meat fresh. Could be this Lancroft guy found it in a forest somewhere after it died of old age. As for how long it's been here, I couldn't tell ya. You're good with computers, right? How about you hack into that one and see if there are any records. If this guy is any kind of Skinner at all, he's keeping a journal." Snapping his eyes toward Cole as if he'd suddenly thought of something more important than what they'd discovered, he asked, "You're keeping a journal, right?"

The question didn't even register in Cole's brain. He stood

near the top of the table, staring down at the massive gaping maw of the Full Blood's mouth. Most of the teeth in its upper jaw had been pulled and the entire lower jaw had been removed. Its tongue had been whittled down to a nub, both of its eyes were gone, the sockets were hollowed out, and a good portion of its skull were emptied. All that remained even vaguely resembling a canine face was a snout and the ridges of its brow.

"This can't be," Cole sighed.

Rico stood up and circled the table to get to the next set of cabinets. Outside, Paige was doing her best to calm down the Dryads. "I know," he said. "When we take 'em down, they at least die fighting. Half Breeds ain't nothin' more than sick, wild animals, and sometimes I still feel bad killin' those in their sleep. This is a whole other story."

Cole looked away from the creature's face and stared down at the spot where the flesh had been pulled away from its arm to reveal bones that were snapped off and scorched at the tips. An acetylene torch rested against the table near his feet, confirming just how tough a Full Blood was even after it was dead. Something registered in his mind that made him reach into the gaping chest cavity and slide his fingers along the top of the rib cage.

"There's plenty for us to use in these jars, Cole," Rico said. "No need to go fishin'."

Now that his hands couldn't get any dirtier, Cole reached all the way in and started feeling for a spinal column. Considering how much had already been removed from the carcass, the task wasn't too difficult. With a little nudge here and a gentle push there, the innards gave way like pieces stuck to a model with glue that hadn't been given a chance to dry.

Finally, Paige appeared at the door. "Elsie and Jordan are the only two Dryads here and they can take us anywhere we want to go. They also say someone's trying to get back here through the curtain, so we need to— Holy shit on a shingle," she gasped when she took in the sight on the table. "What the hell is that?"

Cole's voice was a shaky whisper when he told her, "This is Henry."

Chapter 27

Paige's eyes were focused upon the gruesome sculpture of carnage displayed upon the engraved silver table. The Dryads gathered behind her, peeking into the room before quickly looking away.

"That can't be Henry," Rico said. "There ain't no way this much work was done so quickly. I found a goddamn hacksaw and something that looked like a miniature Jaws of Life in here. It must've taken weeks to do that kind of work. We've just been talking to him, for Christ's sake!"

"We have been talking to Henry," Cole whispered. "But he's right here."

"Are you sure about that?" Paige asked.

Cole looked at the dead creature's face from another angle to imagine if the thing on the table truly could have been the same Full Blood that ran away from him after Misonyk was killed in Janesville. His hand remained buried inside its chest cavity, resting upon a section of broken spinal column that had been rubbed smooth after years upon years of Henry's head swinging like a pendulum.

"It's him, Paige. I can feel where the neck was broken."

"That don't prove jack," Rico grunted. "Damn near everything on this poor bastard is broke."

Paige approached the table and ran her hands over the shaggy fur of the werewolf's leg as though she was comforting a pet that had just been put down. At the midsection, she pulled one of the pins free and examined the flap of skin on the creature's side.

"Coloring of the fur is right," she announced coldly. "According to Gerald's journal, Full Blood fur gets coarse and wiry after they die, so this one couldn't have been dead for any more than a month. Probably less. Here we go," she said while folding the flap of skin over to show Cole and then Rico. "These scars were made by a Blood Blade. They look like the ones on Burkis's face. Same color around the edges, and this is the spot where I cut Henry open in Janesville." Nodding while pointing to spots on the inside of the chest, she said, "Those are bites from a Nymar spore. You and I have seen plenty of those, Rico." Looking to Cole, she added, "Usually, you only see bite marks like this on a Nymar's heart."

Cole wanted to ask how she'd seen a Nymar's heart before it dried up, but quickly decided he didn't want to hear about it until his stomach had settled.

Placing the flap so it covered its section of the werewolf's chest cavity, Paige announced, "This is Henry. What the hell could have done this to a Full Blood?"

"Jonah Lancroft did this," Jordan said from just outside the room. "We were hidden and silenced, but we could hear him in here working . . . sawing."

"Where are the others?" Rico asked.

Jordan locked eyes with him, grateful to have a point of focus away from the table. "What others?"

"The other Dryads. We were told that you two were only the most recent ones that were kidnapped. There's supposed to be more."

"They could be at other places like this," Paige offered. "If Lancroft is able to teleport anywhere there's a temple, he would need other nymphs to keep them working, right?"

"We're the only ones left," Jordan said.

Cole walked over to her and offered her the shirt he wore over his T-shirt. She allowed him to drape it over her shoulders, but wasn't modest enough to close it. "Can you sense your sisters? Are they at another temple?" he asked, hoping that term might spark something in the woman.

Whatever he may have sparked in her wasn't good.

She backed away from the door and then opened the shirt so Elsie could huddle in there with her. Once together, both Dryads put their backs to a wall and lowered their heads. "This is a Skipping Temple," Jordan said. "Lancroft doesn't need another one. It's named that because it can work as a hub like the other temples or it can skip a traveler along to somewhere else like a stone across the top of a pond."

Paige left the examination room and stood beside Cole. "I've already been talking to them about the others, Cole. They're gone."

"Gone where?"

Tightening her grip on his arm, she pulled him all the way back to the workshop. Even then she kept her voice low. "The other nymphs are dead. Lancroft used most of them up for a healing tonic called Memory Water. According to Jordan, enough of that stuff in a properly distilled form could keep a human alive for a long time."

"Like . . . hundreds of years?"

"Longer. He tore some of them up pretty badly and buried them when he was done."

Surrounded by all those carcasses on the benches or the hides that were stretched out to dry, Cole didn't have any problem believing Lancroft could do such a thing to something as naturally beautiful as a Dryad.

"He's been going back and forth using this temple," she continued, "and Elsie said the Dryads that weren't killed to make that memory stuff were kept as an unwilling power source."

"But Tristan and Shae had to sing to get the beads to work," Cole said. "Even Lancroft had to make them sing before he could go through."

"That was in a proper temple, but Lancroft doesn't give a shit about that here. He forces them to transport him however it best suits him. Everything with those purple A-frames—from the architecture to the script on the walls—is to draw and store whatever energy these women produce. Without all of that, this place must be like letting your laptop run on its battery instead of plugging it into the wall. If you're never able to recharge the right way, you need to keep replacing the battery. That's all these women were to this guy, Cole. He used them up and tossed them out after they died from exhaustion."

Cole pulled in a few breaths, looked toward the temple and then studied the workshop. "So Lancroft traps creatures, strips them for parts, uses them up and dumps them. I guess that really does make him a Skinner, huh?"

Paige knocked his shoulder so he was facing her directly. "What the hell is that supposed to mean?"

"Oh come on, Paige. The only reason we don't have a setup like this in Rasa Hill is because we haven't killed a Full Blood yet. The closest we got was watching one get dragged underground by Mongrels in Kansas City, and if you knew where they took him, are you telling me you wouldn't like to dig him up and see how many different uses you could think of for all those teeth and bones?"

"I've never seen anything like what's in that room."

"Yeah? Well I might have believed you were all broken up about it if I hadn't seen you gut a Half Breed in the backseat of your car."

"Half Breeds are different. They're mobile wood chippers with a taste for our blood. Toss in a risk of becoming a wood chipper yourself and I don't see a downside to killing them."

"Killing them is one thing. That," Cole added while waving toward the room with the table, "is something else. I don't even know what that is."

"Hunters hunt," Paige stated. "Werewolves hunt us, and our choices are to hide, die, or hunt them. The Native Americans were Skinners long before us, and I mean that literally. They skinned werewolves the way they skinned buffalo and it worked out pretty well." In a softer tone, she added, "This is the first time we may have spoken to something after it's been laid out, pulled into a thousand separate pieces, and put into jars. Personally, that's freaking me out too."

"He's trying to get here again," Jordan said from the doorway to the temple. "We can delay him long enough for you to leave, but it won't be long before he forces one of our sisters to get here without our help."

"Let him come," Cole said.

Jordan blinked and was moved aside when Elsie poked her head into the workshop. "We haven't heard the Mind Singer for a while, but there can't be much time for us to get away."

"Let him come," he repeated with more conviction. "We came here to get Lancroft, and we're as ready now as we're going to be, right?"

Paige drew her left baton and formed it into a sickle. "If he wants to save us the trouble of tracking him down, I'm all for it. Where's Rico?"

"He's still in the . . . the green room," Jordan replied, obviously making an effort to mention the examination area without actually thinking about what it contained.

Cole walked past the two women, but Paige gathered them under her arms like a mother hen with two nervous hatchlings. "Do both of you need to be here for this temple to work?" she asked.

"No," Elsie replied. "He kept two of us so he always had at least one in case the other passed out or couldn't form the bridge."

"All right, then. I want one of you to get out of here." Both of the Dryads started to protest, but Paige had no trouble in overriding them. "We came here to help as many of you as possible, and we won't risk you both getting hurt now. One goes back now and the other will leave as soon as you can after Lancroft gets here."

"No," Jordan said sternly. "We'll stay to help and that's final."

"You two may fluster the guys, but I'm not as easily swayed as the ones in the next room. Do what I say and don't make me say it again. I need you to tell your sisters what happened here. More importantly, once you're gone, he'll be stuck here. Am I right?"

Both of them nodded. "If he has no sisters here and no sway over the others," Jordan said, "then the temples are useless to him. But you'll all be stuck here. Elsie can leave now, I'll stay to help."

"Fine. Just get moving."

The Dryads huddled together and spoke in a series of words that were either too quick to understand or in some language that Paige had never encountered before. Rather than try to figure it out, she headed for the examination room where Rico was busy pulling open the last set of cabinets and Cole tapped furiously at the computer.

"Hurry up," she warned. "One of our girls is going to leave and then the other will bring Lancroft here. After that, hopefully the word will be spread and there'll be no more magic beads for Jonah Lancroft." There was a crackle of static followed by a flash from the temple behind her, prompting Paige to say, "Did I mention *hurry*?"

Rico dumped the contents of the cabinet onto the floor. "I'm just tryin' to get a handle on what we may be up against. Like if this guy was building weapons or if he might have worked something out to—"

"To what?" she snapped. "Live for three hundred years?"

"Yeah, or drop a Full Blood. Tricks like that would be good to know."

"What have you found?"

Reluctantly, Rico let a metal tray fall from his grasp and said, "A whole lotta nothin'."

"What about you, Cole?"

"I'm trying to get a copy of everything on this computer and send it to my laptop."

"How long will that take?"

"Too damn long," he replied. "I'll get as much as I can, but he may be able to trace it to where I mailed it, so we need to let it run as long as possible and then destroy this computer. I mean really destroy it. No pieces intact."

"That's some tech talk I can get behind," Rico said through a wide grin.

"I just found the Pestilence files!" Cole said. "At least it sure looks like them."

"Can you send 'em somewhere else besides your own e-mail?" Rico asked. "Just in case somethin' happens to us?"

Trying not to think about what that implied, Cole nodded. "Yeah. Like where?"

"One of Ned's hospital contacts back in St. Louis, Dr. Oehler."

Once he'd been given the doctor's e-mail address, Cole made the necessary adjustments and paused before making them final. "You sure about this? There's a lot of stuff in here that we wouldn't want in the wrong hands."

"We can trust the doc," Rico said. "She's one of ours."

After a few more frenzied taps on the keyboard, Cole switched the monitor off and backed away from the computer. The processor was still blinking and whirring, but at least the terminal looked idle from a distance. He then skirted the table without touching the limbs hanging off its edge and dug into his pocket for his cell phone.

"What are you doing?" Paige asked as she checked the temple. Jordan swayed to a song only she could hear, and Elsie locked eyes with her sister as she stepped back through the glowing beads.

Having already speed-dialed, Cole put the phone to his ear and said, "I'm calling MEG."

"Hang that damn thing up and get ready for whatever comes through this freaking curtain!" Paige said with a fury that was equal parts impatience and frustration.

"Henry's body may be dead on that table, but he's still out there!" Cole said over the growing thrum filling the next room. "That means he's a ghost, and ghosts are MEG's territory."

"How much time until our guest arrives, Jordan?"

When the Dryad stopped singing so she could respond, all of the glowing symbols dimmed. "He's trying right now, and if I hold off much longer, he'll know something is wrong."

"Hang up the phone," Paige ordered.

Cole slid his thumb along the side of his phone's case to pop the earpiece from its resting place. "Am I the only Skinner who uses technology from this century?" he grumbled while putting the headset in his ear and the phone into his pocket. The next dial tone was washed out by a rush of sound that originated from one side of the basement, charged through the room, and rumbled several yards beyond the opposite wall. The beads were left crackling and swaying, but Elsie was gone.

"—ranch 40, can anyone hear me?" someone shouted through Cole's earpiece.

"Yeah, is Stu there?"

"I can help you. Do you have a disturbance to report?"

"I don't have time for this. Put Stu on the phone. Tell him it's Cole."

"Cole? Damn it, I told you—" Although Paige stopped scolding him when Cole waved at her to shut up, she most definitely wasn't happy about it.

"Oh," the person answering MEG's phones said. "I've heard him mention you before. Don't you have a verification number or something?"

Cole recited the number from memory while Paige and Rico took defensive positions in front of the beaded curtain. Another wave of energy rushed through the room, this time in the opposite direction than the previous one.

"What happened?" Paige asked.

Jordan was no longer swaying or making any noise. At the end of a long inhalation, she snapped her eyes open and said, "It was a skip. Lancroft used this temple to propel him to another one."

"Could it have been anyone other than Lancroft?"

"Nobody else knows about this temple. My sisters could sense Elsie and me well enough to get you to this house, but if they knew more, they would have sent you straight to this room."

"Did Elsie get out safely?"

Jordan closed her eyes and thought about it. "I suppose I could contact her to find out."

"Do you need to meditate or something?"

"No," the Dryad replied. "I need a phone."

As Paige tossed her cell to the Dryad, a trembling voice came from the workshop.

"Umm, guys?"

It seemed like so long ago since they'd spoken to Daniels that the Nymar's appearance surprised everyone in the basement. Rico was closest to the door, so he headed into the workshop to see what Daniels wanted.

"Cole?" Stu asked breathlessly through the earpiece. "What's the emergency?"

Pressing the earpiece so he could distinguish one conversation from all the others, Cole said, "I need to know how to get rid of a ghost."

"You found a ghost? Sweet! Where? Let me send a team to wherever you are so we can get some recordings first. Maybe some video."

"No time," Cole snapped. "I just need to know how to get rid of it."

For a change Stu didn't need to flip through any papers or tap the keyboard in front of him. Once he'd taken a steadying breath, he slipped right into business mode. "Okay. What sort of ghost is it? Can you see it? Hear it? Does it interact with you or is it more like a recording that just repeats itself?"

"Yes it interacts with us. That's the main problem."

"I can't hold on much longer," Jordan said.

Paige looked at him impatiently, so Cole held up a hand and said, "Quick, Stu. You're the guys who go after these things. What do you do when you need to get rid of one?"

"We don't really run into that sort of thing too often. Mostly just finding them is the tough part. Let's see, you could do an exorcism. I could walk you through it."

"An exorcism?"

"Oh for crap's sake, hang up that damn phone!" Paige growled.

"No exorcism," Cole said. "We're short on priests around here. What else have you got?"

"Is this thing demonic or was it human? Do you know its history?" Stu asked. "From our experience—"

"That's it!" Jordan said as tears rolled down her reddening cheeks. "I can't hold him back!"

Steeling himself for the imminent arrival, Cole turned up the volume of his earpiece. "—problem is that an entity is confused," Stu continued. "The tricky part is communicating with it."

"Just tell me what to do before I hang up and figure something out on my own," Cole urged.

Having organized a small convention on his end of the phone, Stu grunted and wheezed as if about to blow a fuse. A series of loud bumps and cracks were followed by the voice of someone who must have wrestled the headset completely off of him. "Does this entity know it's dead?" the new person asked.

"Abby? Is that you?"

"Yes, Cole. I've got more field experience. Does this entity know it's dead?"

As Jordon fell to her knees and then drooped forward to prop herself up with one hand, a ripple of energy flickered through the beads.

"I don't think so," Cole said as he held onto his spear with both hands and stood between Paige and Rico.

"Then the best thing to do is educate it. After that, it'll probably move on."

"Probably?"

"Either that," Abby said tensely, "or it might really spin out of control."

Since he couldn't think of too many new ways for Henry to lose control, Cole asked, "What do I do?"

"Find its grave, an obituary, a funeral notice, or anything else you can physically show to someone that proves they're dead. The simpler the better. Can you find something like that?"

Shooting a quick glance toward the examination room behind him, Cole said, "Yeah. We've got some pretty solid proof."

"Then try to get the entity to follow you," Abby told him. "But the disturbance may get worse if a grave was defiled or if other changes were made to its home."

"What if its body was dug up?"

"Oh, that wouldn't be good. Especially if the body isn't in very good condition."

Cole winced. "That'll do for now. If I need more help, I'll call you." He tapped his earpiece to shut it off but left it in place. Keeping his eyes on the growing wave of energy building within the curtain, he said, "We're just supposed to get Henry to look at his body. That'll convince him he's dead and banish him, or it'll really piss him off."

"Great girlfriend you have there," Paige said. "Real informative."

Jordan finally collapsed and the beads practically spit out the body she'd been forcing to stay on its side of the bridge.

The long blade at the end of Lancroft's staff emerged first. Rico was closest to the spot where the old man stepped out and didn't get a chance to take aim with his .45 before the blade was shoved into his chest. Rico grabbed the staff, fired a quick shot at Lancroft and fell off the blade before it had a chance to do any more damage.

Paige's sickle cut through empty air as the old man pivoted on his heel to deflect Cole's spear. Lancroft then used the middle portion of his staff to shove Cole into Paige. It was all she could do to keep from slicing her partner to shreds before pushing him out of the way.

"Henry mentioned you'd found this place," Lancroft said as the staff shortened into a pike with dual sharpened ends. Dressed in tweed pants and a matching jacket over a white shirt that was now spattered with Rico's blood, he looked like a college professor at the tail end of a real bad day. The pike whirled in front of him while Lancroft moved toward the doorway with the stark white light flowing through it. "I see you've found my lab. You, more than anyone, should appreciate the accomplishments therein."

Standing near Rico, but keeping her weapons raised, Paige felt a reassuring squeeze on her ankle. The big man was down but only for the moment. "However you're spreading Pestilence, it's got to stop!" she demanded. "People are dying."

"As they always do," Lancroft replied. "Mine isn't the first disease to thin the herd. Isn't it a fair price to pay to rid the country of the shapeshifters and Nymar that have spread thanks to the lackadaisical nature of your generation?"

"Spare me the rants and hand over the antidote. After killing Ned, that's the only way to get out of this in one piece."

Lancroft's eyebrows flicked up and he aimed the pike at

the Skinners. He reached out with his other hand to trace his fingers along some of the runes etched into the wall. "Very admirable, but it's too late for any of that."

Having seen enough to get a feel for what those runes could do, Cole tucked his spear under his left arm and drew the .45 he'd been given. His first shot clipped Lancroft's arm, but Cole wasn't prepared for the gun's recoil and his next round sparked against the wall.

Despite the blood pouring from his arm, Lancroft showed more anger when he surveyed the damage done by the second bullet.

There you are!

The voice echoed inside Cole's mind as well as in the workshop, and came from the same little boy Henry had possessed earlier. He'd pulled away the boards covering the window and, judging by the bloody flaps of skin hanging from his fingers, it hadn't been easy. Hanging halfway in and halfway out of the basement like something being excreted from the wall, the boy smiled eagerly and forced his way inside.

Chapter 28

The instant Lancroft ducked into his lab, Cole fired another shot at him. The Snapper round missed its target but dug deep enough into the stone to break apart some of the runes Lancroft had been tracing. Since Henry was having an easier time clawing his way into the house, Cole guessed those shattered runes were another part of the house's defenses.

Paige knelt at Rico's side. "Here," she whispered as she handed Tristan's flask to him. "Drink this."

"Just send that Nymar down here with some fucking serum," he growled.

"You were hurt too bad for serum. Plus the wound was made by a Skinner weapon. You know those don't heal like regular ones."

Rico grit his teeth and looked down at his bloodied shirt. Allowing his head to fall back and knock against the floor, he spat, "Damn it."

After pulling the stopper from the flask, she jammed it into Rico's mouth almost hard enough to chip some teeth. When she told him what he was drinking. Rico almost spat it out.

Pausing at the door to the examination room, Cole shifted his grip on his spear so he could swing it with his left hand while maintaining his hold on the .45. He fired once into the room, stepped through the doorway, and fired again when he caught sight of Lancroft standing with his back pressed against the wall directly beside the door. He didn't have time to fire another shot before Lancroft dropped straight down and snapped his pike up with a flick of both wrists. The end of the weapon shifted to become as long and thin as a whip, and it cinched tightly around Cole's wrist like piano wire.

"You did a good job, Henry," Lancroft said as he pulled his weapon sharply to send Cole's .45 sailing over the Full Blood carcass. "But you know you shouldn't be down here."

Cole's arm was snapped so violently that losing the .45 seemed more like a favorable alternative to losing his hand. He hopped to one side and swung his arm down to wedge the cord beneath the top of the examination table. "Why don't you come take a look in here, Henry?" he shouted while unwinding himself from the whipcord. "There's a whole secret room you need to see."

From the workshop as well as the back of Cole's mind, the little boy shouted, "I'm not allowed in there."

As soon as the cord came loose, Cole bolted from the examination room so he could check on his partners. Rico was scooting into the corner farthest from the lab, where a dainty hand appeared from over his shoulder to pull him into the wall itself. Cole could only guess that Jordan was behind the cloak in the corner and helping the bigger man into her shelter.

"You three did a very good job finding me," Lancroft said while walking out of the examination room. "I'm actually quite proud of you." His weapon reformed into the single-bladed staff.

"High praise coming from a murdering asshole," Paige snarled as she drew her gun and fired two shots at him. Spending so much time with a gamer had rubbed off on her. Rather than aim for his center of mass, she tried for a headshot, which sailed past Lancroft when the older man quickly hunched over and twisted around. Her next shots were lower and hit him in the upper back, turning bits of his tweed jacket into lint and exposing patches of leather reinforced with a wire mesh.

"That's a new form of ammunition," he said as if admiring a neighbor's riding mower. "Nearly made it through the upper layers of my jacket."

As Lancroft turned around, Cole saw the flaps of leather exposed in the damaged sections of the old man's jacket. It reminded him of the material in Rico's body armor, but was layered like sections in a compressed phone book. However Lancroft had managed that bit of craftsmanship, it might be enough to withstand all the bullets the Skinners had brought.

Cole threw himself at Paige as the whipcord extended from Lancroft's pike. Since he wouldn't get to her in time, he deflected the incoming snare with an upward swing of his spear. Paige dropped to a crouch, tucked the gun away and drew her other baton while running at Lancroft. She feinted with the sickle before swinging the machete, but was blocked by a move that sent a burst of sparks to the floor. Lancroft slashed her elbow, but she twisted all the way around and followed through with a swing from her machete that would have left most other opponents without a head.

Even though Lancroft seemed genuinely surprised by her last attempt, he still managed to duck under it and step away. "It's too late to stop Pestilence," he said while knocking Paige down with a clubbing blow from the shaft of the pike. "I've been infecting Nymar across the country with their portion of the disease since the early 1970s. The component festering in the leeches is derived from pollen. Very sweet, but very toxic. It's only one of several lifetimes of work I've done. Work any Skinner should damn well appreciate!"

Paige rolled to get her feet under her while swinging at Lancroft's legs. When the old man hopped over both weapons, Cole rushed straight at him. Lancroft deflected Cole's spear and then willed his pike to curl around it so he could twist the weapon from Cole's grasp. The thorns in the handle kept the spear in place, but also threatened to pull the skin from Cole's hands in the process.

Paige swung at Lancroft's neck, only to have him skillfully lean away from the sickle. After Cole forced the old man to twist away from a lunging stab with the spear, she hit Lancroft squarely in the back with her machete. It cut through several layers of Lancroft's jacket, exposing the fresh bullet holes. Focusing on one ragged bull's-eye, she sank the pointed end of her sickle into a bullet hole and drove all the way through the protective garment. Beneath that were thin metal plates, layered to protect the old man's back while allowing for complete freedom of movement.

"I want to help, Dr. Lancroft," the little boy said from the doorway connecting the temple to the workshop.

The old man edged along the opposite wall while spinning his weapon in a flow of constant motion to keep Cole and Paige at bay. Rico fired a shot from his corner, which didn't do anything more than turn a few beads into powder and obliterate some more etchings. After that he made certain to keep at least one of the other Skinners between him and Rico's corner. "Of course you want to help," Lancroft said as he poked a shallow hole into Cole's chest with a quick jab from his pike. "Be a good boy, Henry, and bring the others down here. Remember, though, you're not allowed in my lab." While blocking attacks from Cole and Paige, he still had enough speed to take a few swings of his own.

Paige used her machete for defense. Although that arm was getting hit, the hardened limb prevented Lancroft's weapon from cutting too deeply. The pike was a blur and the rest of him moved in a fluid series of unpredictable bobs and weaves.

Fixing an intent scowl on Paige, he said, "Say what you want about my methods, but I *never* would have considered handing over human territory to Nymar vermin or abominations like that pack of Mongrels running wild through Kansas City."

"So instead, you come up with Pestilence," Paige replied. "Real noble."

Lancroft backed toward the examination room. "After spending decades in laboratories without sticking my nose into the sun and hunting creatures that now are only footnotes in the most obscure legends, I would think you'd want to learn from me."

Gunshots sounded from upstairs as hurried footsteps

rushed the door and began stomping down into the work-shop. The other garden-level windows were knocked in, allowing the smaller of the reawakened Mud People to squirm their way into the basement. Their strained wheezes were a foul wind that rolled out of the workshop to sully the Dryad's makeshift temple.

Cole and Paige circled Lancroft so they could catch their breath and try to give Rico a clean shot. While they had used the respite to collect themselves and heal, Lancroft had done the same. All of his wounds were closed, including the ones that would have taken Paige a few days to shake off. As the Mud People started pushing into the temple, Lancroft said, "Wait a second, Henry."

Stop.

All the Mud People obeyed the order.

"Maybe you just aren't aware of what I've created," Lancroft said to the other Skinners. "If you were able to study the bodies of the most recent Half Breed victims, you would have seen the nymph pheromones used to attract them. The same sort of modification will draw the Nymar to their deaths."

"You mean like rat poison stuck inside a piece of candy?" Cole asked.

"Precisely," Lancroft declared. "That way, the Half Breeds are killed as quickly and efficiently as possible. Your generation of Skinners have stopped learning and become nothing but soldiers. Have you even pieced together how the Half Breeds spread their curse?"

"I've seen it happen," Cole said. "Anyone hurt by one of those things will become one."

"Yes, but why do some of the wounded become Half Breeds while others can be healed as if they'd only been attacked by a dog?" Looking back and forth between Cole and Paige, he said, "How are we supposed to do any good if we don't know the root of the problem?"

When he leaned in close to Paige, she lashed out with both weapons rather than listen to whatever he was going to say. Cole wanted to help her, but she'd sparked another blistering series of attacks that turned the space around them into a hissing tornado of wooden blades. Trying to inject himself into that was like deciding how to stick his hand into a rattling garbage disposal, so Cole positioned himself in front of the workshop where several Mud People stood watching. Henry stood there as well. The boy he'd possessed still seemed to have his head connected to his neck.

"It's the marrow," Lancroft snarled. Having reshaped his staff into the oval-shaped weapon he'd used to cut Ned down, he switched his entire stance and fighting style to accommodate the new weapon. "Half Breeds carry their sickness in their saliva, but it needs to make contact with bone marrow for it to take root. Just knowing one simple bit of information like that should make Half Breeds less of a problem. Just as knowing that Pestilence is an exotic virus and not the fabled creeping death of Incan and Mayan mythology."

Panting after the relentless attack, Paige said, "I'll be sure to put that tidbit in my journal and credit it to the fucking asshole who killed Ned Post." She went on the offensive using both of her weapons like a pair of scissors. Her sickle was blocked before cutting Lancroft's throat, but the machete came in to shave large portions of flesh from both of his arms. Even with his advanced healing, a healthy dose of pain flashed across his face.

When Henry saw Lancroft recoil, the boy anxiously bared crooked teeth that were covered in a slick coat of the substance kicked up from the back of his throat.

Desperate to keep the Mud People from charging, Cole decided to give Henry something more pertinent to listen to. "Is this the same offer you gave to Misonyk when you let him infect Henry?"

For the first time since the conversation started, Lancroft appeared shaken. He glanced at Henry, but the strain of the fight made it tougher for him to put on a convincing poker face. "Misonyk was more demon than Nymar. It's because of him that I needed to dispose of my cherished reformatory. I poured my heart and soul into every stone of that institution. There is no way you could possibly know how much good I did there."

Moving so Lancroft was forced to edge away from her

and Cole, Paige imagined Rico's line of fire and inched the old man toward it. She kept him talking in the hopes that he might forget Rico was even there. "I've been to the reformatory," she said. "It's a pit. A den for Half Breeds."

Strangely enough, Lancroft smiled. With Paige standing between him and Henry, he was forced to move away from the door while defending against her incoming blades. Their weapons clacked together in a quick rattle of impacts, each one coming faster than its predecessor. "It was necessary to destroy the entire facility. Such a horrible loss. To be honest, I thought I'd lost the drive to continue my work. And then Henry found me."

The little boy rubbed the door frame and leaned toward the temple, but stopped before crossing the threshold.

Curling his fingers around to brush the scars on his palms, Lancroft glared at Paige and asked, "Where is the Nymar you brought with you?"

Henry's young face twisted around before Daniels separated from the pack of Mud People behind him. When the Nymar grabbed the boy by the shoulders to yank him into the workshop, both Skinners took that as a cue to lunge at Lancroft. Cole almost got close enough to hit the old man before he spotted the bladed oval lashing in a tight arc aimed at his hamstrings. Pure instinct brought his spear down to smack aside the blade that would have crippled him.

"Bring him in here, Daniels!" Paige shouted as she tore after Lancroft.

The Nymar could be seen through the doorway, struggling with the much smaller boy. Even though Daniels outweighed his opponent by a hefty margin, the kid was lean, agile, and powered by something more than the Pestilence running through his veins. "Now you've done it!" the boy screamed in a pitch of the same frequency as an iron glove on a chalkboard. When he shrieked again, his voice ripped through the basement and through all of the minds within it.

I'm not supposed to be here! AND NEITHER ARE YOU!

Daniels and Henry both fell into the temple as Cole raced after Lancroft. The older man may have slipped past him, but he wasn't fast enough to avoid getting tackled by Paige.

When Lancroft was slammed face-first into the wall beside the door, Cole intended on nailing him there with his spear. The sharpened point caught Lancroft in the ribs and tore through the protective jacket to reveal metal plates attached by a series of latches spaced every eight to ten inches vertically along his back. Lancroft quickly twisted around so the spearhead skidded off his back and into the wall. As Paige tried to hit him again, he sent her into the same wall.

Cole swept low, but only scraped Lancroft's ankle before the old man hopped up to avoid the follow-through from the spear's forked end. When Lancroft's foot came down again, it pinned the spear to the floor so his other foot could slam down on Cole's hand. With Cole pinned, Paige kicked straight over his head to pound her heel against Lancroft's hip. Not only did the kick move him away from Cole, but it set him up for a quick attack from both her weapons. The sickle ripped diagonally along Lancroft's chest, while the machete came down toward the base of his neck. He blocked the machete and willed his weapon to close around it so he could ease it safely away as his wound was healed.

"Slower with your right arm, I see," Lancroft said. "That's what happens when you muck about with things you don't understand."

Her right arm was also stronger, and she reclaimed her machete with a quick tug before slashing again and again at Lancroft's face and chest. "Get to Henry!" she said to Cole. "You know what to do!"

The old man defended against the blows and backed toward the examination room. Unable to do more than get in Paige's way, Cole hurried to the workshop to help Daniels.

Henry struggled with the Nymar, but the boy was too small to break free. When Daniels locked him up in a bear hug, Henry exploded from his shell in a burst of energy that smeared through the stagnant air of the basement and was absorbed by one of the closest Mud People. After taking residence in the body of a large man dressed in jeans and a black T-shirt, Henry jumped at Daniels and then abandoned ship so the lumpy body hit Daniels like a couple hundred pounds of dead weight. As soon as the Nymar hit the floor, a blond woman raced over to him and opened her mouth to let more of the mud drip from her mouth onto his face.

The instant Cole arrived, he was assaulted by the Mud People. A short woman wearing butterfly pajamas tried to sink her teeth into his face. He shoved her back and took a few more steps into the workshop before filthy hands grabbed at him and his weapon from all directions. All Cole could do was shift the weapon into its blunted longbow form and push forward. When the Mud People all tried to push him back at once, Cole shifted his balance and twisted his entire body around in a tight circle that sent several of them to the floor.

Mud People stumbled down the stairs into the basement and flopped in through the windows. Although Henry seemed to be spreading himself thin by controlling so many of them, they were effective as a wave of solid bodies and grasping fingers. Two Mud People hung from Cole's back, so he slammed backward against a wall and shook them off. A few older neighbors were easily pushed aside, but a pair of teenage boys had enough strength to pose a threat. One of them cocked his head to the side and loped at Cole in a distinctive way. As soon as the teen pushed off with both feet into a wild jump, Henry ditched that body in favor of another teen dressed in a wife beater and cutoff sweatpants. The human projectile knocked Cole against a bench less than a second before Henry was attacking him in his new body, using flailing arms and snapping teeth.

Daniels wrestled with several Mud People himself, baring his fangs to compliment the savage, hungry look on his face.

"Hey!" Cole shouted. "Don't bite any of them!"

The warning sank in, but not before Daniels was swallowed up by another wave of Mud People. He clamped his mouth shut and rolled onto his belly so he could cover his head with both hands.

Even before the supernatural intervention, the teen in the beater may have been able to wrestle Cole to the ground. When he strained his muscles to the limit, the Skinner felt

a surge through his upper body that allowed him to haul
the bigger guy up and over his hip. Henry's back thumped
against the concrete floor, where he swelled up to the largest
size his human body would allow and lunged at Cole with
the ferocity of a true Full Blood.

Cole drove his shoulder into Henry's gut and then shoved
the teenage body down. Not only did the air leave the teen's
lungs, but Henry flew out of him as well. The Mud People
closed in around Cole as Henry raked the painted nails of an
elderly woman across the Skinner's face. When Cole twisted
around to face the old woman, Henry had vacated her for yet
another body.

A large woman with curly hair jumped onto Cole's back
and screamed in his ear. Before he could force her off, he
was being punched by three other sets of fists. He shook
free just long enough to dodge a punch from a man with a
face that had been completely caked in the crust of Pestilence. The orbs flew from him, leaping from one neighbor
to another. Within seconds after sending two bodies flying
at Cole, Henry used another as a battering ram. Cole ducked
behind a workbench, waiting for the sickening crash of the
clueless body against his makeshift shelter.

This time, however, Henry stayed put for the collision.
"Why don't you cut me, Skinner?" he snarled. "Cut me open
and see what's inside."

The orbs flowed out and behind Cole. When he turned
around, he found the same boy that had crawled through the
window. Although his head was cocked at an angle, it wasn't
dangling from a broken neck. "You don't want to hurt that
kid, Henry," Cole said.

The boy lunged at Cole so quickly that the wood chisel
in his hand was nearly buried into Cole's stomach. Half a
second before the narrow strip of metal sank home, Daniels grabbed the kid's arm, bared his set of curved snakelike
fangs and spat a wad of venom into his eyes.

Henry jerked away from the Nymar and pressed his hands
against his face as all of the Mud People screamed. When
Henry ran out of breath, he sucked in another one and
shrieked into his dirty palms.

Ican'tsee!Whathaveyoudonetome?Can'tseecan'tseecan't see! Stop it! I know you're in my head! Knowyou'reinmyhead! StopitstopitstopitSTOPIT!

For once Cole knew exactly what Henry was going through. Misonyk had been the first one to teach him about Nymar venom. Although intended to be injected through a bite, it could also be collected in the Nymar's mouth and spat. The first method caused sluggishness, dizziness, or even paralysis in the victim. The second allowed Nymar to blind the recipient. If the poison got into someone's eyes, it left them very susceptible to suggestion.

"Don't hurt this boy, Henry," Daniels said.

When Henry frowned and cocked his head in another direction, all the Mud People followed suit. "I got locked up for hurting kids," he said through the boy's mouth only. "I learned my lesson."

In a sterner voice, Daniels commanded, "Let go of them, Henry. Let all of these people go."

Henry tried to wipe the venom from his face, but Daniels held onto both of the kid's hands.

Looming over the kid like a troll from a cautionary fairy tale, Daniels said, "Whatever you're doing to these people, stop it! Let them go."

Lancroft forced Paige toward the lab with a flowing series of attacks that made his staff look more like a crooked windmill. Her sickle rapped against the elongated weapon and the machete raked across his stomach. Paige tried to deliver a stronger swing aimed at the bloody gash she'd just opened, but she was held in place by a muddy hand.

One filthy man in a bathrobe held onto her arm, and when she kicked him away, he fell and grasped her ankle. The foul smell of copper and dirt filled her nose as an entire room full of Henry's playthings screamed and dropped to the floor. Something was happening to them that weakened Henry's control.

She kicked free of the muddy hands and raised her defenses just in time to prevent Lancroft's weapon from taking her head off. The impact rattled through her entire body

and sent her stumbling through the door to the examination
room. Before she could get her bearings, Lancroft knocked
her in the jaw with the middle section of his staff. She staggered back, ducked under another powerful swing and found
herself in the middle of the starkly lit examination room.

"You're an interesting case, Paige," Lancroft said. "With
a little study, I should be able to iron out the kinks of your
botched experiment and solve your mobility problem."

She used the blunt end of her sickle to flip one of the metal
trays into the air and bat it at Lancroft with the machete.
"What mobility problem?" she replied before bringing both
weapons down in a double chop.

Lancroft held his staff across his chest to block her assault
and shifted it so the blades on each end curled into sharp
hooks. With a quick scooping motion, he snagged her leg
and ripped through a small section of flesh. The hook went
in just far enough to get her blood flowing. The following
attacks came in short, chopping blows using the middle section of his weapon or quick slices that scraped across the
hardened flesh of Paige's wounded arm.

She recoiled from the gouging hooks and bounced off the
edge of the large silver table into a row of metal cabinets.
For every attack she blocked, another drew her blood. The
only lull in the fight was when Lancroft knocked one end of
his weapon into a recessed latch on the wall.

Something moved behind her, but Paige wasn't about to
turn her back on the old man. Lancroft put all of his weight
behind a charge that sent her backpedaling through an opening that had previously been hidden by a tall cabinet. Her
foot reached the top of a flight of stairs and the rest of her
fell back into empty air.

Chapter 29

The Mud People dropped to their hands and knees, scraping at the ground as if it was their new enemy. Those who tried too hard to talk were quickly reduced to a heaving pile of muscles that strained to vomit up the substance that had seeped into their throats.

"Good boy," Daniels said.

Henry watched, his eyes wide and mouth agape. The faraway expression and gentle nod made it unclear if his agreement was due to the venom that had been sprayed into his host's eyes or from some other pleasant diversion drifting through his addled brain.

"Are they all free?" Cole asked.

"Yes," Henry replied. "Dr. Lancroft don't need them no more anyhow."

Cole did a quick survey of the people in the basement. Several of them were climbing to their feet and wiping the gunk from their eyes. Others were nursing wounds where their flesh had been cut or scraped away to reveal the hardened, vaguely wooden texture of the underlying muscle. Once Cole told the most alert of the group how to get out, a slow exodus toward the stairs began.

"Shit," he said as the workshop emptied. "I don't hear Paige anymore. They didn't go past us, so there's only one other place down here they could be. Bring Henry."

Daniels held onto the slick little hand and said, "Come with us, Henry."

The boy nodded and held onto him like a well-behaved youngster crossing the street.

"How long will you be able to hold him?" Cole asked as he led the way through the temple and to the examination room.

Daniels replied in a terse whisper, "I don't know. I've never done this on someone like him."

"Just try to hang on."

Walking slowly and staring straight ahead, Daniels obviously wasn't seeing much more than a few steps in front of him. He stepped over a few cowering Mud People only when his foot bumped into them. At times along the way he pulled in a sharp breath and muttered to himself. When the Nymar's lips moved, Henry nodded.

The lab was a mess. Dented cabinets, broken shelves, and spilled jars marked the path to a section in the corner that opened to reveal a flight of stairs. Cole had to choke down the instinct to run toward the sounds of activity that drifted up from the subbasement.

Entering the starkly lit room without truly seeing where he was going, Daniels asked, "What do you want— Good God!"

Cole stood next to the table and patted the massive set of ribs held apart by a set of spanners clamped directly onto the bones. "Henry, look at this."

The boy squirmed and shook his head. "I'm not supposed to be here. Notsupposed to be here. Notsupposedtobe here."

"You need to see this."

"Henry," Daniels snapped. "Look."

Henry looked. The features on his little face twisted nervously before moisture glistened at the corners of his eyes. Mud-stained tears trickled down his face, cutting a path through the caked-on grime.

Meeting the boy's fearful stare, Cole said, "This is your body, Henry. Whatever Lancroft told you, I'm sure he didn't tell you about this."

"You're lying," Henry said. "Dr. Lancroft wants to help me. He saved me from gettin' hung."

Cole shook his head. "Look for yourself. Look what he's done to you."

Daniels moved around behind the boy and nudged him toward the table. "Go on. Do what he says." When the boy resisted, the Nymar shook his head. "I don't know if I've still got him."

The boy's eyes, murkier than the bottom of a lake, flicked open to take in every detail with a hatred that was too vast to reside in such a small body. "Dr. Lancroft will kill you for coming in here," he swore.

If he don't, I will. IwillIwillIwillIwill.

"Lancroft was always hiding things from you," Cole said in a voice that had to be pushed through the oppressive weight in the air. "He's the one who locked you up and made you sit in that corner."

The anger that had filled every inch of the boy's frame shifted into melancholy. "I liked my corner."

"I know you did, but he trapped you in that room."

"I deserved to be there."

Before Cole could respond to that, images flickered through his mind: men in tattered clothes screamed as they were cut down by a Full Blood's claws. Women cowered in root cellars, wrapping their arms around crying children, praying to be pulled apart first so their young ones might have a chance to get away.

Instead of looking at the table, Henry studied the etchings on the walls. His mouth hung open in the same expression the boy might wear at a museum filled with towering displays of dinosaur bones and flying machines. "These are like the scripture written in my old room. They're the words of the Lord."

"No, Henry. They're meant to trick you."

Daniels put a hand on the boy's shoulder and said, "You should listen to him. He's telling you the truth."

Suddenly, Henry spun around to snarl up at the Nymar. "Leeches are vermin! They all need to be ripped apart and flushed away! That's what Liam thinks! That's what Randolph thinks! That's what *all* Full Bloods think!"

Hearing the Full Blood that had been responsible for

bringing Kansas City to its knees mentioned by name was jarring enough. Hearing that name attached to a promise to exterminate his entire species was almost too much for Daniels to handle. Jumping at the first sign of weakness, Henry pulled away from the Nymar and bolted for the door.

Leeches do nothing but LIE! That ain't me. It can't be!

The stairway leading down to the subbasement was short and wide enough for Paige to tuck her head and roll down to the bottom without breaking anything vital. The hallway at the bottom of the stairs was made of solid brick walls and a floor of rough stone. Her blood was already chilled due to all of the serum it was producing, but her wounds were piling up. She needed another injection and doubted Lancroft would be so accommodating as to let her take one.

Using the back of her hand to wipe some blood from her face, she glanced toward the sound of the boy's screams and said, "Your pet Henry is closer than he should be. Think he'll be upset when he finds out you were using him for spare parts?"

"Go back, Henry!" Lancroft shouted. Sweeping his weapon in a motion that scraped the hooks against the floor and wall, he forced Paige a few more steps down the hall and bellowed, "Do what I say and go back!"

Paige brought the machete up to pin one of the hooks against the wall, giving her an open shot at Lancroft's side. The sickle blade cut through his shirt, sliced along the top of a rib, and dug several inches into his torso before coming out.

The old man snarled with a mix of pain and rage. His foot swept Paige's ankles, dropping her to one knee while also forcing her to release the hook she'd trapped. After sucking in a breath, he sent her rolling down the hall with a kick delivered straight to her chest.

Small cells were sectioned off by iron bars at regular intervals along the length of the hall. One contained a Mongrel that was too mangy and sick to do more than acknowledge the combatants with a snuffing breath. Another contained the body of a woman that had decayed to the point where her yellowed parchment skin looked one size too small.

"Do you know how much you can learn from a corpse?" Lancroft asked from directly above and behind Paige. When the hand gripped her hair, she could barely get her legs set as she was pulled to her feet. "Yours probably won't hold up too long, but I'm sure it'll yield some interesting results."

As Paige was dragged down the hall, she swung her machete around to try and strike the man behind her. Lancroft shoved her toward the wall so her weapon scraped against solid brick. A moment later her head was knocked against the same wall with enough force to leave her dangling from Lancroft's fist.

"There is so much you don't know," he mused while continuing to drag her along. "I owe my longevity to a simple discovery made while experimenting in directions that are closed off to minds such as yours. Skinners no longer contemplate the entire spectrum of beasts that live beneath what we know. Even if most people are too blind to recognize Nymar or shapeshifters, Skinners must see more than that. Otherwise," he added while smacking the weapons from her hands, "they don't deserve to survive what's coming."

Lancroft tightened his grip on her hair and tossed her down the hall. As soon as she landed, something that felt like a leather strap cinched around her neck. The strap was an end of Lancroft's staff that had shifted into something more pliable than the petrified wood common to all Skinner weapons. He held it in both hands, shoving her in front of him the way animal handlers forced a wildcat into its cage. "I could have taught you the method of refining my original formula for the healing serum into the one that has sustained me for so long, but there's no need to waste such effort on a simple foot soldier."

Even though she knew there was no chance of breaking the weapon, Paige struggled against it. Her feet skidded against the floor as she tried to push herself upright while also impeding her forward momentum. But she was caught within the snare and, even worse, weaponless.

Lancroft shoved her toward one of the empty cells farther

down the brick passage. "While we were fighting, something occurred to me. Skinner blood combined with that of a shapeshifter might take our healing serum in a whole new direction. A Skinner infected by a Half Breed—under properly supervised conditions, of course—would ultimately yield a new base for the serum that could be passed on through the same methods as the current recipe. Tissue samples taken from your arm before and after the change may unlock some doors I hadn't even contemplated."

Directly across from her was a square cell only slightly larger than a walk-in closet. The Half Breed imprisoned there swiped at her while shoving its face against rune-encrusted bars to drool on the dusty floor. Its body was a withered mass of knotted muscle, and covered with skin that hung loosely on a frame of broken bones. Jagged gouges in the walls, floor, and ceiling told of a tedious, constant effort to escape over the course of what must have been several years.

"Think of this as a learning experience," Lancroft said while straining to shove her closer to the beast. "When the change comes and your bones begin to snap, you'll finally know just how complex your enemy is. I imagine the pain couldn't possibly last throughout the entire process. Or perhaps it does. I'll be sure to chronicle my observations once you take your place upon my examination table."

Daniels trembled and backed away from Henry.

"The leeches were inside me once," Henry said in both his physical and mental voices. Stretching out a filthy little hand, he reached for Daniels's chest and flashed a sludge-stained smile. "I haven't tasted them for a long time."

Cole reached for the kid, but Daniels clamped a firm grip around the boy's wrist. After forcing his grubby fingers away from his chest, Daniels shoved them into the wiry fur of the dead Full Blood splayed out on the examination table. "This is you, Henry!" he said. "Remember the scars you had. Remember the color of your fur, the bumps on your skin, the curve of your nails, just remember anything and see for yourself!"

A rippling disturbance filled the air surrounding the kid's body. But instead of becoming the orbs Cole had seen before, the essence of Henry Bartlett was drawn to the body on the table.

Taking Henry's other hand and pushing it against the Full Blood's exposed rib, Cole felt the kid jerk away from the table as if he'd been electrocuted. "Hold him there, Daniels!" he shouted while Henry's arms flailed and his little feet pushed against the floor.

With Daniels's squat body acting as a barrier, Henry didn't have anywhere else to go. No matter whose spirit was fueling the kid's efforts, his muscles simply weren't up to the task of fighting off two grown men. The wriggling kid swore in ways that were as heartfelt as they were disturbing while he pulled against the thin smear of energy connecting him to the corpse. Cole and Daniels held the boy against the table for a few more seconds before the essence rushed completely out of one shell and into the other. One of the overhead fluorescent tubes flickered and the others died out completely. Cole prayed his e-mail transfer had run its course, because the energy from Henry's reunion with his body fried the terminal along with the earpiece he was still wearing.

Once the transfer was complete, the Full Blood's decimated corpse sat up. Testing the limits of the pegs tacking its skin to the table, it let out a howl that was garbled beyond recognition due to the absence of its lower jaw. The sound it made thundered through the entire house, despite the fact that it emerged from a throat that was not only cut open in several places, but also filled with fluids and loose meat.

The boy fell back, so Cole handed him over to Daniels and said, "Get him out of here."

"Don't you need any help with . . . with that?"

Every move the carcass made introduced it to a new level of pain. Blood trickled from a hundred places despite the lack of a heart to pump it.

"You've already done your part," Cole said. "If there's any Full Blood I should be able to put down, it's this one."

* * *

Henry's garbled howl echoed through the brick hallway like a tidal wave, sending the imprisoned Half Breed scuttling to the back of its cage, where it jammed its rear haunches against the wall and scraped nervously at the floor.

When Lancroft glanced back at the stairs, Paige grabbed the weapon encircling her neck as close to its handle as her arms would allow. Feeling the sting of thorns tearing into her palms, she channeled all of her physical and mental strength into one concerted effort to free herself from the snare. Lancroft was distracted. The Half Breed was gathering its courage, and she only had another second before that slight advantage would be gone. She needed to loosen the snare as quickly as possible.

Loosen the snare.

Loosen it!

Howls continued to roll down from the laboratory, and it wasn't long before the sound of creaking wood mingled with them. As soon as Paige felt the snare loosen, she pushed it up while pulling her head down. Lancroft was quick to reassert his own will and the weapon responded by snapping shut less than an inch over her head, trapping a portion of her hair between its two halves.

"Die as a Half Breed or die as a human," Lancroft snarled while rolling the staff as if he was twirling spaghetti on the end of a giant fork. "Either way, you sure as hell won't die as a Skinner!"

Paige took her knife from her pocket, snapped it open and gave herself the quickest, sloppiest haircut in history. The instant she was free, she rolled past Lancroft and picked her weapons up off the floor. Within moments after the thorns sank into her hands, the sickle shortened to form smaller curved blades at each end. The machete widened into something resembling a butcher's cleaver. Her head was fuzzy from the spill down the stairs, but all she needed was instinct to put her weapons to use.

You did this to me, Skinner!

Henry struggled to sit up, but as he tried to pull himself off the table, he was restrained by the pegs holding the flaps of his open chest cavity to the polished surface. When the Full Blood turned in the other direction, Cole could see that several long strips of flesh starting at Henry's shoulder blade and running to the small of his back had been neatly cut away.

In a matter of seconds the carcass had found the limits of its motion. Whatever pain it experienced before had either subsided or become so overwhelming that it no longer had an effect. Its hands were restrained. Both eyes floated in separate jars. Most of its tongue lay diced in a pan, but its nose was still attached to the end of its snout, and Henry used it to sniff the air frantically.

"You see?" Cole said as he held his spear at the ready. "Lancroft put you here. He locked you away in this room just like he locked you away at the reformatory!"

Either those words got to Henry or the Full Blood had simply run out of steam, because the massive body thumped back down and its limbs hung loosely off the sides. "I . . . eehhhhh . . . err." One more breath shook the carcass and was followed by a surprisingly calm voice in Cole's head.

I remember.

"Remember what?"

Dr. Lancroft told me there was work that needed doing. Said I had to look inside folks and find what he put in 'em. I found it and stoked it like a fire. When I did, they all was different.

"They became Mud People?"

The carcass shifted so its hollowed-out eye sockets were pointed at Cole.

They weren't people no more. Not while that fire was in 'em.

"What about after? Can they be cured?"

They ain't sick. They's changed. Lancroft changed 'em. Everyone I see's been changed. Everyone but Skinners, leeches, and the like.

"So everyone will turn into these Mud People?"

Not unless I'm here to stoke the fire, but I don't plan on bein' here no more. See, I hear the stars now. I feel this wide open space an' all I gotta do is go there. I meant to go there before, but Dr. Lancroft told me not to.

Daniels rushed into the room amid the thump of clumsy footsteps and the clatter of everything shifting within the metal case he carried. Cole waved furiously for him to be quiet, but the noise didn't seem to bother Henry. The carcass was motionless and the pathetic excuse of a face was still aimed at the Skinner.

I won't stoke no more fires. I promise. IpromiseIpromise.

The upper portion of the carcass twitched, and Cole instinctively reached out to hold it down.

You broke me outta one hellhole, Skinner, an' now you busted me outta another. Suppose I should thank you.

"Just tell me how to put an end to Pestilence, Henry. Then we're even."

Daniels stopped trying to get Cole's attention and tried to make sense of the fact that he was having a conversation with a very quiet and very dead werewolf.

Unconcerned with whether the Nymar could hear Henry's voice, Cole said, "Tell me how to get rid of Pestilence!"

Without me, there ain't no Pestilence. Folks'll get sick, but they'll get better so long as I'm gone. They only listened to me. But you gotta swear somethin' to me.

With that, the peeled, brutalized head of the Full Blood slid toward Cole, freezing him in his place and sending Daniels skidding backward into a set of cabinets.

There's somethin' I want you to take so's you can use it to do the Lord's work. I can feel it nearby.

"Take what?" As soon as he asked the question, Cole found the answer tucked neatly into the back of his head.

Talk to yer friend on the floor. He'll tell ya what to do with it, but the rest of me gets buried. You're a good man, but the resta you Skinners is a buncha ghouls. Bury me proper and there ain't no more Pestilence. That's the deal. Break it and I'll know.

"All right. You got a deal."

The Full Blood's snout thumped against the table as if the string holding it up had been cut.

Daniels stood with his arms wrapped around the case that hung open like a street vendor's display of knockoff watches. "Are you still hearing voices?" he asked Cole.

"No. Where are the Mud People?"

"Heading to their homes."

"Are they all right?"

"Well enough to call the cops," Daniels replied. "Can we go now?"

"How's Rico?"

"I went to inject him with some healing serum, but he didn't really need it. He's unconscious and the wound on his chest is . . . fading."

"Fading?" When Daniels nodded, Cole asked, "Is he all right?"

"Sure he is. I wish I had a woman like that stroking my hair and holding me right against her—"

"Okay, then. Get him ready to move and call Tristan. See if there's a way for her to zap you out of here. I'm going after Paige."

Not only was the Nymar sweating profusely, but he shook badly enough to dump half of his supplies onto the floor. "Take some serum in case she's hurt."

Cole gathered up as many of the little syringes as he could find and was about to run through the narrow door beside the computer desk when he spotted another vial. "Is that what I think it is?"

"Leave that," Daniels snapped when Cole took the vial. "It needs to be disposed of properly!"

Despite Daniels's protests, Cole took the vial along with another piece of equipment from that same case. His eyes were then drawn to a rack of long, skinny drawers set against the wall on the other side of the table. There were over a dozen of them, but Cole went immediately to the eighth shelf from the top and pulled it open. The entire tray was covered by a thin metal lid, so he pulled it out and tossed it to Daniels.

"Take that and get the hell out of here!"

The confused Nymar barely managed to catch the tray before Cole hurried down the stairs.

The hallway seemed to stretch for miles, and the farther Paige was forced back, the more the floor sloped beneath her. Lancroft didn't show the first indication of tiring as the battle escalated to a personal war. When his opponent countered his tactics, he simply shifted his weapon along with his fighting style. The rooms appeared at regular intervals on either side of the hall. Some were filled with old crates and others were fashioned into cells. Only a few cells contained living specimens, none of which had any place among civilized man.

"There are others who know about your transgressions," Lancroft said as he swung his weapon at Paige. The staff had become a small halberd to accommodate faster swings in a confined space. "When Kansas City almost fell, there was talk of removing you before any more damage was done."

"Talk is all you do, old man." Paige used the double-bladed sickle to slash at his face, and the cleaver for more solid strikes to his arms and legs. Apart from a number of shallow cuts and a few bleeders, most of her attacks were blocked or dodged. Lancroft was just too quick, too practiced in his style, and too accustomed to his home turf.

When Paige hopped back to avoid being gutted by a vicious swing, she was able to see what was in the alcoves in that section of the hall. The one to her left was filled with clutter, but the one to her right had a metal box attached to the wall. She hit the box with a solid blow from her machete, removing some of Lancroft's advantage along with the overhead lights amid a shower of sparks.

"Stupid," Lancroft snarled. He walked forward slowly and carefully, shifting his weapon into a thin pole with curved blades on each end. The blades were angled forward so when the staff was spun in front of him, it became a meat grinder filling the hallway from floor to ceiling. Anyone close enough to hear the subtle hiss of the blades whipping through the air would quickly feel them chop through flesh and bone.

But Paige didn't need to guess where Lancroft was. She didn't need to listen for his movement or try to get past him. The drops in her eyes allowed her to make out vague shapes in the dark as well as the dim, luminescent scent waves drifting off him. His scent was all over the bricks and bars and floor, lighting up the place for her enhanced eyes like a layer of glowing fungus. Scents from the other creatures floated through the air as well, only to be mixed up by the spinning staff as he cautiously inched down the hall. She knew better than to get overly confident. The old man's guard would be up more now than ever, and if there was a switch to activate any backup lights, Lancroft would know where to find it.

Paige shifted into a sideways stance before extending the cleaver so it cracked against Lancroft's weapon. He responded with a flurry of blows that barely interrupted the circular motion of the staff. Both blades came at her, one after another, end over end. Even though she easily deflected most of the attacks and backed away from the rest, she was about to run out of hallway. Something snarled in one of the cages at the far end of the subbasement to let her know the spinning wooden blades wouldn't be the only threat she would have to face. She couldn't make out much within that cell even with her drops, but the bulky shape was unlike anything she'd ever seen.

"Lancroft!" Cole shouted while racing down the stairs.

In the smeared colors of scent that Paige could see, the old man's head turned to glance back. The trickle of light coming from the examination room was too far away for Cole to get to Paige before she hit the end of her line. Just to be certain, Lancroft pressed forward and willed the blades to extend even farther. Sparks flew as one of them knocked Paige's cleaver from her hand. The thorns in the grip shredded her palm and one even snapped off to become lodged in her flesh.

Suddenly, another scent trail cut through the shadows as Cole rushed down the hall with a last burst of speed from his tattoo. His unnaturally fast footsteps were accompanied by the grating sound of a dentist's drill. Before the old man could angle his weapon to cover his flank, Cole dug the tattoo machine into Lancroft's shoulder. One end of the staff sparked against the ceiling, causing the other to crack against a wall. Now that the whirling barrier was down, Paige took a swing at Lancroft's chest, but was stopped by a thickly callused palm.

The old man grabbed her weapon in one fist. Before he could drive the other into her face, his arm was ensnared from behind and an electric needle was raked across it. As much as Cole would have liked to carve an obscene message into Lancroft's skin, he settled for injecting him with the entire vial of the same defective ink Paige had used in Kansas City.

After slamming Cole into a wall, Lancroft stooped to pick up his weapon. "By opposing Pestilence, you're not just going after me," he said as he grabbed Paige's ankle and flipped her onto her rear. Cole tossed the empty tattoo machine and tried restraining Lancroft by gripping his spear in both hands and dropping his arms down around Lancroft's torso. Before Paige could take a free shot at him, the old man snapped his head back in a clubbing blow to Cole's face and then flipped him over his shoulder. "You're opposing every other Skinner who's helped me throughout the years. I'm doing them a favor by making sure you won't be around to sully our names any longer!" He swung his weapon in an arc angled to separate both of his opponents from their heads. All of those sparring sessions paid off when Cole dropped at the same time as Paige so the halberd could pass over them.

Unlike the previous swings, this one was too powerful to be controlled, and Lancroft wound up driving several inches of his blade into the brick wall. Since he'd easily received four times the amount of ink that had messed up Paige's arm, he went through the change that much quicker. Even with his features crudely outlined in scent trails, Paige could see the confusion on Lancroft's face when she dropped him to one knee with two snapping kicks to the nerve that ran down his leg.

Cole jabbed at him using the forked end of his spear and managed to land several stabs before the old man could retaliate. Lancroft's muscles had become an unknown factor, making each of his punches brutish and overextended. He could no longer get his fingers to close around his weapon, so he balled up both fists and let them fly. Even going by the hazy outline of the scent trails, Cole had no difficulty in allowing each incoming swing to sail past him and answering with a shot of his own.

Paige came at him with another kick that was blocked by the arm that had taken the brunt of punishment from the electric needle. As soon as her shin thumped against the hardened mass of muscle beneath Lancroft's skin, she knew exactly what Cole had done. She tossed a slower kick into Lancroft's chest just to gauge his reaction time, and when the old man tried to block it, she followed up with a quick snapping roundhouse to his face.

In one last burst of strength, Lancroft threw Cole to the floor so he could drop his fist onto him like a sledgehammer. Cole hit the concrete with a thump that knocked the wind from his lungs, and he was barely fast enough to roll away from the fist that sent a tremor through the hallway.

Paige slid into a side kick that caught Lancroft squarely in the chest. The old man planted his feet, absorbed the kick, and dropped his arm to grab her leg. He was too slow, however, to prevent her from burying the curved blade of her sickle into the side of his neck.

Lancroft stood and stared at her for a second, shocked by the blow and weakening from the blood that poured out of him. He reached up with a hand that seemed almost too heavy to lift, pulled the sickle from where it had been lodged and crushed it as if it had been whittled out of balsa wood. Blood sprayed from his severed artery, but was quickly stanched by the healing serum flowing through his body. "You'll never be true Skinners," he croaked as he tore his jacket open to fumble for a pendant that hung around his neck and under his shirt, "but perhaps you'll be remembered as such when you're found here with me."

The little box in Lancroft's hand looked like a remote car door lock. Cole felt the bottom fall out of his stomach as he thought about the collapsed pile of rubble that had once been Lancroft Reformatory. Before this place might be buried in a similar manner, Cole drove his spear straight through the old man's wrist and into his chest. Between the debilitating effects of the ink, the loss of blood, and two such grievous wounds, Lancroft crumpled. His hand was pinned and not functioning well enough to push either of the buttons on the black box. Cole leaned on the spear, twisted it, and pulled it out. With his last spark of life, Lancroft reached for the remote hanging around his neck.

Paige bent down and calmly took it from him.

"Uh . . . guys?" Daniels called from the top of the stairs. "Are you all right?"

When she saw Cole looking at her with that same question written across his dirty face, she rushed to press her body and lips against his. He was surprised at first, but quickly wrapped his arms around her and lifted her off her feet.

"My friend," she whispered, "you won't be able to walk straight for a month after I get through with you."

"Yeah, Daniels!" Cole shouted. "We're fine. Just give us a minute!"

"You don't have a minute," the Nymar replied. "Cops are pulling up to the house, but there's a bridge ready for us."

Paige tensed and bumped her forehead against Cole's chest. "Shit." After taking a moment, she marched down the hall, up the stairs, and straight through the examination room. "How's Rico?"

"Already through. He didn't want to leave you, but I pushed him."

"Damn," Cole chuckled. "I wish I could've seen that."

The beaded curtain was alive with crackling energy. "You guys go ahead," Paige told them. "I'll be right there."

Instead of heroically refusing the offer to leave her behind, Daniels scurried past them both and disappeared through the beads. Cole didn't go anywhere.

Paige jogged through the workshop and ran up to the first floor, and her partner followed. Even before they got to the upper door, he could hear sirens outside the house. "We're not gonna make it," he warned.

"Doesn't matter if we do or don't." Upon stepping through the doorway, Paige jabbed a finger at him and said, "Stay right here and don't make a sound." She then went to a cluster of runes on the wall near the stairway and moved her hand slowly over the blocky symbols.

The street outside was illuminated by headlights and filled

with dozens of dirty, confused people. From what he could see, the former Mud People were barely aware of where they were. "Might want to hurry it up," he urged.

Once she picked out the symbols Rico had toiled over upon their arrival, Paige traced some of them with her fingertips. Cole could see through the little house to the front window, which was enough to spot a pair of police officers approaching the front door. The cops looked through the window and knocked as if they meant to shake the entire house. Paige stepped through the doorway where Cole waited at the top of the stairs. When he tried to shut the door, she whispered, "Don't move. Don't make a sound."

The cops entered the house with their hands on the holsters at their hips and swept flashlight beams back and forth along the walls. "Hello?" one of them said. "Anyone here?"

Even as the cops looked directly at the door, Cole could tell they weren't really seeing it. Their eyes continued to wander along the walls, not even following the lines of symbols etched there.

Slowly, he and Paige went down the stairs as the cops stomped around, and they eventually found their way outside again.

"Next time Rico says I never pay attention to his precious teachings, he can stuff it," Paige said proudly after reaching the temple.

"What just happened?"

"I restored the runes intended to hide that doorway and everything else in the house. All those cops or anyone else will see is what we saw when we first got here, which is a fat load of nothin'."

After the night he'd had, that was all the explanation Cole needed. Before taking the last step that would carry him through the beads, he stopped and nodded toward the lab. "What about this place?" he asked. "The stuff in there? The things down in that hallway?"

Paige took the remote that had been hanging from Lancroft's neck and let her thumb glide over the cover. "I still don't know if I believe he was hundreds of years old, but he came up with some stuff I've never seen before." The remote disappeared in her fist and then into her pocket. "He wanted it destroyed, so I want to keep it around for a while. Hopefully he knows we're sifting through all of his crap. If he's anything like Daniels, that'd be his own personal hell."

"I'm definitely coming back," Cole vowed as he looked toward the stark light cast from the examination room. "I've still got some things to do here."

The front door was pushed open, but the footsteps only stomped around for a minute or two before going back outside, which meant Lancroft's defenses had held up against another set of unknowing eyes. They could hold out a little longer.

Cole stepped through the curtain and emerged in a smaller temple, where he was greeted by an excessively attractive, scantly clad woman with curly pink hair. After a sharp crack of her gum the pink-haired Dryad said, "Hiya. I'm Annie. There's food in the main room."

Paige emerged next and kept walking as if crossing hundreds of miles in a flicker of light had already become second nature. She and Cole followed Annie into a cavernous room filled with five large stages. Reading the confusion on Paige's face, he told her, "This isn't The Emerald. It's Steve's."

"Do you know all of these places by heart?"

"No," he replied as he pointed behind the largest stage to where STEVE'S was written in glowing neon.

Turning to Annie, Paige sighed, "Okay. Where's Steve's?"

"Dallas. Tristan didn't have the juice to bring anyone else into St. Louis. We're running two-for-the-price-of-one lap dances and have enough juice to power the state, so," she added while holding her arms up and out as if posing for the first step in the YMCA dance, "here you are!"

"Are Rico and Daniels here?" Paige asked.

Annie shook her head in a way that made her pink curls wiggle. "They made it to St. Lou."

"Both alive?"

"Uh-huh."

"Perfect. Point me to the buffet."

Epilogue

The cute news anchor with the short brown hair and pretty round face smiled comfortingly at the camera and announced, "Medical teams across the country have reported success in their most recent efforts to combat the Mud Flu. All symptoms ranging from cough and disorientation to the viscous discharge that gave the sickness its name are being cleared up thanks to a treatment developed by Dr. Angela Oehler. One of our correspondents is with Dr. Oehler now at the Pathology Department of Barnes-Jewish Hospital."

A blond woman dressed in a white coat shifted nervously in front of all the cameras and said, "After recently isolating the cause of the flu, we've formulated a treatment that clears up every symptom in all but the most extreme cases. If anyone else is currently affected by the Mud Flu, please contact your physician or anyone here at Barnes to schedule an appointment."

"Dr. Oehler claims similar results have been reported at many other hospitals across the country," the brunette reporter said once she was back on screen. "According to the Centers for Disease Control, the Mud Flu stemmed from an exotic malaria strain brought to the U.S. from a remote region in Ecuador. Hopefully, this marks the end of an epidemic that has claimed a total of sixty-eight lives since the first reported case less than a month ago."

"You hear that, Rico?" Cole asked as he flipped through the channels of Ned's TV using a remote that was heavier than most people's DVD players. "The CDC figured out the Mud Flu!"

"Great," Rico grunted from the broken couch nearby. All that remained of the wound Lancroft had given him was a deep cut that had required just under a dozen stitches to close. "We do the legwork, our friend at the hospital puts it to use, and the feds take the credit. How much you wanna bet the insurance companies and doctors found a way to charge for immunizations of a plague that's been wiped out already?"

"Speaking of medications, how was that Memory Water stuff?"

"Made me remember what it's like to not have a hole punched through my chest. I only took half of what she gave me, though. Gave the rest to Paige so she could try and fix up her arm. Don't know if she took it, though."

"Why don't you take some of those pain pills we found in Ned's collection?"

"I can handle the pain just fine."

"Actually," Cole said, "I was hoping they'd put you to sleep for a while."

"If I'm sleeping, I can't work on your little present."

The big man lay with one leg dangling off the slope-backed couch, and a pile of throw pillows under his back and neck. Rico's grin was wide enough to display a full set of blocky teeth, and it made Cole more uncomfortable than all three sets of a Nymar's fangs. "What present?" he asked hesitantly.

"Don't you remember that case you threw at Daniels while we were leaving Philly?" Rico asked. When Cole furrowed his brow and started to shake his head, Rico propped himself up. Stress lines formed at the corners of his eyes, but he stubbornly refused to ease back down. "If you don't remember, then I might as well keep it for myself!"

"I remember, I remember," Cole said as a way to get Rico

to stop straining the bandages wrapped around his torso. "Wait. I really do remember now."

"You know what was inside?"

"No."

Shifting within the groove he'd worn into the couch, Rico grunted, "Henry's inside, that's what. Pieces of him anyway."

"Oh, hell. I don't even know why I grabbed it, I just did."

"Then I want you pullin' numbers at the next bingo night, because you grabbed enough leather to make one hell of a nice piece of armor. And not just leather," Rico added. "Full Blood hide. Do you have any idea how hard that is to come by?"

"Yeah," Cole said while thinking back to those long strips that had been removed from Henry's back. "I think I do."

"Lancroft must've been tanning it for himself because there ain't no way a Skinner in his right mind would part with something like that."

Crossing the living room to the small desk where Ned's computer was set up, Cole said, "So much for my present, huh?"

"You forgot," the big man said with a waggle of his eyebrows. "I ain't anywhere near my right mind. Plus, you earned it more'n I did. Give me a few weeks, maybe a month, and I'll stitch that leather into something that'll protect your worthless ass better than anything I ever made for anyone."

Ned's Internet connection was passable, so Cole was online and running various key words and phrases through his favorite search engines in no time. "Looks like Lancroft wasn't lying about Pestilence killing off Half Breeds. The only report of any sighting in this part of the country is from some Bigfoot blog in Colorado, and the description isn't anything like a shapeshifter I've ever heard about."

"I was on earlier and saw a few pictures of a big rat thing a few miles away from the KC International Airport."

"Was it digging?" Cole asked.

"Yeah! Only had three legs too. Weird."

"That's Ben. He's supposed to be there. What about dead Nymar? I'd think those would be easy to spot."

Rico propped his foot onto the coffee table and scratched at his bandages. "Nope. They may get hungry, but they're not stupid. One of the bloodsuckers down in New Mexico found a way to sniff out that Pestilence shit and word's spreading. You ask me, they'll be our biggest helpers in making sure us humans gets nice an' healthy in time for supper."

While Rico talked about the coat he was making, Cole continued to search the Web. Other than a bunch of doctors congratulating themselves about wiping out the Mud Flu, the only other hit was from a fresh batch of pictures from Kansas City and Janesville. He was about to pass over one entry on HomeBrewTV.com when he realized it wasn't more wild dog footage from KC, but from Alcova, Wyoming. It was a shaky video file filmed by the passenger of a moving car. About five seconds in, the driver hit the brakes and pointed, screaming for the cameraman to look in the opposite direction. When the camera swung that way, three large figures were crossing the highway. They ran on four legs and resembled small bears. Two of the smaller ones looked like Mongrels and bolted out of frame in a blur. The third was a larger creature with coal black fur that either had trouble walking or wanted to make sure the camera had plenty of time to get a good shot. While the people in the car chattered back and forth, the camera zoomed in close enough to the creature's face for Cole to verify it was missing an eye.

It was definitely a Full Blood. More important, it was the Full Blood that had torn up Kansas City. Cole could almost feel the burning under his scars just by looking at Liam's image on Ned's screen. After a few more seconds the ebon werewolf hung its head and took a few slow steps toward the car. Tires screeched. The driver panicked and nearly ran into a tree. The video ended with a screen swearing the footage was real. Several hundred HomeBrewTV viewers posted their opinions on whether the video was real or one of the many fakes doctored by Cole himself. The prevailing opinion on the site was that the Wyoming video was "fake as hell."

Rico sat up and grabbed his bandaged midsection. "What's that?"

Not wanting to give him a reason to jump off the couch,

Cole e-mailed the video to himself and said, "Just another Mongrel."

The new home page for Digital Dreamers, Inc. had some flashy animations advertising new projects that Cole hadn't even heard about yet. The only mention of the game he'd been consulting on was that it was "alive, but indefinitely postponed."

"Yeah," he grumbled to himself. "I know how that feels."

"Did you hear me before?" Rico growled. "What're your damn measurements?"

"I don't know," he said as he closed his browser and pushed his chair away from the desk. "Take your best guess."

"At least tell me yer coat size."

Standing up, Cole caught himself looking at every one of the room's cluttered shelves and dusty surfaces. If he stared long enough, he could find clean spots that had been left behind by the fingers of its former owner.

"Get me a tape measure," Rico said. "I think Ned kept one in the top drawer of that desk."

Cole opened the top drawer, found the tape measure amid some old lottery tickets and brought it to Rico.

Holding both arms straight out and to the sides, Cole asked, "Where's Paige?"

"Dogtown."

"Is that still in St. Louis?"

After jotting down one set of measurements into his little spiral notebook, Rico grumbled, "Yeah. Just south of Forest Park, right around Clayton Avenue."

"Can you be more specific than that?"

"Sure I can. First let's discuss lining and pockets."

Less than an hour after his session with the ugliest seamstress in history, Cole parked in front of St. James the Greater Catholic Church. He double-checked the address scribbled on the piece of paper torn from Rico's notebook as well as the screen of his GPS. Not even the Cav parked nearby with smashed windows, dented doors, missing bumper, and multiple coats of rust was enough to fully convince him he was in the right place.

St. James was beautiful in the same way that most churches were beautiful. Stained glass caught the sunlight and scattered it throughout a large room filled with rows of pews and well-cared-for statuary. There wasn't a mass being performed, so most of the seats were empty. A small line formed near a confessional, and a priest in his late fifties or early sixties acknowledged Cole's arrival with a curt nod. He returned the nod and spotted Paige sitting just right of center of the sixth pew from the front. As he scooted over to her, he couldn't decide if she was praying, studying one of the leaflets stuck in the hymnal rack in front of her, or sleeping.

A few silent moments passed before he smirked uncomfortably and said, "I never know what to do in Catholic churches. There's all the books and shelves and these folding padded things down there. I guess those are for kneeling."

Her eyes were fixed upon the front of the chapel, assessing the notched altar and the stoic, vaguely distracted faces on the statues around it.

"Speaking of kneeling," Cole fumbled, "I have no clue when to drop down, when to stand up, when to cross myself. Do I eat the bread? Should I pretend I'm singing if I don't know the words or just stand there? When I go by that big water bowl, do I touch it, flick it, make a wish?"

"How did you know I was here?" she asked.

"Rico told me."

"How did *he* know I was here?"

"Was it supposed to be a secret?"

Reaching out to run her finger along the closest hymnal, she replied, "I guess not. Shouldn't you be at Jack in the Box or something? I think Eat Rite is open twenty-four hours."

"I'm not hungry."

Paige looked up at the saints and martyrs frozen in everything from plaster to colored glass. "Good thing I came here. If you're not craving greasy food, the world must be about to end."

Closing his eyes and flattening both hands on the uncomfortable bench, Cole savored the cool touch of the old wood upon his scars. "I had to get out of Ned's house. I know

Rico's still not feeling very good, but he's acting as if we just checked into that place like another hotel room. I see all of Ned's stuff, right where he left it, and think I'm still not allowed to look in those jars. I step over his shoes when I walk past the couch. His clothes are still on the hooks by the door, and I just can't get over the fact that I had to identify his body. Is there even going to be a funeral?"

"No. He was already cremated." Paige didn't have to look at Cole to know what he was thinking. The breath he let out was slow, tense, and loud enough to echo within the quiet calm of the church. "Skinner funerals aren't a good idea," she explained. "Having too many of us together in one spot away from a defensible location is too juicy a target for some Nymar gang looking to prove themselves or someone like Liam or Burkis, who might decide to wipe our slate clean."

"Did you see that video from Wyoming?"

She nodded.

"So you think that's really Liam?"

"Full Bloods don't live so long just because they can. They fight for it tooth and nail."

Too tired to pursue that subject, Cole shifted to the previous one. "Wouldn't you like to say goodbye to Ned? Maybe have a send-off or something?"

"Do you really think something like a funeral matters, Cole? If Ned's going to hear us or see us when we're all crying in our nicest clothes, he'll hear us or see us whenever. He's gone and it doesn't matter where his body is or who gets his stuff. All that does matter is that he accomplished something while he was here. Ned was a Skinner, through and through. So were Brad, Gerald, and all the others who were killed fighting our fight. They made a difference where they could and passed on what they learned. That's all anyone can do."

"What about us?" Cole whispered.

"We did a hell of a lot. No matter who comes after you for any of those files or anything else of Lancroft's, we'll stick to our guns and take each case as it comes."

"What are you talking about?"

"You weren't contacted yet?" Paige asked.

"No. Contacted by who?"

She sighed. "There are other Skinners who want anything Lancroft touched. Journals, notes, records, experiments, you name it. They also know we're one of the few to see his home away from the reformatory."

"So they don't know about the house in Philadelphia?"

"They know about a house and they know it's somewhere in Philly, but that's about it. Lancroft's coming-out party hadn't gotten rolling before we broke it up. Anyway, things may get touchy here between us and the rest of our little community."

"I suppose it may be a bad time to bring this up, but I found some hardcore evidence on the Internet." Reaching out to hold both of her hands, Cole stared into Paige's eyes and told her, "There's been a Bigfoot sighting in Colorado. It . . . looks like a bad one."

After a few seconds she laughed quietly and rested her head on his shoulder.

"How's the arm?" he asked.

"The same. A little stiff. Hurts. You know."

"Rico told me he only drank some of the Memory Water and gave the rest to you."

"I gave that to Daniels," she said. "He knows he's infected with the first component of Pestilence, and after all he did for us, I figure he deserves some peace of mind."

"And you deserve to get your arm back. After all we did for those nymphs, I'm sure Tristan could find some more of that Memory Water for you."

"Oh, she owes us and she's going to pay up. Remember that deal Rico hashed out? We really have been granted access to the A-Frame Airlines. All we need to do is give them some notice and we'll be transported in style. Well, if you can stretch your boundaries enough to call those tacky beaded curtains stylish."

"Fun. So you'll just keep your arm in a sling and feel sorry for yourself?"

Sitting up without leaning on him, Paige let her eyes wander about the huge room, taking in one sight at a time. "No, I'll work through it the hard way. Learn from my mistake, figure out a way to deal with the mess, and move along. That's how it should be." Shrugging, she looked up at the cathedral ceiling and added, "I need a new weapon anyway."

A large man wearing khaki pants ambled down the aisle carrying a box of hymnals and a dozen pens stuffed into the pocket protector of his gray shirt. The glasses sliding down his nose were wide enough to replace the Cav's broken windows, and the eyes behind them showed a hint of friendly familiarity when they spotted Paige. He showed her a crooked smile and started filling the spaces on the racks behind each pew so every parishioner would know the words to their songs.

"When Rico told me you were here," Cole said, "I thought he was kidding."

"Why?"

Lowering his voice to reduce the risk of being struck by lightning, he said, "Because you told me more times than I can count that this religious stuff doesn't work."

"I told you it doesn't work on vampires or werewolves, and it doesn't. It also doesn't work for magic charms. But maybe," she added with a gentle smile, "it works on me."

A special sneak peek at
Book Four in the Skinners series,

VAMPIRE UPRISING

Available Fall 2010!

Alcova, WY

The pickup was covered in a yellow paint that had been faded from decades of punishment from a relentless sun. Even after the sky's glare had faded to a soft, burnt orange, the truck still looked like something that had been flipped out of the proverbial frying pan. Its frame rattled around a powerful engine humming with a dull roar as it slowed to a stop on the shoulder of County Road 407. The passenger side window came down, allowing the driver's voice to be heard as he leaned over and asked, "You need a ride, buddy?"

The man who'd been walking along the shoulder of the road didn't take his hands from the pockets of his Salvation Army overcoat. A mane of tangled, dark brown hair flapped against his face when he turned to fix his blue-gray eyes upon the driver. "No, thanks," he said.

"You sure? It's a few miles until the next gas station."

"I'm sure. Thanks, anyway."

The driver grumbled something under his breath that he thought would go unheard.

Having heard the man's snippy comment just fine, Mr. Burkis turned away from the truck and let it move along.

"Funny," said a voice from the hills amid a rush of bounding footsteps and the skid of heels in rocky sand. "After all the death that has been brought to them from strangers, they still justify stopping to ask for more from a monster walking along the side of the highway."

The County Road cut through a section of exposed rock that made the area seem like something closer to a desert than a place within range of so many rivers and dams. No running water could be seen from this stretch of road, although both of the men who now faced each other could smell moisture in the air as easily as they could feel the fading sunlight upon their faces.

"Hitchhiking, Randolph?" the vaguely amused voice asked in a guttural cockney accent. "You've never been one to indulge in the finer things, but surely you don't need to travel on human roads."

The man in the overcoat wasn't impressed by the display of speed that had brought the other man to his side. He merely stuck his hands deeper into his pockets, turned away from the road and started walking at a normal pace into the surrounding wilderness. The new arrival fell into step beside him, wearing a set of rags that wrapped around his waist and hung over his chest thanks to the good graces of a few stubborn sections of leather and canvas. He wore no shoes. The hair sprouting from the top of his head hung in strands that looked more like greasy wires. A jagged scar traced a line down the side of his nose, but that was the least of his injuries. His right eye socket was filled with a mass of hardened flesh resembling wax that had been stirred right until the point of hardening.

"I stuck to the roads because I knew that's where I would find you, Liam."

"Have I become so predictable?"

"Ever since you became famous." After cresting a small rise, Burkis removed his hands from his pockets so he could cross his arms sternly over a chest that was thicker now than it had been a few moments ago. "Didn't you get enough camera time in Kansas City?"

Liam smiled wider than any human could. The corners of his mouth stretched almost back to his ears and a few of his teeth flowed into fangs as if melting down to points. "I made a damn fine run of it there, didn't I?"

"You made a mess and stirred up the Skinners, just like I said you would."

"Always know best, eh Randolph? Remember when you were the one listening to what I had to say?"

"That was a long time ago."

"And in that time, you've become the one with all the answers, have you?"

"This is my territory," Burkis snarled. "No matter what our history may have been, you don't get to come here and sully it by terrorizing humans for no reason. Feeding is one thing, but you're—"

"Sending a message," Liam snapped in a way that sent his last syllables rolling along the tops of the hills. Immediately aware of the impact he'd made upon his environment, the man in rags lowered his chin as well as his voice. "If you've picked up the same rumblings from the east that I have, something out there may very well have gotten that message of mine."

Burkis pulled in half a breath and grimaced. "You reek of Mongrels."

"Of course. The filthy buggers escorted me out of Kansas City. To be honest, I think they might have gotten closer to finishing the job than that group who cornered me in Whitechapel. I always knew the Mongrels were opportunistic little shits, but I never banked on them working with the Skinners."

"That has yet to be determined," Burkis said. "How did you get them to take your side?"

"A wild stab on my part. Common greed on theirs." Casually shifting his gaze to the east, he squinted at the darkest horizon as if he could make out what was happening on the other half of a map. "I told the lot of them that Full Bloods are created when one of us bites one of them."

Burkis recoiled as if he'd picked up the scent of cotton candy amid the desolate stretch of hardened terrain. "They believed you?"

"One of them did. That's all it took to carry me away before I was damaged any further. After that, I suppose the fellow with the ambition to move up a rung or two on the food chain convinced some of his mates to join him because that's all they could talk about when I was able to open my eyes."

"Please tell me you didn't."

"I did," Liam said with a wink. "Nipped at one or two as soon as I was able. Of course, the first one didn't make it. Seems those Mongrels aren't put together as well as they like to think they are. Their strength is in numbers, though, so they kept me from getting away. I needed a few more days to heal and then I bit the few who stuck around for their chance at immortality. Only took some fingers and half an arm. Doesn't do the trick unless you get to the bone."

"I know that. What happened then?"

"What do you think happened? They changed."

"Into what?" Burkis asked.

"Into something that's close enough to a Full Blood to fool the likes of them." Seeing the other's glare, he explained, "They're stronger and bigger than what they started as, but they're also a little slower. Takes away some of their advantage. After word spreads, Mongrels in this precious territory of yours may come to trust me."

"You honestly believe they'd trust you after the history of blood spilled between our kinds?" Letting out a cynical snuff from flared nostrils, Burkis said, "They took you away from the Skinners to use you and they'll keep using until they figure out a way to be rid of you."

When Burkis started walking even further from the road, Liam dashed around to get in front of him. It took next to no effort to cover the short distance in a flicker of motion. "I know what I'm doing, Randolph. If you found me to try and show me the error of my ways yet again, you can stuff it up your self-righteous arse."

"What I want is for you to help me find someone that can give us some of the answers we've all been after for longer than these cities have been scattered across this country. The one that may have gotten your message."

Not only did that cause Liam to straighten his posture, but it put a curious tilt into the way he held his head. "Go on."

"I also want to meet the ones you created. I've seen your appearance in those videos that have been making the rounds."

"Ah yes. That motorists with the cameras. They all have cameras these days, don't they?"

"And they spread their pictures like rumors over a campfire," Burkis said.

"Have the Skinners seen my movies?"

"I'd wager so. But right now, that's not your concern. You were seen traveling with Mongrels, so I'm assuming those are the ones you altered. Any others wouldn't split from their pack and they sure as hell wouldn't defer to you the way those did."

"What makes you think they're still with me?"

"Because you're a terrible liar, that's what."

"Wouldn't be so sure about that." Filling up the massive lungs within his chest, Liam expelled his breath and said, "But I could hardly ever slip one past you, Randolph. They're not far from here. Maybe ten or twenty miles up in the mountains."

"Take me to them."